The Trun

The Truman Gumshoes

*The Postwar Detective Fiction
of Mickey Spillane, Ross Macdonald,
Wade Miller and Bart Spicer*

J.K. Van Dover

McFarland & Company, Inc., Publishers

Jefferson, North Carolina

Library of Congress Cataloguing-in-Publication Data

Names: Van Dover, J. Kenneth, author.
Title: The Truman gumshoes : the postwar detective fiction of Mickey Spillane,
Ross Macdonald, Wade Miller and Bart Spicer / J. K. Van Dover.
Description: Jefferson, North Carolina : McFarland & Company, Inc., Publishers, 2022. |
Includes bibliographical references and index.
Identifiers: LCCN 2022001637 | ISBN 9781476688022 (paperback : acid free paper) ∞
ISBN 9781476645414 (ebook)
Subjects: LCSH: Detective and mystery stories, American—History and criticism. |
American fiction—20th century—History and criticism. | Noir fiction, American—
History and criticism. | Private investigators in literature. | Spillane, Mickey,
1918–2006—Criticism and interpretation. | Macdonald, Ross, 1915–1983—Criticism
and interpretation. | Miller, Wade—Criticism and interpretation. | Spicer, Bart,
1918–1978—Criticism and interpretation. | BISAC: LITERARY CRITICISM /
Mystery & Detective | LCGFT: Literary criticism.
Classification: LCC PS374.D4 V366 2022 | DDC 813/.087209—dc23/eng/20220121
LC record available at https://lccn.loc.gov/2022001637

British Library cataloguing data are available

ISBN (print) 978-1-4766-8802-2
ISBN (ebook) 978-1-4766-4541-4

Front cover image © 2022 Fer Gregory/Shutterstock

Printed in the United States of America

McFarland & Company, Inc., Publishers
Box 611, Jefferson, North Carolina 28640
www.mcfarlandpub.com

For Bruce and Cindy

Table of Contents

Preface

Having emerged as a popular development in the genre of detective fiction in aftermath of the First World War, the hard-boiled detective story apparently had two directions in which it could develop as it entered its second generation after the Second World War: it could play its hardness either piano or forte. Its most popular practitioner, Mickey Spillane, opted for forte: Mike Hammer would be more tough, more violent, more regardless of bourgeois niceties, more lusty than his prototypes from the 1920s. Its most respected practitioner, Ross Macdonald, would play piano: Lew Archer would still be tough enough to administer a beating and to endure one, but he would always be thoughtful and sensitive and never over-confident about his own rightness. *The Truman Gumshoes* explores these two opposite directions as they emerged during the late 1940s and early 1950s. A close examination of the early novels of Spillane and Macdonald is supplemented by a look at the work of two of their important contemporaries—Wade Miller and Bart Spicer—whose private eye novels offered visions of who the new hard-boiled detective might be and what he might do that lay somewhere between the poles inhabited by Mike Hammer and Lew Archer. *The Truman Gumshoes* looks at the different ways these writers imagined the hard-boiled private eye and his world.

The introduction provides some context for the work of Mickey Spillane, Ross Macdonald, Wade Miller, and Bart Spicer, by placing them in the history of the country and the history of the genre during Harry Truman's time in office, 1947–1952. It is followed by four chapters, each examining all of the novels featuring a series detective that one of these four writers published during the Truman presidency: the first six Mike Hammer novels by Mickey Spillane (plus a seventh novel whose publication was delayed until the 1960s), the first six—which is to say, all six—Max Thursday novels by Wade Miller, the first four Lew Archer novels by Ross Macdonald, and the first five Carney Wilde novels by Bart Spicer. Some reference is made to the later developments in the careers of Mike Hammer, Lew Archer, and Carney Wilde, but the focus is upon how these four writers adopted and

1

changed the conventions of hard-boiled detective fiction that had been established in the 1920s and 1930s. Certain themes emerge, and certain comparisons and connections are discussed, but this is not a thesis-driven analysis and each chapter tries to look at what the writer was trying to do and what he achieved. His connections to and his departures from the hard-boiled writers of the pre–World War II generation—especially Carroll John Daly, Dashiell Hammett, and Raymond Chandler—and to his three hard-boiled contemporaries are emphasized.

These chapters are followed by a long essay which does focus, not too tendentiously I hope, on a theme: the detective as anti-organization man. It explores the varying sorts of self-sufficiency (and corresponding aversion to joining organizations or networks) that, until the 1970s at least, seemed a signature quality of the character of the fictional detective. It is a quality that was emphasized by Edgar Allan Poe in the first detective stories; it was developed in one direction by the classical form of the story, and then it was given a different color by the hard-boiled model. It seems to have had a special resonance in post–Depression, post–World War II America. The four Truman writers take quite different attitudes toward the detective's relation to others—both his wariness in associating himself with others in intimate, private relationships and with others in broader social, political and economic matters. These differences do not constitute a revolution, but they do herald the radical change that would be sounded in the 1970s and change the fundamentals of the genre.

The Truman Gumshoes is, in a sense, a sequel to my earlier book, *Making the Detective Story American: Biggers, Van Dine, Hammett and the Turning Point of the Genre 1925–1930* (McFarland, 2010). The work of Spillane, Wade, Macdonald, and Spicer between 1947 and 1952 does not quite constitute another major turning point. That would occur three decades later when the private eye not only ceased to be defined by versions of white heterosexual masculinity, but when the detectives—whatever their sexual, racial, ethnic, religious, or class identity—began to think about these identities and to engage in multiple long-standing relationships with partners and friends that served as essential markers of their authority as a detective as well as his or her virtue as a person. The communities to which they belonged and the families that they created became the apparent basis of their authority to solve crimes. Successfully exposing the consequential connections in other people's lives was no longer enough; the detective needed to demonstrate an ability to connect with people in his or her own life and to see that all connections were colored by the country's broader social arrangements. Good detectives were good because they were anchored in lasting relationships. Exposing the perpetrators of specific legal crimes, while still a generic obligation, was no longer sufficient; the detectives needed to move beyond a naive acceptance of their nation's current legal standards of what constitutes a crime and reflect upon the social conditions that lay behind the crime at hand.

The Truman gumshoes were still working within the paradigm that the *Black Mask* writers had produced. They were practicing "normal" hard-boiled fiction, discovering original angles but not challenging the existing premises. Their private eyes were still men cast in the lonely tough guy mold. Emotional attachments to families of any sort would not serve as the basis of their virtue; to the contrary, such attachments would fatally weaken them. Or would they? The premier writers of the period—Spillane and Macdonald—seem to adhere, in quite different ways, to the premise of their models: the detective's necessary self-sufficiency precludes any attachment beyond masculine comradeship (and limits even the reach of that comradeship). Wade Miller and Bart Spicer begin to ask whether there might be a place for detectives to define themselves as tough men who might engage in longstanding personal relationships and still retain the necessary character to act alone. But it would take another few decades before the genre was prepared to insist that relationships were not just acceptable, they were essential.

* * *

In a fairly long academic career, I have had happy associations with nine universities, and I will take this occasion to express my gratitude to all of them. I earned degrees at Lafayette College and Bryn Mawr College; I have taught at Lincoln University (the nation's oldest Historically Black University) for 38 years; and, largely through the good offices of the Fulbright Program, I have been invited to teach for a year, a semester, or a half-semester at the University of Tübingen, the University of Stuttgart, Nankai University, the University of Vienna, Comenius University (Bratislava), and (not through the Fulbright Program) the University of Mannheim. Additionally, I have benefited from attending (largely through the good offices of the National Endowment for the Humanities) summer seminars at Harvard University, the Newberry Library, Yale University, and New York University (the NYU seminars being offered through the Faculty Resource Network). I am grateful for the experiences I have had at all of these institutions, though only one—Robin Winks's summer seminar on Detective Fiction and the Historian—bore directly on the material discussed in this book, and even then, none of the four Truman writers made the reading list. I do not fill this page with the names of individuals only because inevitably I would recall omitted names only when the printed book was in my hand. But I am grateful for a lifetime of education provided me by my teachers, my colleagues, and my students.

Though I have no formal connection with the University of Delaware, its Morris Library has continued to be a resource for me, at least until the pandemic barred its doors in 2020.

And, as always, I would like to acknowledge some very important non-academic influences on my life. First among these would be my parents and my siblings. I have already dedicated books to my father and my mother; this time I mark the influence of my brother and sister, both of whom have excelled in science and in academics: Bruce in physics and materials science at Cornell University, Cindy in marine biology (especially deep sea biology) at Duke University. Their significant contributions in their respective fields are best measured by their peers. I am only qualified to testify that their willingness to engage in extended non-acrimonious discussion and argument with their brother, in childhood and ever since, has been an invaluable gift.

Finally, I want to mention a set of four friends and a spouse, whom I join in various settings, but who, every spring, share with me the Green Bunny meal (at which no rabbit has ever been consumed): Iris and Jörg, Lisa and Bruno, and Sarala (who all agree is my better half). Neither they nor Bruce and Cindy should be blamed for any shortcomings in me or in my writing. My errors are my own.

Introduction
Four Post–World War II
Approaches to Detective Fiction

Prologue: Presidents and Private Eyes

Walt Whitman might speak of "Presidentiads," but, generally, American literary movements have not been usefully identified themselves with Presidents. Unlike British monarchs, who seem frequently to reign over cultural "Ages" (Elizabethan, Jacobean, Victorian, Edwardian), American Presidents, with one exception, have never presided over the nation for more than eight years, and even the most influential have rarely been identified with specific literary developments. But the evolution of the American detective story can be described as a punctuated equilibrium, with the major changes occurring in brief bursts of innovation during which a set of writers seem deliberately to redefine the detective's relation to his or her country and its social structures. Such a burst famously occurred during the Presidency of Calvin Coolidge (1923–29) and a second significant burst occurred during the Presidency of Ronald Reagan (1981–89), though the Reagan development was anticipated by a few writers in the mid–1970s. The Truman Presidency (1945–1953) cannot be said to have fundamentally altered the shape of the genre, but it did demonstrate that the hard-boiled model introduced by the Coolidge writers could be pressed in different, even contrary, directions, and it laid the groundwork for the more radical rethinking that emerged during Reagan's Presidency.

President John Tyler and the First Detective

The initial appearance of the fictional detective in Poe's Dupin stories belongs to the relatively undistinguished administration of the Whig, John Tyler, who took office in 1841 in same the month the first Dupin tale,

5

"The Murders in the Rue Morgue," was published, and left shortly after the last Dupin tale, "The Purloined Letter," appeared in 1845. M. Dupin is, of course, French, not American, and even if the Paris of "The Mystery of Marie Rogêt" seems very New Yorkish, it *is* in Paris—with its Prefects and its Rues and its "royal personages"—that Dupin detects. Critics have connected the orangutan that climbs the lightning rod at the rear of the L'Esplanaye's building on the Rue Morgue with Poe's attitudes toward (and anxieties about) African Americans, and John Tyler was a slave owner and a defender of States' Rights. But the connection is tenuous and Poe's whole art of fiction tends—except occasionally in satire—to avoid the pedestrian realities of the politics and sociology of America.

Later developments in the genre did begin to anchor the romance of the detective's investigations in the social realities of the time—the realities of Second Empire France (Emile Gaboriau) or Victorian England (Arthur Conan Doyle). But it was during the term and a half—1923–1929—that Calvin Coolidge served as President of the United States that the detective story made its most radical turn, replacing as the central feature of the story the reader's wonder at the impressive analytical skills of the Great Detective with the reader's admiration for the all-too-common detective who manfully maneuvers through the vividly represented mean streets of urban America to uncover the truth. The everyday disorder of those streets governed as much by a disciplined underworld as by a corrupt political order makes visible the special power of the tough detective to meet and overcome all obstacles. The detective's authority derives less from the way his gray cells can decipher the plot by which a corpse comes to lie in a locked room than from his ability to face guns and recover from beatings.

Calvin Coolidge's Private Eyes

It was in 1923, the year Coolidge inherited the Presidency upon the death (by cardiac arrest) of Warren G. Harding, that *Black Mask* introduced this new hard-boiled style into the genre, with, most notably, the first Race Williams short story by Carroll John Daly (in the June issue) and the first Continental Op short story by Dashiell Hammett (in the October issue). The somewhat more realistic Private Eye replaced the Great Detective as the defining figure: the standard investigator would be the wage-earning tough guy, not the brilliant amateur. In 1929, the year Coolidge was succeeded by Herbert Hoover, both Race Williams and the Continental Op found themselves involved in novel-length cases, and the hard-boiled detectives moved from pulp magazines into books, a format in which, through the 1930s and 1940s, they prospered. There is little to connect the puritanical and taciturn

Vermont President directly with the hard-edged detectives who worked the mean streets of his America. The world of Race Williams and the Op—and a host of pulp fiction stable mates—is the Roaring Twenties, with its Prohibition, its bootlegging and its gangsters, its flappers and its flivvers. It was a world presided over by Silent Cal, but it was not a Calvinist world. The detective of the Coolidge Presidentiad would not be a peculiar individual marked by his violin and cocaine—or by his priesthood, his Belgian origins, his medico-legal credentials, or his status as the favorite son of the Dowager Duchess of Denver—as somehow distinctly removed from the vulgar crowd and able, from his distance, to perceive what the crowd could not, and thus clarify the disorder that dismayed the crowd.[1] The vulgar electorate might in 1920 elect the Harding-Coolidge ticket, preferring its promise of a return to "normalcy," over the promise of James M. Cox and Franklin Delano Roosevelt to advance the Progressive agenda that had been espoused by Woodrow Wilson between 1912 and 1920, but having made the world safe for democracy and embedded the morality of the Women's Christian Temperance Union in the nation's Constitution, a large segment of the population was now discovering the excitement of indulging in prohibited behaviors—of drinking, smoking, gambling, and, if one were female, of baring one's hitherto well-concealed limbs.[2] And the Coolidge detective immersed himself in this destructive element. He drank, smoked, gambled, and admired exposed limbs. He was of the vulgar crowd, and this was his strength. He was marked as normal; he was not eligible for admission to any well-credentialed brain trust assembled in Washington, D.C., to apply its intelligence to correcting the injustices that history had introduced into American social, political, and economic arrangements. He did not have the credentials, and he was not, in any event, the sort to join any trust or any club. He was a common man.

Ronald Reagan's Private Eyes

The next significant development in the genre would be less specifically American, though American writers were central in its emergence. The detective having been demoted from being an extraordinary man to being an ordinary man would now in the 1970s and 1980s be figured an ordinary person. The most accurate identifier of the period would be the cumbersome "Nixon-Ford-Carter-Reagan Presidencies." But given that Ronald Reagan began his ascendency with his challenge to Gerald Ford in 1976, that the full flowering of the new model took place in the 1980s, and that the defining characteristic of this new model was its reaction against what it took to be the reactionary politics that Reagan embodied, it seems that the Reagan Presidency may properly stand as its location in history.

The new model retained the hard-boiled emphasis on the common man combating crime and corruption of the mean streets of urban America (though the mean streets would now often be mapped in smaller cities and towns, with regional differences mattering). But he ceased to be predictably white and male. And his or her commonness became less a matter of his or her private integrity, and more a matter of his or her relationships with friends and lovers and his or her commitment to social justice. The drinking, smoking, and gambling, the dalliances with women ("frails," "twists") and the disdain for ethnic minorities that once marked the detective as a man of the people disappears. He may be a former hard drinker, now committed to Alcoholics Anonymous (e.g. Lawrence Block's Matt Scudder, 1970); more likely she now enjoys a glass of wine with meals. She never chain smokes; she never smokes at all. Of course, she dispenses with sexism, and with racism, homophobia, anti–Semitism—with all of the implicit biases that had bonded the hard-boiled detective to his initial audience of hard-boiled readers of pulp magazines. Instead, the detective now embraces a progressive agenda that bonds her or him with her or his progressive audience that buys hardcovers and paperbacks. The common person is now an enlightened person (indeed, in the absence of other clues, unenlightened attitudes are sure markers of guilt), and she engages herself in cases that expose the oppressions that powerful unenlightened people impose on the disadvantaged members of society. And she is much less likely to be a *lonely* common person: she is engaged in a variety of intimate personal relationships that model the sort of beloved community that is possible when people of goodwill find each other.

This emergence of the engaged yet fairly tough private eye began in the 1970s and was crystallized in the early 1980s with the first novels of Sue Grafton and Sara Paretsky. The Reagan Presidency has some claim to be the central moment when diversity—gender diversity, sexual orientation diversity, racial diversity, ethnic diversity—became the hallmark of the genre, as the most popular writers and their detectives ceased to be a cadre of uniformly white, heterosexual men. If the original hard-boiled detectives of the 1920s were the unlikely offspring of a President who was weaned on a pickle (as Alice Roosevelt Longworth is reported to have said of Coolidge), the new hard-boiled detectives of the 1980s and after became expressions of a definite reaction against the President and the conservative values proclaimed by the Reagan Revolution. Implicit critiques of what a Missing Persons policeman in Raymond Chandler's *The Big Sleep* would call "the way we run our country" become explicit: after the 1980s, it seems, many detective novel series would begin with a well-defined sense of what is wrong with the country and then imagine the sort of detective who might involve himself or herself in the sorts of cases that expose the wrongness.

To be sure, some important and well-received detective novel series begun well before the Reagan revolution had taken social injustices suffered by different categories of the citizenry as the essential premise of their novels: Chester Himes in the Gravedigger Jones and Coffin Ed Johnson novels (African American detectives, debuting in 1957), Joseph Hansen in the Dave Brandstetter novels (Gay detective, 1970), Tony Hillerman in the Joe Leaphorn novels (Native American detective, 1970), Marcia Muller in the Sharon McCone novels (female detective, 1977). Robert B. Parker's Spenser debuted in 1973 as the very model of a modern progressive (but still tough) white male private eye. But the Reagan presidency saw a proliferation of new scenes of meanness in which new sorts of detectives from various intersections of male and female, black and white, gay and straight might pursue justice for the oppressed. Grafton's Kinsey Millhone and Paretsky's V.I. Warshawski, both debuting in 1982, embody the virtues of the new wave. Grafton's novels became reliable bestsellers, year after year, in hardback and paperback. Kinsey Millhone remains still a tough, independent investigator who always discovers whodunit, but she also, over the course of 25 novels, acquires a community of friends and lovers and family. And the evolving community, and the central values that it embodies (diversity, tolerance, equality), becomes for many readers an important secondary source of the series' appeal. That Millhone always perseveres and always solves the crime at hand remains primary. But the detective's character is now defined not just by her success in investigations, but also by her success in personal relationships—with success requiring that the detective embrace the right people the right way, while always maintaining her integrity. Paretsky's novels—quite popular, though not to the degree achieved by those of Grafton—similarly feature a tough, independent investigator who also always discovers whodunit but who discovers a community of friends and lovers and family. Warshawski is more overtly political in her commitments.[3] She wears her enlightenment brightly.

Harry Truman's Private Eyes

Midway between the concentrated toughness of the white male hard-boiled detectives who investigated the America of Calvin Coolidge in the 1920s and the flowering of less tough, more tolerant—often very much more tolerant—and very much more diverse detectives in the 1970s and 1980s, there was, during the Truman Presidency (1945–1952), a noteworthy transitional phase in which a second postwar era encouraged a new generation of writers (like their detectives, still white and male) to rethink the model of American detective that had been codified by the *Black Mask* boys in the Coolidge era.[4] They did not propose the sort of radical rethinking of the type that would later occur in the Reagan years, but they did prepare the ground for that rethinking—by pressing the hard-boiled detective in two contrary directions. Mike Hammer looked backward toward the very first tough American detective as Mickey Spillane pushed Race Williams's appetite for rapid movement and unapologetic violence to a new level and achieved unprecedented popularity. Yet despite his extraordinary success, Mike Hammer embodied the direction that the mainstream of the genre would *not* take.[5] It would be Ross Macdonald (Kenneth Millar) whose slow, incremental advance toward literary legitimacy and bestseller status blazed the trail that many of the Reagan writers would acknowledge as their inspiration.[6] Macdonald offered Lew Archer as a successor to Philip Marlowe, as a detective moved not just by judgment against general injustice and specific misbehavior, but as well by a deep sympathy for the victims of various sorts of oppression and discrimination, a sympathy that would become de rigueur in the 1980s.[7] Other writers such as Bart Spicer, Thomas B. Dewey and Wade Miller (Robert Wade and Bill Miller) filled the spectrum between these extremes, generally leaning forward with Macdonald and adding dimensions to the detective's character that Macdonald chose to neglect.

All of the postwar detectives still operated in big cities—New York, Philadelphia, Chicago, Los Angeles, San Diego.[8] All were men who still met the Chandler call for detectives who were complete men and common men and yet unusual men, taking no man's money dishonestly and no man's insolence passively. But the mean streets down which they went, neither tarnished nor afraid, were different from the streets down which Race Williams, the Continental Op, Sam Spade, and Philip Marlowe had to go. All of the postwar writers had been born in the mid– to late–1910s; the Great Depression had colored their youth; the Second World War had colored their young manhood; and they began writing in the immediate aftermath of the war which had ended the Depression and elevated America to economic and military supremacy in the world. Their protagonists— always roughly of an age with their authors—were men who had seen the nation and then the world dramatically fall apart and then be restored by, it seemed, a combination of American grit, American productivity, and American armed force. And the social contract between individuals and government had been irreversibly altered by the innovations of the New Deal and the strictures of the war economy. The original hard-boiled detectives had enjoyed a similar euphoric moment after those American virtues had made the world safe for democracy, but the American Normalcy that

Harding and Coolidge (and then Hoover) presided over was a reactionary normalcy. The normalcy that prevailed after Hiroshima was for most Americans an even happier recovery of material prosperity, but it was a post–New Deal normalcy that had, whether one liked it or not, changed the social and economic world that the new hard-boiled detectives had to navigate.

The Truman Presidency

Harry Truman's Presidency began with the unexpected death of Franklin Roosevelt at Warm Springs, Georgia, on 12 April 1945. Less than a month later, on 7 May, he inherited the German surrender in the European theater of the Second World War. In August, he approved the dropping of atomic bombs on Hiroshima and Nagasaki, which led, another month later, to the end of the war in the Pacific. When the Japanese formally surrendered on 2 September 1945, having served less than five months in office, Truman found himself Commander-in-Chief of the world's only military armed with atomic weapons and leader of an economy that was, by far, the world's strongest. The Red Army had performed heroically and the sun still did not set on the British Empire, but the United States could congratulate itself in late 1945 on being the pre-eminent nation in the immediate post-war world. If in the first half of the 1940s America had been consumed by the arduous struggles first against the devastating economic depression that had devastated the country (and the world) since the beginning of the 1930s and then against the aggression of the Axis powers in North Africa, Europe, and the Pacific that had interrupted almost everyone's life (and ended the lives over 400,000 Americans), the second half of the decade could claim the reward of an ultimate triumph in both of those struggles and be devoted to the satisfaction of personal needs that had had to be suppressed through 1945. A relatively affluent polity was now ready to consume what American factories (and American studios, now both cinema and television) could produce. During the last two years of the war, Americans had saved 25 percent of their take-home pay; they had $140 billion in liquid assets, most of it in small (under $5,000) accounts (O'Neill 84). The demand for consumer goods (and other markers of a good lifestyle) was seemingly insatiable.

Not everyone participated equally in the prosperity. African Americans might be encouraged by President Truman's desegregation of the military in 1948, but they still found themselves denied rights and privileges assumed by white Americans. And women who had entered the work force in large numbers often found themselves pressured to resume more traditional roles. The seriousness of the Cold War grew, with significant intensifications in 1949, when Russia exploded its first nuclear weapon and Mao Zedong declared mainland China's affiliation with the Communist world order, and in 1950, when 75,000 North Korean troops crossed the 38th Parallel and began a conflict that eventually would cost over 30,000 American lives. But when contrasted to the prior decade and a half—1930–1945—with its seemingly global traumas that afflicted nearly all levels of society, the Truman years were very good years. They constituted the strong beginning of the decade and a half that William L. O'Neill calls *American High: The Years of Confidence 1945–1960.*

The military, which had expanded to a force of more than 12 million at the end of the war, was quickly reduced to just over 1.5 million by June 1947. Millions of new civilians provided the incentive to convert existing factories from the production of war materiel to the production consumer goods, and, with new factories employing new workers, markets were filled with commodities for those workers to purchase. The G.I. Bill (the Servicemen's Readjustment Act of 1944) made low interest mortgages available to veterans (as well as the celebrated and often life-changing stipends for college and trade school education), and a boom in housing construction followed; a total of 15 million housing units were built between 1946 and 1955 (O'Neill 19).[9] And every house required new appliances. Virtually no new civilian vehicles had been produced in 1943 or 1944; by 1951, over five million civilian vehicles were being produced annually. The automobile was no longer the emblem of liberation (to many, dangerous liberation) that it had been after the First World War, but, with its chrome and its aerodynamics, it was a very visible emblem of an increasingly affluent society. Between 1949 and 1959 the number of television stations rose from 69 to 566, and the number of households with television sets rose from 940,000 to 44,000,000 (O'Neill 80). The large new middle class could view every night the habits and the possessions proper to the new middle class. Economic security and ever-expanding creature comforts seemed assured.

Geopolitical security was less assured. Even before the detonation of the Soviet Union's atomic bomb and the triumph of the People's Army in mainland China there had been the Berlin Airlift in 1948, and the Korean War would outlast Truman's administration. Even sooner than it had after the First World War, it became clear that the world was still not definitively safe for democracy. And there was, as well, an emerging awareness of the threat of an internal fifth column. Traitors had subverted the American monopoly of nuclear weaponry (Julius and Ethel Rosenberg were executed in 1953), and someone had lost China. Senator Joseph McCarthy's speech to the Ohio County Women's Republican Club in Wheeling, West Virginia, in February 1950 in which he announced possession of a list of 205 members of the Communist Party currently employed in the U.S. State Department can be taken as the moment when the Red Scare began to move to the center of national consciousness. It would remain a central topic of political affairs at least until the Army-McCarthy hearings of 1954.

But there were other indications that the prosperity of the Truman years, while great, was not universal. There was significant labor unrest: Truman felt compelled to authorize federal intervention in a railroad strike in 1950 and in a steelworkers' strike in 1952. And although the next important landmarks in the Civil Rights Movement would emerge during the Eisenhower Presidency with the Supreme Court's 1954 *Brown v. Board of Education of Topeka, Kansas*, decision and the 1955 Montgomery Bus Boycott, the Truman years saw violent racial unrest in Columbia, Tennessee (1946), Peekskill, New York (1949), and Cicero, Illinois (1951) make the national headlines. Productive industries and expanding suburbs did reward a very large and confident middle class, and without Prohibition and Depression, there was no widespread, very visible challenge to the new prosperity, but not everyone felt included in what emerged through Truman's Fair Deal.

Detective Fiction in the Truman Presidency

The hard-boiled detectives who debuted in the late 1940s were created by men who had grown up experiencing economic depression as boys and young men, and a world war against fascism in their mid- and late twenties. They returned from war to write primarily for other men who had also been through both trials and who were now engaged in pursuing happiness in union jobs or in gray flannel suits. It was, in some obvious respects, a quite different world than the one that their hard-edged predecessors had encountered in the 1920s or that their softer-edged, more socially conscious heirs would encounter in the 1970s and 1980s. The inaugural private eyes of the Coolidge era had undertaken their investigations against a background of dramatic postwar social change. As corsets were discarded and dresses were shortened, as alcohol became illegal (and more widely consumed than ever), as mobs and bankers prospered, as Hollywood manufactured movies, and movie stars, and scandals, tough guys with guns drove from scene to scene throwing wrenches into the machinery in an effort to discover whodunit. The first major novel in the new genre that reflected that world was Dashiell Hammett's *Red Harvest* (1929). In it, the Continental Op tried to navigate between competing criminal gangs, each specializing in a field of illegal activity such as gambling or bootlegging, as he worked to restore the mining city of Personville to the management of its aging magnate, who had lost control after labor unrest. As W.H. Auden wrote, in "The Guilty Vicarage" (1948), the fiction of Raymond Chandler (and, clearly, though Auden doesn't mention him, Dashiell Hammett) is set in The Great Wrong Place—as opposed to the Great Good Place that Auden argued is the primal scene of the classical British detective story. The milieu of Mike Hammer, Lew Archer, Carney Wilde, and Max Thursday in the late 1940s is still a Wrong Place; crime is still an endemic social problem, *not* "shockingly out of place, as when a dog makes a mess on a drawing room carpet"; murder occurs in the streets, not in vicarage libraries. But the Wrongness of the late 1940s seems a bit less raw, a bit less a matter of the greed and the lust of unrestrained individuals—magnates or gangsters, and a bit more baked into the complex class, racial, and gender structures of the American socio-economic world.[10] Social structures—whether civilian (the multitude of acronymic federal agencies spawned by the New Deal) or military (the armed forces or factories geared to mass production of war materiel)—were much more pervasive and much more visible in 1947 than they had been in 1923. And the detective is, consequently, a bit more openly critical of these structures. He tends to see—and talk about—injustice as well as crime.

This trend would emerge as the keynote of the next turning of the genre. Writers of private eye fiction began explicitly to prioritize injustice over crime: they identified classes and categories of abuse based on class, race, and gender, and they created detectives, crimes, and criminals that illustrated these abuses suffered by disadvantaged members of society. (Abuse of the natural environment also came to the attention of many of the engaged detectives of the 1980s and after.) The private eyes of the late 1940s—as homogeneously white and male and tough as their predecessors of the 1920s—were (Mike Hammer excepted) making tentative steps toward the diverse socially conscious detectives who would prevail a few decades later. All of them were naturally ex–GI's; though they would not sympathize with oppressed communities as vigorously as the Reagan detectives, their army (or navy) experiences with a band of brothers made them to some degree resistant to the 1920s model of the lone wolf who never commits to any friendship, to any marriage. Unlike Race Williams, the Continental Op, Sam Spade, or Philip Marlowe, they were open to a measure of emotional investment in the people they encountered. And they could begin to see broader implications to the problems of individuals.

The New Private Eyes of the 1940s

A number of new hard-boiled detectives joined the existing roster of private eyes in the immediate post–World War II period. Their authors would be competing not just with the acknowledged master, Raymond Chandler, but with a surviving host of first-generation hard-boiled writers who had continued to publish fiction through the war and would continue to be active. Although the widely admired Dashiell Hammett had stopped publishing novels with *The Thin Man* in 1934 and Carroll John Daly—less widely admired by those who publish their admiration, but still, on the basis of his priority and his popularity meriting the title "The Father of the Hard-boiled Private Eye"—had issued the eighth and last Race Williams novel in 1940, but he would publish ten more Race Williams short stories between 1948 and 1955. Robert Leslie Bellem would publish more than a dozen additional "Dan Turner, Hollywood Detective" short stories between 1946 and his final appearances in 1950. Cleve Adams would publish *Death at the Dam*, the fifth of his six Rex McBride novels, in 1946. The more prolific Brett Halliday, who had begun his Mike Shayne series in 1939, the same year that Philip Marlowe debuted, would publish nine further Mike Shayne novels between 1946 and 1952 (and a further eight before turning the series over to ghostwriters). If readers wanted to see how tough-guys who had matured in the Depression years could handle crime in the post–World War II crime, they had many to choose from. For the most part, these detectives continued to follow the trails that they had blazed in the 1930s.[11]

The new detectives were imagined by men who were clearly working within the parameters defined by Hammett, Daly, Bellem, Chandler, Halliday and others. They did not make dramatic departures from their predecessors, but they did nudge the genre forward, with detectives fresh from the extraordinary regimentation of the war confronting familiar hard-boiled types—tough gangsters, grasping women, aging millionaires—in prosperous post-war America. But the gangsters could no longer rely on bootleg liquor for their profits; the women were grasping for executive positions, not just money; the millionaires could no longer be plausibly restored to their "natural" authority.

Principal Post–World War II Hard-Boiled Detectives

Author	Birthdate	Detective	Debut Novel
John Evans[12]	1908	Paul Pine	1946
Frank Kane	1912	Johnny Liddell	1947
Thomas B. Dewey	1915	Mac	1947
Ross Macdonald[13]	1915	Lew Archer	1949
Mickey Spillane	1918	Mike Hammer	1947
Bart Spicer	1918	Carney Wilde	1949
Henry Kane	1918	Pete Chambers	1947

Author	Birthdate	Detective	Debut Novel
Wade Miller[14]	1920	Max Thursday	1947
Richard S. Prather	1921	Shell Scott	1950

Ross Macdonald and Mickey Spillane

Of these, Mickey Spillane and Ross Macdonald were clearly the most influential. Mike Hammer almost immediately thrilled unprecedented millions of readers (most of them presumably fellow ex–G.I.s), and appalled dozens of reviewers, and then, through the early 1950s provided intellectual observers of mid-century American popular culture with a touchstone for the degeneration of the taste of the mass of American readers. Ross Macdonald from the beginning attracted a decent readership and excellent reviews and he eventually, in 1969, received the distinction that had eluded both Hammett and Chandler: an escape from being reviewed in a "Criminals-At-Large" column onto a front-page article in *The New York Times Book Review* and regular appearances on the *Times*'s bestseller list. For a few years at least he could claim consideration not as a fine genre writer, but as an American novelist.

But each of the remaining seven writers has a claim to attention. Each managed to produce a series of novels that consistently attracted a sufficiently wide readership.

John Evans and Richard Prather

John Evans and Richard Prather were both successful writers in the hard-boiled genre—Prather especially—and both have admirers. But both lie somewhat outside the mainstream. Evans was a decade older than the others, and thus experienced both the Depression and the War at a significantly different age. He published only four hard-boiled Paul Pine novels, three of them in the Truman 1940s, and while they clearly demonstrate Raymond Chandler's continuing strong influence on the genre, they reflect the response of an older writer.[15] Richard Prather, by one year the youngest of the writers, had a long and distinguished career, publishing dozens of Shell Scott novels between 1950 and 1987. But the Shell Scott novels belong to a particular line of hard-boiled detective fiction that employs a touch of comic excess. Robert Leslie Bellem's Dan Turner novels pioneered this tradition; other precedents might be found in Norbert Davis's Doan and Carstairs novels and Craig Rice's Jake Justus-Helene Brand-John Joseph Malone novels. It is a line that deserves recognition, and Shell Scott's long and steady appeal is surely due in part to Prather's exuberant play with the adventures and misadventures of his detective. Decades of reliable sales suggest that a playful take on the business of being hard-boiled struck an appealing chord in the postwar approach to violence and morality. But the comic tone sets the series apart from the mainstream narratives of hard-boiled detection.

Frank Kane and Henry Kane

Frank Kane and Henry Kane each produced dozens of novels featuring their detectives. They were solid workmen in the vein of Brett Halliday, and a study of their fiction over the decades (Frank Kane's last Johnny Liddell novel appeared in 1967; Henry Kane's final Pete Chambers novel in 1972) can also be rewardingly studied on its own terms; it opens a useful window on the way its regular readers saw (or wanted to see) the way Americans lived and worked and murdered. Each writer produced at least a volume a year, and often more: a total of 31 featuring Peter Chambers and 30 featuring Johnny Liddell.

Thomas B. Dewey, Wade Miller, and Bart Spicer

The post-war private eye fiction of Thomas B. Dewey, Wade Miller, and Bart Spicer was somewhat more ambitious in significant ways than that of Evans, Prather, Kane and Kane. Their fiction did not match the popularity of Spillane's and they did not appear to set themselves to surpass the artistry of Raymond Chandler, as Ross Macdonald did.[16] But all three produced a series of novels that present versions of the new normal for the private eye of the late 1940s.

Thomas B. Dewey

Thomas B. Dewey began his Mac series in 1947, the year that Mike Hammer and Max Thursday also debuted, and two years before Bart Spicer introduced Carney Wilde and Ross Macdonald introduced Lew Archer. Like Hammer and Archer, Mac would have a long career—some seventeen novels, ending with *The Taurus Trap* (1970). Mac begins as a Chicago private eye in *Draw the Curtain*, but as early as the second novel, *Every Bet's a Sure Thing* (1953), he travels to the West Coast, and several of the later novels find Mac relocated in California. Dewey's interest in generational issues makes him an especially useful contrast with Macdonald, who also centered much of his fiction upon the strains between children and parents. But sixteen of the seventeen Mac novels were published after the end of Truman's second term, and Mac cannot be counted a principal private eye of the period.

WADE MILLER

Wade Miller has perhaps the best claim to have produced a thoroughly Truman detective: all six of the Max Thursday novels were published while Harry Truman was president. Miller introduced Max Thursday in 1947, the same year as Mickey Spillane introduced Mike Hammer. The two collaborators who wrote as Wade Miller had, in fact, published a debut novel in the hard-boiled genre the prior year, *Deadly Weapon* (1946). It featured private eye Walter James, who comes to San Diego in pursuit of his partner's murderer. James happens upon another murder in the first chapter, and the San Diego homicide detectives assigned to investigate that murder— Lt. Austin Clapp and his partner Jim Crane—will be the officers with whom Max Thursday will work in all six of the novels in which he appears. Wade and Miller would produce dozens of crime novels published between 1946 and 1961 and would use a number of different pen names (Dale Wilmer, Will Daemer, Whit Masterson), but the Max Thursday novels are their most important contribution to the genre.

And the six novels do compose an innovative series: there is an underlying arc of action that gives shape to the sequence. In the first novel, a drunken, armed Thursday is called by his happily remarried ex-wife to rescue their son. In the middle novels, having shot and killed four people, he resolves never to carry a gun again, and he develops a new romantic relationship with a feisty newspaperwoman. In the final novel, he is once again alone, having lost the affection of newspaperwoman. Thursday has thus an evolving life in a way that none of the original *Black Mask* detectives had. In another gesture toward novelty, the series takes as its scene an American city—San Diego—not famous for mean streets, and it takes San Diego seriously, precisely locating the action on the real streets and in the real buildings of the city. Finally, Wade Miller chose to write the series in the third person; though not unprecedented, third-person narration was rare in the late 1940s: Evans, Dewey, Macdonald, Spillane, Spicer, Henry Kane, and Prather all preferred the first person; only Frank Kane's Johnny Liddell series was narrated in third person.

BART SPICER

The Carney Wilde novels of Bart Spicer, though the final two of the seven were published during the Eisenhower presidency, seem to be the new series that can be most usefully set against the appealing violence of Spillane's innovations and the appealing sensitivity of Macdonald's. The first Carney Wilde novel, *The Dark Light*, actually won Dodd Mead's Red Badge prize ($1,000) for the best first mystery novel in 1949.[17] The Carney Wilde novels share the some of the same virtues of the Max Thursday novels. Wilde's Philadelphia is another city hitherto undetected by a tough private eye. Spicer, to be sure, is not as careful in creating the tangible city as was Wade Miller, but Wilde's Philadelphia usefully contrasts with Hammer's New York and Archer's Southern California. And Spicer was considerably more careful in projecting the realistic development of Carney Wilde's personal and professional career, as the detective acquires a wife and expands his agency, an especially useful contrast to isolated lives and careers led by Mike Hammer and Lew Archer. Finally, two novels in the Carney Wilde series feature African American characters in central roles, something unprecedented in the hard-boiled world.

The Four Key Writers of Hard-Boiled Detective Fiction, 1947–1952: Macdonald, Spillane, Spicer, and Miller

Kenneth Millar/Ross Macdonald, Mickey Spillane, Bart Spicer, and Wade Miller (both Robert Wade and Bill Miller), then, were just some of the veterans, all in their early thirties, who returned to civilian with the notion that the hard-boiled detective novel series offered a young writer a viable path to make a living as an author—and, for Ross Macdonald certainly and perhaps for Bart Spicer and others—to make art as an author. Spillane and Macdonald already had some experience with professional writing. Spillane had enjoyed some success writing for the comics before the war, and Macdonald had published four non-series hard-boiled novels during and immediately after the war. Wade Miller's first Max Thursday novel would build upon the author's first collaboration, published in 1946; Bart Spicer's first Carney Wilde novel would be his first publication. All four now proposed to introduce private detectives who might serve as the protagonists of an extended series of novels that exploited the new ubiquity of cheap paperback fiction.[18] Their detectives would themselves be veterans of the war; they would be investigating crime in a country full of veterans returning to civilian life and able to afford cheap paperback fiction. They chose four different cities in which to place their detectives and the crimes that they would confront: Mike Hammer would drive his heap up and down the avenues of dark, rainy New York City and occasionally into its Long Island and upstate periphery; Max Thursday would drive his Oldsmobile through the streets of San Diego and its immediate surroundings. Lew Archer would locate himself in Los Angeles but would range throughout the sunny country of the southern Californian coast, from Santa Teresa (Santa Barbara) to Mexico. Carney Wilde would establish his detective enterprise in what hard-boiled detective fiction had hitherto regarded as the undistinguished environs of Philadelphia[19]; on rare occasions he crossed the Delaware River, driving into New Jersey and up to New York City (and once flying to Arizona).

Spillane would eventually publish 13 Mike Hammer novels: six phenomenally popular books in the Truman years between 1947 and 1952.[20] Then, after a ten-year hiatus, he resumed the series, producing nine more Hammer novels between 1962 and 1996 (also popular, though less phenomenally so).[21] During the second phase of productivity, Spillane would also write several non–Hammer novels set in the hard-boiled milieu, including four Tiger Mann novels between 1964 and 1965, aiming to attract readers of Ian Fleming's James Bond novels. Wade Miller published all six Max Thursday novels (plus eight other thrillers) during the Truman administration. As it happened, they too took a brief one-year hiatus, publishing no novels in the final year of Truman's presidency. Ross Macdonald published the first four (of eighteen) Lew Archer novels between 1949 and 1952, with a four-year gap before the fifth Archer novel, *The Barbarous Coast*, appeared in 1956. Macdonald himself saw the publication of *The Galton Case* in 1959 as a major turning point in his career as a writer of detective fiction, but the first four novels fairly establish the parameters of Lew Archer and his world. (Ross Macdonald also sought to escape the limitations of Lew Archer in two other hard-boiled novels, the first *Meet Me at the Morgue* coming in 1953 during Archer's hiatus, and then in 1960, after reviving Archer in 1954, with *The Ferguson Affair*). Bart Spicer would publish seven Carney Wilde novels between 1949 and 1959, five between 1949 and 1952, with the final two novels, which tie up Wilde's career as an active detective, appearing after gaps of two and five years in 1954 and 1959.[22] The inauguration of Dwight Eisenhower as President thus saw the end of one series (Max Thursday), and a hiatus of between two and ten years in the careers of the other three series (Wilde, Archer, and Hammer).

During the Truman years, then, these four writers would publish twenty hard-boiled detective novels in four series that established one of them as, in his time, the model of the excellence in the genre; one of them as the model of the worst in the genre; and the other two as examples of largely well-received and then largely neglected series in the genre.

	Mickey Spillane	Wade Miller	Ross Macdonald	Bart Spicer
1947	*I, the Jury*	*Guilty Bystander*		
1948	[*The Twisted Thing*]	*Fatal Step*		

	Mickey Spillane	Wade Miller	Ross Macdonald	Bart Spicer
		Uneasy Street		
1949			*The Moving Target*	*The Dark Light*
1950	*My Gun Is Quick*	*Calamity Fair*	*The Drowning Pool*	*Blues for the Prince*
	Vengeance Is Mine	*Murder Charge*		
1951	*One Lonely Night*	*Shoot to Kill*	*The Way Some People Die*	*Black Sheep, Run*
	The Big Kill			*The Golden Door*
1952	*Kiss Me, Deadly*		*The Ivory Grin*	*The Long Green*

Note: *The Twisted Thing* was originally written as the second Mike Hammer novel but was published later.

The six Mike Hammer novels made Mickey Spillane notorious, a notoriety that made the novels by far the best-selling titles on the "Mystery/Crime Fiction" bookshelf for decades and, at the same time, provided critics with a handy shibboleth to distinguish tasteful popular fiction from tasteless popular fiction. Ross Macdonald's four Truman-era Lew Archer novels, considerably less popular with readers—Pocket Books declined even to issue a paperback of the fifth Archer novel, *Find a Victim* (1954)—became, for contemporary critics the standard against which hard-boiled detective novels should be measured. Bart Spicer's five Carney Wilde novels, sometimes twinned with Macdonald's as exemplars of tasteful hard-boiledness, faded from all but the most comprehensive accounts of the genre, as did Wade Miller's once quite popular Max Thursday novels.

1

Mickey Spillane's
Mike Hammer

Mickey Spillane emerged as an unparalleled phenomenon as the mass market paperback became, by the early 1950s, the way to reach a wide audience of readers. He was the bête noire of the cultural custodians of postwar America. It was not just reviewers who patrolled the mystery columns of the book reviews that were appalled by the crudity of Spillane's prose and ethics. His peers in the genre shared the disdain: "everybody in the Mystery Writers of America and all the critics of that time [the 1950s] loathed Spillane and hated his books and thought they were vile and, if not obscene, certainly reprehensible and of little or no redeeming value" (Pierce). Ross Macdonald referred to Spillane as "the poet laureate of sexual psychopathy," and in 1951, disappointed by the sales of the first three Lew Archer novels, he promised to work on another good novel, the alternative being to "have a prefrontal lobotomy so I can write like Mickey Spillane" (Nolan 89, 128). The next year, Raymond Chandler wrote, "This Spillane, so far as I can see, is nothing but a mixture of violence and outright pornography" (*Selected Letters* 311). It was the altogether unprecedented sales of the series of Hammer novels that provoked the outrage. Upon his debut in 1947, *The New York Times Book Review*'s mystery column, "Criminals at Large," actually took a relatively neutral view of the first Mike Hammer novel, *I, the Jury*, describing it as a tougher-than-usual crime novel: "Mr. Hammer bludgeons the males, captivates the females, and goes about his business in a rousing, slashing, smashing manner." The review concludes that the novel will appeal to readers "who must have the impact 'right between the eyes'" (3 August 1947: 14). But when *My Gun Is Quick* appeared three years later and Spillane's immense popularity had to be addressed, the tone of "Criminals at Large" shifted dramatically: "This brew of sadism, eroticism and the glorification of 'the thrill of running something down and pumping a slug into it' is enough to make the staunchest member of the American Civil Liberties Union waver just a second in his opinion of the Watch and Ward

Society" (12 February 1950: 183). The Hammer books are now such a danger to society that they justify a half-serious preference for the Victorian decencies upheld by Anthony Comstock's notoriously censorious society. When Anthony Boucher, the doyen of American crime fiction critics from 1951 to 1968, took over the "Criminals at Large" column, he continued the castigation of Spillane's moral imagination and its regrettable influence: reviewing *The Big Kill*, he reports that "the usual Spillane sex cum sadism is here blended with crude sentimentality and much pretentious talk about social responsibility (vigilante style) to make the mixture even more repellent than usual" (5 August 1951: 185).[1] Max Collins and James L Traylor summarize the consistent response of contemporary middle brow intellectuals to Spillane's vision: "starting in February 1952, a series of articles in *Harper's*, *Saturday Review* and *New Republic* blamed practically everything that was going wrong with American society on Mickey Spillane" (*One Lonely Knight* 25).

I, the Jury *(1947)*

When he sat down to write *I, the Jury* in 1946, Mickey Spillane was not proposing to engage in the project of making serious literature of detective fiction, a project that both Dashiell Hammett and Raymond Chandler had expressed in letters to Blanche Knopf and that Ross Macdonald would soon claim as his own ambition. Spillane wrote for "customers," not critics; and he was selling them "the chewing gum of American literature" (Severo). Mike Hammer was designed to please the customers for the emerging market in paperback thrillers that was served by publishers such as NAL's Signet Books (which published Spillane's novels) and Fawcett's Gold Medal Books. Spillane composed *I, the Jury* as the likeliest device to supply the $1,000 that he required to complete the construction of a house on a plot of land he had purchased near Newburgh, New York, in 1945. He took as his model Carroll John Daly's Race Williams, who had most reliably pleased the customers who purchased copies of *Black Mask*. "Yours," he once wrote to Daly, "was the first and only style of writing that ever influenced me in any way. Race was the model for Mike [Hammer], and I can't say more in this case than imitation being the most sincere form of flattery" (quoted in Etheridge). Spillane had already enjoyed success writing for the comic books before his service in the war, and that experience in blocking out sharp panels of action, along with the precedent provided by Race Williams's confident and constant motion through the streets of New York City, prepared Spillane to write fiction that would capture and hold the attention of his readers.

Mike Hammer would indeed resemble Race Williams in his supreme—and invariably justified—confidence in his own moral authority. He could echo Race Williams' claim, "My ethics are my own," though Hammer, like Williams, clearly assumes that, in fact, his readers will share his values. But where Race Williams follows a detective story convention— observed by both M. Dupin and Sherlock Holmes—of prefacing both his first short story and his first novel with brief expositions of his method, Mike Hammer simply declares his extreme moral self-confidence.[2] The difference is slight, but significant. Race Williams begins with an argument, however thin, for his authority, then narrates the events in which he exercises that authority. And then, immediately, he is in motion, walking down "a dirty little street of the lower East Side" (*Snarl* 2), when he is accosted and attacked by the "Beast." He doesn't stop until the Beast is dead, with Race Williams's bullet in his brain.

In his opening paragraphs, Mike Hammer enters a murder scene, insists upon uncovering the body of his murdered comrade, curses, and declares his intention to race the police to catch the criminal: he and the police will "work together as usual, but in the homestretch, I'm going to pull the trigger" (6-7). Without moving from the room where his comrade's body lies, Hammer spends the entire first chapter of his first novel declaiming a passionate tirade against the murderer, and it is this excess of passion—a private thirst for revenge that even Captain Pat Chambers, who also was a comrade of Jack Williams but is now a public servant, cannot match—that constitutes Hammer's signature virtue as a detective, his equivalent of a Science of Deduction or little grey cells. Mike Hammer always begins with a personal animus. He is always personally angry about the crime he is investigating, whether the victim he is avenging is a close friend who made a great wartime sacrifice for him or, in the next novel, a former prostitute whom Hammer has only briefly encountered one night.

Having discarded Race Williams's vestigial discourse on method (and, as well his residual Victorian diction and Victorian mores), Mike Hammer would adopt Race Williams's version of the standard hard-boiled method of discovering truth: confident forward motion and violent confrontation. The motion need not be mindful; the final chapter explaining everything often relies upon luck as a paste to bind the actions of the villain and the detective into a plausible (often barely plausible) plot. The motion did need to be quick, and the action violent. And violence—physical assaults administered and suffered by the detective (with a corresponding regimen of aggressive sexual encounters)—became, for many, the Spillane brand.

The first chapter of *I, the Jury* does offer some relevant information about the manner in which Jack Williams met his death, but its principal function is to immerse the reader in Hammer's emotional response to that death. In Chapter Two, Hammer begins to move, and he never stops moving until he corners the killer at the novel's end. He climbs into his jalopy to drive to his office, and for the rest of the novel, he seems not to pause in any one location for more than a few pages. Every new scene serves as a stage for the detective to assert his dominance over whomever he encounters—criminals, cops, attractive women, befuddled bystanders—and to acquire a new direction in which to rush. The constant motion finally ends when he stops to spend most of the final chapter in Charlotte Manning's living room, working himself up to his climax.

But if Spillane looked to Carroll John Daly for the essence of Mike Hammer's toughness and his drive to extract information through physical intimidation, the plot that he devised for Hammer to solve in *I, the Jury* is as clearly a borrowing from the plot that Daly's principal rival for *Black Mask* supremacy, Dashiell Hammett, had devised for Sam Spade in 1929. It was the *Maltese Falcon* that Mickey Spillane kept in mind when he devoted nine (or, by other accounts, nineteen) days to the composition of his first novel. His redaction of what many regard as the greatest of the hard-boiled detective novels would attract readers in unprecedented numbers. The hard-cover 1947 edition would sell a respectable 15,000 copies, but the paperback issued in 1948 would quickly sell two million copies, and eventually top eight million in sales. Mike Hammer's single-minded pursuit of the killer of his army comrade would make him as much an icon as Sam Spade had become. If Spade stood as a pulp hero who seemed to cross the border between lowbrow fiction and highbrow, Hammer would stand as a paperback hero who disdained the highbrow and remained resolutely working class in his morals and his tastes.

In part, the difference is a matter of style. Hammett embellished his hero's voice with sardonic wit. Sam Spade demonstrates his mastery of situations physically, like all hard-boiled detectives, but also verbally.[3] Spillane stripped his hero down to a brutal simplicity and directness, both physical and verbal. Hammett's decision to move from the first-person narration of the Continental Op stories and novels to the third person narration of Sam Spade's words and actions placed Spade at a crucial distance from the reader. Like all first-person narrators, Mike Hammer erases that distance, but from the first pages Hammer is especially insistent not only that the reader be limited to his point of view, but that the reader share the emotion with which Hammer views things. That the surnames of both detectives refer to tools is doubtless a coincidence, but a telling one. "Spade" surely makes reference to digging for the truth. "Hammer" speaks to the way that Spillane wants to bludgeon the reader into turning the page.[4] Hammett uses Spade's verbal agility as a signature tactic in the tough guy's confrontation with his adversaries. Spillane has Hammer speak most effectively with the unsubtle weapons of his fist, his feet, and his gun. Hammer remains, in this respect, very much the heir of Race Williams. He has no time for clever phrasing; when he speaks, it is always with force and directness.[5] Even *Red Harvest*, the Hammett novel that comes closest to the fast-paced violence of Carroll John Daly's fiction, the Continental Op is more thoughtful and more articulate than Race Williams or Mike Hammer. Williams's motto—"With me the thought is the act" (*Snarl*, 12)—would serve Mike Hammer as well: his virtue as a detective lies in his reflexes. These reflexes serve him in fisticuffs, but they also propel his investigation. Williams declares, "I am a man of action but I can think occasionally" (63). Mike Hammer occasionally indulges in a paragraph of thought, briefly outlining a set of suspicions, but action is his métier.

But aside from the radically different styles, the parallels between *The Maltese Falcon* and *I, the Jury* are extensive. Both detectives run their own private detective agency, one in San Francisco, the other in New York City. Both employ loyal secretaries, unlike Chandler's Philip Marlowe, who operates an agency of one. Both Sam Spade and Mike Hammer are confronted with the murder of a close associate: Spade's partner, Miles Archer; Hammer's comrade, Jack Williams. Both detectives find that the case involves themselves deeply with a beautiful and strong woman (Brigid O'Shaughnessy, Charlotte Manning). Both detectives declare their love for the woman (Spade with crucial qualifications; Hammer with an unqualified proposal of marriage). In the end, both discover that the murderer of their partner/comrade is the beautiful woman. And both choose to sacrifice love to justice.

Hammett's novel is, of course, more artful in its development and more complex in its portrayal of characters and the choices that they must make. The core murder plot (Spade-O'Shaughnessy-Archer) is balanced with the fantastic conspiracy to possess the marvelous falcon (Gutman, Cairo, Wilmer, Jacobi, O'Shaughnessy).[6] Spillane intensifies the emotions of the core plot: Hammer's devotion to Jack Williams is as far from Spade's disdain for Miles Archer as Hammer's besotted love of Charlotte Manning is from Spade's deep and deeply uneasy relation with Brigid O'Shaughnessy.[7] There are, of course, distractions from Hammer's intense hatred of Jack's killer and his intense love of Charlotte, but they are diverse. Some—such as the Hal Kines-George Kalecki subplot are tangentially related to the central Mike Hammer-Charlotte Manning plot; some—such as the antics of Mary Bellamy or the action at the Hi-Ho Club—have no direct bearing on the central plot and serve only to amplify the magnetism and the prowess of the detective. Spade has to puzzle through the multifaceted problem of the Maltese Falcon before he can identify the murderer of Miles Archer;

Hammer has to beat up or kill or sleep with a variety of individuals before he can identify the murderer of Jack Williams.

This marks the fundamental difference in the progress of the two parallel plots. Spade is always cool and thoughtful. He maintains an emotional distance from everyone, not just from Miles and Brigid. His affair with Iva Archer illustrates the same quality: she is violently in love with Spade, and believes he is so violently in love with her that he might have murdered Miles; frustrated by his coolness, she attempts to have Spade charged with the crime. Spade does seem to express anger once, when he engages in a threatening rant against Caspar Gutman at the end of their first meeting. His face is "pale and hard"; he speaks "in a low furious voice"; he turns "with angry heedlessness" and shatters a glass; he slams the door when he leaves (*Complete Novels* 485–87). And then, riding down the elevator, he grins and says "Whew!" It has all been a performance, a tactic to elicit more information from Gutman. Spade may feel genuine emotion—as he says, perhaps he does love Brigid O'Shaugnessy. But he never expresses genuine emotion.

Mike Hammer constantly expresses extreme emotion. His first gesture in *I, the Jury*, after entering the room in which his friend, Jack Williams, has been murdered, is to comfort Williams's fiancée, Myrna; his second is to intensify his anger at the situation: he insists upon uncovering the corpse of his friend to view the great wound in his abdomen and the trail of blood that he left attempting to crawl toward his own gun. Hammer explicitly disavows any desire to be "cold and impartial" (as juries are supposed to be): "this time I'm the law and I'm not going to be cold and impartial. I'm going to remember all those things" (7). He explains to his friend, Homicide Capt. Chambers, "I hate hard, Pat…. Some day, before long, I am going to have my rod in my mitt and the killer in front of me. I'm going to watch the killer's face. I'm going to plunk one right in his gut, and when he's dying on the floor, I may kick his teeth out" (8). Sam Spade feels the obligation to apprehend his partner's murderer; Mike Hammer feels the desire to kick the dying murderer's teeth in. In contrast, Spade regards Miles Archer as "a son of a bitch." Within a week of establishing the partnership, Spade realized that he was going to have to get rid of Archer (581). Jack Williams was not just Hammer's "best friend"; he was a wartime comrade who lost his arm in the South Pacific parrying a Japanese bayonet that would have killed Hammer.

Hammer discovers, as Spade did, that the killer is the woman whom he has formed a deep connection with during his investigation. Spade actually has a sexual encounter with Brigid O'Shaughnessy (and then, while she sleeps, cold-bloodedly sneaks to her apartment and searches it). Where Spade is cool (yet promiscuous), Hammer is hot (yet virginal). Hammer virtuously declines premarital sex with Charlotte Manning, but he repeatedly talks about the desire that her beautiful body (he specifies her legs, stomach, breasts) arouses in him, and that his rugged manliness arouses in her. He proposes marriage, and the couple begin to plan their future life together. She will, of course, give up her profession as psychiatrist, and she agrees to pursue only hobbies that she can afford on the salary of an investigator's wife.

Spade's consistent ambiguity and Hammer's consistent simplicity lead to clearly different conclusions. Both plots end identically: the detective reveals to the woman whom he loves that he knows she is the one who killed his partner/comrade, and that he will not protect her from the consequences of the homicide that she has committed. Spade's exchange with Brigid O'Shaughnessy is famous: although he says that he does not expect her to understand, he offers her seven reasons ("Maybe some of them are unimportant") why, despite perhaps loving her, he must turn her in to the police. She pleads that if he loves her—and she rejects his claim that he doesn't know if he loves her—love should oblige him to spare her. In the end, he won't let her go precisely "because all of me wants to—wants to say to hell with the consequences and do it—and because—God damn you— you've counted on that" (583). He won't play the sap for her.

Mike Hammer's final exchange with Charlotte Manning is notorious. Although, while waiting for her to return to her apartment, he promises himself, "I'll make the killer sweat—and tell me how it happened, to see if I hit it right" (165), when he does confront Charlotte after her return, he doesn't allow her to say more than "But...." Instead he speaks: twenty paragraphs of narrative in which he reviews what *must* have happened. Interpolated in this narrative are a half dozen italicized paragraphs in which Charlotte silently removes all of her clothing. When he has completed his account and she is completely nude, she leans forward to kiss him (and, he later realizes, to reach for a gun she has presciently stored in a rubber plant pot behind him) and Hammer shoots her in the abdomen, as he had promised to do in Chapter One. "How c-could you," she gasps; "It was easy," he says (174).

The uneasiness of Sam Spade's final exchange with Brigid O'Shaughnessy—an uneasiness emphasized by the reaction of his ever-loyal secretary, Effie Perine ("I know you're right. You're right. But don't touch me now" 584)—exemplifies the quality of *The Maltese Falcon* that has made it, for many readers, rank as one of the greatest of all detective stories. Sam Spade has had to make difficult choices; his world is full of complications. Beams fall from high buildings, and when they just miss a prosperous businessman, the businessman abruptly and radically alters the way he lives— until he gets used again to beams not falling, and he resumes a lifestyle very much like the one he abruptly abandoned. But the easiness of Mike Hammer's final exchange with Charlotte Manning should not be undervalued. It exemplifies the quality that made *I, the Jury* by far the best-selling detective novel of its generation. The novel presents a world of complications, but the complications are *always* resolvable, the choices are *always* clear and easy, at least to a man with complete self-confidence, a muscular build, and a .45 caliber gun. Whether he suffers an unprovoked attack by two Negroes armed with knives in a Harlem bar or he is surrounded by a college dean and four college kids with rifles after he has broken into a dorm room and shot dead its occupant, Hammer knows he is right and knows how to impose right upon others: the two Negroes are brutally beaten; the dean and students are given instructions that they instantly follow. In a Harlem bar or a college in rural Packsdale, Hammer can do what needs to be done, and doing it always restores order. Sam's Hi-Ho Club and Dean Russell Hilbar's college are clearly better places after Hammer's violence has purged their rooms, even if the local thugs in the bar or the mid-level gangster at the college have no direct connection to the murder that the detective is investigating.

This is the burden of all of the rapid sequence of events in *I, the Jury*. Hammer rushes from scene to scene—uptown, downtown, out into the countryside—and always meets individuals who either instinctively acknowledge his authority—deans and college students, nymphomaniacs and morons, prostitutes and homosexuals—or who can be beaten into appropriate submission to his authority—the two nameless Negroes, or the one-time bootlegger George Kalecki, or the mastermind of a white slavery ring, Hal Kines. Sam Spade's calculating toughness enables him to survive in a world that successively destroys Miles Archer, Floyd Thursby, Capt. Jacobi, Caspar Gutman, and Brigid O'Shaughnessy. Mike Hammer's hot, impetuous, and always overwhelming toughness allows him not only to survive, but, again and again, leave behind him a succession of scenes of justice achieved. Not everyone survives; there will always be collateral damage in his world: decent people—in addition to the victim whose death precipitates all of the action (Jack Williams in *I, the Jury*)—do die: Myrna Devlin, Bobo Hopper, and Eileen Vickers are virtuous persons simply caught up in the carnage consequent upon Charlotte Manning's murder of Jack. The two women are in the process of recovering from criminal pasts for which they are not entirely responsible, and Bobo is a mentally handicapped tool of a drug ring. But Hammer's mission will always be to avenge the initial crime death as well as explain it, to be judge, jury, and executioner as well as detective. It is not enough for Hammer to know; he must punish as well. *I, the Jury* presents world that is dark in all its corners, not just darkened by the murder that "is shockingly out of place, as when a dog makes a mess on a drawing room carpet" (Auden), but Mike Hammer can confidently enter every corner and dominate it and rectify it as he races to eliminate the murderer who has committed the initial crime.

A Note on Race in *I, the Jury*

Mike Hammer has little to do with African Americans or any other racial minorities. The New York of the first five novels is almost entirely white, and with the exception of a few marked Italians and Slavs, almost entirely non-ethnic. The sole important appearance of African Americans in Hammer's experience occurs in their entirely gratuitous roles in *I, the Jury*.

They appear in the form of the "big black buck" and the "high yellow" who attempt to rob Hammer in the back room of the Hi-Ho Club (57). Although they are armed with knives, Mike Hammer is able, in two brief paragraphs, to kick out the teeth of one, smash the nose of the second, and leave both unconscious on the floor. The episode has nothing to do with Hammer's investigation; the two men have simply seized the opportunity to rob what they assume will be an easy target. They have no names, just Hammer's disparaging description of their pigmentation. The scene is unapologetically racist. Its only function can be to demonstrate Hammer's prowess: at one end of his competence, he can defeat the devious schemes of an over-educated female mastermind; at the other end, he can, with his bare hands (and shod foot) defeat the combined muscle of two unintelligent, Black thugs.

There is, however, a third African American in the scene. "Big Sam" is the bartender at the Hi-Ho Club. He has once in the past backed up Hammer in some gunplay, and Hammer has killed a hood who demanded protection money from Sam. Sam is, to Hammer, a "Negro," and Hammer gives Sam as much respect as he gives anyone. Sam permits the two men to enter the back room because he is confident that Hammer can handle them; indeed, he bets on Hammer's success and collects from his patrons who thought two armed Black men could handle a single white man. But Sam is still a stereotype, and he talks like one: "What's up, Mistah Hammah? Somethin' I can do fuh yuh?" (52).

The fourth African American in *I, the Jury* is also a stereotype. Charlotte Manning's "darky maid" (59), Kathy, talks like Big Sam: "Sho' nuff, Mistah Hammah" (136). There is no reason for her to be—or not be—African American. Because she is incurious about the mechanics of Charlotte's doorbell, she helps to supply Charlotte with an alibi, but aside from receiving the condescension that any maid might receive, her race only serves to provide entertaining mispronunciation of English.

The racism in *I, the Jury* is not excusable because it is incidental. Big Sam's satisfaction at Hammer's demolition of the two men may be meant to suggest a mutual, inter-racial bond between the two strong men who both recognize the folly of the two knife-wielding Black thugs thinking that the white man would be an easy target. But Hammer's pleasure, after beating one of the thugs unconscious, at smashing a beaten man's face—"That guy was a lady killer in Harlem, but them days were gone forever" (57)—is an ugly and specifically racist exercise. The best that can be said is that nothing similar ever happens again.

The Twisted Thing *(1966)*

The next published Mike Hammer novel would be *My Gun Is Quick*, which appeared in 1950, three years after *I, the Jury*—after *I, the Jury*'s moderate success as a hardback had been followed by its stunning success as a paperback. But between those two novels, Spillane had composed and submitted to his publisher a manuscript entitled *Whom the Gods Would Destroy*. It involved Hammer with a brilliant scientist who was raising his fourteen-year-old son as a prodigy. Hammer's first assignment is to recover young Ruston York, who has been kidnapped. After restoring Ruston to his father, Hammer must discover the murderer of the scientist, Rudolph York. E.P. Dutton apparently found the premise of scientist and prodigy "too fantastical" (Collins & Traylor, *Mickey Spillane on Screen* 8), and Spillane set the manuscript aside. In 1966, after Hammer's decade hiatus had ended, he published it as *The Twisted Thing*.

It is not clear how much editing or rewriting Spillane did for the 1966 publication, but as published, *The Twisted Thing* shows a surprising willingness to experiment with the model introduced in *I, the Jury*. Hammer's secretary and would-be fiancée, Velda, a key character in every other Mike Hammer novel, is completely absent. And the principal scene of the action is not New York City. *I, the Jury* had twice sent Hammer upstate—once to the college town of Packsdale and once to the country estate of the Bellamy twins, but it was clearly the mean streets of New York City that constituted Mike Hammer's home territory in his first case. He does briefly return to the City in *The Twisted Thing* (in Chapter 8 of 12), where he does briefly meet up again with Capt. Pat Chambers, but virtually all of the action takes place in the vicinity of the small town of Sidon, where Rudolph York's estate and laboratory are located. Sidon has its brutal policemen; Officer Dilwick is as sadistic as the worst misfit on an urban force. And it has its good policemen; Sergeant Price is as tolerant of Hammer's unorthodox methods in the countryside as Pat Chambers is of Hammer's methods in Manhattan.

Still, it is strange to see Hammer navigate in a terrain of beaches and small towns instead of nightclubs and slums.

But the original conception remains. The action begins, as it does in all of the early Hammer novels, with a primal scene of victimization. In *I, the Jury*, the victim, Jack Williams, is dead, having been murdered sadistically by Charlotte Manning. The violence of the scene lies in Hammer's reconstruction of the torture that was imposed upon his friend and comrade, and, even more, in the emotion of Hammer's response to the reconstruction. In *The Twisted Thing*, the victim is Billy Parks, a pathetic former criminal who is trying to go straight and who has used his one phone call to plead with Hammer for help. Billy's victimization is in progress: Hammer arrives to rescue Billy from the terrible beating that Dilwick is administering to the "nice little ex-con" (11), in the basement of the police station. Billy's situation will not become the central motivating fact as Jack Williams's murder was, nor will Dilwick emerge as the homicidal villain at the center of the mystery. But Billy's suffering does suffice to confirm that Hammer's rages for justice are always instigated by an initial episode of violence against a defenseless victim.

And, as always, Hammer subdues all whom he encounters. The men bend to his will, and the women desire him to dominate them. Spillane always inserts complications. Hammer is often clubbed into unconsciousness, though always from behind, and he always recovers incredibly quickly (or, occasionally, when the beating is especially bad and he spends a day recovering, just unusually quickly).[8] And while Ruston York's governess falls into Hammer's arms and bed, Rudolph York's laboratory assistant, a lesbian, does prove immune to Hammer's appeal. Nonetheless, whether in the heart of the dark city or in the dark countryside, Hammer never doubts his own righteousness, and events never fail to justify his confidence.

My Gun Is Quick *(1950)*

The second published Hammer case opens with another variation on the precipitating victimization. Here the initial victim is female, a red-haired, slightly bedraggled "fluff"—a prostitute—who begs a late-night cup of coffee from Hammer in "an all-night hash joint" under the Third Avenue El (6). When she is accosted and threatened by a "tall, dark and greasy looking" thug, Hammer rises chivalrously to her defense, punches and slaps the thug, and then, when the thug reaches for a gun, Hammer draws his .45 and points it at the man's forehead. The man faints, Hammer hands him over to the police and, before departing, gives the woman $150 of the $2,500 fee he has just earned. The next morning, Hammer reads in the newspaper that the woman—he knows her only as "Red"—has been killed in a hit and run accident.

Hammer dedicates himself to the mission of identifying the woman and seeing that she gets a proper burial. Because the thug—Feeney Last—turns out to be the chauffeur of Arthur Berin-Grotin, a proud and wealthy philanthropist and a member of the New York social elite, Hammer drives to Berin-Grotin's Long Island estate and secures Berin-Grotin's sponsorship of his mission to properly identify and bury Red. If Shorty's hash joint under the El constitutes one pole of Hammer's world in *My Gun Is Quick*, Berin-Grotin's elegant estate and the nearby cemetery where his even more elegant marble tomb is under construction constitutes the other. Red has no name, and without Hammer's intervention will be assigned to an anonymous plot in a potter's field; Berin-Grotin makes a fetish of his hyphenated surname and possesses the means to erect a permanent memorial to it. This neatly constructed contrast between the nameless and the nameful, the poor and the rich, the streetwalker and the philanthropist, the parent of a stillborn child and the parent of a disowned child, and—not least—between a victimized woman and a victimizing man gives *My Gun Is Quick* a vivid moral structure and provides Spillane a surprise ending with a satisfying irony.

If *I, the Jury* derives its central action from Hammett's *The Maltese Falcon*, the situation in *My Gun Is Quick*—a criminal chauffeur is employed by a sympathetic man of great wealth—echoes at least faintly the situation of Raymond Chandler's first Philip Marlowe novel, *The Big Sleep*. That both novels provide the wealthy man with a disreputable and troublesome daughter/granddaughter adds another parallel. But the divergence is great. There is nothing romantic about Feeney Last; he is an unmitigated thug, not, as Rusty Regan was, an ex-bootlegger and one-time member of the Irish Republican Army, who entertains his wife's invalid father, General Sternwood, with tales of the Irish revolution. Although Berin-Grotin professes horror at having employed such a person, Feeney Last proves to be a useful tool in the prostitution ring that Berin-Grotin runs; Rusty Regan is—like the General, the General's butler, and Marlowe himself—an imperfect man with "the soldier's eye." General Sternwood has two delinquent daughters, Vivian and Carmen, the latter a pathological murderer; he despairs of their behaviors, but he will not disown them. Berin-Grotin disowns his granddaughter when she gets pregnant while unmarried, driving her into desperation and prostitution; eventually, to protect his name and his operation, he orders Feeney Last to kill her.

What was for Sam Spade hard remains for Mike Hammer easy. *My Gun Is Quick* pushes the easiness further. Spillane's characters are morally simple: Feeney Last is, from the moment he enters the hash joint to the moment Hammer smashes his head to a pulp a thoroughly despicable human being. Rusty Regan and his soldier's eye may, for some readers, embody the sort of sentimentalism that distinguishes Chandler from Hammett, but in his decision to marry Vivian Sternwood and to stay married to her, he makes a complex choice. Red (Nancy Sanford, Berin-Grotin's granddaughter) is a fallen woman, instantly redeemed by the chivalric gesture from Hammer and then murdered by her family-proud grandfather. She is the necessary victim who will justify the crusade that Hammer undertakes to clarify her death and secure her decent burial. Carmen Sternwood is a nasty creature, with an unfettered libido, an infantile selfishness, and an inclination to see murder as a solution to her problems (and she is, for some readers, a proof of Chandler's gynophobia), but she is also a victim as well as a protected victimizer. Marlowe doesn't, in the end, shoot her or even turn her in to the police; she will be placed under medical supervision.

Mike Hammer needs Nancy Sanford to be simply a victim and thus the excuse that legitimates every violent thing he does. And, as a prostitute, she is a soiled victim, the victim of a vicious grandfather, but also a victim of a city and a civilization that allows corrupt men to operate corrupt prostitution rings (and corrupt men to patronize those prostitutes) and that allows fallen girls no alternative to prostitution. So Hammer's few minutes with her late at night—buying her a cup of coffee, protecting her from an attacker, giving her $150—makes him her avenger. Arthur Berin-Grotin and New York City might not offer Red a second chance, but Mike Hammer does. He gives her dignity in those few minutes and alters her life. She writes to him, "When I met you, Mike, I was tired.... Now I'm not tired at all and things are clear once more.... Until now there has been no one I could trust and it has been hard.... You don't know what it means to me to have someone I can trust" (33–34). Women seem uniquely able to reverse the course of their lives in Hammer's world, usually through Hammer's intervention. Men—and most women—in Spillane's fiction seem to have fixed moral identities (though, of course, if they are the primary villain, they necessarily conceal that character until the detective exposes it at the end). But Hammer's generosity and his masculinity do have the power to redirect the lives of women who have succumbed to immoral lives in the brutal world. Red—Nancy Sanford—is one of those women. But having redeemed her character, Hammer cannot save her life. She is murdered immediately after sending the letter, and Hammer can justify her trust in him only by the rampage which eventually leads him to kill both the man who killed Nancy Sanford and the man who ordered her killed.

Everything in Spillane's fiction—action as well as character—works with a fatalistic inevitability in which the good always suffer and the bad are always punished. Readers willing to enter Mike Hammer's are assured that while the world contains crude brutes (Hal Kines, George Kalecki, Dilwick, Feeney Last) and sophisticated deviants (Charlotte Manning, Ruston York, Arthur Berin-Grotin) who cause the suffering, it also contains Mike Hammer, who invariably ensures that they too suffer. There is pathos in the deaths of the sheep—the incidental victims like Bobo Hopper (*I, the Jury*) or Lola Bergin (*My Gun Is Quick*) as well as the precipitating victims (Jack Williams, Red)—but there will also be the justified deaths of the goats, and not just of the principal goat, but of a series of incidental goats.

And in Hammer's world everyone—the sheep and the goats—seems to die in the end. Only Hammer, Pat Chambers, and Velda survive the holocausts of a Mike Hammer investigation. Toward the end of *I, the Jury*, Hammer reviews the events thus far with Charlotte Manning. "Sounds sort of scrambled, doesn't it?" she says. He agrees, but adds, "as the plot thickens it thins out, too" (106). Indeed, Hammer solves all of his cases through a sort of harrowing which certainly thins the cast of characters and through which everyone is eventually fixed with a definite identity—fixed because everyone is dead. Of the four most plausible suspects in *I, the Jury*, three (Hal Kines, George Kalecki, and Myrna Devlin) are dead when Hammer confronts and kills the fourth (Charlotte). Eileen Vickers and Bobo Hopper have also been eliminated along the way. The Bellamy twins are the only featured characters to survive, and while Mary has figured as a nymphomaniac who verifies Hammer's overpowering sexual appeal (and also exemplifies the usually suppressed wantonness of her own sex), Esther is little more than a name.

Hammer's purging of his world is given a thematic unity in *My Gun Is Quick* through the opening and closing scenes. In the first chapter, Hammer meets the anonymous "Red" in an anonymous hash joint, and he frames his mission as restoring a true name and decent resting place to her corpse. In the last chapter, Hammer and the name-proud Berin-Grotin lie trapped in the burning Seaside Hotel. Hammer explains to the dying Berin-Grotin that he will see that Red—identified as Berin-Grotin's granddaughter Nancy Sanford—will be interred in the marble tomb that Berin-Grotin has built as monument to his name, and it will be Berin-Grotin whose unidentifiable charred corpse that will be planted in a potter's field. Red recovered her true self through Hammer's intervention and will be buried permanently under her true name; Berin-Grotin lost himself and will remain forever nameless.

Vengeance Is Mine *(1950)*

The third Hammer novel to be published is a curious reprise of the first. Both books open with Hammer standing in a room containing the corpse of a friend and comrade; both novels end with Hammer holding a gun on the most fascinating woman he has met, delivering a reconstruction of the events that demonstrates her guilt, and then firing a fatal shot into her naked body. The most obvious purpose of duplicating *I, the Jury* is the final line of *Vengeance Is Mine*, a line Spillane saw as a demonstration of his virtuoso skill with surprise endings: Juno Reeves, the statuesque woman who has attracted, intrigued, and always slightly discomforted Hammer, is, he declares in italics, "*a man!*"

But the parallels allow Spillane to explore a number of other variations. Chester Wheeler is no Jack Williams. Williams was close comrade who sacrificed an arm to save Hammer's life and who was a cop before the war and, though disqualified by his injury, he retained his cop attitude (and his cop gun): "his heart was with the force" (9). Jack, like Pat Chambers and Mike Hammer, is part of a special band of brothers. Chester Wheeler spent the war as an Air Force captain in Washington; Hammer met him in Cincinnati in 1945 after returning from the Pacific, and they bonded over drinks. Wheeler is not a cop; he runs a family department store in Columbus, Ohio, and when he arrives in New York City on a business trip, he looks Hammer up. Despite the novel's title, avenging Wheeler's murder is *not* Hammer's principal motive; there is no Chapter One philippic in which Hammer vows to catch the killer and impose a slow painful death. Rather, Hammer pursues the case to clear his own name and save his investigator's license: the district attorney believes that Wheeler committed suicide with Hammer's gun while Hammer lay in a drunken stupor and that Hammer's carelessness with his weapon is sufficient grounds for withdrawing his license.

The chief variation that *Vengeance is Mine* plays upon *I, the Jury* is, of course, the figure of Juno Reeves, who explicitly recalls Charlotte Manning to Hammer's mind. He explains to Juno the significance of Charlotte in his life: "She was the most gorgeous thing that ever lived and I was in love with her. But she did something and I played God; I was the judge and I the jury and the sentence was death. I shot her in the gut..." (62). Later, talking with Velda, he recalls Charlotte and as well, Lola from *My Gun Is Quick*: "I keep thinking of the women who died," and he makes the pointedly ironic vow, "God, if I ever have to hold a gun on a woman again I'll die first, so help me I will" (101). When Hammer finds himself confronting Juno in the end, he is indeed paralyzed. "I pointed the gun at her head and sighted along the barrel and said, 'My God, I can't!'" Before his eyes, Juno seems to transform into Charlotte ("I was seeing Charlotte's face instead of hers" 139). He is spared dying only by that ultimate revelation that "*Juno was a man!*" Juno's sex permits him to pull the trigger.

The links between Charlotte Manning and Juno Reeves are complex.

Both are (or appear to be) strong women. Each operates a prosperous business: Charlotte is a psychiatrist; Juno runs her own modeling agency. Both use their business as a front for criminal activity: Charlotte is an efficient drug-dealer; Juno is an efficient blackmailer. Both are very attractive and both are immediately very attracted to Mike Hammer. And Mike Hammer is very attracted to both of them, though he proposes marriage only to Charlotte. Both relationships are so important to him that he refuses to engage in sex with either of them—he refuses sex with Charlotte because his code requires that he not know his wife until their wedding night; he refuses sex with Juno because at moments of intimacy he feels an indefinable uneasiness—not, he explains, because she seemed to be a female crouching away from an aggressive male—but because "there was something else again I couldn't understand and it snaked up my back and my hands started to jerk unconsciously with it" (106). What he can't understand, but somehow intuits, is that Juno's creamy skin, "breasts of youth—high, exciting, pushing against the high neckline of the white jersey blouse" (28), and round thighs are the features not of a gorgeous woman, but of a gorgeous man wearing "falsies."

Juno Reeves's profession corresponds to her/his distinctive quality. Charlotte Manning had become a drug dealer and a murderer because her intellectual training had taught her contempt for "the frailty of men." "You no longer had the social instinct of a woman," Hammer tells her; her overdeveloped intellect has destroyed the natural female instinct "of being dependent upon a man" (167). Charlotte's deviance was mental, the result of mind misshapened by over-education. And her narcotics ring plays upon the dependency of the weak-minded addicts she serves. Juno Reeves profits from the physical beauty of sexually attractive young women. She runs a modeling agency that employs girls' bodies for advertising. Her criminal enterprise—her blackmail ring—depends upon photographing the bodies of wealthy men and attractive girls as they engage in illicit trysts. And Juno's criminal character finally centers upon her/his deviant body—the body of a man sheathed in a woman's most seductive attire, attire accentuating those round thighs and high exciting breasts of youth. *I, the Jury* is a fable of a woman's viciously deformed mind; *Vengeance Is Mine* is a fable of a "woman's" viciously deformed body.

One Lonely Night *(1951)*

One Lonely Night, like its predecessors, opens with a victim whose demise inaugurates a Mike Hammer crusade. Spillane has alternated the gender of the victims—male (Jack Williams), female (Red), male (Chester

Wheeler)—so, as might be expected, the victim precipitating the fourth published case is female. The initial novelty in *One Lonely Night* is that her murderer is Mike Hammer. She and Hammer, meeting on the lonely walkway of the George Washington Bridge on a snowy night, are approached by a man with a gun; Hammer naturally protects her (and himself) by killing the man with his .45. The rescued girl then looks into the face of her savior and finds it so frighteningly inhuman that she leaps to her death.

Of course, Hammer is not a villain. He may be the immediate cause of her leap, but the true cause—the true murderer—is the Communist Party. *One Lonely Night* is the novel upon which Spillane's reputation as a right-wing, McCarthyite ideologue rests. And anti–Communism is indeed the touchstone for decency in the novel. Every non-evil character in the novel is not just anti-Communist; he or she is strongly and unquestioningly anti–Communist: Mike and Velda and Pat, but also cynical New York City journalists and politicians. Hammer himself actually professes no positive political affiliation. He tells a journalist, "I haven't voted since they dissolved the Whig party" (24). But even Whigs can be outraged by the infiltration of the American by foreign Communism. There is a sense in which, by attacking Communism, Hammer is avenging Paula Riis, the girl on the George Washington Bridge: she is a decent girl from the American Midwest who has come to New York City. She has been seduced by the Communist Party's deceptive appeal, but she has finally realized the malignancy that the Party represents and has come to the George Washington Bridge expecting to meet the police and give information against the Party and its front men. She has been followed by a brutal Communist agent, who has been sent to liquidate her. When she is rescued by an equally brutal, but quicker at the draw, American, she sees both armed men—the Communist and his antagonist—as comparable threats, and she leaps to her death.

But although he recalls Paula Riis's revulsion from his face several times in the course of the novel, the image that haunts Mike Hammer throughout *One Lonely Night* is the face of the American judge who is presiding over Hammer's trial for "knock[ing] off somebody who needed knocking off bad" (6). After reviewing Hammer's violent actions in earlier investigations, the judge finds himself compelled to exonerate Hammer because the circumstances proved it was a justifiable homicide, but he nonetheless seizes the opportunity to castigate Hammer publicly for his violent behavior. "He went on and on, cutting me down until I was nothing but scum in the gutter, his fists slamming against the bench as he prophesied a rain of purity that was going to wash me into the sewer with the other scum" (6–7). The verbal assault has unsettled Hammer, and though he always asserts that he kills only those who deserve to be killed and that he *likes* killing those who deserve to be killed, he does wonder whether he has indeed lost his moral bearing, whether he *is* scum.[9] Hitherto, he has justified his violence as vengeance for the violence perpetrated against vulnerable victims—a one-armed war veteran, a beaten down prostitute, an inoffensive Midwestern businessman. In *One Lonely Night*, the justification is the brutality of the Communist Party—a brutal ideology being executed by bestial Russian MVD agents[10] and a cadre of soft-hearted American adherents. The righteous wrath of the judge is decisive in a world of courtrooms governed by centuries-old legal traditions, but in the streets of New York City, the only righteous response to the brutality of the Soviet Communist threat is the antithetical brutality of the American patriot. Mike Hammer sets himself directly against Joseph Stalin—"cruddy Uncle Joe" (95); by extirpating an entire cell of subversive actors, he demonstrates that individual Americans are still able to out-brutal the Soviets.[11] The emblematic scene occurs toward the end of the book, when General Osilov and his drooling lackeys have kidnapped Velda and taken her to a remote abandoned warehouse. There they have hung her naked from the ceiling and are whipping her with a knotted rope, demanding that she reveal the location of the plans of America's newest super-weapon. Using a Russian machine gun, Hammer kills them all and rescues the American virgin.

In the first and last chapters, Hammer is responsible for the death of representative of each of the three categories of Communist subversive. The killings all occur on the middle of the George Washington Bridge. In the first chapter, he kills the MVD agent (with his Russian stainless-steel teeth) sent to liquidate Paula Riis. Then Paula Riis, (the naïve American seduced by Communist propaganda) leaps to her death. In the last chapter, he returns to the hump of the bridge and executes the third type of subversive, the mad and power-hungry American politician, Lee Deamer, who has been running for office on a platform of anti–Communism and anti-corruption, but sees the Communists as his avenue to supremacy. In the first instance, Hammer removed all identifying features of the MVD agent—even using the frozen walkway to rub the skin off of his fingers before shoving the corpse into the Hudson River. He takes the opposite tack after killing Lee Deamer at the novel's end, insuring that Deamer ironically becomes a patriotic icon by making his death on the bridge seem a heroic and successful sacrifice that prevents the super-weapon plans from reaching Moscow.

In Lee Deamer, Spillane again indulges his habit of having as his principal villain a character who, in any other fiction, would be rejected as perversely absurd. Identical twins were a long-standing staple of detective fiction, and, by 1950, a much discredited one. In 1928, SS Van Dine had, in Rule 20 of his "Twenty Rules for Writing Detective Stories" forbidden "the final pinning of the crime on a twin, or a relative who looks exactly like the suspected, but innocent, person." Yet Spillane seems to employ this generic chestnut in *One Lonely Night*. In Chapter 2, some witnesses confidently identify Lee Deamer as the murderer of a known Communist, while other witnesses can testify that Lee Deamer was giving a speech (attended by, among others, Pat Chambers). Spillane has Hammer immediately raise the possibility that the noble Lee Deamer has an evil twin. Soon the police confirm that, in fact, Lee *does* have a twin—an evil, insane twin, Oscar. Before either Hammer or the police can apprehend the mad Oscar, he is killed and mutilated beyond recognition by an oncoming subway train. This would seem to conclude Spillane's venture into the deployment of "a twin, or a relative who looks exactly like the suspected, but innocent, person." But, in fact, Mike Hammer discovers that Oscar Deamer was Lee's *fraternal* twin, not his identical twin. They do *not* look alike (which is why the twin's body had to be mangled in the subway). Spillane is *not* availing himself of the generic chestnut. Oscar did murder the Communist, but he had employed the barely credible device of hiring an aged actor to impersonate him and deliver the speech. Then, having murdered the Communist in front of witnesses, he rushed to the dinner meeting in time to replace the actor and shake everyone's hands. (Later, of course, he murders the aged actor.)

A detective, a girl, and a Soviet assassin *might* find themselves all alone on the George Washington Bridge; snow *does* inhibit pedestrian traffic. But the saga of the Deamer twins defies plausibility not just because of Oscar's very well-timed and poorly noticed replacement of his surrogate. After escaping from a Midwestern insane asylum, Oscar had arrived in New York City, embraced Communism, adopted the identity of his sane brother, Lee, and run for the New York State Senate on a reform platform (exactly why election to the Senate in Albany is a goal of the Soviet secret service, or why a New York State Senator is seen by cops and journalists as a bulwark against Communism is not clear). Paula Riis, who happens to have worked in that Midwestern asylum and, by chance also come to New York and also (naively) joined the Party, recognizes Oscar and calls upon the hitherto oblivious and decent Lee Deamer back in the Midwest to leave his farm and come to expose his brother. Oscar kills Lee by pushing him onto the subway tracks so that the arriving train obliterates Lee's identity and can thus preserve the illusion of identical twins. When he dies on the George Washington Bridge, Oscar Deamer is performing a double pretense: he pretends to be Lee, and he pretends to be a modest patriot. Mike Hammer ensures that his two pretenses, the personal and the political, are both recorded in history as the truth. And thus the mad Communist traitor to America dies as a heroic martyr to the anti–Communist cause.

Oscar's death on the bridge named after the founder of the American republic has obvious significance. Opening and closing the novel on the same bridge has obvious significance. The snow that falls throughout the novel (replacing the rain that seems to fall in most of the early Hammer novels) has obvious significance (to state the obvious, it evokes both the Cold War, and the deceptive white cloak beneath which objects true outlines—Communists, mad twins—can be concealed). The novel's deliberate progress from Hammer's lonely night of self-doubt caused by the judge's diatribe to his discovery of the redeeming virtue of his vigilante crusade is obvious enough. The judge exercises verbal authority within the ceremonial confines of the courtroom; Mike Hammer exercises the physical authority of fist and automatic and machine-gun out on the mean streets where only physical authority is recognized.

The novel's absurdities are obvious enough: details such as Oscar hiring an actor to masquerade as him for the first half of a campaign rally and then, in timely fashion, replacing him for the glad-handing afterward, or, even more incredible outside the forward pressure of the narrative, Hammer's vaunt that his crusade will shatter cruddy Uncle Joe's illusion that Americans have lost their manhood and that the Kremlin will have an easy path to dominance of the United States. But the narrative does press forward, and readers at all willing to suspend disbelief will be carried efficiently along another fable of Mike Hammer's ability to pound a path to discovering truth, executing justice, and preserving the American way, even against the bestial viciousness of Soviet agents and the mad conceit of American traitors.[12]

The Big Kill *(1951)*

The Big Kill abandons Mike Hammer's brief excursion into geopolitics and returns him to exercising his wrath upon the local sources of nefarious activity. The background vice in *I, the Jury* had been drug-dealing; in *My Gun Is Quick*, it had been prostitution; in *Vengeance Is Mine*, it had been blackmail. *The Big Kill* takes gambling as the contextual vice, with an element of blackmail added in the end. The victimization scene that begins Hammer's crusade is an especially pathetic one: William Decker, a defeated man, sets his one-year-old son down in a bar that Hammer happens to be drinking in, and then walks out onto the street where he knows he will be killed. A precocious boy had been the central figure in the unpublished manuscript of the second Hammer novel; the boy in *The Big Kill* is much younger than Ruston York, but he too will be precocious in a singular way.

The novel sustains the rhythm of alternately male and female precipitating victims. The male victim here is divided into William Decker and his infant son. Decker is a petty criminal trying to go straight. His wife dies after the birth of their son, and he is maneuvered into committing one more burglary which leaves him in possession of evidence that will incriminate the gangsters who run New York City's gambling racket. Knowing he will be murdered, he tearfully kisses his son goodbye and walks out to his death. Hammer takes custody of the one-year-old and undertakes to investigate Decker's murder and to avenge the crime. Though it is unlikely that a homicide detective, even Pat Chambers, would award temporary custody of an orphan child to a bachelor private eye with a long record of homicidal anger (and no record of childcare), Hammer does take William Decker, Jr., back to his apartment. This sets up the neat ending of the novel in which William Decker (junior) fires the bullet that kills the person responsible for killing William Decker (senior).

The rhythm of ultimate villains is also sustained: in *The Big Kill*, it is the turn of a female to be identified as the ultimate villain. Marsha Lee does commit several murders, though she does not, like Charlotte Manning and Juno Reeves, actually kill the precipitating victim. Marsha Lee has the glamour of a former Hollywood movie actress who is currently investing herself in theater production in New York City. Like her predecessors, she is magnetically drawn to Hammer's masculinity, but she is a less vivid character. There is a sense in *The Big Kill* that Spillane is content to do well what he has done spectacularly before.

An odd feature of *The Big Kill* is the vanishing of Velda. Having elevated her in *One Lonely Night* to the status of Hammer's fiancée, she is now dispatched to Florida. Hammer sees her off at the airport, and when she has completed her principal assignment, he instructs by phone to carry on a further investigation in Cuba. On the one hand, it is another confirmation of Velda's autonomous authority: she too is a very competent P.I. who operates successfully on her own. On the other hand, having just made a point of signaling a progress in the relationship between the detective and his secretary—a point that Erle Stanley Gardner avoided making in the 82 novels that he wrote featuring Perry Mason and *his* secretary—Spillane now sidetracks the relationship. It does free Hammer to be open to the sexual availability of the exceedingly attractive women whom he meets. The double standard regarding male and female promiscuity would have permitted Mike (but not Velda) to stray from the commitment implied when he put the engagement ring on Velda's finger but having Velda out of sight perhaps makes the masculine prerogative even less objectionable.

Kiss Me, Deadly *(1952)*

Kiss Me, Deadly ended Spillane's initial string of unprecedentedly popular hard-boiled novels in the Truman years. By June 1952, the first five

Hammer books had sold over 11 million copies (Collins & Traylor, *On Screen* 9). His reason for abandoning Hammer for nearly a decade is not certain, though it has been attributed to his joining the Jehovah's Witnesses in the winter of 1951.[13] But it also seems true that Spillane had pretty much exhausted the vein he had been mining. *Kiss Me, Deadly* strains for novelty. Whereas in earlier novels he seems to be playing with themes and situations he had used before—Juno Reeves is a clever variation on Charlotte Manning; *My Gun Is Quick* and *The Big Kill* both begin with chance encounters between Hammer and a vulnerable individual in a bar or restaurant—the repetitions in *Kiss Me, Deadly* seem forced, and at times pointless.

Hammer is, in *Kiss Me, Deadly*, disarmed for the second time. Because his gun had been used in the apparent suicide of Chester Wheeler, Hammer had lost his license to carry a weapon in *Vengeance Is Mine*. In *Kiss Me, Deadly*, the authorities—for no specific reason—withdraw both his license and Velda's, so now they are doubly disarmed. Velda will, in fact, continue to carry a gun, though she will not use it. Hammer, however, abides strictly with the legal ruling. This does not mean he does not shoot people; he does, usually aiming for their eyes. But he does so by wresting their weapons from the professional killers who are holding on him.

Hammer meets the usual number of sexually attractive women in *Kiss Me, Deadly*, and his magnetic virility continues to subdue them all. But this time, though he expresses flashes of desire for them, he sleeps with none of them. None of them shed her negligee in a gesture of invitation. Velda, who had been dismissed to Florida and Cuba in *The Big Kill*, is restored to her status as visible fiancée, with a reference to the ring Hammer put on her finger in *One Lonely Night*. She again plays an active role in the investigation, and—despite a toughness that makes her a suitable match for Hammer—she does once more need to be rescued by him, though this time she is in a strait jacket and taped to a chair instead of being hung naked from a ceiling. And when Hammer finds her, she is sitting there, sallow, fearful and shrunken after having been interrogated; in *One Lonely Night*, she was being actively being interrogated, and with a whip. In both novels, Hammer immediately wrecks vengeance on the violators of his secretary: spraying machine-gun bullets against the drooling Communists in *One Lonely Night*; firing a single bullet into the eye of her interrogator in *Kiss Me, Deadly*.

The major parallel between *Kiss Me, Deadly* and *One Lonely Night*, however, is the nature of the adversary. In the earlier novel, inspired by the McCarthy hearings, the underlying villain was the Communist Party, both the Russian masters and their American dupes. In *Kiss Me, Deadly*, inspired by the Kefauver hearings, it is the Mafia.[14] The moral of the fable is the same in both novels: a vicious organization that threatens to strangle the American Way cannot be defeated by law enforcement at the local or federal level, but only by a single, strong, unbound American man. And Mike Hammer, without a gun of his own, does exterminate a number of Mafia enforcers. He also manages to execute a couple of the bosses, including suave Carl Evello, who, at the beginning of the novel is identified as potentially the capo di tutti capi ("The others are pretty big too, but not like him" 25), but is eventually exposed as "only the boss locally" (136).[15] And Evello's death is not the climax of the novel. It is immediately followed by Hammer's execution of the man—Dr. Soberin—who interrogated Velda, and *that* execution only leads to the ultimate execution of Lily Carver, the woman who abetted Dr. Soberin, by committing murder and by appealing to Hammer's protective instincts. Lily Carver—actually "Lily Carver," as she has murdered the actual Lily Carver—follows in the line of Charlotte Manning, Juno Reeves, and Marsha Lee. As with Juno Reeves, Spillane manages a visceral shock to accompany the revelation of the woman's vicious duplicity. Juno was disrobed to reveal that she was a man; Lily disrobes herself to reveal a body repulsively deformed by the scars from a fire.

But if "Lily Carver" is ultimate villain, she is not the principal villain. She is explicitly the accomplice of Dr. Soberin, whom she loves, and even *he* is not the principal villain; that would be the corporate villainy of Mafia, and the closest to decapitating that octopus came when Hammer set up the execution of Carl Evello ("only the boss locally") in the penultimate chapter. Oscar Deamer was not Joseph Stalin, but in *One Lonely Night*, he was indeed the chief Communist villain in the novel. Dr. Soberin and Lily Carver are related to the Mafia only by their desire to locate the $2,000,000 cache of Mafia narcotics that has been hidden since 1940.[16] The final page death of Lily Carver is, thus, not a useful symbol of the demise of the Mafia in Mike Hammer's America; she is not Mafia at all. But her death does fit the sequence of final-page female deaths. It was, in his first case, easy for Hammer to shoot the woman who had murdered his best friend, and it was easy for him in his third published case, to shoot the woman who was exposed as a man (and who had murdered an old acquaintance); in Hammer's fifth case, Spillane arranged final-page shooting of a homicidal woman so that the one-year-old son of the initial victim actually fires the fatal bullet. In this sixth case, just after she has wounded him and the moment before she pulls the trigger to kill him, Hammer uses his cigarette lighter to ignite Lily Carver's alcohol-soaked robe. He staggers from the room with the woman's body aflame behind him. Lily Carver may not neatly end Hammer's crusade against the Mafia, but it is the culmination of the hate half of his love-hate relation with women.

Lily Carver's last-page immolation points to another oddity of *Kiss Me, Deadly*. The novel breaks the pattern that began with *I, the Jury* of alternating the sex (or apparent sex) of the initial victims and final villains. *The Big Kill* opened with the murder of William Decker, so it was predictable that *Kiss Me, Deadly* would open with the murder of Berga Torn. But Berga Torn, unlike all of the preceding initial victims, male or female, is not a pathetic victim. She might have been. She flags Hammer down on the highway, and at a police roadblock he learns that she must be a just-escaped patient at a nearby mental hospital. Hammer does not turn her over to the authorities, though more because he instinctively objects to the demands of authorities than because of any deep sympathy with Berga Torn. And, after she is murdered and he is badly beaten, Hammer learns that Berga Torn is not an oppressed prostitute (like "Red" in *My Gun Is Quick*), nor a disillusioned Communist dupe (like Paula Riis in *One Lonely Night*). She is a tough consort of Mafia men and is killed because she knows the location of the missing parcels of narcotics. Hammer is never engaged in a mission to redeem the death of Berga Torn. She is the occasion of his crusade against the Mafia, as Paula Riis was of his crusade against the Communists, but there is no pathos in Berga Torn's violent death; it does not specifically motivate Hammer's rampage. In *Kiss Me, Deadly*, a more generalized anger at the corruption of American values replaces specific outrage at the death of a vulnerable individual with whom Hammer is personally involved.

Truman's Mike Hammer

Mickey Spillane repeatedly produced narratives of roughly 175 pages that kept millions of readers turning those pages. Within a consistent framework—an opening occasion for the motivating anger that propels the detective onward and a shocking ending in which the detective metes out capital punishment—he produces a rapid succession of encounters in which the detective confronts and overcomes a series of adversaries: tough bad men, less tough than he; decent men, either more timid than he, or more bound by social constraints; and women, who find him irresistibly attractive, even when his declared mission is to punish the perpetrator of crimes that they have perpetrated. The hard-boiled style had always assumed that the detective succeeded because he, although he was only ordinarily intelligent, was extraordinarily tough. He always possessed the courage to, in Sam Spade's famous phrase, "heave a wild and unpredictable monkey-wrench into the machinery" and the reflexes to insure that "none of the flying pieces" hurt him (*Complete Novels* 465). Instead of heaving monkey-wrenches, Mike Hammer wields his .45 Army Colt (and his fist, and his shoes): the violence is immediate and direct. And it recurs frequently. Spillane condenses into a page or two confrontations that other writers extend into full chapters intended to reveal nuances of character in the detective and the various characters who spar with words. Hammer's verbal exchanges are pithy, almost stichomythic. His physical battles, while gory in detail, rarely last more than a page. Every encounter is essentially an occasion for Hammer to master the person he faces, and—with the exception of the occasional moments when Hammer is momentarily outwitted and savagely beaten, moments from which, after a brief or extended period of sleep, he arises fully ready to resume his crusade—Hammer always rises to the occasion.

This insistent pattern of a rapid succession of short, sharp verbal/physical confrontations takes place within a consistent larger pattern of initial victimizations and last-page executions. There is a distinct, almost mechanical rhythm to Spillane's choice of initial victim and final surprise villain. Narratives with a male victim and female villain alternate with narratives of a female victim and a male villain. Only the final novel breaks the pattern, with a female victim and a female villain, and even here the execution of the surprise female villain (Lily Carver) is immediately preceded by the execution of the expected male villain (Carl Evello) and the surprise male villain (Dr. Soberin).

The Rhythm of the First Six Mike Hammer Novels

Novel	Precipitating Victim	Ultimate Villain
I, the Jury	**male** Jack Williams	**female** Charlotte Manning
My Gun Is Quick	**female** Red (Nancy Sanford)	**male** Arthur Berin-Grotin
Vengeance Is Mine	**male** Chester Wheeler	**female** Juno Reeves
One Lonely Night	**female** Paula Riis	**male** Oscar Deamer
The Big Kill	**male** William Decker	**female** Marsha Lee
Kiss Me, Deadly	**female** Berga Torn	**female** "Lily Carver"

On the one hand, Spillane's variations on his basic model could become tiresome, as Mike Hammer repetitively bludgeons his way through dozens and dozens of miniature confrontations. There is *always* an underserving victim to ignite Hammer's righteous wrath; there are *always* minor thugs only incidentally involved in the case but there to be colorfully subdued by Hammer's fist, shoe, and gun; there are *always* women with generous breasts and legs and hearts (or libidos) that instantly respond to Hammer's virile attractions. Always the fable justifies the authority of the just man over all villainous conspiracies; he is the infallible judge, jury, and executioner. On the other hand, Spillane does find dramatic variation. The six ultimate villains are, in order: an intellectual psychiatrist, a vain old man, a transvestite, a madman impersonating his brother to advance Communism, a Hollywood actress, and a greedy woman devoted to the doctor who has saved her fire-ravaged torso. Though it hardly composes a fair anatomy of evil in mid-century America, it is certainly a diverse group. The context of the investigation may be kept within a private arena, or it may extend to the public threat of International Communism or of Organized Crime. Like all detectives, Hammer demonstrates that every death is explicable and every individual murderer accountable, but he also demonstrates that no leviathan is immune to the authority of the detective. The Hammer novels may be chewing gum, but, as Anthony Boucher acknowledged, they are chewing gum of extraordinary quality.

2

Wade Miller's Max Thursday

Max Thursday was not Mike Hammer, though he may have been meant to be. The young two young men who collaborated to create Thursday in 1947 surely enjoyed his considerable popularity—the back cover of the 1957 Signet edition of *Shoot to Kill* boasts that Wade Miller sales in Signet alone exceeded 2,000,000 copies—and they surely would have welcomed an even greater measure of Hammer's phenomenal success popularity (*I, the Jury* alone had sold 3,500,000 copies by 1953)—if not of Hammer's notoriety. Robert Wade and Bill Miller were, like Mickey Spillane, returning veterans producing fiction for a market of returning veterans. They were even quicker than Spillane to attempt to do so. In 1946, a year before Mickey Spillane issued *I, the Jury*, they had published their first venture into hard-boiled fiction with *Deadly Weapon*, and thereafter every year except 1952 would see the appearance of at least one Wade Miller (or Will Daemer or Dale Wilmer or Whit Masterson) novel. Some years saw three (1953) or even five (1951). They published a total of 33 novels between *Deadly Weapon* and *Evil Come, Evil Go*, published in 1961, the year of Bill Miller's death. (Robert Wade would continue to write another thirteen novels between 1963 and 1979.) By comparison, Mickey Spillane had, by 1961, published a total of nine novels, Ross Macdonald a total of fourteen, Bart Spicer a total of sixteen (five of them in collaboration with his wife), and Thomas B. Dewey a total of twenty. Wade and Miller were certainly a productive team of writers.

But although their total sales did not match the sales of Mickey Spillane, and their art of fiction may not have matched that of Ross Macdonald, they did produce, in the six Max Thursday novels, a well-written and, in some important respects, an innovative contribution to hard-boiled fiction. They adopted the less-favored third-person narration that Hammett had used for *The Maltese Falcon*, and that Brett Halliday had adopted for his long series of Mike Shayne novels. More interestingly, they dated and timed each chapter of every Thursday novel, a device that emphasized the pace at which the detective's cases moved (and, incidentally, the quite remarkable speed with which he recovered from some of his more severe beatings). But most importantly, they made Max Thursday grow in ways no other private eye had ever grown. On the first pages of the first novel he is a drunken has-been, divorced and alone, living in a bare hotel room; on the last pages of the last novel, he is again alone, though now with a license and an office. In between, he kills four people and then gives up ever carrying a gun; he meets an attractive and clever journalist and engages in a long-term, multi-novel relationship with her; he expands into providing security services for San Diego businesses and employs four part-time agents; and then he loses the attractive and clever journalist, finding himself obligated to exculpate the man she now plans to marry. Max Thursday does not develop the complex life story that detectives of the 1970s and after would offer to readers, but the arc of his life over a sequence of novels begins a movement in that direction.[1]

Guilty Bystander *(1947)*

Max Thursday will later (in the second novel in the series, *Fatal Step*) refer to the action of the first novel, *Guilty Bystander,* as the "Manila Pearl business." It is the case which brings him back to sobriety and back to work as a detective. It was, he says, "just a dirty gang war with no holds barred." This is true. In *Guilty Bystander*, competing gangsters vie to acquire a set of valuable pearls that have been smuggled into the country. They are willing to betray one another, to kill, to kidnap, and to torture to gain the pearls. Victims include employers and employees; they also include bystanders. One of the bystanders is Dr. Homer Mace, a decent physician whose partner, a less decent physician, has become involved in the hijacking of the pearls. Another bystander is Dr. Mace's stepson, who is kidnapped to secure Dr. Mace's cooperation. And that stepson's birth father is Max Thursday. When his former wife in desperation calls upon him to save their son, Thursday abruptly stops drinking and recovers his identity as a tough private eye. It may be "the Manila Pearl business" six months later, in *Fatal Step*, but in *Guilty Bystander*, the Manila pearls are a side issue; the main business is the recovery of a son.

The reason for the retrospective shift from seeing *The Guilty Bystander* as a kidnap-centered case to recalling it as the "Manila pearl case" would seem to lie in the decision to drop, without comment, Thursday's ex-wife and son from his life. Georgia, and their son Tommy, never appear again in the series. Wade Miller evidently wanted Max Thursday to revert to the normal hard-boiled dick, free of attachments, and especially free of his ex-wife and child. Saving his son and avenging himself against the son's kidnapper is Thursday's primary goal in the novel; in retrospect, the primary goal is shifted to more traditional hard-boiled detective actions: defeating gangsters, recovering pearls, securing rewards. But "Manila pearl case" does—if very faintly—recall the Maltese Falcon case: exotic jewels (Mediterranean or Philippine) pursued by competing conspirators are central to the action of both novels, while the detective's personal loss (murdered partner, kidnapped son) has the most meaning for the investigator. But the parallels are slight compared to those between *The Maltese Falcon* and the jewel-less *I, the Jury*.

But the parallels between the premise of *Guilty Bystander* and that other 1947 debut, *I, the Jury*, are more remarkable. Both Mike Hammer and Max Thursday engage in an investigation with a strong personal motivation. The initial crimes—murder in *I, the Jury* and kidnapping in *Guilty Bystander*—harm persons to whom the detective is deeply attached, and both men react with fierce determination to solve the case themselves. They both acknowledge that the authorities—the police—will work earnestly to secure justice, but they both insist that they themselves must pursue their own investigation, and that their outrage at the violence done to a loved one will be give them an advantage denied to the police. (They both have allies on the police force, though Lt. Austin Clapp is less accommodating of Max Thursday than Pat Chambers is of Mike Hammer.[2]) Their initial losses, however, are significantly different. Hammer has lost a wartime comrade, and specifically, a comrade who sacrificed an arm to save Hammer. The obligation to avenge this irreparable loss drives Hammer to pursue any means necessary to find and to execute the murderer. Thursday has lost his son, who has been kidnapped. The loss is not irreparable; in fact, Thursday does rescue his son. Hammer races against the police: if he wins, he gets to kill the murderer. Thursday races *with* the police. Both are rushing to prevent the ever-increasing likelihood that the kidnappers' will find it most expedient to kill their captive. If Thursday or the police win, the son's life will be saved. Both novels assert the superiority of the personally motivated individual over the well-meaning organization: it is, of course, the private eye, not the police force who discovers the villain in the end. But Max Thursday never rises to Mike Hammer's high passion; he never assumes that the urgency and the justice of his cause excuses any act of violence in pursuing his goal.

The bond with a son may surely be as intense as the bond with a comrade, but Thursday, living a derelict life in the Bridgeway Hotel, has not, in fact, seen his five-year old son for three years. His wife, Georgia, the boy's mother, has remarried, and her new husband, kindly Dr. Homer Mace, has been the only father Tommy has known. Thursday shows himself willing to employ violence—and to suffer violence—in his mission to save his son but saving his son—not destroying the captors—is his primary motive, and he does not seem to enjoy the necessary violence of the investigation the way that Hammer does. The genre presumes sympathy for a measure of excess when avenging a comrade or rescuing a son, but Hammer's excess is, for most readers, extraordinary; it is either, by Spillane's readers, justified as righteous wrath or, by Spillane's critics, denounced as pathological sadism. Max Thursday is also capable of extraordinary behavior in the crisis—he abruptly (and permanently) ends years of alcoholism in a matter of days, but he does not approach Mike Hammer's extreme embrace of physical violence—fists and guns—as the right means to his righteous ends.

Thursday does, however, finish the novel committing an execution that parallels the end of *I, the Jury*. In the last lines of the novel, Thursday, like Hammer, shoots and kills the murderer, a murderer whom the detective has trusted throughout the narrative. Indeed, the woman whom he kills on the last page has been one of the most trusted persons in the detective's life.[3] Hammer has proposed marriage to Charlotte Manning; they have already enjoyed domestic moments (she fries chicken for him) and have been planning their life after the wedding. Thursday has relied upon Smitty for his job (she runs the Bridgeway Hotel and hires him) and, as well, for information and support throughout his investigation. But again the differences are telling. Both killings can be justified: in both cases, the woman whom the detective shoots has committed multiple murders, and she is, when he shoots her, an immediate threat to the detective. To be sure, Mike Hammer realizes the threat *after* firing the fatal bullet into Charlotte Manning's belly: he then discovers that she had been reaching for a gun hidden behind a plant. When Max Thursday shoots his son's kidnapper (and, as well, the murderer of two other persons), Smitty is actually holding a gun on him, and is about to fire at him. His claim of self-defense is not an afterthought.

Spillane makes his ultimate villain an unnatural woman: Charlotte is a sadist (having tortured Jack Williams as he lay dying); more broadly, she is without what Hammer takes to be the social instinct of a woman (i.e., the instinct to subordinate herself to a man). She uses her mind (as a brilliant psychiatrist) and her body (as a beautiful blonde) to compel men to submit to her will. She is preternaturally evil. Smitty, by contrast, is a quite natural woman; she is a concerned mother, doing her best—to be sure, her amoral best—to protect a daughter whom she knows as little as Max knows his son. She is willing to commit any crime to find the funds to give that unknown daughter the best opportunities. Her means (killing, kidnapping) are evil, but her end—unlike Charlotte's—is natural. Killing her seems not to be hard for Thursday, but it is not "easy."

Still, the peculiar parallels between the main plots of *I, the Jury* and *Guilty Bystander* only emphasize the broader differences. *Guilty Bystander*, with its third-person narration and its precisely dated and timed chapters, deliberately avoids the hot temperature of *I, the Jury*. Max Thursday feels the need to act: he knows that the longer his son is held, the less likely his son will survive. But the reader is not immersed in his passion, and, in fact, as the various facets of the complex crime are exposed, Thursday has, occasionally, to remind Lt. Clapp—and the reader—that in kidnap cases, speed is essential. Max Thursday's San Diego is not an operatic setting constantly evoking an emotional response in the detective. The action of *Guilty Bystander* is mapped objectively on the actual streets and in some of the actual buildings of San Diego. And Max Thursday himself is a more complex character. Mike Hammer has a fairly simple back-story: a detective who went to war in the Pacific and returned to his office and his secretary. Max Thursday's back-story is somewhat more complicated: a detective got married, had a son, went to war in the Pacific, returned home, got divorced, lost his license, and became an alcoholic house detective. This story is never told in more than a few sentences, but it establishes that Max Thursday's world cannot be reduced to simple good and evil.

Fatal Step *(1948)*

Gangs and gangsters did play a role in *Guilty Bystander*, and they will appear in most of the Max Thursday novels, but the gangs and their pursuit of the pearls were secondary to the problem of the missing son. *Fatal Step* itself, however, does center upon "a dirty gang war." Mickey Spillane always repeats Mike Hammer's intense personal involvement in every case; each novel begins by establishing Hammer's emotional engagement with a victim. In the second Max Thursday novel, Wade Miller retreats from the personal. Although Hammer's relationship to Red in the second Hammer novel is considerably less developed than his relationship with Jack Williams—she is a prostitute with whom he spends a few minutes in a diner; he was an old friend, an ex-cop, and a man who had sacrificed an arm for Hammer in the war—Hammer's intense commitment to securing justice for each of them is the same. In every novel, Hammer's passion is fully ignited in the first chapter. *Fatal Step* erases the passion of *Guilty Bystander*; Max Thursday's son and ex-wife simply vanish from his life. He does, in the course of the novel, make a new emotional connection, but although Merle Osborn will reappear at least briefly in all four of the following novels, Thursday's romantic connection with her never takes on the importance of his paternal concern for Tommy in *Guilty Bystander*. Until the final novel, the Thursday-Osborn romance is largely taken for granted.

It is, in *Fatal Step*, gang warfare lies behind all of the murders. The principal gang is run by Ulaine and Larson Tarrant, a wealthy and mismatched couple—he is a louche sadist, she is wealthy and tough. They run a string of legal draw poker parlors, each with an adjoining illegal stud poker parlor. They employ a team of their own brutal enforcers and, as well, a professional security organization, the Hempstead-Young Merchants Patrol. Although there are interesting diversions—several key scenes take place in a San Diego amusement park named Joyland, and a subplot concerns a Chinese elder's concern for the reputation of his murdered son—the main action of the novel revolves around the Tarrants and the co-owners of Hempstead-Young. The wealthy clubman Parker Hempstead and tough Al Young prove to be odd partners, just as the Tarrants prove to be an odd couple. Each of the four is willing to employ violence to advance his or her individual interests, and each is an individual. Al Young comes closest to the stereotypical mob boss, and even he develops a distinct character.

Max Thursday's involvement comes through David Lee. Having revived his detective skills in "the Manila Pearl business," Thursday has reactivated his investigator's license and opened an office on the fourth floor of the Moulton Building. The painter is still lettering the office door. There will be a measurable development in Thursday's career; he will not begin each new case from exactly the same premises. He has had at this point only two paying cases, with a total remuneration of $50. David Lee makes an appointment to meet the detective at the amusement park but is killed while Thursday is riding the Loop-o-plane on which they were supposed to meet. Thursday is then hired by David's father, Song Lee, to clear his son's name. Where, in *Guilty Bystander*, solving a series of murders seemed secondary to rescuing a kidnapped boy, in *Fatal Step*, Thursday's nominal assignment is simply to secure a signed statement from Larson Tarrant, declaring that David Lee was engaged in no shameful activity when he was murdered. Thursday does force Tarrant to write such a statement, and Song Lee accepts it as a vindication of his son. It is a slender basis on which to keep Thursday involved in an investigation in which a number of men are killed.

The most important addition to *Fatal Step* is Merle Osborn. She is a professional journalist, covering the crime beat for a sensationalist paper, the *Sentinel*. She got the job during the wartime manpower shortage and has held on to it through competence. She is presented as a flawed, independent woman. She has taken pay-offs from the Tarrants in return for not publicizing what she knows of their operations; by the novel's end, she has ended the arrangement. She is attractive but takes no care to accent her attractiveness. She comes to appreciate Max Thursday during the course of *Fatal Step*, and will even lie for him, but she never adores him in the manner of Mike Hammer's Velda. And—also unlike Velda—she does sleep with the detective, even without the seal of a wedding ring.

Uneasy Street *(1948)*

The third Max Thursday novel, *Uneasy Street,* is another interesting homage to *The Maltese Falcon.* Nearly all of the key elements assembled by Hammett are repeated. The significant omission is the absence of a partner (a murdered partner), and thus of what Sam Spade has to remind Brigid O'Shaughnessy—and the reader—is the novel's central crime. (Where Spillane eliminated the valuable-work-of-art aspect of *The Maltese Falcon,* Wade Miller eliminates the murder-of-the-comrade.) In *Uneasy Street* the fabulous piece of ownerless art is Velázquez's *El Bobo de Coria,* a painting which, like the Maltese Falcon, is pursued across an ocean and a continent by an international cabal of conspirators—including, in this case, a Spanish art expert, an Austrian "exporter," and an American art dealer, and a femme fatale. But although the cast of characters and the driver of the action—betrayals and murders in pursuit of possession of a very valuable work of lost art—all nod to Hammett's novel, the development of the plot moves in new directions.

El Bobo de Coria (The Fool of Coria, also known as *El Bufon Cala-bacilla)* is an actual painting by Diego Rodriguez de Silva y Velázquez that actually hangs in the Museo del Prado in Madrid.[4] The novel's conceit is that what hangs in the museum is a facsimile, and that Velázquez's original painting was discovered in a wine merchant's house that was bombed during the Spanish Civil War by Abrahán Niza, "an important official at the Prado Gallery in Madrid." With the assistance of Count Emil von Raschke, an Austrian "exporter" (who here plays the role of Casper Gutman), and his associates, April Ames and Gordon Larabee ("one of the biggest fine art and antique dealers in Southern California"), Niza has brought the painting to San Diego, where the eccentric millionaire, Oliver Arthur Finch, has agreed to pay $100,000 to add the painting to his secret hoard of objets d'art. Finch, an 80-year-old recluse, made his fortune by building a dry goods store into a chain of several hundred five-and-ten stores that litter the Pacific Coast. He has now retired to his mansion on the Point Loma Peninsula west of central San Diego where he lives with an aged secretary, a nurse, and his dissolute son, who has become infatuated with April Ames.

April Ames shows the greatest debt to Hammett. She is, like Brigid O'Shaughnessy, an adventuress willing to seduce anyone who can further her ambition and to betray anyone who obstructs her pursuit. Like Brigid O'Shaughnessy, and unlike Caspar Gutman (or Count von Raschke), she desires not the work of art, but the money it represents. Brigid O'Shaughnessy secured the assistance of Captain Jacobi; April Ames secures the assistance of Finch's son, Melrose, who is usually found on his boat, moored on Cormorant Island, just beyond the Finch mansion. April flirts with Max, but the relationship never reaches the point where he wonders whether she loves him or he loves her. Max Thursday permits April Ames to escape, and to escape with the antique music box that has held the one hundred $1,000 bills. He has, however, surreptitiously removed the money, so her only profit is the music box itself. Letting her go is easy. Unlike Brigid O'Shaughnessy, April Ames has not murdered anyone. Her holding a gun on the others gathered at the Finch mansion and then driving away with the music box is not problematic. It solves the problem: the winsome and amoral April Ames is gone, and Max Thursday is left able to complete his assignment, with Oliver Arthur Finch in possession of his $100,000, Count von Raschke in possession of *El Bobo de Coria*, and Thursday in possession of the murderer, Lucian Pryor.

Finally, it might be noted that *Uneasy Street* anticipates by two years the surprise ending of Mickey Spillane's *Vengeance Is Mine*. Spillane was quite proud of his ability to shock on the last page. The exposure of Juno Reeves as, beneath her provocative gowns, a man does shock as well as surprise. Wade Miller aims only at surprise. When Max Thursday reveals that the murderer is the artist Lucian Pryor, who has been impersonating his villainous sister Gillian, most readers will be surprised. But Pryor appears not as the bold and transgressive transvestite that Juno Reeves was, but as a weak and troubled person: "Lucian probably does think of his real self as either male or female. He's always envied his sister's ruthless life and so when he put on Gillian's dress and that blonde wig all his repressions came bursting out." Thursday is not excessively sensitive; he can say, "I don't mean he's a fag." But having caught the murderer, he can begin to try to understand his character. Spillane disdains complexity. Juno Reeves's confused sexual identity simply adds a final touch to the depravity that Juno has already demonstrated through blackmail and murder.

An additional interesting aspect of Lucian Pryor as an artist is his decision to use his knife—the knife he has used attempting to murder his way to possession of the $100,000—to destroy all of his own paintings, paintings which he had recently shown at the National Gallery in London and was now preparing to show at the Fine Arts Gallery in San Diego. When Max Thursday asks him why, he replies, "You don't see the point at all, do you? Great works are never appreciated until they are centuries old. What good comes to the creator then? No, the only persons who benefit from great talent are the merchants, the criminals like Raschke…. That can never happen to my works now. I made them and destroyed them." However pathetic he appears in the end, this seems a grand gesture. It is, however, apparently a misguided one. In fact, the "great merchant" in *Uneasy Street*—the 5-and-10 tycoon Oliver Arthur Finch—is a miserable invalid who squirrels away his acquisitions—everything from cheap bric-a-brac to (as he hopes) a Velázquez—in a disordered storage room; his collection is not for display. His vanity is petty and foolish—a five and ten cent vanity. And the criminal von Raschke, though his bravado is at times impressive, ends up in a very questionable possession of the painting. His claim will doubtless be challenged. As an artist, Lucian Pryor could create paintings museum-worthy paintings; with his knife, he has now destroyed both the art and the artist. Having slashed all of his canvases and having murdered Mrs. Wister, Gordon Larabee, and Abrahán Niza, he has reduced himself to nothing more than a small, confused, and uncreative villain.

Uneasy Street is set during the Christmas season (7:45 p.m. December 23 to 3:15 a.m. December 25). There are intermittent references to Santa's and gift-buying. San Diego's routines of holiday celebration contrast with the ugly, homicidal greed of everyone involved in the case. There is a touch of humor in Max Thursday's brief excursion to Tijuana, but no one—not the sometimes humorous von Raschke, not even the sprightly April Ames—emerges as other than mercenary. The happy ending—the painting and the money recovered, the villain identified and under guard—is really satisfactory only for the detective who solved the mystery and completed his commission.

Calamity Fair *(1950)*

After publishing two Max Thursday novels in 1948, Wade Miller published a gangster novel in 1949: *Devil on Two Sticks*, also set in San Diego, but not featuring Thursday. In 1950, Max Thursday's career resumed with *Calamity Fair*. The detective's initial commission echoes that of Philip Marlowe in *The Big Sleep*—he is called upon to recover a woman's unwise signing of gambling IOUs. Later, he will be called upon to recover a wealthy young woman's nude photographs. In *The Big Sleep*, a single woman—the psychopathic Carmen Sternwood, the privileged daughter of General Sternwood—signs the IOUs and sits for the photographs; in *Calamity Fair*, two quite different women are involved, one who proves to be an entirely decent wife, the other to be a criminally minded child of privilege. The situation quickly evolves in entirely different directions than that faced by Marlowe, as Wade Miller again confronts Max Thursday with a gang of thieves among whom there is no honor. Still, there is a distinct touch of

Marlowesque chivalry in Thursday's behavior, and a touch of Chandleresque sentimentality in the end.

The main plot concerns a blackmail syndicate that operates under the cover of the Night and Day, an exclusive agency that sells "personal services" (76). The glamorous Quincy Day is the face of the agency (one surprise at the end of the novel is the identity of "Night").[5] She is a sort of establishment Brigid O'Shaughnessy: Max and Quincy are clearly attracted to one another, but their fundamentally different moral orientations divide them. Max sleeps with Quincy, as Sam Spade slept with Brigid, and in both instances, the detective awakens first and makes a clinical search of the woman's rooms while she sleeps. Both couples enjoy domestic moments, but both women have chosen to involve themselves in conspiracies that set them irrevocably against the standards of the detective. Hammett chose to place Spade in a position where, in the end, he had to choose between his standards and his love; with great difficulty, he chose his standards. Wade Miller was kinder to Max Thursday: in the end, Quincy is fatally shot by her co-conspirator, and, accompanying her in the ambulance, Max is able to hold her hand and reassure her, as she dies, that he does care for her.

Calamity Fair takes a flashback form, uncommon in hard-boiled fiction. In Chapter 1, dated Saturday, August 13, 6:00 p.m. (making the year 1949), Thursday is on the run, evading detection by the police; Chapter 2 shifts to five days earlier—Monday, August 8, 12:00 noon—to the beginning of the case, when Thursday visits a client who hires him to recover IOUs that she had signed in a spree of illegal gambling. Not until Chapter 29 (of 34) does the reader learn that Thursday's first chapter avoidance of arrest follows his leaping from the window of the San Diego District Attorney's office after learning that D.A. Leslie Benedict has sufficient evidence to warrant charging Thursday with the murder of Col. Ellis Fathom, who has been identified as an accomplice in the blackmail syndicate. In the novel's final five chapters, Thursday discovers that the syndicate is keeping its incriminating evidence in a frozen meat locker. He is himself nearly frozen to death, but he survives to comfort the dying Quincy Day and then to visit each of fifteen blackmail victims and—for a $100 finder's fee—hand them the evidence to destroy. This exercise—first securing a commission from each of the fifteen victims (he will receive $100 from each if he can gain possession of the incriminating photos or IOUs); then gaining possession of the material; then delivering the photos or IOUs and watching them be destroyed by the victims, and finally collecting the $100—is different from the practice of the criminals, who plan to bleed their victims for much more money over a very long period of time. It is quite different, but not totally different. The exercise occupies only a couple of paragraphs and could have been omitted; Wade Miller surely wants to suggest how close the detective can come to crossing the line between tough private eye and tough gangster.

Because there were many victims of high social status and because the D.A. can't be sure Thursday has indeed found and destroyed the evidence, Benedict declines to prosecute the detective. But he is not a happy District Attorney. Benedict would have been even less happy had he known that Thursday's initial client, being blackmailed over those gambling IOUs, was Benedict's own wife. She had not revealed her true identity when she hired Thursday, and Thursday manages to preserve her secret, even when he has to call upon her for assistance. Benedict—though not his wife—will return in both of the remaining two Thursday novels, always as an antagonist suspicious of Thursday's motives and actions.

And Merle Osborn, introduced in *Fatal Step*, makes her third appearance in *Calamity Fair*. As in *Uneasy Street*, it is a brief appearance. She is now Thursday's reliable girlfriend, largely taken for granted. She is still a journalist covering crime and can be called upon to provide the detective with an alibi or information. She will return again in a brief role in *Murder Charge*, and then, in the final novel, *Shoot to Kill*, she will appear as a major figure.

Murder Charge *(1950)*

Murder Charge was the second Max Thursday novel to be published in 1950.[6] And once more, Wade Miller offers something new. In *Calamity Fair*, it was the flashback form that opened with Max Thursday on the run, evading the authorities: the detective as villain in the eyes of the law. In *Murder Charge*, the experiment is having Thursday actually become a gangster: the detective as villain in the eyes of the lawless. Because of his physical resemblance to an important gangster who, having just arrived from the east, has been shot by local rivals, Lt. Clapp and the F.B.I. plan to confine the wounded gangster—Harry Blue—in the hospital while Max Thursday impersonates him in order to discover why Blue has come to San Diego. Blue, a one-time associate of such famous mobsters as Johnny Torrio, Al Capone, Lucky Luciano, and Jake "Greasy Thumb" Guzik, has been sent by "New York, Cleveland, Miami interests" (16) to San Diego to scout the possibilities for reorganizing and expanding mob operations in the city. He is ambushed outside his hotel on the day of his arrival, and—with the unenthusiastic cooperation of D.A. Leslie Benedict—Lt. Clapp and Joseph Maslar of the F.B.I. want Thursday to undertake the impersonation for a few days in order to find out New York, Cleveland, and Miami have planned for San Diego, and what local criminal talent he can identify.

As a result, Thursday spends most of the novel acting as a brutal mob capo, intimidating with a Mike Hammer panache the members of the San Diego underworld whom he encounters. The mob assigns him a bodyguard, and that gunman will casually execute two local gangsters on what he takes to be a hint from "Mr. Blue." Thursday will thus be in some measure responsible for the two murders, even though at the novel's end, he expressly disowns accountability for any of the six deaths that have occurred. Thursday, as Blue, even presides at a mob banquet given in Blue's honor. Blue's wife shows up; she doesn't expose Thursday, but she does complicate the situation. (In the end, Thursday abets her escape from San Diego.) Although D.A. Benedict is outraged by the six murders, he is compelled to admit that Thursday's impersonation has taken down a new prostitution ring, exposed a corrupt vice cop, and, for the moment at least, kept the national mob out of San Diego.

The premise is, of course, improbable.[7] But Thursday carries it out plausibly, and in the process he demonstrates, as, in a different way, he had in *Calamity Fair*, that the line between the detector of crime and the committer of crime is a thin and permeable one. In *Calamity Fair* Thursday can behave so as to persuade the District Attorney that he is a criminal; in *Murder Charge* he can behave so as to persuade the gangsters that he is a criminal. Yet he never actually becomes a criminal. The detective can cross over and operate efficiently on the other side; it is his moral center that distinguishes the one from the other.

Murder Charge brings back familiar faces. Merle Osborn appears briefly, but, as a journalist, she is necessarily shut out from the undercover impersonation. D.A. Leslie Benedict continues to disapprove of Thursday but remains powerless to enforce his disapproval in any way. Lt. Clapp is, as always, the supportive official.

A final innovation appears in the first and final chapters. All of the Max Thursday novels are narrated in the third person, almost always from Thursday's point of view. The initial chapter of *Murder Charge* is narrated from the point of view of Mr. Blue's unnamed, would-be assassins, who wait in a car and race off after shooting him when he exits his hotel. The final chapter is narrated from the point of view of Mr. Blue, who is attempting to get out of San Diego when another assassination team catches him in a remote phone booth and succeeds in killing him.

Shoot to Kill *(1951)*

The last of the Max Thursday novels returns to the temper of the first: the detective is again has a deep personal investment in the case he is investigating. He still does not rise to the self-righteous passion of Mike Hammer; indeed, the circumstances of the crime make him unusually dubious of his own motives. And his self-doubts are justified. The novel opens with him—the sharp-eyed detective—being surprised that not only has Merle Osborn chafed at what she regards as being taken for granted in their relationship, but that she has decided to end it, has, indeed, already engaged herself to marry another man. The final novel of the series replays a version of the back-story of the first novel. The Max Thursday novels are bookended by women who once chose Max Thursday now choosing another man.

Merle Osborn's new man—sporting goods retailer, Bliss Weaver— has actually been employing Thursday's five-person agency (which now includes Thursday and four part-time agents) for store security. When Thursday follows Weaver from Merle Osborn's apartment to Weaver's wife's apartment and, immediately after Weaver leaves, discovers Weaver's wife's corpse, he makes a gesture toward framing Weaver for the crime (which he believes Weaver has in fact committed). The gesture quickly backfires, and Thursday spends the rest of the novel questioning his own motives and working to exonerate Weaver with the same earnest commitment he worked to rescue his son in *Guilty Bystander*.

The plot of the prior Thursday novel, *Murder Charge,* depended upon an unlikely set of circumstances: the physical resemblance between Thursday and a mob gunman, the unsuccessful assassination attempt, and the universal unfamiliarity among a diverse body of San Diego gangsters with the voice and manners of that famous gunman. The plot of *Shoot to Kill* requires an even greater suspension of disbelief. A pair of violent thieves happens to practice their craft in Bliss Weaver's wife's apartment building the day that Merle Osborn declares her intent to marry Weaver. One of the thieves happens to look like the large, blond Weaver, and he is the one who strangles the occupant of the apartment, who happens not to be Weaver's wife, but Weaver's wife's sister, who happens to have arrived from the east that very day, and, when Weaver's wife departed for an assignation, the sister happened to decide to wear try on the wife's dress and jewelry, and thus her corpse happens to be identified as Weaver's wife (and the wife, upon learning of the misidentification, happens to prefer appearing dead to identifying her sister's corpse). When Weaver is arrested, the police car carrying him happens to have an accident that permits Weaver to escape, and Weaver happens to have a place where he can hide undetected for the duration of the novel. A lot happens in the novel.

Added to the improbabilities of the main plot are the improbabilities of the principal subplot: in addition to the usual competition between the individual private eye and the organized men of the establishment law enforcement, *Shoot to Kill* brings in a private, organized force. Kelly Dow, having made a fortune with his chain of restaurants and having once chanced to find the body of a crime victim, has organized a group of armed men on horseback—"my Sunset Riders" (63). In the present case, Dow and his men are not looking for evidence; they are looking for Bliss Weaver, whom Dow simply assumes is the murderer. Official law enforcement may resent interference from lone detectives; it is even less happy with the assistance provided by this mob of vigilantes. A series of happy events—Thursday befriends a paraplegic bookie who provides him with a clue that leads him to identify Dow as the backer of a bookmaking operation—exposes the restaurateur-cum-vigilante as more than a blowhard; he is himself a criminal, and Thursday has the satisfaction of being obliged to bludgeon Dow in order to follow up on a hot lead. It is the private eye—that complete, common, yet unusual man that Chandler eulogized, that *solitary* man—who legitimately discovers truth overlooked by official law enforcement. No private organization—no Sunset riders—organized by a vain man who plays at law enforcement and at law breaking has a useful role to play.

And yet the virtues of the series are also present in the final novel. San Diego is again clearly mapped as the scene of the crime. Lt. Clapp, naturally disinclined to accept all of the happenstances that Thursday's theory of the crime requires, continues to challenge his friend productively, and when it is he who discovers Thursday's misbegotten attempt to frame Weaver, he conceals the falsified evidence and delivers a proper dressing down of his friend. Merle Osborn surprises Thursday (and the reader) with her preference of Bliss Weaver over Max Thursday. As a remarkable woman who has made an unusual success in a man's profession, the adventurous Merle seemed to be the right partner for the adventurous Max. No woman ever drops Mike Hammer; it is the detective who does the dropping. But Merle chooses the comfort of marriage to a businessman to an apparently unending affair with the detective. And yet she does not convert into a housewife. When Thursday discovers a tip that may lead to Weaver's exoneration, Merle Osborn is not only active in the search, she boldly follows a lead into a deserted neighborhood and is nearly killed. Though she will enjoy the secure comforts of being Bliss Weaver's beloved wife, she remains Merle Osborn, intrepid journalist. The arc of her life is not a retreat into mere domesticity. And the detective will return to the lonely life he led when *Guilty Bystander* began; Max Thursday ends emphatically as an isolato.

Truman's Wade Miller

> The fox knows many things, but the hedgehog knows many
> things.—Archilochus

Wade Miller produced a popular detective by sticking to the basic hard-boiled formula: a solitary detective travels the mean streets asking tough people tough questions, pushing and being pushed, often violently, and, in the end, discovering whodunit. But the two writers kept experimenting with formal and thematic innovations. They made the choice to narrate in the less common third person, remaining always—almost always—with the detective's point of view. They dated and timed every chapter. They gave the detective an ex-wife and a son, and then they took them away. They gave the detective a girlfriend in the second novel, kept her in the background in the next three novels, and then took her away in the final novel. They had the hard-boiled detective renounce the possession of a firearm (though he would continue to find occasion to employ a firearm). They had the detective fleeing the law at the beginning of one novel and, at the beginning of the next novel, being solicited by the law to impersonate a major gangster. The initial sequence of Mike Hammer novels played an almost mathematical set of variations on a single theme—very tough, very confident detective is aroused to wrath and bludgeons his way to the execution of the person who, in a shocking finale, proves to be the murderer. The Max Thursday novels have their continuity—the streets and scenes of San Diego, Lt. Austin Clapp and his sidekick Jim Crane, D.A. Leslie Benedict—but each successive novel seems to move in surprising new directions.

Wade Miller clearly knows many things. But Mickey Spillane knew one big thing, one really big thing. Righteous wrath as the motivation, violent physical encounters (fisticuffs and guns; discarded dresses and hard kisses) as the process, shocking surprise as the end: it might be a simple formula, but it was a formula that a very large segment of Truman's reading public clearly preferred. Mike Hammer possesses something of the grand monomania of Melville's Captain Ahab: he defies all normal constraints as he pursues the object of his passionate hatred. There is, as with Ahab, who lost a leg to Moby Dick, always a personal element to the passion, but Hammer, like Ahab, sees himself pursuing justice in an indifferent universe. But Hammer's is not the natural universe of the vast sea; it is the urban world of tough guys and dangerous dames that hard-boiled fiction portrayed, full of victims and dupes incapable of confronting true villainy and needing a monomaniac to secure justice. Ahab was a profoundly equivocal hero; Mike Hammer is not. But his simplicity can be deceptive.

Though it might seem easily imitable, it was evidently not. Spillane's succession of brilliantly forward-moving narratives—whatever their moral or literary defects—were what an astonishing number of readers discovered they had been looking for in the postwar years. A respectable number of readers would embrace the somewhat more complex urban world, somewhat more complex crimes, and somewhat more complex investigator created by Wade Miller—and by Ross Macdonald and Bart Spicer, and a host of others.

3

Ross Macdonald's
Lew Archer

If Mickey Spillane was the hard-boiled detective story writer that the custodians of culture in the Truman era loved to hate, Ross Macdonald was the one they loved—if they loved any hard-boiled detective story writers— to love. Ross Macdonald counted himself among the haters: in an interview, his biographer, Tom Nolan, reports: Macdonald said that he felt that Spillane "did not have moral or aesthetic control. [Millar] made careful distinctions between the hard-boiled school that Hammett founded, and these other people [like Spillane] who had sort of taken the lurid or violent aspects of the hard-boiled school and abused them, as he saw it" (Pierce). Ross Macdonald committed himself to practicing a moral and aesthetic control that exceeded even that of the prior masters, Dashiell Hammett and Raymond Chandler.

Ross Macdonald had already published four hard-boiled novels before he composed his first Lew Archer novel.[1] He had begun by writing spy thrillers: the first, *The Dark Tunnel* (1944), set in a version of the University of Michigan, where Macdonald had been working for his doctoral degree in English, and the second, *Trouble Follows Me* (1946), set in Honolulu, Detroit, and San Diego, reflecting in part Macdonald's experience as a naval officer in the Pacific. Each of these novels was narrated by a different protagonist—doctoral student Robert Branch in *The Dark Tunnel*, Navy Ensign Sam Drake in *Trouble Follows Me*—but the official investigator in both novels was an F.B.I. agent, Chet Gordon. For his next two novels, Macdonald experimented with different forms of hard-boiled fiction. *Blue City* (1947) is a solid version of the fable of the stranger who enters a corrupt town, disrupts the prevailing misrule, and restores at least a degree of order. It is somewhat in the vein of Hammett's *Red Harvest*, but the differences are crucial: John Weather is not a professional detective; he is the estranged son of the murdered businessman and community leader J.D. Weather. His one-man crusade against the city's official and unofficial power structures is, therefore, deeply personal as well as civic-minded. It is a situation that Mickey Spillane would explore in the non–Hammer novel, *The Long Wait* (1951). Finally, *The Three Roads* (1948) follows a naval officer, Bret Taylor, investigating the murder of his wife while suffering from traumatic amnesia. It is ultimately an Oedipal story—the title refers to the meeting of three roads as the location where Oedipus killed his father, and is thus an early, explicit instance of Macdonald's lifelong interest in Freudian psychology.

It was at this point that Macdonald produced the first of what would be a 17-novel series of Lew Archer private eye novels. It is another movement in a new direction. Robert Branch and Sam Drake had been private individuals who—in the tradition of John Buchan—found themselves caught up in international conspiracies (the ultimate villains in *The Dark Tunnel* are the Nazis; in *Trouble Follows Me* they are the Japanese). The heroes are men in a network of intimate relationships who must struggle to save themselves, their friends, and their country. John Weather and Bret Taylor had been individuals with troubled histories; Weather must discover the truth about his father; Taylor must discover the truth about himself. Mystery does not happen to them; they are themselves the source of the mystery.

But Lew Archer would, until the very last novels, remain a detached individual. Macdonald sketches a background for him in *The Moving Target*: recently divorced, five years with the Long Beach, California, police department, intelligence officer in the war. But he never engages in the variety of personal relationships that Sam Spade endures: no Miles Archer, no Iva Archer, no Sid Wise, no Mr. Freed, no Tom Polhaus, no Effie Perine. Even the Continental Op, who had little personal life, did have an extended professional community of Continental agents. (And Ned Beaumont and Nick Charles, protagonists of Hammett's final two novels, are embedded in a whole set of personal relations.) Mike Hammer, for all his self-centeredness, has ongoing relationships with Pat Chambers and Velda (to whom he eventually proposes marriage). And Max Thursday devotes much of his first investigation to working out his relationship to his ex-wife and his son. Lew Archer's ex-wife is a wraith who is recalled on occasion, but who never appears, never speaks. And Thursday will continue, over the course of five novels, to develop a relationship with Merle Osborn. Archer, in his first case, does already know Albert Graves, the lawyer who brings him into the case; he has worked for Graves in the past, and, in *The Moving Target*, he regards Graves as something more than an acquaintance. But Graves exits Archer's life at the end of the novel, and Archer remains essentially alone in the world. In this respect, as in many others, Macdonald adopts the Chandler model of very lonely detective, sans boss, sans secretary, sans friends, sans wife or children.

The Moving Target *(1949)*

Although he came to resist acknowledging a greater debt to Raymond Chandler than to Dashiell Hammett, when Ross Macdonald began the first Lew Archer novel, it was Chandler who, from the first pages, haunted the narrative. Macdonald does not adapt the basic plot of a Chandler novel, as Spillane adapted Hammett's *The Maltese Falcon*.[2] But he does certainly declare his intention to compete with Chandler as an artful writer of detective fiction. *The Moving Target* opens with the same cinematic scene as Chandler's first novel, *The Big Sleep*: the detective approaches the mansion of his prospective client, with the mansion and its grounds constituting a display of conspicuous wealth, while the detective's voice conveys his self-confidence despite his conspicuous lack of wealth.

Thomas B. Dewey's first Mac novel, *Draw the Curtain Close* (1947), had also opened with a nod to Chandler's *Big Sleep*. The Warfield estate just outside Chicago, like the Sampson estate and the Sternwood estate, has been designed to impress: the library into which Mac is introduced is "a room which resembled the main concourse of the Chicago Public" (8). Warfield's fortune was—unlike Sampson's or Sternwood's—not made in oil; it was made in a criminal career on a scale of Al Capone's, and, in fact, Warfield's birth name was Luigi Scarpone. There are, however, further acknowledgments of the debt to Chandler. General Sternwood hired Marlowe to protect his wayward daughter; Warfield says that he wants to hire the detective to protect his alienated wife. Mac declines, but then, when Warfield's butler later brings him a commission on behalf of the wife, Mac does accept it.

Both Dewey and Macdonald emphasize the variations from the Chandler original, and they are significant. But that they both chose to begin their series with same juxtaposition that Chandler began his Marlowe series—the uncommon common man enters an extraordinary estate to be hired by aging plutocrat (or by the plotocrat's wife)—indicates that they conceived their investigators in the Marlowe mold. The Truman novels betray an interestingly similar twist: in 1939, Marlowe had to deal with General Sternwood's two delinquent daughters, one of them a cynic with redeeming qualities, the other irredeemably corrupt. In 1947, Mac had to deal with the well-born, attractive, and victimized wife of Warfield; in 1949, Archer had to deal with the well-born, attractive, and emotionally vulnerable daughter of Sampson. Both men end their novel renouncing these attractive women. Chandler has been charged with misogyny; Dewey and Macdonald might be charged with sentimentality.

And, following Chandler's insertion of the stylized gangster, Eddie Mars, in *The Big Sleep*, Macdonald does include a stylized gangster in *The Moving Target*: the "Italianate Englishman" (52) called Dwight Troy.

Troy's criminal operation, involving the transport of illegal migrant labor, remains a nebulous affair. It turns out to have no direct connection with the crime Archer is hired to unravel: the kidnapping (and eventually the murder) of Ralph Sampson.

Macdonald's variations from his Chandler prototype are significant and begin almost immediately. Philip Marlowe's client had been the aged General Sternwood, an infirm but straightforward man with whom Marlowe—and Norris the butler, and Regan the bootlegger—could share a male bond, what Norris calls "the soldier's eye." Archer's client is the infirm but not-so-old Elaine Sampson, whose character remains questionable throughout the narrative. Her primary motive seems to be to outlive the husband whom she seems to despise. General Sternwood had two daughters, both of whom he disapproves; Mrs. Sampson has a stepdaughter, Miranda, with whom she has an uneasy relationship. One of General Sternwood's daughters has had a brief flirtation with the family chauffeur; Mrs. Sampson's stepdaughter is infatuated with the family chauffeur. In the course of *The Big Sleep*, Marlowe kills a gangster's enforcer, the only time Marlowe ever kills anyone; in the course of *The Moving Target*, Archer kills a gangster's enforcer, the only time Archer ever kills anyone. The echoes cannot be accidental, but Macdonald so varies the details that he cannot be said really to be rewriting Chandler. But he is clearly aligning Lew Archer with Philip Marlowe as a self-aware, lonely man completely dedicated to solving problems.

One of the first and clearest differences emerges in the relationship between the detectives and the daughters. In both novels, there is an erotic element to the relationship. But General Sternwood's daughters are aggressively sexual; Marlowe has to defend himself from the direct assaults of the pathological Carmen Sternwood, once violently, and, less violently, he has to parry Vivian Sternwood's deployment of her physical attractions. Lew Archer consistently takes a less combative, more sensitive, more paternalistic interest in the vulnerable Miranda Sampson, though he is tempted by her nubile sexuality in a way that Marlowe was not by the infantile Carmen or the sophisticated Vivian. This sensitivity of Archer becomes his signature quality. Where Marlowe seems to look for conflict in all of his encounters—with men as well as with women—Archer's usual response is to look for a basis in sympathy. If Mickey Spillane pushed the hard-boiled detective toward utterly confident self-assertion that enabled him to command every situation he finds himself in, treating all whom he meets as naturally subordinate to his authority, Ross Macdonald pulled the detective toward self-questioning and emotional outreach to anyone who seems victimized by circumstance. Lew Archer remains tough—he endures beatings and he administers beatings, but he often makes an effort to put himself inside the experience of others.

The central problem in *The Moving Target* is different from that in *The Big Sleep*. Chandler's novel, constructed by cannibalizing two short stories, featured two plots: first, an extortion plot relating to gambling, pornography, and the younger of the General's two daughters; and second, a missing persons plot relating to the husband of the General's elder daughter. Lew Archer's problem initially seems to be a reversal of Chandler's second plot: it is the father, Ralph Sampson, who is missing, and his daughter, Miranda, who assists in the search for him. But the case turns into a matter of kidnapping and ransom and, finally, murder; and whereas Philip Marlowe discovers that the missing man for whom he has been searching was murdered before he began to search, Lew Archer discovers that Ralph Sampson is murdered only at the very end of the novel, moments before Archer reaches him. In lieu of a second plot, Macdonald expands the dimensions of Ralph Sampson's life to include an association with an actress, a gangster, and a hermit, each of whom provides the occasion for Archer to explore another aspect of postwar California.

Spillane reduced New York City to an expressionist landscape of heightened scenes of wealthy penthouses and poor tenements, fancy nightclubs and greasy spoon diners, and always dark and rainy streets. Wade Miller mapped Max Thursday's world precisely on the actual streets of San Diego. Macdonald places Lew Archer in a recognizable Los Angeles but has him cover a wide range of southern California, always with an eye for distinctive detail. Specific locations are often fictionalized: the Sampson mansion is on the coast in Santa Teresa, California, Macdonald's version of the Santa Barbara where he lived most of his adult life.[3] Archer ranges widely in his first case. He visits the gated estate of his client and the dingy cottage occupied by one of Troy's accomplices, a Hollywood studio, the mountain retreat of a dubious guru, fancy Los Angeles nightclubs, and cheap piano bars. On the one hand, the variety of sharply observed scenes, while impressive, seems gratuitous: it is not clear why Troy, an elegant gangster who runs illegal agricultural workers from Mexico to Californian farms, would engage as his principal partner an aging movie star with an interest in astrology and as his transit manager an aging, long-haired, would-be bodhisattva. The core conspiracy—the kidnapping of Ralph Sampson—was executed by three persons, one of whom lives at the Sampson estate and none of the three have nothing to do with Hollywood, mountaintop temples, astrology, or illegal migrants. Macdonald's broadening of the horizons of his investigator's commission permits him to exercise his talent for evoking the textures of midcentury American lifestyles, and it also allows him to extend his judgment upon the society that nurtures those lifestyles.

Thus Fay Estabrook, the aging Hollywood star, enables Lew Archer to notice the garish, astrologically decorated bedroom that she has designed for Ralph Sampson, to visit a Hollywood set and observe the way a director treats his actors, to banter with a gossip columnist who introduces him to Fay, to escort Fay to a succession of fashionable Hollywood nightspots, and to listen to a fading actress's self-pity. It also provides an occasion for him to squirt oil into a tough guy's face, and eventually to meet the suave gangster who, however improbably, is partnering with Faye to smuggle illegal workers into California. And, as he deliberately gets the old actress drunk in order to get information from her, Fay Estabrook lets him express his disgust at his own behavior, at what his occupation compels him to do.

Though he will later downplay it, in *The Moving Target*, Macdonald has Lew Archer declare that his principal source of employment is securing evidence for divorce court, the sort of sordid work that actual private detectives presumably rely upon, but that fictional detectives usually deplore. Archer is, of course, as high-minded as the best of the fictional detectives; his disparagement of the low practices that he is driven to pursue only confirms that high-mindedness. To say that his awareness of his own flaws is greater than that of Mike Hammer is to say little; Hammer has no flaws to be aware of. But Archer's consciousness of his occasionally ignoble actions or ignoble thoughts marks him as more sensitive than most of his hard-boiled peers.

The Estabrook-Troy-Claude secondary plot also provides a clear opportunity for Archer to express a judgment about social and economic corruption of California society. Fay Estabrook's apparently sincere astrological fantasies and Claude's perhaps less sincere performance as an unkempt guru satirize the Californian appetite for the occult that hard-boiled fiction had always found useful, witness the Haldorns of Hammett's *The Dain Curse* and Jules Amthor and Second Planting of Chandler's *Farewell, My Lovely*. But it also allows Archer to look into the basis of wealth in California. The exploitation of illegal Mexican laborers is an ugly business that proves sufficiently profitable to be Troy's primary criminal activity. And it is specifically an ugly business from which the kidnapped Ralph Sampson has profited. Although Sampson's wealth derives originally from Texas oil, he now operates farms in California, and when his underpaid workers go on strike, he hires illegal labor from Troy. "He's doing everything he can to starve them out and break the strike. He can't seem to see that Mexican field-workers are people," reports his daughter, Miranda (88). Archer does not directly denounce at length either the folly of astrology or the evil of smuggling human beings. He certainly disapproves of both, but the impulse to deliver hectoring sermons about such things is absent until the later novels of the 1960s and 1970s, when Macdonald's outrage at, especially, environmental degradation does lead him to have Archer issue explicit condemnation of various systemic manifestations of injustice.

If Archer is a little more searching in his self-criticism than most hard-boiled detectives and perhaps a little less inclined to righteous criticism of the errors of others, he is surprisingly dismissive of the police. Hard-boiled detective fiction, like all detective fiction in which the detective is not himself a policeman, necessarily requires that the police be in some measure incompetent. And the police may be corrupt—more often in the hardboiled mode than the classical (though in the two dozen Continental Op stories prior to *Red Harvest*, with its very corrupt police force, the Op had encountered only more or less competent cops, all of them well-intentioned). Mike Hammer regards most policemen as hamstrung by rules and regulations, but he respects their motives and—Pat Chambers being the constant example of the almost-as-good investigator—their abilities. When he encounters a corrupt cop, like Dilwick in *The Twisted Thing*, he treats him as he treats all miscreants, kicking him in the groin in the first chapter and shooting him to death in the penultimate chapter. The one corrupt cop whom Max Thursday encounters (in *Murder Charge*) plays a very minor role. Otherwise, Thursday is given no reason to express anything other than a general respect for the competence and the probity of the police.

Macdonald has Lew Archer condescend toward the cops. When a sheriff proposes setting up a roadblock to cut off the kidnappers, Archer responds, "'We can't do that,' I said in words of one syllable. 'If we do, we can kiss good-bye to Sampson'" (106). Later, when a plainclothes policeman asserts, not unreasonably, "I got a good mind to put you under arrest," Archer replies, "You got a good mind period." And when the policeman threatens to slap him, Archer warns him not to; the cop asks why, and Archer declares, "Because I've never killed a cop. It would be a blot on my record" (116–17). Mike Hammer would have said it and meant it: he *would* kill the cop who slapped him. Lew Archer comes off as smug in these exchanges. One of Raymond Chandler's charges against Macdonald in his 1949 letter about *The Moving Target* was that the author used pretentious diction: "Scribblings on toilet walls are 'graffiti (we know Italian yet it says); one refers to 'podex osculation' (medical Latin too, ain't we hell?)" (*Selected Letters* 164). "Graffiti" no longer seems especially Italian, but "podex osculation" *is* pretentious. Archer is explaining why he left the Long Beach police force: "I couldn't stand the podex osculation. And I didn't like the dirty politics" (107). It is Macdonald's graduate school version of Philip Marlowe's explanation to General Sternwood of why he left working as an investigator for the District Attorney's office: "I was fired. For insubordination. I test very high on insubordination, General" (*Stories & Early Novels* 594). Marlowe's line sets up the General's unexpected response—"I always did myself"—and establishes the essential bond between the honorable men of the novel—the men with the soldier's eye. Archer's line only marks him and the few readers who do not need to resort to a dictionary as a club of individuals who know an elegant periphrasis for "ass kissing." Archer will always be an educated investigator, plausibly capable of making recondite allusions, but he will not always feel obliged to express his intellectual superiority to the dumb cops who fail to grasp situations as quickly as he does.

The deeper significance of the condescension to the policemen is that it indicates that Archer does not share that male bonding embodied in the "soldier's eye." In *I, the Jury*, the war provided the setting for the ultimate proof of a man's sacrifice for a comrade: Jack Williams loses an arm to a Japanese bayonet that would have taken Mike Hammer's life. Hammer and Jack (and Pat Chambers) are bonded for life, and after Jack's death, Hammer and Pat are Jack's unrelenting avengers. The war alienates men in *The Moving Target*. The death of Ralph Sampson's son seems to have driven the millionaire into the arms of Fay Estabrook and the consolations of astrology. Alan Taggert, a heroic pilot in the war, feels himself diminished as he now drives Sampson's car and flies his plane. He has lost his moral compass and is thus willing to consider marrying Miranda for her wealth although he does not love her, or to conspire to kidnap her father for a $100,000 ransom. Albert Graves, a decent District Attorney before the war and someone Archer knew and worked for and respected, served honorably running a town in Bavaria for Military Government. But upon his return to Santa Teresa, he shifted to private practice with the ambition to acquire wealth. In the end, he is willing to commit murder to acquire the wealth.

Lew Archer is the one man who returns from war and, despite a broken marriage (it is not clear exactly when Sue disliked the company he kept and divorced him), pursues his mission. He explains that after a youthful conviction "that evil was a quality some people were born with," his mature view is that "evil isn't so simple"; criminal acts may be affected by a number of factors: "Environment, opportunity, economic pressure, a piece of bad luck, a wrong friend" (87). Archer's awareness of influences such as these not only precludes him from easily shooting a comrade's murderer in the belly, it underlies the sympathy with which he approaches all of the frail human beings whose misbehavior he observes. That sympathy becomes his signature quality, and the quality most admired and most imitated by the writers of the 1970s.

A Note on Style

The essence of the detective story is its moral plot: crime-confusion-clarity-justice. Consequently, writers of detective fiction tend to be praised as masters either of the confusion and clarity components or the crime and justice components. They are singled out for the fertility with which they construct baffling puzzles for their detectives to disentangle, or for their humane vision of what constitutes true crime and what constitutes true justice in the society in which they place their criminals, victims, and detectives. Of course, all stories in the genre must contain both of these essential aesthetic and the moral elements: there must always be a surprise at the end of even the story most laden with sociological observation or ideological argument, and the purest puzzle requires characters of identifiable gender, ethnicity and class who operate with intelligible motives in imaginable circumstances. But in addition to the particular puzzle aesthetic of plot that the genre demands, there are the broader aspects of prose style that all fiction writers must face. The contrast between the prose of Mickey Spillane and that of Ross Macdonald could not be greater. Simply put, Spillane— who demonstrated a genius for a surprise at the end and who proposed a coherent (nearly solipsistic) moral regime that either seduced readers or repelled them—wrote hurriedly and badly; Ross Macdonald wrote carefully and well. And this can be most clearly seen in the way they depict the setting of the action.

But this simple contrast requires at least this qualification: Spillane may never have paused to ponder le mot juste, but the words he did type into his manuscript never distracted the reader from the forward rush of the narrative. The stark scenery of the New York City that Mike Hammer inhabits may lack texture, but it always has just enough detail to keep the reader oriented and able to read the environment. The detail certainly draws on clichés, which are by their nature easy-to-read guideposts, and Spillane's cityscape is always painted in primary colors, with lines clearly drawn. Everything exists as a sufficient stage for the important physical and emotional action that Mike Hammer engages in.

I, the Jury opens in Jack Williams's apartment. The apartment has, we learn in the second paragraph, a studio couch against one wall. A few short paragraphs later, Hammer observes that it also has a throw rug, a rocking chair, an artificial arm, and a gun; the throw rug has been twisted by Jack's dying effort to crawl toward his service revolver, which hangs from the chair. And that is it. The rest of the chapter consists of Hammer's inference from the rug and chair—that the murderer tortured the dying one-armed man by slowly pulling the chair out of his reach—and Hammer's vow to exact comparable pre-mortem suffering from the villain. How Jack died matters; how he lived doesn't, and Spillane wastes no time on the accouterments that might give the reader a deeper sense of Jack's character or of the way a bachelor in a New York City apartment lived in 1947. It is enough to know that in the war Jack sacrificed his arm for Hammer; that now he lives in a modest apartment; that he has died painfully in his apartment; that Hammer is outraged.

The first chapter of *The Moving Target* is much more attentive to the natural and social environment. The first sentence brings Archer's cab "round the base of a brown hill into a canyon lined with scrub oak" (1) as he heads toward the Sampson estate in an exclusive reserve on the coast of the Pacific Ocean. As he approaches, he smells the sea and feels the coolness. There are "ordered palms," "Monterey cypress hedges," "lawns effervescent with sprinklers," "white porches," "roofs of red tile and green copper." The description continues, ending with a flourish of Archer attitude: "Private property: color guaranteed fast; will not shrink egos" (1). Archer's first spoken words in the novel are an exchange with the cab driver about whether he wants to be dropped off at the service entrance of the mansion. This combination of observation of precise details and remarks suggesting an awareness of the subtle—and the less subtle—nuances of social class is typical of Macdonald's style.

It was, of course, typical of Raymond Chandler's style. But Philip Marlowe's approach to the Sternwood estate in *The Big Sleep* is more sharply focused. That novel opens with a paragraph of self-observation (powder-blue suit; dark blue shirt, tie, and handkerchief; black brogues, etc.) and self-deprecation ("I was everything the well-dressed private detective ought to be," *Stories and Early Novels* 589). Then there are three full paragraphs of description, including that of the much-discussed stained glass portrayal of a knight and a naked lady. There is the brief interlude with Carmen, the daughter whose misbehavior begins and ends the action of the novel. And then Marlowe is guided by the butler, Norris, into the vividly evoked greenhouse where Marlowe meets the invalid General Sternwood and receives his commission. Two principal effects are achieved. The first is of the General belonging to a class of enormous wealth and of Marlowe not being nonplussed by the evidence of all that wealth. The second is of the comradeship of Marlowe and the General (and, incidentally, that the comradeship includes Norris and excludes Carmen). Despite the difference in their social status—a matter of wealth, but also of rank and age and family and health—Marlowe and the General recognize each other as honorable men, men with the soldier's eye. All of the detail and the dialogue work to impress these two effects upon the reader.

Archer's entry into the Sampson estate is less focused. The presence of the cab driver makes the exclusivity and wealth of the family less of a challenge directly to the detective. Both the driver and the detective share a view of how the other half live. Archer is greeted by Mrs. Kromberg, the housekeeper: there will be no gender-specific union of detective, butler, and old man. Mrs. Sampson's bedroom is described in some detail: "a high white room to big and bare to be feminine. Above the massive bed there was a painting of a clock, a map, and a woman's hat arranged on a dressing table. Time, space, and sex. It looked like a Kuniyoshi" (2). The painting stands in for the Sternwoods' stained glass, but where the knight being untied by a long-haired, naked lady resonates throughout the novel (including a very precise echo in the scene when a clothed woman in a silver wig has to untie the detective), the three items in Mrs. Sampson's painting have the broadest of meanings, which Archer carefully specifies—time, space, and sex. That the painting is a Kuniyoshi suggests that Mrs. Sampson or her decorator have a fine taste in oriental art and, perhaps more importantly, that Lew Archer recognizes at a glance the style of Utagawa Kuniyoshi (1798–1861). And then Archer is escorted out onto a sundeck to meet Mrs. Sampson and receive his commission. Mrs. Sampson, unlike the General, appears to be a faux invalid; and where the General had two quite different reasons for calling on Marlowe (ostensibly to protect Carmen from extortion, but with an unspoken desire to locate his son-in-law, Rusty Regan), Mrs. Sampson simply wants to know where her wealthy husband (whom she intends to beat by outliving) is.

Upon leaving the General, Marlowe is diverted to the room of the General's other daughter, Vivian, and in a bit of smart repartee learns a bit more about that unspoken commission—Rusty Regan is Vivian's husband—and begins his relationship with a woman for whom he will come to have a measure of respect and even attraction. Upon leaving Mrs. Sampson's sundeck, Archer descends to a patio where he has lunch with Sampson's daughter, Miranda, and his driver-pilot, Alan Taggert. These two persons, much more than Mrs. Sampson, will be characters with whom Archer will be engaged throughout the novel. Taggert proves to be a somewhat complicated veteran of the Army Air Forces, and Miranda becomes, for Archer, the central emotional figure in the entire drama.

Each of the scenes—Mrs. Sampson's bedroom; her sundeck; the patio; the pool below the patio—is closely observed. The dialogue between the characters of different rank—the cabdriver, Mrs. Kromberg, and Felix the Filipino houseboy representing the lower class of workers; Alan Taggert and Archer himself placed in quite different ways in the middle; and Mrs. Sampson and Miranda representing the upper class of privilege—brings out distinct strains of pride and desire and resentment. Macdonald's characters, even minor ones, seem multi-dimensional, and principal figures—the triangle of Miranda Sampson, Alan Taggert, Albert Graves—seem not just complex in their motives, but themselves not entirely certain of who they are and what they really want.

As a result, where Spillane pressed backward toward the simplicities of Carroll John Daly, Macdonald presses Chandler's sophisticated blend of well-phrased observation and vivid dialogue into an even more nuanced appreciation of the complicated lives people lead. Lew Archer loses some of the authority of Philip Marlowe's assertive moral judgment, but his self-subordination enables him to remain open to the mixed nature of the people whom he meets.

The Drowning Pool *(1950)*

Like *The Moving Target*, *The Drowning Pool* presents two plots, one domestic and one gang-related. But where the Sampson kidnapping bore no direct relation to the Troy-Estabrook-Claude-Puddler migrant worker smuggling in *The Moving Target*, in *The Drowning Pool*, the death of the Slocum family matriarch *is* related to the machinations of the unsavory gang that operates under the direction of Walter Kilbourne. The connection is embodied in Pat Reavis, a small-time grifter whom Kilbourne has placed as chauffeur to the Slocum family. Reavis courts the Sampson daughter, Miranda, causing an eruption from her father. Reavis later falsely claims to have killed old Mrs. Slocum in order to secure money from Kilbourne; and he is finally executed by thugs at the California-Nevada border acting under Kilbourne's orders. The Kilbourne gangster plot provides melodramatic scenes of the sort that the genre prescribed: nighttime encounters in bars in California and Las Vegas; the violence at the border; a tense interview on a yacht; and most extravagantly, Archer's incarceration in the sanitarium of Dr. Melliotes, one of Kilbourne's accomplices, where Archer is tattooed with water from a high-powered hose and then imprisoned. He manages to escape by filling his cell room with a twelve-foot depth of water, the weight of which bursts open a locked door. But it is the private, family melodrama at the Slocum estate that principally occupies Archer's attention and foreshadows the sort of mystery that will come to preoccupy him for most of his career.

The Sampson family in *The Moving Target* had been mismanaged by a wealthy patriarch with a weak moral compass that led him to consort with astrologers and gangsters, and to neglect his bitter, handicapped second wife and his nubile and confused daughter. The Slocum family in *The Drowning Pool* is mismanaged by a wealthy matriarch, Olivia, who takes far too much interest in her household, especially her son, James, who seems very much to have remained under his mother's thumb. He briefly attempted an escape by marrying Maude while in college, but he has returned with her and their daughter Cathy to the estate his mother has inherited from his father. Although the acreage appears to be rich in oil, and Walter Kilbourne's Pareco (Pacific Refining Company) is interested in exploiting it, Olivia will not permit drilling to mar her views of the landscape, and she holds James, Maude, and Cathy to a tight budget. James has artistic ambitions as an actor, and seems most closely connected to Francis Marvell, a playwright who encourages him. The relationship between the two men is clearly in some degree a homosexual one. An old friend of Maude's asserts that James always had a "faggot tendency" (183) and although there is nothing like the scene in *I, the Jury* when Hammer performs "a good gag" by pouring a pitcher of water on the heads of a pair of quarreling "pansies" and sends them running away crying in falsetto (146), no one, including Archer, seems to have sympathy for James's orientation.

The Slocum family, which will eventually include Sheriff Ralph Knudson, the unacknowledged biological father of Cathy, is portrayed in a largely negative light. The domineering and inconsiderate Olivia appears only briefly before being drowned in her swimming pool, and James is certainly petty and weak. Knudson seems to be a decent man caught in difficult circumstances, but he is ineffectual in supporting either his daughter or her mother, and he needs the catharsis of a fistfight with Archer to clear his conscience over his role in the investigation of Mrs. Slocum's drowning. The teenage Cathy is largely portrayed as a pathetic victim, although she acts viciously toward first her mother, then toward her grandmother and toward her chauffeur. Only Maude, Archer's initial client, seems consistently well-intentioned. But like Knudson, she is ultimately ineffectual in protecting her daughter. She sacrifices herself to save Cathy from being identified as a murderer, but the sacrifice is vain. Macdonald seals a positive view of her by having Archer, after her suicide, interview an old friend who testifies that Maude was indeed a smart, generous, loyal, loving person who always did her best to fulfill the obligations that she undertook.

The Drowning Pool has a curious ending. Maude, Archer's client, commits suicide, hoping to divert suspicion from her daughter, whom she realizes is the murderer of Olivia Slocum. James Slocum, whom Archer blames for driving his wife to suicide, is last seen solacing himself in intimate company with Francis Marvell and arguing that he has been the unhappy victim of a wife who committed suicide after murdering his mother. Ralph Knudson, having purged himself through a brutal fight with Archer, has resigned from the police force and plans to take Cathy to Chicago for treatment. Cathy, the actual murderer of Olivia Slocum, escapes punishment. In order to secure sole possession of her father's affections, she had initiated the entire problem by sending him a poisoned pen letter accusing her mother of infidelity. When Maude intercepted the letter and hired Archer, Cathy pushed her grandmother into the swimming pool, hoping that her parent's access to the hitherto withheld wealth of the estate would enable her mother to run away and leave Cathy with James, the man she believes to be her biological father. And to complete her scheme, she attempted to frame the chauffeur, Pat Reavis, with whom she had been flirting. Yet there is no penalty for any of these misdeeds: Knudson has arranged—and Archer accepts—that Cathy will leave the toxic Slocum estate in California and restart her life in the Midwest. She will go with a man whom she has disliked all her life, but whom she now placidly accepts as her father.

It is not exactly a conventionally just conclusion. There is, perhaps, an echo of the ending of *The Big Sleep*, where Philip Marlowe, having railed against the rich and their privileges, permits Carmen Sternwood, a pathological killer who has murdered Rusty Regan and tried to murder both Joe Brody and Marlowe himself, to escape the justice system and be placed in an institution. Marlowe proposes this solution to Carmen's sister, Vivian: "Will you take her away? Somewhere far off from here where they can handle her type, where they will keep guns and knives and fancy drinks away from her? Hell, she might even get herself cured, you know" (*Stories & Early Novels* 763). If Carmen is ill, not evil, this is surely the most humane response to a person who cannot control her impulses. Knudson does not have the means to place Cathy Slocum in an institution—he is technically still married to a wife who lives in Oakland, and he is without a job. But Cathy is not a pathological case, at least not to the degree that Carmen is. She is not obviously an ongoing danger to others. Permitting her to attempt to restart her high school years in a distant place is the humane response, even if it is not a just one.

And earlier in the novel, Archer made a relevant point to Maude Slocum, who saw in Archer "a passion for justice." "I don't know what justice is," Archer had responded. "Truth interests me though. Not general truth if there is any, but the truth of particular things. Who did what when why. Especially why" (124). Archer interviews Maude's old friend specifically because he needs to know why Maude committed suicide. And once he knows why Cathy committed the crimes that she did, he has completed his assignment. Truth—and especially the truth of deep motives—is Archer's ultimate goal. Not only does he not want to be the executioner, he does not want to be the judge or the jury. Mike Hammer offered readers the satisfaction of knowing that misdeeds could—*would*—be avenged: someone can bludgeon his way to discovering whodunit, and, knowing whodunit, can mete out just deserts. Lew Archer always fulfills the detective's contract to find out whodunit, but his real success lies in finding out *why* whoever did it did it. It is more important—it becomes essentially important—to discover why the misdeeds occurred. Understanding motives matters much more than identifying actors, and certainly more than apportioning punishments. And this is why Macdonald can de-emphasize the consequences for the person ultimately identified as the principal murderer. On occasion,

Sherlock Holmes could dramatically excuse a criminal—examples include "The Adventure of the Beryl Coronet," and "The Adventure of the Devil's Foot"—and facilitate his escape from judicial review. Mike Hammer never excuses a murderer and always pre-empts judicial review with his gun. Beginning with *The Drowning Pool*, Lew Archer's practice is *always* to care less about subjecting any criminal to the formal judgment of his or her peers than about understanding why he or she has behaved in the manner he or she has.

Behind this lack of interest in society's prerogative to judge and punish misbehavior lies, at least in part, a sense that society—writ large in its socio-economic structures or writ small in the pressures within a family or community—is itself an instigator of crime. Its arrangements may even be the principal villain. Cathy, who commits the murder, is a victim as well as a villain; Maude Slocum, who is murdered, is a villain as well as a victim through over-mothering her son and then tying him, his wife, and daughter too tightly to her control. Although the Pacific Refining Company is headed by an explicitly villainous gangster, Pareco's designs on the oil lying under the Slocum estate are not directly related to the central criminal action. In his later fiction, Macdonald will make exploitative Pareco-like organizations more clearly major villains whose predations lie behind the specific acts of violence Archer has to investigate. And this view—that families and corporations and governments are fundamentally implicated in the misguided actions of murderers—becomes, by the 1970s, a common theme in the new models of private eye fiction. A .45 caliber bullet cannot terminate the true cause of the crime that the detective is investigating because the true cause is institutionalized in bullet-proof social structures.

The Way Some People Die (1951)

In his first two Archer novels, the ultimate villain proves to be a sympathetic character. This is obviously the case with Cathy Slocum; there is never a point when she is viewed as other than a victim. Her confession is pathetic—"From the moment I decided to do it, I've felt as if I was cut off from every human being. I know what they mean by the mark of Cain, I have it" (193), and she rejects the consolations offered by her father and by Archer. Albert Graves, in *The Moving Target*, briefly sinks from Archer's ally to the greedy killer of Ralph Sampson, but his decision to turn himself in to the District Attorney restores him to a status of a decent man who yielded to the multiple temptations embodied in a lovely, rich, young girl. In *The Way Some People Die*, Archer finally confronts a depraved killer who, for $30,000, has murdered her husband, a man who loves her, and her husband's brother; she would have murdered Archer too, had she not emptied her gun of bullets. Yet even here, Archer's last gesture is to give the murderer's devoted mother money to be used for legal fees. Mike Hammer found it easy to execute a woman who committed multiple times; Lew Archer finds it easy to subsidize the defense of a woman whom he knows is "guilty as hell" (185) of multiple murders.

The girl is Galatea Lawrence, an attractive young nurse who decides to advance in the world by exploiting men. She chooses first a tough young thug who is a rising figure in the local underworld, and then a weak young would-be actor who assists her in disposing of the corpse of the thug before himself being murdered by her. This is the third—and last—Lew Archer novel in which old-style gangsters figure prominently. Heroin smuggling is the principal vice that the gang caters to. It is headed by Dowser, who, with his gunman Blaney, is cut from the familiar cloth of early hard-boiled gangsters. Galley encounters Dowser's organization when one of its agents, Herman Speed, is hospitalized with a gunshot wound. Speed's subordinate, Joe Tarantine, has betrayed his boss and arranged to hijack two kilos of heroin that Speed had been transporting for Dowser. Visiting Speed in the hospital after the hijacking, Tarantine meets and impresses Galley, who marries him and then begins to plot against him, using the susceptible actor, Keith Dalling. The novel's plot grows very complicated. Herman Speed, recovering from his wounds and using the name Col. Henry Fellows, marries a wealthy recent divorcee. Absconding with $30,000 she gave him to invest, Speed purchases the hijacked heroin from Joe Tarantine, and plans to sell it for well over $100,000. Archer locates Speed and takes the heroin from him. (Speed then commits suicide.) Archer returns the heroin to Dowser, and immediately thereafter, by arrangement, the police raid Dowser's estate. After killing Joe Tarantine with Dalling's assistance, Galley has killed Dalling, and then left the $30,000 that Tarantine had received from Speed with her mother. Joe Tarantine, Keith Dalling, and, for good measure, Joe's brother Mario are all killed by Galley; Galley is presumably arrested and charged with murder; Dowser and his gunman Blaney are presumably arrested and charged with drug smuggling; the heroin is in the possession of the authorities; and the $30,000 is left with Galley's mother, who, against Archer's advice to turn it in, plans to spend it on Galley's defense.

On the one hand, the gangster plot is not, as it was in the first two novels, a secondary subplot; it is at the center of *The Way Some People Die*. Archer's case begins as what the Continental Op called a wandering daughter case. But by Chapter 4, when Archer visits the boxing arena once run by Herman Speed and now by Joe Tarantine, the gangster hierarchy—with Dowser and his gunman and his moll at the top; the small-time extortionists and drug dealers, Ronnie and Mosquito, at the bottom; and the upward-looking Speed and Tarantine in the middle—constitute the core actors in the action. They are none of them quite as tough as gangsters are supposed to be: Dowser proves to be unexpectedly afraid to be alone; Speed commits suicide; when cornered by Archer, Ronnie and Mosquito prove themselves pathetically weak. But they all have the natural greed expected of gangsters, and their limitless pursuit of money helps to conceal the unnatural greed of the true villain in the case, the young nurse who has been raised by a medical father and a pious mother, but who is more ready to use people (and kill people) than the professional criminals.

The coherence, however complicated, of the central plot and its thematic resonance highlights the additional pleasures of Macdonald's narratives. There are a number of minor characters who are introduced to supply the necessary information to advance Archer's investigation, and many of them are nicely rounded in the few pages that they have to respond to the detective's questions: Galley's roommate Audrey Graham, with her lack of self-awareness; Galley's wise old landlord, Mr. Raisch, who worries about nothing; Simmie, the young Black boxer, who trains in Joe Tarantine's gym. At least one secondary character is interesting, but also a bit improbable: unhappy in her Toledo marriage to well-to-do businessman, George Barron, Marjorie Barron came to Reno for a divorce; there she met Col. Henry Fellows and married him. Troubled by her new husband's behavior, she attempts to follow him, and happens upon the unconscious Archer. Eventually she hires Archer to locate Henry Fellows, who has absconded with her $30,000. Archer finds Fellows, and finds that he is Herman Speed, who, after recovering from the bullet wound received when the heroin was stolen from him, evidently rushed to Reno, assumed the identity of Henry Fellows, and now intends to use Marjorie's $30,000 to buy back from Joe Tarantine the heroin that Joe stole from him. Marjorie's story ends quite happily, with George Barron having rushed to Los Angeles to recover his wandering wife, and the couple seem very happily reunited when Archer last sees them. Macdonald was a careful plotter, and doubtless Herman Speed's brief career as Col. Henry Fellows could be fit into the novel's timeline, but there does seem a good deal of serendipity in its quick arc.

Finally, Macdonald adds a few more details about the background of his detective. Archer remembers eating greasy potato chips as a grade school kid in Oakland (163). His abrupt transition from officer in the Long Beach Police Department to private investigator is given more detailed explanation: "You wouldn't take Sam Schneider's monthly cut, and he forced you out" (115). He now lives in "a five-room bungalow on a middle-class residential street between Hollywood and Los Angeles" (112). District Attorney Peter Colton reappears to provide Archer with a character reference. But most significant are the references to his prior cases. He is initially brought into the search for Galley Lawrence because Joshua Severn remembered *The Moving Target*'s Miranda Sampson singing Archer's praises and therefore Severn recommended Archer to Keith Dalling, who then recommended Archer to Mrs. Lawrence. Late in the novel, talking with Peter Colton, Archer brings up his contribution to the arrest of the gangster Dwight Troy in *The Moving Target*. Poe's Dupin had initiated the genre with a detective who, in his third case, could allude to events in his prior cases; the device adds a small degree of depth to the detective's character—it is a sign that he has a past—and incidentally it informs the reader pleased with the present case that there are others available for purchase. Conan Doyle had Holmes or Watson occasionally refer to prior cases, and he gradually sketched in a back story to Sherlock's Holmes's life. The hard-boiled style had largely eliminated any reference either to the detective's personal past or to his prior cases. Though he will never approach the degree of self-revelation embraced by the detectives of the 1970s and afterward, Lew Archer does make tentative steps toward presenting himself as a man with childhood and youth that contributed to making him the man that he has become, and as a detective whose past cases may have some relevance to his present case.

The Ivory Grin *(1952)*

The Ivory Grin has two distinctions: it presents Macdonald's fullest treatment of African American experience in the Archer series, and it is the last novel in which that staple of the original hard-boiled—the gangster— plays a significant role. Ross Macdonald—as Kenneth Millar—aligned himself definitely with mid-century American liberalism; he wept the night Stevenson lost the Presidency to Eisenhower. He was, in his fiction, certainly sympathetic to the situation of African Americans and other minorities (such as the Mexican migrants exploited in *The Moving Target*), but he was properly cautious about representing the African American experience (or, for that matter, the Mexican American experience). And while mobsters continued to concern the American public—the Kefauver Hearings into organized crime were televised live in 1951 to an audience estimated at 29 million (and Spillane would exploit the mob in his 1952 *Kiss Me, Deadly*)—Macdonald would begin his turn toward locating the sources of the crimes that interested him in family histories, not in the city-wide (or nationwide) underworld.[4]

Private eyes did not generally concern themselves with the racial problems in urban America. The detectives, victims, and villains, like the authors and, presumably, the readers of hard-boiled fiction, were normally white. Chester Himes (1909–1984) would not publish *For the Love of Ima-belle* (*A Rage in Harlem*), the first in his series of Harlem novels featuring Grave Digger Jones and Coffin Ed Johnson, until 1957.[5] When African Americans did appear in hard-boiled fiction, it was usually in walk-on roles as porters and elevator boys, and they were usually referred to with demeaning epithets. The gratuitous racism of Mike Hammer's encounter with the "big black buck" and the "high yellow" in *I, the Jury* is extreme, but not unprecedented. The brief appearance of a Black preacher and one of his parishioners in *Shoot to Kill* show that Max Thursday's San Diego has its African American community; neither the Reverend Terhune nor the grocer, Ebbie White, speak in dialect (as did Charlotte Manning's maid, Kathy, in *I, the Jury*); they are simply honest citizens reporting information that Thursday and Lt. Clapp can use to find a killer. Macdonald clearly intends to counter the genre's casual disregard of Black identity by giving African Americans a higher profile in Lew Archer's Southern California.[6]

African Americans had played a minor role in the third Archer novel, *The Way Some People Die*. As Archer explores a criminal hierarchy that placed Dowser at the top, with Speed as Dower's opportunist subordinate, and Joe Tarantine as Speed's opportunist subordinate, a bottom rung was occupied by Simmie, a young Black man who works as the janitor in the arena that Tarantine runs for Speed. Simmie is in training and has the ambition of working his way up as a boxer. In the few pages in which he and his girlfriend, Violet, are given a voice, he provides Archer with some useful information, and Archer expresses some sympathy for Simmie's dream—and some condescension: "If he was really good, he might be airborne for ten years, sleeping with yellower flesh that Violet, eating thick steaks for breakfast, dishing it out. Then drop back onto a ghetto street-corner with the brains scrambled in his skull" (17). Less sympathy is shown by other whites. When, later in the novel, Simmie is attacked by Joe Tarantine's brother, Mario, white bystanders immediately take racial sides: "Attaboy, Tarantine. Go and get the black bastard" (87).

Macdonald's fullest attempt to engage with African American experience occurred in the pre–Archer novel, *Trouble Follows Me*. There, one of the principal villains is the sailor Hector Land. Land is subjected to a baseless racist attack from Mrs. Merriwell, who accuses him of murder because he is Black. Land did not, in fact, commit that crime, but he does turn out to be a key member of a conspiracy to sell tactical information to the Japanese. And his treason is directly linked to his radicalization following the Detroit race riots of 1943.[7] His brother was killed in the riot, and Land reacted by joining Black Israel, "a violent and subversive organization" (123). He was, therefore, susceptible when he was recruited to supply an espionage network with U.S. Navy data that he obtained from his fellow sailors. Macdonald makes clear an understandable basis for Land's decision to prefer the Japanese over the Americans, although, in a wartime novel, Land's treason is, of course, condemned. Macdonald even offers Land a small measure of redemption: it is Land who shoots and kills the mastermind of the espionage conspiracy before himself dying of his own wounds.[8]

In *The Ivory Grin*, Archer's initial commission is to trace the movements of an African American nurse, Lucy Champion. His client is Una Durano, an unattractive woman who eventually proves to be the very tough sister of a Detroit mobster, Leo Durano[9]; Lucy Champion proves to be a very attractive young woman who finds herself involved in two difficult situations that seem to have no connection: she has been hired by Una to attend to Leo, who is in the final stages of paresis, a condition his sister is concealing from his underlings in Detroit, and, while working for Dr. Samuel Benning, Lucy has observed Dr. Benning seize an opportunity to murder his wife's current lover, Charles Singleton. Lucy tries to escape from both Una Durano and Samuel Benning but is murdered in a motel room before she can get away.

Lucy Champion is a lightly sketched character; she is primarily a plot device that connects the gangster Durano siblings, the unhappy married couple of Dr. Samuel and Elizabeth Benning, and the missing Charles Singleton. To Lt. Brake, the investigating officer, her murder is just another "dinge cutting" (150); to Archer she is a victim whose life needs to be understood. Alex Norris, the young man who is so taken with Lucy when she moves into his mother's house that, against his mother's strong prohibition, he engages himself to marry her two weeks after meeting her, is also barely realized. He serves as a focus of Archer's sympathy, partly because he suffers as a distraught youth, alienated from his judgmental mother, accused of murdering the woman he loves, and even briefly handcuffed to Lucy Champion's corpse in the morgue as a way of forcing him to confess. But Archer also sympathizes because he is the Black youth who is presumed guilty by the authorities as much for his race as for the circumstances that suggest his complicity.

It is, rather, with the incidental portraits of two elderly Black women that Macdonald most successfully individualizes his African American characters. Aunty Jones is a disabled neighbor of the Norris's, a gentle woman who provides Archer with some useful information. Mrs. Norris herself, as she confides in Archer after her son's arrest, also emerges as a pious, well-intentioned woman. Ross Macdonald, raised in Canada and inhabiting a consistently white American world, may not have the deepest insight into the African American experience, but he does make an effort to represent it.

The Duranos work nicely as Macdonald's farewell to the American gangster. Leo Durano's mob history is condensed into a telegram sent by a Detroit detective agency to the shady California detective Max Heiss. Heiss gets himself killed while trying to extort money from the Singleton family or the Duranos (or both); Archer inherits the summary: Leo has faced charges of assault, kidnapping, and murder; he was a member of the Detroit's Purple Gang and then of a "goon squad" in Chicago; he set up a Detroit-based numbers ring and still receives a cut of the proceeds (195–196). In order to conceal his mental deterioration, Una has brought Leo to California, where she enables him to act out violent fantasies. Leo Durano is the ghost of mobsters past, and his breakdown into idiocy marks the end of Macdonald's use of active California gangs as a context for violence and corruption in Lew Archer's world. In 1956 Macdonald could still add a soupçon of organized crime to the Hollywood and country club milieu of *The Barbarous Coast*, but Carl Stern's mob credentials are even less impressive that Leo Durano's. Like Durano's, Stern's racketeering record is pasted in at the end of the novel in an effort to make him belatedly a more formidable participant in a set of crimes that he is only incidentally involved in. The Mob ceases to be a central factor in the commission of crime in Lew Archer's California.

Truman's Lew Archer

Mickey Spillane claimed to dash off his novels in just a few days—nine (or nineteen) for his first novel, *I, the Jury*. Ross Macdonald's final novel, *The Blue Hammer*, seems to have gestated in Macdonald's mind for fifteen years before it was finished and published in 1976 (Pierce). Hurried composition may explain Spillane's mechanical alternation of the sex of his victims and his villains. It forced him into an artificial variation (a variation that went unnoticed by critics who made it a charge against him that his nasty villains were all women whom the misogynist Hammer enjoyed exterminating in the end). The sex of Macdonald's victims and villains is less unpredictable.

The First Six Lew Archer Novels: Sex of Victims and Villains

Novel	Chief/Initial Victim	Ultimate Villain
The Moving Target	**male** Ralph Sampson	**male** Albert Graves
The Drowning Pool	**female** Olivia Slocum	**female** Cathy Slocum
The Way Some People Die	**male** Keith Dalling	**female** Galatea Lawrence
The Ivory Grin	**male** Charles Singleton	**male** Dr. Samuel Benning

Novel	Chief/Initial Victim	Ultimate Villain
	* * *	
Find a Victim [1954]	**male** Tony Aquista/	**female** Hilde Church
	female Anne Meyer	
The Barbarous Coast [1956]	**female** Gabrielle Torres/	**male** Clarence Bassett
	male Lance Torres	

The alternations seem more organic than mechanical.

Given Macdonald's obsessive focus in his later novels upon the damage that dysfunctional families impose upon the members of their younger generation, perhaps more interesting is the sequence of the ages of the murder victims and of the murderers in the early novels.

The First Six Lew Archer Novels: Age of Victims and Villains

Novel	Chief/Initial Victim	Ultimate Villain
The Moving Target	**old** Ralph Sampson	**old** Albert Graves
The Drowning Pool	**old** Olivia Slocum	**young** Cathy Slocum
The Way Some People Die	**older** Keith Dalling	**young** Galatea Lawrence
The Ivory Grin	**young** Charles Singleton	**old** Dr. Samuel Benning
	Post-Truman Novels	
Find a Victim [1954]	**young** Tony Aquista/	**older** Hilda Church
	young Anne Meyer	
The Barbarous Coast [1956]	**young** Gabrielle Torres/	**old** Clarence Bassett
	Young Lance Torres/	
	Hester Campbell	

The young in Macdonald's fiction are quite young: late teens, early twenties. "Older" signifies the later twenties. The first two principal victims—Ralph Sampson and Olivia Slocum—are of a kind in that they are quite old and quite powerful. Ralph Sampson has built his fortune first upon oil in Texas and then upon agriculture in California; he has lost an adult son and acquired a second wife. And his will clearly dominates the lives of his family members and employees. Olivia Slocum is equally dominant and willful; she has over-mothered her gay son and confined the life of her daughter-in-law. Domineering elders were a staple of the detective story: their broadly oppressive bearing provided plausibly homicidal motives for a variety of oppressed dependents. Macdonald was being very traditional in this regard.

And then he stopped. Domineering elders persist in Macdonald's later novels. Their wealth and their crotchets *do* supply motives. But they are much less likely to be the victims, and more likely to be the killers. The murders are committed not to acquire the old person's wealth, as in *The Moving Target*, or to break up a poisoned household, as in *The Drowning Pool*. Rather, the murders occur because powerful persons in a family have distorted the lives of the young and press the young into committing acts that eventually ramify into murder. Albert Graves is not simply greedy; even in his first case, Archer recognizes complicated motives behind his friend's impulse to homicide. Cathy Slocum is not simply hoping to banish her mother and secure her father when she kills her grandmother. But the later novels do shift toward making the unhappiness of the younger generation the central problem: their unhappiness may have its source in unfair treatment by a repressive older generation or in their own unreasonable ambitions for expensive lifestyles, but in either case, their situation is not simple, and Archer must unravel its complexity to solve the crimes he is commissioned to investigate.

The shift is visible in the third and fourth novels. The elderly in *The Way Some People Die* are represented by Mrs. Lawrence and Dowser. She is the widow who preserves the obsolete piety of her husband (and as well the superannuated furnishings of the house he has left her). She cares about her daughter but has no knowledge of her daughter's true character. Dowser is the aging gangster, with his trophy girlfriend and his fear of being alone. He is tough, or at least was once tough, but he too has outlived his time in power. (The Duranos of *The Ivory Grin* carry this particular form of superannuation to its ultimate conclusion.) Neither the old widow nor the old gangster is a central actor in the murder plot. The victims and the villain in *The Way Some People Die* are all young, and it is their youthful ambition and youthful folly that drives the action.

The Ivory Grin might seem a step backward, with the distinctly mature Leo and Una Durano and Dr. Samuel Benning playing crucial roles. But they are the villains, not the victims (Una does die in the end, though only after killing Elizabeth Benning). And they are more pathetic than domineering. The Duranos are in hiding, hoping to conceal a little longer the devastating weakness that prevents Leo from exercising the authority he once commanded. Dr. Benning is the old man who keeps taking back his young wife and doing whatever he can to protect her and hold onto her. The active characters who push the complex plot forward are young and in search of something that will enhance their lives: Lucy Champion, Alex Norris, Charles Singleton, Elizabeth Benning, Sylvia Treen. Macdonald does not fully enter their lives. Charles Singleton remains a cipher. Lucy Champion and Sylvia Treen remain one-dimensional. Alex Norris's brief play with Lucy set against his conflict with his mother and his grief at losing Lucy do give him some substance. And in her final conversation with Archer, Elizabeth Benning sketches a troubled life history that makes her a more complex character that the mere object of several men's desire.

The two Archer novels that follow *The Ivory Grin* confirm the shift in Macdonald's pattern. The main victims are all young and their motives and actions—benign or malign—lie at the center of the problem that Archer must solve. Hilda, the older sister in *Find a Victim* (1954), is finally seen as a disturbed woman who cannot be held fully responsible for her actions, even if those actions include three homicides. In the end, she is as much a victim as her younger sister, who was sexually abused by their father, and who, prior to being murdered, had embarked on a life of dangerous behavior. Tony Aquista, who appears fatally wounded on a roadside in the first chapter, is a simpler case: his life has been distorted by his Mexican heritage, which he blames for his failure to win Anne Meyer. In *The Barbarous Coast* (1956), the cousins, Gabrielle and Lance Torres, along with their friend Hester Campbell, compose a trio of three young people without means trying to live rich in the world of Hollywood and country clubs. Archer first sees them in a photograph in which all three are leaping from a high diving platform. As it happens, one old man—in a sense, a very old man, who traces his family's origins to Boston in 1634—murders all three, but it is clear that other old men—Simon Graff, Leroy Frost, Carl Stern— are as culpable. The young are never innocent in Macdonald's world, but their sins are always more forgivable than those of the old.

Macdonald's aspiration to find in the genre of hard-boiled detective fiction a vehicle for serious art may lie behind this trend toward focusing upon the misguided actions of young people whose lives have been distorted by their environment. That environment is, for Macdonald, as it was for many American writers, what was taken to be the characteristically American culture that values material possessions and celebrity—that measures success in terms of lifestyle. But it was also, increasingly for him, the intimate family environment in which successful but troubled adults impose great psychic costs upon their young.[10]

Macdonald establishes two other significant aspects of his vision of the hard-boiled detective and his world. The detective is himself more lonely than ever. Chandler had pared away the social connections that tied all of Hammett's detectives to bosses, and colleagues, and secretaries, and partners, and wives. Philip Marlowe has always operated as a lone agent; Lew Archer is the more lonely because he often recalls that was once married. Marlowe's loneliness becomes the proof of his integrity; he will not, until the final novels anyway, surrender *any* of his principles; he will not make the compromises required of friends or lovers. Archer's past marriage to Sue is proof of his willingness to try to compromise, and in every case he finds himself wanting to make a personal connection with at least one— and usually more than one—individual whom he encounters. He is open to emotional commitment, but never (again, until the last novels) actually engages in a deep mutual exchange of trust and love.

The other notable distinction of Lew Archer's world is its setting. Lew Archer is, like Philip Marlowe, a citizen of Los Angeles. His home and his office are in the city. But his territory is all of Southern California. He spends time on the coast and in the mountains; and his cases take him to small towns and large cities, to college campuses and to Hollywood studios. He will eventually be affected by oil spills in the Pacific Ocean and wildfires in the hills beyond Santa Teresa (i.e., Santa Barbara). Philip Marlowe also moved beyond Los Angeles, with cases taking him to Bay City and Little Fawn Lake, and these enable Chandler to broaden his survey of the Californian version of the American Dream. But from *The Moving Target*— in itself something of an anatomy of California cityscapes, seascapes, and mountainscapes—onward, Macdonald sends Archer on centrifugal expeditions into the various natural and social terrains of southern California. The hard-boiled detective was essentially a creature of the metropolis, even if he did venture for a number of chapters into the bucolic scenery of Little Fawn Lake (or even into the Ruritanian world of Muravia, where Hammett once deposited the Continental Op). Macdonald moved toward making the detective's world a region, not a city, and this development would bear fruit in the generation of writers who followed him.

4

Bart Spicer's Carney Wilde

Mickey Spillane and Wade Miller opened their hard-boiled detective series with scenes of emotional intensity designed to establish the passion with which the investigator pursues his investigation—revenge against the murderer of his comrade, rescue of his kidnapped son. Ross Macdonald and Thomas B. Dewey adopted Chandler's device and opened their series by situating the investigator morally as a high-minded, low-paid professional confronted with the trappings of great wealth. Bart Spicer adopted a very traditional detective story opening for his first Carney Wilde novel, *The Dark Light*, a situation frequently encountered by Sherlock Holmes, Nero Wolfe, and a host of other classical detectives: a new client comes to his office. The most unusual thing about Carney Wilde's first meeting with a client is that his new client is African American.

Andrew Jackson's race proves to be irrelevant to the content of the case of the missing minister. The minister is white, as is the patroness of his church mission, the minister's key assistant, his wife, and all of the other important characters in the novel. But Spicer's decision to make the reader's first impression of Carney Wilde be defined by his relationship with a humble but strong African American client—and not by his emotional attachment to a comrade or son, or to a social and economic "superior"—marks Wilde as a peculiar tough guy. The world of hard-boiled fiction was still, in the 1940s, an almost exclusively white world. And on the rare occasions when African Americans were depicted as more than ancillary elevator boys or Pullman car porters or—as in *I, the Jury*—dim-witted thugs, the authors opened themselves to accusations of perpetrating stereotypes. Raymond Chandler's depiction of an African American bar and an African American hotel clerk in *Farewell, My Lovely* (1940) illustrate the problem. Ross Macdonald cautiously introduced Black characters into Lew Archer's world, but Bart Spicer placed an African American prominently on the first page of his first novel. Spicer cannot be said to plumb African American experience; no white writer could claim to do so. Carney Wilde does not avoid condescension to Andrew Jackson, though he is at least at times aware that he has been condescending. But Spicer was willing to acknowledge that, by the 1940s, African Americans made up a large portion of the urban population in the United States. And he would portray them in some diversity—poor, like Andrew Jackson, in *Dark Light*, but in later novels also as medical doctors, celebrated musicians, policemen, and political radicals.

In this and in a number of other ways, Bart Spicer advanced the possibilities of the hard-boiled genre. The Wilde series never develops the intensity that Spillane forced into each of his Hammer novels, nor does Carney Wilde's Philadelphia ever acquire the topographic precision that Wade Miller built into Max Thursday's San Diego. Nor, though he can write a sharp line of dialogue or description, is his prose as vivid as is that of Ross Macdonald. But he does expand the human terrain that the detective explores. And, when the seven-volume series was complete (in 1959), he had produced an unprecedented account of the private eye as entrepreneurial businessman.[1]

Spicer's achievement was recognized early. In addition to winning Dodd Mead's Red Badge prize, his first Carney Wilde novel was recognized by reviewers for precisely its humane values. In *The New York Times*, the "Criminals at Large" column praised *The Dark Light* for its "fresh approach" and its "qualities of warmth and humanity" (25 September 1949). And by 1951 Anthony Boucher would be bracketing Spicer with Ross Macdonald as the progressive alternative to the regressive phenomenon of Mickey Spillane: "Along with John Ross Macdonald, Bart Spicer has led this renascence of the tough detective," finding in *Black Sheep, Run* "a greater depth of humanity and warmth, a richer understanding of social responsibility and of the psychological and sociological meaning of crime" than could be found in the work of Dashiell Hammett ("Criminals at Large," 18 November 1951: BR 28). Ross Macdonald's addition of a sensitive heart to the hard-boiled detective's still tough core had been immediately identified as a significant move forward in the maturation of the subgenre, and not just as a post–Spillane return to the status quo ante. The 1949 debut of Bart Spicer's Carney Wilde was seen to reinforce this forward movement.[2]

The Dark Light *(1949)*

Carney Wilde finds Andrew Jackson waiting for him on the floor outside Wilde's newly opened office. Jackson's skin "was almost pure black," his eyes "were staring into a world I never saw" (3). He is the deacon of the city Mission of the Church of the Shining Light. The church itself is located in suburban Marion; the Mission serves the inner city. Jackson is troubled by the unexplained disappearance of the founder and pastor of the

Church, the Rev. Matthew C. Kimball, and offers Wilde $43 in well-worn bills to look into the matter. Jackson guides Wilde to the Mission, where Wilde meets the Reverend Kimball's assistant, Gerald Dodge. It is Dodge who leads Wilde out to Marion, where the Church has been built on the property of the wealthy widow, Mrs. Prentice, who has embraced the Reverend Kimball's social mission, and, with her daughter and son, provides it with financial backing and social respectability. Mrs. Prentice takes over employing the detective, and Andrew Jackson, who is murdered in Chapter 8, plays no further active role in the narrative. (Jackson's brother, Henry, appears briefly, to hand a crucial manuscript to Wilde and to disdain Wilde's offer of help with Andrew Jackson's funeral expenses.) The Church's Mission is not a benevolence specifically directed toward the African community; Andrew Jackson simply seems to admire the Rev. Kimball for his character (as do all of the persons of good-will). Jackson is presented as conscious of racial difference. Walking with Wilde to the Mission, he stays a half step behind Wilde. Wilde observes, "I could ignore him if I wanted to and pretend I didn't know him. Jackson's technique was smooth and long practiced. He was the honor graduate of a tough school" (6). On the one hand, he quietly accepts Wilde's patronizing epithet, "General Jackson"; on the other hand, he can reproach Wilde when Wilde speculates groundlessly about the Reverend having misbehaved or is careless with his cigarette ashes in the mission.

Spicer's decision to open *The Dark Light* with an African American client is a small but revealing instance of the sort of innovation he is willing to experiment with. The crime itself is fairly standard. Wilde uncovers tangible clues—revised and unrevised manuscripts, eyeglasses, hair dye stains in a sink. There is a red herring in the misbehavior of the Prentice son and a romantic interest in the person of the Prentice daughter. The city, though it is never named, is clearly Philadelphia, but many locations are identified with pseudonyms (the actual Lancaster Pike becomes "Manchester Pike"). It will take time for Wilde's urban landscape to approach the specificity of Max Thursday's San Diego. The discovery of the murderer is achieved in that most familiar of detective story devices, a gathering of all of the suspects, with the guilty person blurting out a confession. Spicer also indulges in the self-referential allusions that the detective story genre encouraged, with Alicia Prentice several times playfully calling Wilde "Sherlock" and Wilde repeating his response, "Don't call me Sherlock." Sam Spade and Philo Vance are also alluded to. These overt gestures toward the generic conventions are not pursued beyond *The Dark Light*.

But there are other signs of the originality that Spicer will bring to the series. That the victim is a minister is remarkable. There had, of course, been religious detectives. G.K. Chesterton's Catholic Father Brown and

Melville Davisson Post's Puritan Uncle Abner had established the type early in the twentieth century. But non-religious detectives, and especially hard-boiled detectives, rarely intervened in religious affairs. They might, on occasion, find themselves involved with cults, such as the Temple of the Holy Grail, which complicates the Continental Op's efforts on behalf of Gabrielle Dain in *The Dain Curse*. But they did not investigate priests and ministers. The Reverend Kimball is a peculiarly American minister: a former tire salesman, Kimball seems to have had a sudden and genuine spiritual awakening and has founded his new ministry with a social gospel that reaches out to a broad community. Everyone admires his sincerity. Kimball inspires Wilde to reflect on his own faith: "a long and colorful Sunday School record," followed by quitting the church at sixteen, experimenting with visits to charismatic Hollywood Bowl Easter Services, Catholic masses, synagogues, and Buddhist temples, and concluding, "It's all jake with me" (97–98). No other hard-boiled detective had recorded such a spiritual history or made such an explicit profession of tolerance.

Carney Wilde is an unusually ordinary detective; he does not appear to rely upon dramatic cases of kidnapping, blackmail, and murder to pay his bills; he does not do divorce. The essential mainstay of his newly established agency is a retainer to provide store security for Eli Lazarus, owner of the largest department store in the city.[3] Eli Lazarus (or, in later novels, Eli Jonas) will remain a constant in Wilde's world, calling upon the detective as a contract employee to investigate thefts in his store or problems in his personal life. Wilde's contract with Lazarus/Jonas remains a steady source of income for his expanding agency. No other hard-boiled detective agency relies so clearly upon such a plausible, quotidian line of investigative work.

Wilde's relation with his designated cop-companion is also distinctive. It is not a pre-existing condition; he has not known Lieutenant Grodnik prior to their encounter in *The Dark Light*, and it is an evolving relationship of growing mutual respect. Mike Hammer's Capt. Chambers was a long-standing friend; Max Thursday's Lt. Clapp and Mac's Lt. Donovan were mentors to the private eyes. Each P.I.-cop pair has a well-established personal relationship before the first novel opens. Established P.I.-cop relationships at some level were a staple of hard-boiled fiction: Sam Spade's with Sgt. Polhaus and Lt. Dundy or Philip Marlowe's with Bernie Ohls. But the Truman cops always play recurring roles, unlike those who, in the early hard-boiled novels, might appear in a single novel or two. They appear in *every* Hammer, Thursday, and Wilde novel.[4] They are consistently loyal to the private eye, though they do at times express officialdom's distress at the interference from unofficial investigators. Wilde is unique in that he meets Grodnik for the first time in the course of *The Dark Light*. And their intimacy develops over the course of time. Grodnik grows to appreciate Wilde as a detective and as a man, and in one novel even embraces him as a prospective son-in-law. Although Grodnik's main function is that of all cop-companions—to facilitate the detective's investigation (and to render it a bit more plausible)—Spicer makes Grodnik a slightly more complex, autonomous figure than usual.[5]

Spicer follows a principal genre motif by providing his detective with a love interest in *The Dark Light*. Mike Hammer and Mac find themselves attracted to mature women in their first novels. Hammer famously feels compelled in the end to execute the woman to whom he has been attracted. Mac, more in the Spade/Marlowe vein, in the end renounces the woman to whom he has been attracted; they belong to different and incompatible milieus.[6] Lew Archer and Carney Wilde find themselves attracted to more nubile women, the young daughters of the wealthy Sampson and Prentice families. (Max Thursday is as virile and heterosexual as any of his peers, but in *Guilty Bystander* he is focused on his role as a father and an ex-husband.) Archer makes a point of rejecting Miranda Sampson's advances toward him, regarding them as the impulses of a young and vulnerable girl. By virtue of a brief mention in *The Way Some People Die*, she will, however, be one of the very few characters to appear in more than one Archer novel. Wilde is more open to the appeal of the gamesome Alicia Prentice, who is young, but more assertive than vulnerable. Yet whatever the promise of their relationship at the end of *The Dark Light*, she is completely forgotten in the next novel. Carney Wilde will, indeed, eventually develop an extended relationship with a woman—indeed, he will marry that woman—but that will occur in the novels published after the Truman years.

Carney Wilde is, like Mike Hammer, Max Thursday, and Lew Archer, a veteran of the Second World War. He was an officer in the Army's Criminal Investigation Department and served five years in the South Pacific (35). He is never called upon to avenge the murder of a comrade who saved his life, but the camaraderie of service does mean that when he needs to solicit help from a New York City detective agency, he can call upon Bob Medary, who had been his first sergeant during the war and who now works as a detective for the Metropolitan agency. The Second World War plays a somewhat larger role in the experience of the second generation of fictional private eyes than the First World War did in the lives of the first generation. It may have a dramatic effect: Jack Williams's corpse is the focus of Chapter One of *I, the Jury*. It may supply background motivation: Alan Taggert's participation in the kidnapping of his rich employer in *The Moving Target* is attributed in part to his inability to settle into civilian life after the excitement of his career as a war-time aviator. Carney Wilde's call to Bob Medary illustrates another after effect: the war bonded men in a mutual trust that can in later years be drawn upon.

Blues for the Prince *(1950)*

Blues for the Prince turns the Wilde series in a new direction. It is not just that the novel now features African American characters in nearly all of the major roles. The novel is as much a celebration of a key aspect of the African American experience as it is a murder mystery. Bart Spicer clearly writes the novel to advocate the specific virtues of hot jazz as it was performed in postwar America. The two characters who attempt to articulate the richness and complexity of the sound are both white: Wilde, who loves the music, and his friend, Manny Brenner, an accomplished clarinetist and owner of a jazz club, Manny's Hot Box. Spicer again wisely does not presume to speak from within the African American experience, but through the responses of these two men, he does try to express what jazz can do while writing for what must still have been a readership of largely white men.

The plot does involve a spectrum of Black characters. At the center is the victim, Harold Morton Prince, a renowned jazz composer and pianist. Wilde says that learning that the Prince had been shot was for him comparable to hearing, on the island of Morotai in the South Pacific, that Roosevelt had died. The Prince is survived by an elderly and ailing father and an alienated daughter. His wife had died when, touring the South, she was injured in an automobile accident and did not survive the trip to a hospital that accepted Negroes. The Prince's father has a young, well-educated and under-employed protégé, Randolph Greene, who represents the Black militancy of 1950. The daughter, Martha, has a fiancé, Dr. Lawrence Owens, who is the one who contracts the services of Carney Wilde. He is the accomplished Negro, who, having earned his medical degree, has to deal with the indignities that even northern medical institutions imposed upon African Americans. The apparent villain, a man who once made music with the Prince and who now claims to have written some of the Prince's most popular compositions, Stuff Magee, and his accomplice/wife Arabella Joslin Magee, are both African American. Finally, there is Sgt. Connolly, the new—and very rare—Black addition to the Homicide Division of the police force, working under the familiar (and enlightened) Lt. Grodnik.

The novel opens with Lt. Grodnik having solved the murder to the satisfaction of the authorities: Magee was attempting to extort money from the Prince; the Prince, with a record of irrational rages, had refused; Magee had shot the Prince with the Prince's gun. Sgt. Connolly had captured and subdued Magee, though at the cost of sending him to the hospital in a coma (as Lt. Grodnik says, given "the racial angle," it was a good thing that Connolly was a Black officer). Although Magee has yet to be questioned, the case seems closed. Upon Grodnik's recommendation, Dr. Owens hires Carney Wilde to pursue the question of the authorship of the Prince's music. Though Martha Prince professes not to care about her father's reputation, Dr. Owens wants no shadow cast upon the Prince's originality. Wilde's investigation leads him to discover the crucial evidence that proves Magee's attempt at extortion had no basis in fact; the Prince *is* the Prince, author of his own innovative style. But it also leads him to discover that Magee's accomplice, Arabella, who has confessed to murdering Manny Brenner and seems to have confessed also to murdering the Prince, did not fire the shot that killed the composer. That shot was fired accidentally by the Prince's father when he struggled with the enraged Prince. The father is near death; he had been struggling with his son to preserve his son's good name for the sake of the race when the gun accidentally went off. Wilde decides to burn the father's written confession so that the old man can die peacefully in his bed—a bed which once belonged to the man who owned his grandfather.

There is a measure of sentimentality in the progress of the action. The celebrated art of the Prince is, of course, stands on its own. But the effort to preserve the image of the sometimes-violent Prince and the untroubled end of the proud father's life are purchased at the expense of Arabella Joslin Magee being held responsible for a murder that she did not commit as well as for a murder that she did. (The fate of Stuff Magee is left undefined; he will presumably be charged with attempted extortion). As Wilde tells the father, the Prince "wasn't just your son. He was a symbol of pride to his people" (242), and this justifies the deception. The bitter daughter is reconciled to her father after his death; she comes to understand the medical issue—a brain tumor—that drove him to drink and to rage, and she plays beautifully at an all-night jam session in his memory. She is also readily reconciled with Dr. Owens, a man whose steady decency marks him as model representative of his race.

There is again a measure of condescension in Wilde's treatment of Randolph Greene, whom he refers to as "Sonny." Greene's race pride—expressed in what Dr. Owen takes to be very offensive terms—leads him to foolish, even improbable actions: hoping to save the Prince's father, he attempts to deter Wilde's investigation first by making muffled threats on the phone, then by sapping the detective. It is Dr. Owens, not Carney Wilde, who actually strikes Randolph Greene, knocking him unconscious when he refers to Wilde as an "ofay clodhopper" and Owen as "a cringing field hand" (107, 108). But it is also Dr. Owens who explains that the only work that Greene could find after graduating college was working as an elevator boy. Wilde's "Sonny"—like his references to Andrew Jackson as "General" in *The Dark Light*—can be justified as natural terms of disdain in the first instance and affection in the second, but they both sound patronizing coming as they do from a white man. Yet Spicer's knowledge and appreciation of the African American contribution to the American musical tradition is impressive. He knows the important names and the dominant trends in the popular music of the postwar period. And, especially in Wilde's account of the memorial evening when the players celebrate the Prince's life and work, Spicer is strong in his attempt to evoke in words the effect the music itself has upon Carney Wilde.[7]

In other respects, *Blues for the Prince* continues the development of Carney Wilde as a private investigator. He is still working in an indistinct Philadelphia. There is a reference to "Fairview Park" (44), clearly a stand-in for the actual Fairmount Park, a Philadelphia landmark. His office still depends upon a retainer from Eli Lazarus's grand department store. He has his office in an unimposing building, with a discreet Carney Wilde Investigations painted in gold on the door. Lt. Grodnik still has the policeman's wary regard for private eyes, but he does recommend Wilde to Dr. Owens, and he and Wilde do grow to respect and even like one another. Wilde is given another attractive woman for company; appropriately she is a more than competent jazz singer. But it is the music that makes *Blues for the Prince* a notable achievement.

The Golden Door *(1951)*

The Golden Door is more focused upon Carney Wilde's investigation of crimes than was *Blues for the Prince*, but once again Spicer draws attention to a broader issue. In *Blues for the Prince*, the wider issue had been primarily aesthetic—the art of jazz—though it certainly also connected that art with its source in the African American experience. In *The Golden Door*, the topic is primarily social: the suffering of displaced persons and the problems with legal (and illegal) immigration to the United States. The title announces this theme: "the golden door" is the final phrase in Emma Lazarus's poem, "The New Colossus," which, cast in a bronze plaque, hangs inside the Statue of Liberty in New York Harbor. The U.S. government's largely unwelcoming approach to refugees—especially Jewish refugees—from Hitler's Europe had been controversial before and during the Second World War; after it war it was even more problematic as knowledge of the extent of the Holocaust became more widely known. The central crime in *The Golden Door* turns upon the actions of a small group of refugees—Jewish and non–Jewish, legal immigrants and illegal—connected with a small organization dedicated to facilitating the transition of new citizens into the American economy.

One of the principal developments in *The Golden Door* is the fleshing out of the owner of the grand Philadelphia department store for whom Carney Wilde has supervised security since *The Dark Light*, and whose retainer has been Wilde's most significant and reliable source of income as he tries to establish himself as a private investigator. Although his business has expanded steadily and he is now looking at plans for his own office in his own building, Wilde still operates primarily from his office in the department store. The owner's name—Eli Lazarus in the first two novels— now appears as Eli Jonas. Jonas is still a tough-minded businessman, but also a kind-hearted and generous man. *The Golden Door* opens with details of Wilde's successful investigation into the disappearance of thousands of dollars worth of stock from the cosmetics department of the Jonas store, an investigation which involves Wilde's deployment of a team of adjunct agents and auditors. There is a dramatically abrupt closing of the department, but the process of investigation is largely an unexciting matter of doggedly eliminating possibilities and narrowing in on the actual method of the theft. When Wilde identifies the culprit as Willie Jacobs, a low level stockroom clerk, Jonas's response is more sorrow than anger.

Jonas's son, Jack Jonas, is introduced in *The Golden Door*, and it is he who then hires Wilde to undertake a separate, private investigation. Jack Jonas fought with the British against the Nazis during World War II, and then against the British in Palestine as the State of Israel was, with some violence, being created within the British Mandate in the Middle East after the war. Jack, who is Jewish, then married Lida, a Catholic survivor of a Nazi concentration camp, and he has used Jonas money to establish "Future Americans," an organization that supports refugees—evidently most of them from Poland—by assisting them to acquire education and employment in America. (The employment element is through work in the Jonas store; Willie Jacobs has been one of the beneficiaries.) Future Americans keeps a card file of past, current, and future immigrants, and a handful of these cards with important personal information has gone missing. Carney Wilde, for $50 a day plus expenses, agrees to attempt to recover them.

In the end, Willie Jacobs's thefts from Eli Jonas's store and the missing cards from Jack Jonas's foundation prove to be connected. The key trio of characters proves to be three women who bonded in the concentration camp during the war: Jack's wife, Lida; Monique Fornier, who had been active in the French Resistance; and Mia Jacobs, who married Willie, and now works for Future Americans. Also involved are three very tough former members of the Polish Resistance, one of whom is in the States legally, while the immigration status of the other two is less clear. All ought to be bonded by their common anti–Nazi past, but the unexpected prospect of one of them inheriting a fortune (the Portemain fortune of over seven million dollars) leads to division and death. Carney Wilde clearly sympathizes with the immigrant cause. He comes to like and respect the very tough Jack Jonas; he comes to respect, though not to like, the very tough Rudi Grecov (the legal Polish Resistance leader); he recognizes the terrible experiences that have darkened the lives of Lida Jonas and Mia Jacobs (he never meets Monique Fornier). But he also sees that suffering does not invariably produce admirable characters. Those who have suffered greatly may be seduced by greed or fear into ignoble betrayal. Emma Lazarus's famous lines "Give me your tired, your poor, / Your huddled masses yearning to be breathe free, / The wretched refuse of your teeming shore. / Send these, the homeless, tempest-tost to me, / I lift my lamp beside the golden door!" are vindicated by the generous behavior of some of "wretched refuse" aided by Future Americans but are betrayed by the actions of the weak and the selfish. Spicer's representation of African Americans in *Blues for the Prince* was almost entirely admiring; his representation of the immigrants in *The Golden Door* is divided: they include true heroes, but also true villains.

Much of the novel returns to the matter of detection. Concrete clues are presented and then eventually decoded by Carney Wilde: burs ("usually called beggar's ticks or devil's pitchforks" 74) that catch on pant legs, a torn jacket, a large perfume bottle labeled *Memoire d'Amour* but containing attar of roses. The last clue is key to a subplot only tangentially related to the main plot. The first chapters detailing the accounting procedures and the process of elimination required to determine the location of thefts from the cosmetics department demonstrate that not all of a private eye's work consists of driving to dramatic confrontations that call upon sharp words, quick fists, and fast guns. Careful execution of routine procedures is also necessary.

The main plot, of course, does involve dramatic confrontations, and in one of them, Wilde shoots and kills a gunman who has fired upon him. It is the first time Carney Wilde has killed a man. Philip Marlowe and Lew Archer both kill a man in their first novel, but then manage almost entirely to avoid repeating that ultimate act of violence. Max Thursday kills four people in his first novel, and though he does kill again, he never again carries a firearm. Mike Hammer invariably kills multiple men and women in every novel. Spicer waits until the third novel before he puts his detective in a position where he must, in self-defense, shoot to kill. At the novel's end, Lt. Grodnik warns Wilde that the act has marked him, and that consequently he now should carry it for protection on all occasions. Committing even a justifiable homicide alters a man's world.

Black Sheep, Run *(1951)*

Spicer returns to relatively straightforward hard-boiled detective fiction in *Black Sheep, Run*. There is no larger social issue underlying all of the action. Carney's Wilde's agency continues to grow and his connection with Lt. Grodnik (and with Lt. Connolly) deepens, but the story focuses upon traditional hard-boiled topics: gangsters, gambling, and police corruption. The appearance of something approaching a vigilante enterprise—the Minute Men—on the periphery of the action does add an interesting note.

The steady expansion of Carney Wilde's agency is unprecedented in the hard-boiled genre. The Continental Op remains always a subordinate agent; Philip Marlowe and Lew Archer remain always unaffiliated loners. Sam Spade actually moves in reverse: from partner to sole proprietor. Max Thursday does eventually retain some useful part-time employees, and so moves in the direction of becoming a businessman, but it is Carney Wilde who makes the growth of his business a central motif. When *Black Sheep, Run* opens, five years after beginning his solo career as a private eye, he has just opened Carney Wilde, Inc. ("Investigations, Licensed, Bonded"), moving into the new, larger quarters that he had been contemplating in *The Golden Door*, with new furniture and a suite of offices. Wilde has hired his assistant at security in the Jonas Department Store, Penn Maxwell, as his full-time associate in the new firm. In the course of the novel, he will add Lt. Grodnik's attractive daughter as the agency secretary. And at the novel's end, the publicity derived from the case at hand means that he will be hiring additional employees. The detective as successful entrepreneur is something quite new.

What is also new in *Black Sheep, Run* is the identity of Carney Wilde's city. It is now explicitly Philadelphia, with references to actual Philadelphia streets and sites. What had been "Fairview Park" in *Blues for the Prince* (44) now receives its proper name, Fairmount Park (181). Wilde's Philadelphia will never be as concretely detailed as Max Thursday's San Diego, but much of the action can now be mapped.

A last novelty in *Black Sheep, Run*: Spicer brings in the American trope of the vigilante. The version here is a mild one. Eminent lawyer (and special friend of Lt. Grodnik), J. Franklin "Joe" Quiller, is organizing businessmen disturbed by the apparent corruption in city government to clean up Philadelphia: "We have the vilest water in the country ... inadequate police and fire protection, no control over gangsters and gambling" (102). In a parallel development, the patrician F. Lindsey Olmsted has organized the Action Committee of the Minute Men to assist in the cleansing.[8] Neither extra-governmental effort has a practical impact, but both prove relevant to

Wilde's investigation. The Minute Men hire a shady private eye whose murder complicates the action, and Joe Quiller proves to be a central figure in the conspiracy that drives the plot.

Wilde's client in the case at hand is Lt. Connolly, who has collected $500 to hire Carney to investigate corruption charges that have compelled Lt. Grodnik (now Acting Captain Grodnik) to take an enforced vacation while the situation is investigated by the city. A fellow cop, Chesty Chestow, has apparently committed suicide and has apparently left a note that seems to suggest that Grodnik has accepted a $525 bribe from gambling interests controlled by Bernie Sokol.[9] Grodnik appears passively to accept the suspicion that he is under, and declines to assist Wilde's private investigation, but Wilde persists and, building his case upon a single clue—one of Sokol's special matchbooks, he solves the case and vindicates the Captain. In the course of the action, Wilde finds himself plausibly (though, of course, incorrectly) identified as the murderer of another private eye, and consequently has to avoid arrest as he pursues his investigation. The detective compelled to avoid being apprehended for committing the crime that he is investigating while he is investigating the crime is not an unprecedented occurrence in detective fiction.[10]

Wilde's engagement on behalf of Capt. Grodnik—despite Grodnik's initial rejection of Wilde's or anyone else's assistance—deepens the relationship between the two men. Their bond was never a given; it has been earned over the course of several novels. Here it grows to include Grodnik's rather colorless wife and Grodnik's quite colorful young daughter. By the end of the novel, it appears that Carney Wilde is on track to become Grodnik's son-in-law.

And finally, again suggesting that Spicer is pausing to re-establish Carney Wilde as a private eye who investigates crime and corruption in a city of mean streets (as opposed, say, to a sensitive auditor with admirable taste in contemporary jazz, who investigates cases of aesthetic plagiarism), the plot of *Black Sheep, Run* takes Wilde from his new offices to Grodnik's lower middle class duplex; to Bernie Sokol's roadhouse, with all the accouterments of the hard-boiled roadhouse; to F. Lindsey Olmsted's grand estate; and to a number of other Philadelphia area scenes. And the plot, when it is finally unraveled, turns out to adhere to the least-likely-suspect so favored by the classical detective story. Spicer makes some effort to have Grodnik provide a psychological explanation of the reversal necessary for a respectable character who has, after a long struggle, won his way from impoverished outsider to admired insider with a profitable law practice then to Mr. Hyde pursuit of criminal activity. There is, in the end, perhaps more surprise than plausibility.

The Long Green *(1952)*

The Long Green takes Carney Wilde to an entirely new scene, the outskirts of Tucson, Arizona. Desert landscapes replace mean streets; a tough Deputy Sheriff replaces the tough Capt. Grodnik. And the presence of Indians permits Spicer to add an extended look at the situation another distinct community to his broadened portrait of ethnic America, to which he had already devoted a novel to African Americans and a novel to recent immigrants.[11]

The central crime in *The Long Green* is kidnapping. In a somewhat strained set-up, Eli Jonas has taken an extended vacation, renting a well-appointed adobe mansion that a local deputy sheriff inherited from his prominent family. Jonas has brought with him his five-year-old granddaughter, Bibi, and it is she who has been kidnapped, with a ransom demand for $50,000. Jonas calls Carney Wilde in Philadelphia, and Wilde boards the next available flight to Arizona. Jonas is devastated by the crime, and Wilde himself displays an unprecedented emotional engagement with the case. He is unusually tough with anyone whom he sees as impeding his single-minded effort to recover Bibi.

The intensity of Wilde's engagement with the crime of kidnapping recalls that of Max Thursday in his first case, *Guilty Bystander*. There it was Thursday's own son who was taken, and the boy suffered near fatal consequences from his captivity. Jonas's granddaughter, it appears, has had such a painless (though certainly strange) experience in her few days of captivity that Wilde and Jonas are able arrange the legal issues following upon the death of the kidnapper so that Bibi will never even realize she had been kidnapped. Without diminishing the intensity or the legitimacy of Wilde's personal engagement, Spicer's version of the detective's heightened emotional investment in his case seems a degree below that of Max Thursday, which, as has been observed, is itself a degree (or two) below that of Mike Hammer in *I, the Jury*. Spicer, Wade Miller, and Spillane have chosen, in these extreme cases, to produce distinctly different versions of the wrathful detective. The stimulus for emotional investments of Max Thursday and Carney Wilde—the victimization of small children—making the investigation a sort of crusade, is something that would be developed by later writers (with Andrew Vachss being the outstanding example).[12]

Spicer's treatment of the Indians lacks the cultural sensitivity displayed by Tony Hillerman (in *The Blessing Way*, 1970, and seventeen other Leaphorn and Chee novels) and the writers, often themselves Native American, who followed him. But Spicer is careful not to represent Native Americans as a monolithic ethnic culture. Wilde receives important assistance from Jeremiah Schuyler, who claims to be a full-blooded Mohawk (with, admittedly, an infusion of his Schuyler ancestor's presumably Dutch blood) and the son of a Sachem. Schuyler has an admirable vision of expanding the cultivation of Pima cotton in the area and employing as his labor force the members of the impoverished local tribes. He guides Wilde on a visit to the nearby reservation, and he recruits three Apache men—two of them named (Tahzay and Ponsonay)—to assist in the pursuit of the kidnapper. And the villain of story turns out to be a deracinated woman of Native American ancestry who goes to extremes to erase any sign of her Indian ancestry, bleaching her skin and insisting upon riding horses with an English side saddle.

The Long Green, though it takes Wilde away from Philadelphia for nearly all of the action of the novel, continues to chronicle the expansion of his business. Carney Wilde, Inc. now employs, in addition to Penn Maxwell, two full-time operatives, with four more on retainer (15). Carney Wilde is proving himself to be a savvy entrepreneur as well as a tough investigator. Although Wilde's work on the kidnapping case in *The Long Green* is explicitly a matter of his personal relationship with Eli Jonas, not of his professional duties as CEO of Carney Wilde, Inc., Spicer once more emphasizes that the basis of Wilde's prosperity lies definitely his contracts to provide routine store security at now a number of Philadelphia department stores, with, of course, the Jonas store as "my favorite and best-paying client" (15).

A final observation about the first five Carney Wilde novels: an interesting pattern in the motivation of the principal villain emerges. In the first two novels the motives are specific to the peculiar situation. In *The Dark Light*, Gerald Dodge murders the Reverend Kimball and then the Reverend's wife in order to conceal the fact that he has impregnated Mrs. Kimball. In *Blues for the Prince*, the Prince's father accidentally kills his intermittently violent son in a struggle. But in the next three novels, all the principal villains commit murder in the course of attempting to improve their social status. Mia Jacobs, in *The Golden Door*, is driven to murder because, unlike the two women—her closest friends—whom she nursed in the European concentration camp, she has remained essentially a poor pensioner in America. One of those women married the heir to the Jonas Department Store fortune; the other happened to be the only heir to the Portemain fortune. Mia finds herself stuck with a husband whom she despises, a man content to be a low-level clerk and a petty thief, so she extorts the assistance of two tough illegal immigrants who also want more of the good life promised by the American golden door. To acquire the Portemain millions, they will arrange to seduce and murder Monique Fornier, the legitimate heir to the estate, and then, to preserve their safety, to murder Mia's failure of a husband. In *Black Sheep, Run*, Joe Quiller has risen from being a rough-edged new lawyer from outside the city ("a Carbon County jerk" 206) to one of Philadelphia's most eminent attorneys, but he has purchased that status by engaging in corrupt gambling practices, and to preserve his reputation, he commits a series of murders. Finally, in *The Long Green*, Mrs. Rector tries to escape from her Native American heritage into what she takes to be the magic of the Anglo world—pale skin, English hunting prints, English side saddles. When Gilbert Rector proves unable to supply that status—he has to rent out his family's mansion and, with his wife, to live in a comfortable but not elegant adjoining building—she seizes the opportunity to kidnap a millionaire's son and to attempt to extort the $50,000 that she believes will enable her to live in the style to which she believes she is entitled. Mia Jacobs, Joe Quiller, and Mrs. Rector all act not simply out of greed, but out of resentment at a world that has not granted them the means to live in the high style appropriate to their self-images. It is not just wealth that they desire; it is the social status that, in America, only "the long green" can provide.

Truman's *Carney Wilde*

When Maj Sjöwall and Per Wahlöö launched the Martin Beck series of police procedurals with *Roseanna* in 1965, they began with a plan for a ten-novel, 100-chapter opus that would carry Beck and his police comrades through a series of crimes and life changes that would constitute an anatomy of what the authors took to be the failures of the Swedish experiment in social democracy. Bart Spicer did not, it seems, plan the Carney Wilde series with such an ambition, but he did, from the beginning, intend the series to present more than just one case after another, with the detective beginning each installment as a tabula rasa. This is clearest in the matter of business affairs: Wilde does not, like most hard-boiled detectives, remain consistently a lone operator or, like some hard-boiled detectives, consistently the employee of a larger operation. He steadily expands his company, basing its success not upon serendipitous commissions from well-heeled yet troubled clients, but upon the mundane business of providing security for an expanding roster of Philadelphia department stores. Spicer may not have known the full arc of Carney Wilde's life when he began *The Dark Light*, but he evidently did have in mind a concrete progress in Wilde's professional life. He would not follow the usual one-case-after-another pattern of the private eye's career. And Wilde's steady, irreversible rise up the economic ladder would be, in the final two Wilde novels, both published during the Eisenhower presidency, supplemented by an unusual development in the progress of his private life as well. Spicer's insistence upon development in the detective's professional and personal life makes it useful to look briefly at the way the series ends.

Carney Wilde, Inc. continues to grow in the final two novels. In *The Taming of Carney Wilde* (1954), the firm's roster of clients on contract includes the Department Store Association and "approximately fourteen others as well" (107). No other hard-boiled detective had successfully completed every investigation that he is called to undertake (or that he happens upon) *and* built a successful and growing commercial enterprise. At the ends of their careers, Mike Hammer, Lew Archer, and Max Thursday are still solitary agents working from their basic or minimal offices.[13] By the time of the last novel in the series, *Exit, Running* (1959), Carney Wilde, Inc.—with offices on Broad Street, opposite the Union League—is so prosperous that the action opens with Wilde negotiating the acquisition of a major competitor, the store security service run by Quentin Christie. Wilde borrows $250,000 to purchase Christie's payroll and equipment (including a fleet of radio cars), and merging them into "Wilde Protective System, Inc." Wilde still relies upon Penn Maxwell as his second-in-command, but he now has an efficient secretary, Agnes, and hundreds of employees on his payroll. He is still a tough guy in physical confrontations, and he is still a sharp observer of clues, but unlike any detective—hard-boiled or classical—he is also the CEO of a prospering corporation.

Not only does Carney Wilde end the series as much a successful businessman as a successful investigator; he ends up a successful husband as well. He meets Ellen Jane Pomeroy, a commercial photographer in *The Taming of Carney Wilde*, and almost immediately falls in love with her. (It is she, of course, who does the titular taming.) The novel ends with their intention to cross the Mississippi to Algiers, Louisiana, for a quick marriage. When *Exit, Running* opens, the married couple is enjoying a September vacation in the Poconos, with Carney returning to the city to close the deal on his acquisition of Christie's company. Happily married couples are not entirely unprecedented in detective fiction. Nick and Nora Charles (*The Thin Man*, 1934) certainly lie in the background, although Spicer does not play up the clever exchanges between the two spouses in the manner of Hammett or the screenwriters of the many films. And the Mr. and Mrs. North series of novels produced by Richard and Francis Lockridge (1934–1963) might also be cited. But Nick Charles has already retired from detection (and has already married) in the single novel in which he and Nora appear. And the Norths are amateur detectives, which places them in a different category (one that includes Agatha Christie's five experiments with Tommy and Tuppence, 1922–1973). Ellen Pomeroy Wilde is not merely a decorative addition to the detective's lifestyle; she remains a professional photographer after her marriage, continuing to operate from her center city studio—Ellen J. Pomeroy and Associates.[14] She and Carney live in a building on Rittenhouse Square, and he is still as besotted with her as he was in *The Taming of Carney Wilde*.

Business and marriage complicate Wilde's life. But Carney Wilde does not, in the end, simply retreat into the available identity as businessman and husband. He remains as well the confrontational investigator that his hard-boiled heritage baked into him. When Wilde and Captain Grodnik arrive at the apartment of the murderer at the end of *Exit, Running*, Wilde charges into the killer's room and then realizes he has done so without a gun. To please his wife, he has, since their marriage, refused to carry a gun. The last line of the novel has Ellen accepting that her husband will always live in a sometimes-violent world: she reports Grodnik's advice that she never let Wilde go out the door without his gun. Carney Wilde may be married and he may be a CEO, but he will not wear a gray flannel suit; he remains a man who will find himself in situations when he needs a gun.

And so, despite his unusual growth as a man, developing longstanding relationships with men (Captain Grodnik, Eli Lazarus/Jonas, Penn Maxwell, Lt. Connolly) and women (Jane Grodnik, Ellen Pomeroy) and building a large and profitable business, Carney Wilde ends as the hard-boiled, manly man he was when he debuted in *The Dark Light*. He is a more complete man than he was then, but he still is essentially a man who knows he has to walk the mean streets, and that walking the mean streets requires masculine toughness and courage, and a gun.[15]

5

The Solitary Detective Against the Organization Man: From Dupin to Lew Archer

The first major series of postwar private novels—the Mike Hammer novels of Mickey Spillane and the Max Thursday novels of Wade Miller—appeared in 1947. In that year, John Steinbeck published *The Wayward Bus,* and among the passengers and workers that he assembled for the cast of his novel was an embodiment of the new type of American business executive.

> Mr. Pritchard was a businessman, president of a medium-sized corporation. He was never alone. His business was conducted by groups of men who worked alike, thought alike, and even looked alike. His lunches were with men like himself who joined together in clubs so that no foreign element or idea could enter.... Wherever he went he was not one man but a unit in a corporation, a unit in a club, in a lodge, in a church, in a political party.... He did not want to stand out from his group. He would like to have risen to the top of it and be admired by it; but it would not occur to him to leave it [26].

Mr. Pritchard is a successor to Sinclair Lewis's George F. Babbitt, though he is a secondary character, and not the novel's eponymous hero. Both are prosperous businessmen with obvious weaknesses. Both are governed by a desire to belong. Lewis's pre-war businessman was an insecure consumer of status markers and a conformist booster of local Americanism. A generation later, Mr. Pritchard, who looks like Harry Truman (25) and who enjoys a prosperity greater than that of Mr. Babbitt, is even more desperate to submerge himself in social groups that provide him with a validated identity—corporations, clubs, lodges, churches, political parties. He is an organization man. And the nature of "The Organization Man," the title of William H. Whyte Jr.'s 1956 bestseller, had become a much-discussed American problem in the Truman years. The parallel and unprecedented expansion of regimented government bureaucracies (civilian under the New Deal and military in the Second World War) and regimented corporate bureaucracies seemed too many to be extinguishing what had been taken to be the signature American type of the self-reliant entrepreneur.

The hard-boiled detective as he emerged in the 1920s was the very model of the self-reliant entrepreneur. His distinction is that he does *not* club with like-minded men; his strength lies in his ability to draw useful information from conversations with persons of all races and classes. He does *not* anxiously take his values from his peers; he lives according to a minimal code of personal values. He does *not* confine himself to "groups of men who worked alike, thought alike, and even looked alike"; rather, he presumes to enter—and master—any of the diverse micro-environments of his city. On the rare occasions when he is an employee of a larger organization—Dashiell Hammett's Continental Op, Norbert Davis's Doan—he is an unruly employee. He is, as Raymond Chandler says in "The Simple Art of Murder," even when he is an employee, "a lonely man" ("and his pride is that you will treat him as a proud man or be very sorry you ever saw him," *Later Novels* 992). This loneliness—this aversion to identifying with any marked social group—had been built into the DNA of the detective by writers like Poe and Conan Doyle; the hard-boiled writers simply made it the loneliness not of aloof aristocrats like Chevalier C. Auguste Dupin or bohemian descendants of the English squirearchy like Sherlock Holmes, but the loneliness of the common man (Raymond Chandler: "He must be a common man or he could not go among common people," *Later Novels* 992). He was, in the late 1940s a distinct antithesis to the Organization Man, especially if his indifference to the herd manners and morals of his fellow citizens was as exaggerated as that of Mike Hammer. But even in his most polished form— that of the humane and articulate Lew Archer—the private eye's essential independence of the systems that defined "success" in America made him an attractive alternative to the men in the grey flannel suits.[1]

Organization Men and Other-Directed Men

In 1956, William H. Whyte, Jr., published a thick (nearly 500 page) volume of popular sociology to explore what lay beneath the flannel. *The Organization Man* also became a best-seller, selling over two million copies. Whyte was a writer for Henry Luce's *Fortune* magazine, and he studied the sorts of lives led by men who intended to advance in the emerging American business-scape dominated by huge corporate entities. Large companies and predatory monopolies had been features of the American economy since the Gilded Age, but the Second World War had fostered an increase in their numbers and in their sizes, and the post-war boom had only further accelerated their prominence in the country. Whyte's concern was that the employees of these vast concerns—especially the middle-class, white-collar employees, virtually of them men—didn't just work for their corporations; they *belonged* to their corporations; they—and perforce their spouses—embraced the total culture of expectations that the organization established.

It was a peculiarly American problem because, as Whyte explained, the American creed has always assumed a fundamental individualism: "Officially, we are a people who hold to the Protestant Ethic…. Whatever the embroidery, there is almost always the thought that the pursuit of individual salvation through hard work, thrift, and competitive struggle is at the heart of the American achievement" (4–5). The new organizational ethos appeared to assume that different virtues would now lead to success and happiness: against hard work, thrift, and struggle, it prioritized belongingness and togetherness. The admiration once awarded to the risk-taking entrepreneur is now awarded to the cooperative co-worker. A facility for subsuming self to group becomes the desideratum. "It is the organization man … who most urgently wants to belong…. The group that he is trying to immerse himself in is not merely the larger one—The Organization, or society itself—but the immediate, physical group as well: the people at the conference table, the workshop, the seminar…. It is not enough now that he belong; he wants to be *together*" (52). Whyte is careful to say that "this book is not a plea for nonconformity" (11). Organization, belonging, togetherness—all are valuable, even necessary things. Whyte's concern—and that, presumably of his contemporaries—is that the pendulum had swung too far in a worrisome direction, and Americans—the broad middle class of Americans whom Americans have traditionally seen as the core of the American identity—had become too willing to sacrifice other valuable and necessary virtues in order to belong.

David Riesman (with Nathan Glazer and Reuel Denney) had been equally cautious in *his* earlier best-selling work of popular sociology, *The Lonely Crowd* (1950), though he too was seen as exposing an anxiety about a conformist trend in contemporary American culture. Riesman's anatomy of the three types of character—tradition-directed, inner-directed, and other-directed—was sometimes taken to be an unqualified disparagement of the other-directed type that he describes as "emerging in very recent years in the upper middle class of our larger cities" (34). The "tradition-directed" type posed no threat; it was, Riesman argued, prevalent in stable societies with "a relatively unchanging" social order (26); it seemed more or less alien from the perpetually dynamic American culture. "Inner direction" would correspond roughly to Whyte's original Americans: "inner-direction is the typical character of the 'old' middle class—the banker, the tradesman, the small entrepreneur, the technically oriented engineer, etc." It is the character that Americans have liked to think is essentially American. "Other-direction" is that type of the "new" gray flannelled middle class: "the bureaucrat, the salaried employee in business, etc." (36). Members of this class find themselves obliged to submit "to the requirement of more 'socialized' behavior both for success and for marital and personal adaptation" (37); they must, to prosper, conform.

Riesman is not, however, simply denigrating other-directed conformity. He points out that the other-directed person is in some respects similar to the tradition-directed person: both types develop their senses of themselves by responding to signals from their community. The difference lies in the community. The tradition-directed person attends to stable signals from a coherent, long-standing culture, signals received first through his or her family and then from the wider population that shares (and has shaped) the family's values. The other-directed person focuses upon vibrations from his or her immediate surroundings, detecting and responding to whatever waves the current mode circulates. He or she "must be able to receive signals from far and near; the sources are many, the changes rapid." (42). Instead of a steady gyroscope cultivated by the inner-directed person, the other-directed person acquires a sensitive radar that recognizes attitudes and behaviors the day demands and thus enables the person to profit by assuming them. Whyte's book expressed the fear that, in the 1950s, organizations seemed to provide the securest avenues to success, and that organizations rewarded those who most quickly sensed the expectations of their superiors and their coworkers and adjusted their public selves to meet those expectations. But there was still alive the American cultural bias toward admiration of men (once more, usually men) of gyroscopic bent, men who defied conformity, whether they be Natty Bumppo or Huckleberry Finn, Frederick Douglass, or Thomas Alva Edison.

The fictional detective has, from his very first incarnation, been a gyroscopic man.[2] He does possess sensitive radar for detecting anomalies (footprints, cigarette ashes, oddly placed mirrors, but also revealing phrases and gestures). But he *uses* the anomalies he perceives to interpret the world, not to calibrate his own behavior; he never adjusts himself to fit himself into the prevailing ethos. Rather, he fits whatever his radar detects into a clear understanding of what must have happened to cause that ash to fall *there*, that phrase to be spoken by that person at that time. With his radar, he discovers the bases for reconstructing what has happened in his world; he himself remains inviolable, unwobbling, untouched by events.

And, again from his origins in the Paris of the Rue Morgue, he is always set against organization men pursuing the same goal. They are, most concretely, the men (and eventually the women) of police organizations—the Sûreté of Inspector G—, Scotland Yard of Lestrade and Gregson, the San Francisco Police Department of Sergeant Polhaus and Lieutenant Dundy. And at times he is set against an organized underworld—Sherlock Holmes will encounter the Ku Klux Klan, a German espionage ring, and, above all, the network of Professor Moriarty. Organizations are seen as at best inhibiting the efficacy of virtuous actors, at worst of enhancing the potential for disruptive action on the part of bad actors. But as well, the detective is set apart from his society as a whole—radically in the case of the deliberately anti-social Dupin, relatively in the case of the bohemian Holmes, but also in the case of the hard-boiled detective who is, in Chandler's phrase, complete, common, and *yet unusual*: he—or she—may be common, but he or she will never wear a flannel suit.

Private Eyes Against the Organization

In the middle of *The High Window* (1942), Philip Marlowe confronts a pair of LAPD homicide detectives who are questioning about the murder of a young man. Marlowe recites an anecdote from the recent past to justify his reluctance to share details with the police. It concerns a murder-suicide in which two young men are found dead in a mansion: a rich man named Cassidy and his male secretary.[3] Guided by deference to the desires of the rich for discreet closure rather than to conclusions drawn from the evidence, the police declare the crime solved: the secretary murdered wealthy Cassidy and then committed suicide. The District Attorney's office and the police, Marlowe asserts, both knew that this solution did not fit the facts, but they didn't want the truth "because Cassidy was too big." And so Marlowe declares, as an independent investigator, he will not cooperate with Detective Lieutenant Jesse Breeze:

> Until you guys own your own souls you don't own mine. Until you can be trusted every time and always, in all times and conditions, to seek the truth out and find it and let the chips fall where they may—until that time comes I have a right to listen to my conscience, and protect my client the best way I can. Until I'm sure you won't do him more harm that you'll do the truth good [*Stories and Early Novels* 1072].

Listening to his own individual conscience has always been an essential quality of the fictional detective, as has been the essential inefficacy of the official police. But Marlowe's contention is not that the police, who, the genre usually concedes, are competent to investigate ordinary crimes, are necessarily incompetent even when faced the peculiar circumstances of the mystery at hand. His contention is not that they couldn't reach the correct solution, but that they couldn't announce the correct solution. Because they belong to an organization vulnerable to pressure from certain quarters, they "do not own their own souls." Their defect is not the inability of their pedestrian, systematic investigative methodology to penetrate to the truth. It is that their investigations are governed by a higher principle than the discovery of truth. They are cogs in a vast governing machine that often values truth, but always values political expediency. It is not that they cannot discover whodunit; it is that the state which employs them prioritizes service to its most powerful clients over any commitment to "the truth." Marlowe may care about the feelings of the secretary's mother, sister, or sweetheart when they hear he has falsely identified as a murderer; the state does not, and it does not permit its agents, the police, to carry their investigations through to their logical conclusion.

Marlowe's defense of his choice not to cooperate with the police is thus based on the assumption that private eyes are fundamentally free agents and policemen are fundamentally not. Because they have enlisted as members of a larger social apparatus, the cops have given up their moral autonomy. In the hard-boiled American world, under pressure the police are in the first place, servants of the system, not free investigators. The system, not the evidence, can dictate the outcome of the investigation. Lt. Breeze ultimately agrees. In the final chapter of *The High Window*, he tells Marlowe that he has tolerated Marlowe's irritating independence because he has himself seen a "Cassidy case" ("under another name"): "I sometimes give a guy a break he could perhaps not really deserve. A little something paid back out of the dirty millions to a working stiff—like me—or like you" (1176–77).

"Working stiffs"—Breeze or Marlowe—are set against the corrupt state. Both see "the system" as decisively favoring the rich. Breeze does his best within the organization; Marlowe does his best against the organization. It is, of course, the man against the organization who is the hero of the detective story. This is fundamental to the genre: the organization men may lack the method or the grey cells (Inspectors G—, Lestrade, Japp) or they may lack the moral freedom (Lt. Breeze). Or, as we shall see, they may simply be villains (Prof. Moriarty, Arnold Zeck, Eddie Mars). The immediate heirs of Philip Marlowe—the private eyes of the late 1940s—found themselves working in a world where more and more organizations seemed to be more and more limiting the moral freedom of Americans generally.

Max Weber's analysis of three types of legitimate social authority may be useful here: traditional authority ("sanctified through the unimaginably ancient recognition and habitual orientation to conform"), charismatic authority ("the authority of the extraordinary and personal *gift of grace* [charisma])," and rational or legal authority ("by virtue of the belief in the validity of legal stature and functional 'competence' based on rationally created *rules*") ("Politics as a Vocation" 78–79). Traditional authority, at least in the realm of judicial investigation, had lost its hold by time the detective debuted; the faith that "mordre wol out" was replaced by systems of investigation and systems of jurisprudence. Those systems relied upon rational/legal authority, and are, in detective fiction, naturally embodied in the representatives of official police. Rational/legal authority is, as Weber explains in *The Theory of Social and Economic Organization*, the basis of the modern bureaucratic administrative state (329–41). His third category—charismatic authority—Weber associates with shamans, prophets, and certain intellectuals (those who are "carried away with their own demagogic success" *Theory* 359). The detective is not charismatic in exactly this sense. Although he routinely astonishes his fellow citizens with the infallibility of his insights, he does not inspire a cadre of devoted admirers. He does, especially in his form as Great Detective, often secure a single devotee—a Watson, a Hastings, but generally he astonishes people only once, and in a single instance. He is not a demagogue and does not covet followers or political power of any sort. Moreover, and precisely in the Great Detective form where awe is most invoked, the Great Detective always attributes his success not to his personal "gift of grace," but to his method, which he enjoins upon his companion, insisting it is a transferrable gift.

Nonetheless, the detective possesses a charisma of sorts that sets him apart. Both Marlowe and Lt. Breeze know that Marlowe is special. However much he insists he is just a methodical man (or, in his hard-boiled form, a common man), the detective's inevitable last-chapter explanation of who-how-when-where-why must impress all of those who could *not* explain these things—which is to say, everyone. The rational/legal authorities, with all their bureaucratic facilities to call upon, could not explain it. And as "method" fell into disuse as the detective's putative source of excellence, and the hard-boiled detective's character—his or her toughness, intuition, sensitivity, perseverance, experience of oppression, whatever—became the key to his or her peculiar ability to penetrate appearances and discover truth, the charismatic element grows. The ne plus ultra of charismatic, in this sense, detectives—at least for those who can accept his premises about the nature of virility, femininity, and American exceptionalism—might be Mike Hammer, who presents himself as something of a prophet of the virtue of unbound individualism, a prophet who never doubts himself, who awes everyone whom he encounters, and who is always vindicated by events.

The First Detectives and the First Organizations

With the exception of the sideshow of the police procedural (an important sideshow, to be sure), the detective story has been consistently the fable of the power of the individual to know hidden moral identities, and, as a necessary corollary, of the relative impotence of designated groups of individuals to attain that knowledge.[4] Whatever his or her method—ratiocinative analysis or hard-boiled persistence or forensic expertise—the detective demonstrates his or her peculiar aptitude for seeing behind appearances that neither professional investigators (the police) nor casual observers (such as the reader) can penetrate. He or she alone discovers whodunit (and how/when/where/why it was done). A villain contrives to manipulate the evidence so as to baffle the community, and the detective unravels the deliberately raveled skein. This unraveling is naturally more impressive when it surprises not only the community in general, but especially the community's authorized unravelers—its police force and its prosecutors and district attorneys, with all the resources that they command. The consistent failure of the organization highlights the triumph of the individual.

This contrast was built into the first detective stories and has persisted—with varying emphases—throughout its history. C. Auguste Dupin is not just the impoverished scion of an illustrious family, a sort of poète-analyste maudit. Dupin chooses to isolate himself in the "long-deserted" mansion in "a retired and desolate portion of the Faubourg St. Germain" that he permits his one companion to rent on their behalf. Where his equally impoverished contemporaries—the poètes maudits of Henry Murger's *Scènes de la vie de bohème* (1847–49), for example—gathered in a community of happily shared misery, Dupin dramatically asserts his alienation from all but a single acolyte. And Poe emphasizes the virtue of his withdrawn detective by contrasting it to the determined, competent, and always ineffectual efforts of the police force. Dupin's remote genius is always set against the bustle of Inspector G—and his minions of the *Sûreté*. In "The Purloined Letter" the police exercise in vain the full resources of their manpower and their technology (microscopes, probes) to discover where the villainous Minister D—has hidden the purloined letter. Their systematic searches of his apartment and his person are fruitless, and it is only the eccentric genius of Dupin, the poet-mathematician, that can locate and recover what has been hidden in plain view.

The Sherlock Holmes saga reiterates the message. Dr. Watson's first knowledge of Holmes comes as the invalided doctor is seeking "a fellow-lodger." Young Stamford, an old medical school crony of Watson, suggests Holmes as a possibility, but warns that Holmes is peculiar in his habits. He may not be deliberately as irregular as the nocturnal Dupin, but among the students at St. Bartholomew's Hospital, he is a notoriously irregular figure. His medical studies are "very desultory and eccentric," definitely not "systematic" (I.16); he follows no comprehensible professional track. Organized study of medicine is as antithetical to the student Holmes as organized policing is antithetical to the professional Holmes. He has baffled Stamford, and in their first weeks of joint occupancy of 221B Baker Street, he baffles Watson. Watson will come to admire his companion's "Science of Deduction" and its unique power to dissolve perplexing mysteries, but he will always find aspects of Holmes's character odd. As in the Dupin tales, this evidently symbiotic combination of distinctive authority and distinctive eccentricity is set against the more common combination of pedestrian skills and pedestrian character embodied in the official police, who have been trained systematically and who operate systematically. Lestrade, Gregson, Hopkins—the professionals of Scotland Yard are well-meaning, decent men and their methods are successful in the pursuit of commonplace criminals, but they are frustrated when confronted with the sorts of three-pipe problems that Holmes makes his specialty.

Another sign that the detective is above organization is the brief career of "the Baker Street division of the detective police force" (I.42 Baker) whom Holmes introduces to Watson in the first novel, *A Study in Scarlet*. He also employs them in the second novel (*The Sign of Four*) calling them the Baker Street Irregulars (the title of Chapter 8). And then, in the fifty-eight succeeding stories and novels, he refers to them only once, and then obliquely ("my Baker Street boys"), in "The Adventure of the Crooked Man." Conan Doyle saw that the detective hero may need a narrator; he does not need accomplices, and certainly not a set of accomplices on retainer. (And in fact, the Baker Street Irregulars were on call, not on retainer. Even in their three appearances, Holmes calls them up for a specific task and pays them for piecework. They are not regular employees; they are not part of a team.) Holmes declares that he is unique: "I have a trade of my own. I suppose I am the only one in the world. I'm a consulting detective, if you can understand what that is" (I.24). He is singular in the sort of work he does, and he does his work as a single individual.

On the other hand, villainy may well involve a community. Most of the criminals that Holmes encounters are also individuals, motivated by personal motives and executing their crimes without assistance. The studies in scarlet that the detective must unravel have generally been raveled by greedy, lustful—or in *A Study in Scarlet*—vengeful men and women who act alone. But organized criminality on a large scale sometimes looms in the shadows—the Ku Klux Klan in "Five Orange Pips," the Molly Maguires in *The Valley of Fear*, the Mormons (a brutal organization as portrayed by

Conan Doyle) in *A Study in Scarlet,* German spies in "His Last Bow." The archetypal criminal gang of the Holmes saga is, of course, the one headed by the Napoleon of Crime, Prof. Moriarty. When Conan Doyle wanted to imagine a criminal worthy of the ultimate sacrifice of his detective hero on a ledge at Reichenbach Falls, he imagined a meek looking former university professor who himself does not commit crimes, but whose organization facilitates the crimes of others. The antithesis of the detective is the bureaucratic chief of an organization who oversees, through a cadre of violent lieutenants such as Col. Moran, a wide corps of criminal specialists.

The Golden Age Detectives and Organization

The cascade of amateur detectives who follow Holmes all commit themselves to unabetted investigation,[5] and they generally find themselves in a similar relation to the official, organized detectives of Scotland Yard or the New York City Police Department. They often indulge in eccentricities that mark them as men apart; they always operate as individuals[6]; and while they too express respect for the official police as well-meaning decent men—though, in the manner of Dupin and Holmes, often (but not always) disparaging their abilities—they always demonstrate that, in extreme cases—the sort of cases they inevitably find themselves involved in—the intelligence of the odd individual always prevails over the systematically trained intelligence and well-staffed offices of the Criminal Investigation Divisions and Homicide Squads.

Of course, a large number of the best-known heirs of Sherlock Holmes did chose careers within the organization. Inspectors Joseph French, Roderick Alleyn, Alan Grant, John Appleby, all worked within the system as members of Scotland Yard. But with the exception of the workmanlike Inspector French, they wore their officialdom lightly. The aegis of Scotland Yard granted them privileges—citizens *must* respond to their interrogations, whereas the amateur detectives must presume on courtesy of witnesses (or exercise their own subtlety in asking the questions)—and it made the detective's frequent encounters with murder in mysterious circumstances plausible. It rarely compelled the high-minded, well-educated inspectors to follow tedious investigatory procedures. That these inspectors are usually English, not American, usually well-born, and usually university-educated (and obviously university-educated) emphasized that they, like their amateur peers, were marked as distinctly separate class from their uniformed police associates. They did need to observe certain legal limits; they were not free, as Sherlock Holmes felt himself to be, to burgle houses or seduce maids. But as compensation, they could threaten arrest and imprisonment to encourage cooperation from suspects, something Holmes could not do. In the end, they were, like the amateurs, Great Detectives, dependent essentially upon their native genius, not their official organizations.

The exceptionally workmanlike Inspector French, featured in 28 novels (1924–1957) by Freeman Wills Crofts, admired by many readers (and by many writers) of Golden Age detective fiction, makes the point. He is *not* an auteur inspector, in the manner of Alleyn or Grant or Appleby, but neither is he a prototype for the procedural policeman who emerged in America in the 1950s. On the one hand, he is indeed thoroughly ordinary, with no Oxbridge degree, no aristocratic connections, and no untoward addictions; on the other hand, although he is a member of a professional, bureaucratically structured organization, in practice he functions as an individual investigator, not as a member of a team following established police procedures. He finds that doggedly following a series of leads culminates in the discovery of the identity of the criminal, and it is his personal doggedness that makes for his success. His affiliation with Scotland Yard—along with his not unrelated sturdy moral decency—distinguishes him from the hard-boiled detectives that were emerging contemporaneously in *Black Mask*, but his method has a good deal of the pedestrian (and automotive) qualities that work so effectively for those private eyes. As a civil servant, he has none of the impatience of the hard-boiled detective, and no inclination to accelerate his investigation with violence.[7]

The Hard-Boiled Detectives and Organization

The hard-boiled detectives who emerged in the 1920s in pulp magazines like *Black Mask* could not airily dismiss the authority of police departments and district attorney's offices and insist upon those organizations acknowledging the natural superiority of men distinguished by their breeding or their formidable intellects, nor could they, like the Golden Age policemen (either the auteur inspectors or the dogged inspectors), work their magic within those departments and offices. They were working men,[8] never wealthy, never well-connected. The police were more likely to threaten them with arrest than to solicit their assistance. They were entrepreneurs operating from small, poorly furnished offices, only rarely employing a secretary. Their status was always vulnerable to challenge; they needed to earn a living by operating under the limitations that their licenses imposed upon them.

They almost never worked in teams. Too much can be made of the rugged individualist as a peculiarly American figure, but as the dime novel detective began to take form in the 1880s (Old King Brady, from 1885; Nick Carter, from 1886), the emerging type of the distinctly American private eye emphasized the man's self-reliance. Old King Brady was "a rough, tough, dogged and determined American who always got his man." And he was not a genius belonging to the social elite: Old King Brady was "an experienced detective, a former investigator with the NYPD, who solves his cases the old fashioned way: through legwork, brains and persistence" ("Old King Brady").

The American detective was a man of the city; he was not averse to neighbors in the manner of Natty Bumppo, but he was nonetheless a loner, more of a loner than his predecessors. Dupin might first appear as ostentatiously averse to the society of his Paris, but he does embrace his admiring roommate. Sherlock Holmes is first seen as an isolated figure in the chemical laboratory of St. Bartholomew's Hospital, but his first action is to solicit a roommate, and while he never pursues a spouse, he does sustain a relationship of some degree of intimacy with his landlady, Mrs. Hudson. Poirot has his Hastings, his valet George, his secretary Miss Lemon. These attachments do not enmesh the detectives in a thick social fabric; they remain relatively isolated individuals, and their detective skills are purely their own. But, until the dramatic development of his/her character in the 1970s, the tough American detective who emerged in *Black Mask* and other pulp magazines in the 1920s never seeks a roommate, and never has any ongoing friendships, and certainly not with a landlady or a valet.

In addition to his regular competition with the organized detectives of the city police departments, the private eye does, at times, confront an organized antithesis—an antithesis made all too familiar in newspaper headlines of the 1920s. Dr. Moriarty's extraordinary network of villainy, finds its successor in the all too ordinary gangsters that populate hard-boiled fiction. These gangsters are rarely the central villains,[9] but their regular appearance seems a reminder, especially emphasized in the American 1920s and 1930s (and continuing into the 1940s and 1950s as national attention was drawn to the operations of the Mafia), that malignity, like incompetence, is associated with organizations. Men in groups are not to be trusted. It is the individual private eye that can join efficacy to virtuous purpose.

The two prototypical *Black Mask* P.I.s both made their debuts in 1923. Carroll John Daly's Race Williams—most strongly embraced by the magazine's readers—first appeared in the 1 June 1923 issue[10]; Dashiell Hammett's Continental Op—most strongly embraced by the magazine's editors—first appeared four months later in the 1 October 1923 issue. The first Race Williams story makes the point about organizations most emphatically as Race Williams confronts a form of corporate villainy in "The Knights of the

Open Palm." Hammett's Op appears as—apparently—the representative of corporate detection in "Arson Plus."

Carroll John Daly: Race Williams

Race Williams introduces himself as a very much an American man: a man alone and as a man opposed to men together. He may begin a paragraph admitting, "Of course I'm like all Americans—a born joiner," but he ends the same paragraph, "No, I like to play the game alone. And that's why I ain't never fallen for the lure of being a joiner" (19). His justification of the contradiction may be unpersuasive: joining a group, Race declares, might someday inhibit him from killing a villain whom he recognized as a fellow member of the group, which might permit that villain, who failed to recognize Race's membership (or who lacked the inhibition), to kill Race. But Daly makes his point: Race Williams is, by nature, American, but he is, by profession, loner. To succeed—to survive—as a detective in America, he must forgo the gratification of joining any organization. And because he doesn't "belong to any order" (19), Williams has no problem agreeing to rescue Earnest Thompson's son, who has been kidnapped by the "Knights of the Open Palm"—the Ku Klux Klan.

But not only does Race Williams not belong to nefarious "orders" like the Klan; he distances himself equally from the state-authorized orders. Hence the first sentences of "Knights of the Open Palm": "Race Williams, Private Investigator, that's what the gilt letters spell across the door of my office. It don't mean nothing, but the police have been looking me over so much lately that I really need a place to receive them" (18). Race is, he insists, "what you might call a middleman—just a halfway house between the dicks and the crooks" (18), and unlike M. Dupin and Sherlock Holmes, he will not receive either the crooks or the dicks in his private chambers. His aloneness is more radical than theirs. Dupin welcomed Inspector G— to his decayed mansion; 221B Baker Street was open equally to the clients who employed Holmes and to Gregson, Lestrade, and other Scotland Yard inspectors who consulted him. Race Williams needs to keep his home space free of both clients and cops. The unimposing, usually unoccupied office is his necessary alternative. The office is a functional space only, revealing nothing of his character. There is no secretary; there are no irregulars (he will acquire a chauffeur, Benny, but Benny is more a thinly sketched functional device than a person).

The adversary in "Knights of the Open Palm," however, is very much a corporate entity. The June 1923 issue of *Black Mask* in which the story appeared took the Ku Klux Klan as its theme, and a "Klan Forum" in which readers could participate was continued in succeeding issues.[11] The revival of the Ku Klux Klan had begun on Stone Mountain in 1915, and by 1921, it was enjoying a widespread, well-organized expansion through much of the country, with thousands of Klaverns and millions of members. Although not immune to the racial prejudices of the time, Daly chose to set Race Williams firmly against the populist Klan. Race is not much interested in the requirements for membership ("you got'a be white and an American and a Protestant—and you got'a have ten dollars—though if you've got the ten the rest of it can be straightened out" 21); his animus is directed toward the dangerous nonsense of its organization ("Exalted Cyclops, Klaliff, Klokard, Kludd, Kligrapp, Klabee, Kladd, Klexter, Klolkann, Kloran, and a host of others" 21). It is, in his view, an elaborate and useful cover for all sorts of petty criminals—"burglars, counterfeiters, and check-raisers welcome— also arson might be appreciated—I don't know" (21). And it draws on that inborn American passion for joining.

> The real fellows who just enter the Klan because they are joiners don't know half the time why they are beating up some helpless old man or weak woman. They just do it. Why—God alone knows. They forget their manhood and listen to all the wind about cleaning up the world and making it safe for the white race [30].

Joiners forget their manhood: this is the fundamental principle of "Knights of the Open Palm" and the fundamental value asserted by Race Williams in his debut. The joiners embrace childish nonsense—Klaliffs, etc; secret salutes; coded greetings; foolish costumes—and mindlessly follow leaders who exploit their baser instincts. Neither Daly nor Race Williams pays regard to the ideas that the Klan claimed to embody; the Klansmen are not despicable for their views on race or community; they are despicable because they fall for the lure of gaudy ranks, gaudy paraphernalia, and gaudy ceremonies.

Half the population of Clinton (a county seat "in the west") has fallen under the spell of the organization; most of the other half is intimidated by it. The unintimidated exception is a radically different sort of organization: the Jabine family. Buck Jabine and his two sons—and his equally self-reliant womenfolk ("they were sure some Amazons" 37)—live outside the town. When they walk down the street, the Jabine men all openly carry guns. Buck himself has a record of having killed three men, and the Klan evidently doesn't dare to threaten him or his family. And this admirably empowered family unit can recognize the virtue of the empowered individual and offers Race Williams a refuge in a town otherwise divided between joiners and cowards. It is, significantly, a refuge Race never really needs. His is the only gun required to deflate the pretentions of the Klan. Daly inserts the Jabines into the story to present an alternative source of moral authority: an organic, patriarchal, tradition-oriented family can match the strength of the man alone. The difference is that the family remains inward-looking; it focuses upon preserving its rough autonomy and leaves the larger society to solve its own problems. The man alone can be hired to work on behalf of the intimidated community.

Race Williams defeats the Klan with his gun. When threatened in his hotel by a delegation of Klansmen, he outdraws the leader and unmasks him. He easily penetrates a Klan ceremony. He rescues Thompson's son, killing three of the four Klansmen who are about to execute the boy. And later he kills the fourth, who turns out to be the leader whom he had earlier unmasked. Daly's final comment upon the folly of joining occurs when he has Race, having shot the leader at the station just before the arrival of Race's train out of town, claim the assistance the train's conductor, a Klansman who, recognizing Race's salute and coded greeting, welcomes him onto the train. The conductor saw a body on the platform, but he prefers loyalty to the code of his group to the arrest of an apparent murderer. The weak-willed joiner thus facilitates the escape of the strong-minded loner.

Daly uses the antithesis of a malignant corporate entity in his first Race Williams story to establish the contrasting virtue of his solitary hero; it does not become a routine device (though, in fact, the villain in the second Race Williams story, "$3,000 to the Good," is a corrupt union official). In the first Race Williams novel, *The Snarl of the Beast*, serialized in four installments of *Black Mask* (June–September 1927) and then published the same year as a book, Race's adversary is a monstrous figure, closer to the Ourang-Outang of "Murders in the Rue Morgue" than to Professor Moriarty. But although The Beast, as he is identified by everyone in the novel, has subhuman qualities—long, powerful arms, a snarling voice, and (more superhuman than subhuman) an apparent invulnerability to bullets fired from Race's unerring gun—he does have a human motive and he does claim to have "a great organization" working for him (213). That "organization," however, has none of the sophistication of Moriarty's, nor even that of the serried ranks of the Klan. Just as Race Williams employs Benny as his useful chauffeur and eventually engages in a tactical alliance with the NYPD's Inspector Coglin without diminishing the impression that Race is a man alone in the dark city, so the Beast's various accomplices do not diminish his stature as a nightmare figure who is persecuting his enfeebled stepson in order to access the wealth of his deceased wife. If in the first Race Williams story, Daly established the strength of his detective's singular competence by juxtaposing it to the weakness of the Klan's mass (and masked) *incompetence,* in the first Race Williams novel, Daly sets the self-reliant detective against an equally self-reliant villain.[12]

The Snarl of the Beast opens with Race Williams reiterating his self-placement in the amoral space between the moral police and the immoral criminals.

> The police don't like me. The crooks don't like me. I'm just a halfway house between the law and crime; sort of working both ends against the middle. Right and wrong are not written on the statues for me, nor do I find my code of morals in the essays of long-winded professors. My ethics are my own [1].

There is, of course, no problem with a private investigator being disliked by crooks; it is Race's equal satisfaction with being disliked by the police that distinguishes him. Hitherto the police in detective fiction may have been baffled by the detective's genius and, having experienced its superior efficacy, may at times acknowledge its superiority by deprecating it. Prefect G—may laugh at Dupin's affectations and paradoxes, and Dupin may disparage the Prefect's acumen, but both the Prefect and Dupin know that they share the same ethics. Race Williams possesses no baffling genius to distinguish him from the G—s, the Lestrades, and the Japps. When Inspector Coglin asks him, "Did you learn anything—see anything?" he does not respond with a cryptic remark about the curious incident of the dog in the night. He declares, "I'm not that kind of detective.... There might be a hundred clews around and I'd miss them. I've got to have a target to shoot at" (174). Action, not thought, is his métier.

Early in the novel, Race declares with evident pride, "With me the thought is the act" (12). When the cops are pursuing him from behind and the Beast is fleeing ahead of him, the realization that there is "only one way of escape" (the thought) and dashing in that direction (the action) occur simultaneously. Throughout the novel Race unerringly perceives his target and, in the same instant, fires his gun.[13] This confidence in the validity and the efficacy of his unitary thought-action—justified in his very first encounter with the Klan leader in his hotel room and reiterated endlessly throughout his long career—lies at the root of his authority. His quick reflexes, not his grey cells, secure Race's successes, and reflexes are unique to the individual. The results achieved by grey cells can be explained. Though he could not himself perform the analysis, Dr. Watson can grasp every step of Holmes's thinking when Holmes eventually explains it to him. The Great Detective's genius lies in sorting the essential clues from the red herrings, but the sequence of his thought must be comprehended and accepted as conclusive by the ordinary minds (including the reader's) when it is laid out at the narrative's end. The hard-boiled detective's method lies in his ability to persist in a series of hazardous (and revealing) confrontations which he survives through his quick reactions and his extraordinary resilience.

This will remain a fundamental principle of the hard-boiled detective's method and a fundamental principle of his radical individualism. Private

eyes considerably more sophisticated than Race Williams adopt the principle: Sam Spade's "My way of learning is to heave a wild and unpredictable
monkey-wrench into the machinery. It's all right with me, if you're sure none
of the flying pieces will hurt you" (*Complete Novels* 465) expresses the same
method. The detective's reflexes—his ability to duck the flying pieces—ensure
his success, and his slower allies, like his slower adversaries, can only wonder at his instinctive actions. Great detectives interrogate the evidence—the
physical clues and the testimonies of witnesses, and if the interrogation is
fairly presented, the reader, like Dr. Watson or Hastings, can, in the end, feel
that he or she too could have drawn the correct conclusions. Hard-boiled
detectives disrupt the evidence—occasionally concealing the physical evidence, but always challenging the men and women whom they encounter:
they wield their weapons and their wisecracks to provoke revealing (and
often dangerous) responses. Hard-boiled detectives have no Watsons because
their success does not depend upon a sequence of inferences that Watson
(and the reader) could have made but did not make. Their success depends
upon heaving wild and unpredictable monkey-wrenches into the machinery,
precipitating (and surviving) a sequence of violent confrontations that the
reader could never make in places the reader would never go.

Dashiell Hammett: Sam Spade and the Continental Op

Hammett–Sam Spade

But if Sam Spade is like Race Williams in relying upon a detective
method that depends upon reflexes that cannot be imparted to others, he
is, on the surface, less isolated than Race Williams. Race has his functional
chauffeur; otherwise, he is insistently alone. Spade has a partner and a secretary; he has a lawyer; he is running a business with an office. In his personal life, he has a lover that he is discarding as *The Maltese Falcon* opens,
and another that he acquires in the course of its action. Like Race Williams
and all hard-boiled private eyes, he has an uneasy relation with his city's
civil authorities—in *The Maltese Falcon*, both the district attorney and the
police. But he seems himself emotionally enmeshed in both commercial
and personal communities.

He is not. The novel presents his progressive shedding of all of these
associations, beginning with the death of his partner in Chapter Two and
ending, on the last page, with the alienation of his hitherto unquestioningly loyal and affectionate secretary. The losses may be casual—the separation from Iva Archer and the death of Miles Archer take no apparent

emotional toll on the detective—or they may be difficult—his handing Brigid O'Shaughnessy over to the police is famously complicated, and Effie Perine's ultimate revulsion from him clearly hurts—but Spade accepts them all as necessary to his success and his survival. That the final action of the novel is Effie Perine's "small flat voice" announcing the unwanted return of Iva Archer only emphasizes how alone Spade is.

The villain in *The Maltese Falcon* is not a single individual, but more a collective than an organization. Its central figure, Casper Gutman, never imposes upon his co-conspirators the discipline that Dr. Moriarty imposed upon his gang, or even that the whiskered Klan leader imposed upon his klavern. Rather, the "gang" members—Joel Cairo, Brigid O'Shaughnessy, Capt. Jacobi, Wilmer—combine and separate as their individual interests move them. They are *not* organization men (or women); they do not subordinate themselves, and Spade's success depends upon his ability to exploit the fault-lines in Gutman's imperfect organization.

The two novels that Hammett wrote after *The Maltese Falcon* do complicate the loneliness of the life of the detective.[14] Ned Beaumont, the protagonist of *The Glass Key*, is throughout the novel identified with an organization: the corrupt party that run by the political boss, Paul Madvig, who is Beaumont's intimate friend as well as his employer. The malignant opposition is, of course, a rival party run by the gangster Shad O'Rory, but O'Rory is no Dr. Moriarty; the contest is not between the solitary consulting detective and the organization of the Napoleon of Crime; it is between two more or less corrupt organizations—O'Rory's or Madvig's. Beaumont investigates on behalf of Madvig's party and, graphically, he suffers for it. In the end, he abandons Madvig, the party, and the city. Like Spade, he seems to have given up all the social connections that had defined him. But by having him take Janet Henry with him as he departs town, Hammett gives Ned Beaumont a hope for connection that was denied to Sam Spade by Effie Perine's "small flat voice." Even in leaving the community that has defined him, Ned Beaumont is not alone. *The Thin Man*, Hammett's last novel, moves toward a detective further toward convivial integration into a community, and especially into a marriage. Nick Charles debuts as happily married at the beginning of the narrative and remains happily married throughout, and his circle of friends and acquaintances seems wide. But Nick Charles is a *retired* detective, and he retired *because* he got married. Active detectives never marry.[15]

Hammett—The Continental Op

But if, in the three novels that constitute the second phase of his detective fiction (*The Maltese Falcon*, *The Glass Key*, *The Thin Man*, 1929–1934),

Hammett explored the lives of detectives with increasingly more complicated relations to their friends and lovers, their cities and their classes (and
their gangs), it was in the longer first phase of his fiction—28 short stories and two novels (1923–1929), all featuring the Continental Op—that
really established in *Black Mask* the major alternative to the Race Williams
model of the hard-boiled detective. It was the Op, based most directly upon
the author's actual experience as a practicing detective (Hammett worked
for the Pinkerton National Detective Agency between 1915 and 1922), who
made the solitary hard-boiled detective most plausible. If Race Williams
engaged in melodramatic contests in which he defeated bullet-proof Beasts
and a Klan that claimed the allegiance of half of county seat, the Continental Op would achieve the same victories with somewhat less simplis-
tic melodrama; only somewhat—*The Dain Curse* has much the exotic
romance and the gothic mystery as *The Snarl of the Beast*, and *Red Harvest* has the lone detective defeating gangs considerably more violent than
the Klan in "Knights of the Open Palm." The Continental Op achieves his
success—discovers the truth—by acting alone; he too is willing to heave
monkey-wrenches into the machinery and he too is able to survive. But,
as his name suggests, his essential character seems to lie in himself being
part of a machine: he never, in 28 short stories and two novels, claims either
a first or last name. He is always only a cog in an organization is not local
(Spade & Archer), not even national. He is a functionary of the Continental Detective Agency.

And Hammett insists upon the authority of the Agency. A half dozen
other employees appear in various stories. Fellow agents include Dick Foley
(in ten stories and both novels), Bob Teal (three stories), Jack Counihan
(two stories), Mickey Linehan (two stories and both novels). Tommy Howd
the office boy (three stories) and Fiske the night man (four stories) also
appear. To be sure, they operate as little more than as enhanced (and reg-
ularized) Baker Street Irregulars. They display no initiative of their own
(as do, for example, the secondary team members in a police procedural);
they are instruments sent by the Agency to work with—and take direction
from—the Op. They *are* enhanced: they do not simply collect evidence;
they execute the Op's assignments by applying their intelligence (and their
facility for avoiding exploded parts of the machines into which he heaves
his monkey wrenches—and, indeed, they do not always survive). And they
may even reject Op's authority, as Dick Foley does in *Red Harvest*, when he
refuses to declare his faith that the Op is not a murderer, and the Op sends
him home. Their presence is a concession to the sort of realism that Hammett prized. A modern American detective rarely has the resources to sustain a private agency or to carry out the investigations that he is hired to
perform. But while close readers of the Op stories might be able to name

Dick Foley, the Agency employees are not memorable as individuals. They may contribute to the forward movement of the plot, but they do not solve cases, and they are not even sufficiently realized to provide Watsonian ejaculations of awe at the Op's final solution. They render the Op and his sequence of investigations more plausible without diminishing the Op's claim to full credit for discovering the truth.

The role of the Old Man is more complicated. Like the Op, he never acquires a personal name; he is a function, and his is the superior function. He is manager of the San Francisco office of the Continental Detective Agency, the office to which the Op is attached. He thus places the Op in the middle of an extended bureaucratic hierarchy: at the top are the national CEO and his officers; then there is the local CEO (the Old Man), then the Op and his fellow agents, then the night man and the office boy. Though he does not appear until the eighth Op story, "The Zigzags of Treachery" (*Black Mask*, March 1924), the Old Man will appear in 11 Op stories and both novels. Almost always his principal function is to allocate resources. When the Op requires assistance—to have someone shadowed, to have inquiries made by Continental offices in other cities—the Old Man provides the assistance.

The Old Man is also the guardian of the institutional ethics, which matters most dramatically in *Red Harvest*. To cleanse Personville, the Op heaves a number of monkey-wrenches into the machinery, leading the major criminal gangs and the corrupt police force to slaughter one another. (The Personville gangs are more disciplined than Casper Gutman's. The members of each gang stay loyal to their group. The Op succeeds by manipulating one gang to fight another.) When the final gangster has died, the Op spends a week "trying to fix up my reports so that they would not read as if I had broken as many Agency rules, state laws and human bones as I had" (*Complete Novels* 186). The novel's final paragraph reports the judgment upon the Op's successful cleansing. He does not, it seems, have to answer to the state, but upon his return to San Francisco, he is arraigned by the Old Man: "I might as well have saved the labor and sweat I had put into trying to make my reports harmless. They didn't fool the Old Man. He gave me merry hell" (187).

Although the Op is clearly the hero of his own stories, he is not the completely free agent that Race Williams or, for that matter, Sherlock Holmes or Hercule Poirot is. His practical subordination within the Continental Detective Agency is superficial: *he* solves his cases, not the Agency that pays him his salary and provides him with support in the occasional instances where support is needed. But he is, in the end, subject to rules in a way that even Holmes and Poirot are not. When Holmes, as he does on more than one occasion, decides not to hand over a thief ("The Adventure of the Blue Carbuncle") or a murderer ("The Adventure of the Devil's Foot") to the ministrations of the judicial system, he does so without qualms. Philo Vance may take the detective's moral autonomy to a Nietzschean extreme, but all classical detectives presume that their auditors and readers would accept the values that the detectives embody and embrace. The Op makes the same presumption, and readers are surely expected to agree that Personville was indeed a Poisonville that demanded a strong antidote. (They may also agree that restoring the city, "all nice and clean," to the control of Elihu Willsson means only that it is "ready to go to the dogs again" [176]). The Old Man's "merry hell" does not diminish the Op's rule-breaking triumph in Personville, but it is a reminder that organizations do have rules and that the Op can be judged by the propriety of his methods as well as by the happiness of his results. Beginning with Dupin, all non-organized detectives could simply justify their methods—Dupin's analysis, Holmes's science, Poirot's grey cells, Race Williams's quick gun—by the outcomes achieved. An organization man is also measured against the additional standard of agency rules.

His employment by the Continental Detective Agency thus complicates the Op's moral authority; unlike Race Williams, who accepts no external judgment of his actions, the Op's performance is always subject to the Old Man's review. And the Old Man himself in his review must apply Agency rules that he himself did not make. Of course this Agency review process is a very rare occurrence, and even in *Red Harvest* the Old Man's outrage at the violation of the rules serves primarily to endorse the Op's irregular improvisations: had he followed prescribed directions, he probably would be dead, and Personville would be as unclean as ever.

Two other organizations further complicate the Op's world. Police departments are, in hard-boiled fiction, a good deal less incompetent (and a good deal less deferential to the private detective) than in prior detective fiction, and the criminal gangs are a good deal more common, more ambitious, and more violent than hitherto. Leroy Panek has observed that, until *Red Harvest*, when he encounters the corruption of the thuggish police force that Chief Noonan heads in Personville, the cops with whom the Op finds himself working are, in fact, uniformly competent and friendly. "Without exception, the Op stories before Hammett's first novel present the police at every level as honest, hard-working, diligent, law-abiding, mostly intelligent, responsible men" (Panek 130). And they are working policemen, not Oxbridge scholars who have decided to donate their uncommon talents to Scotland Yard. Even more than the Op, they are governed by rules, but they are not feeble Lestrades or Japps. They possess roughly the same abilities that the Op claims for himself: "such results as I get are usually the fruits of patience, industry, and unimaginative plugging, helped out now and then, maybe, by a little luck" (*Crime Stories* 100). (The Op does then add, "but I do have may my flashes of intelligence," and these "flashes"— the birthright of all detectives—align him with his predecessors; like all fictional detectives who can attract readers repeatedly, however pedestrian he may assert his abilities are, the Op always achieves an insight denied to the police and the readers.)

Agency oversight may occasionally seem to impose some limits on the Op's freedom to detect malefaction, limits that other detectives escape. And the elevation of police competence means that the Op's superiority to state-sponsored organized investigation is marginal, not, as in the comparison between Dupin and Inspector G—, radical. But the Op stories compensate for these qualifications of the Op's individual brilliance by facing him with far more gang-related malefaction: the police and the Continental Detective Agency may in some small degree inhibit the Op's initiative, but organization flourishes in the underworld that Op confronts. This is obviously true in *Red Harvest*, where Personville is depicted as an anarchy in which competing gangs specialize in various underworld activities: Max Thaler's gang controls gambling, Pete the Finn's controls bootlegging, Lew Yard's controls loan sharking. Noonan, the Chief of Police, and his Department (itself an organized criminal gang) cooperate most closely with Lew Yard (and toward the end, with Reno Starkey, one of Yard's men who attempts to usurp Yard's place). Against these openly criminal gangs Hammett sets two other organizations. The first is the once all-powerful organization headed by Elihu Willsson, who is the owner of the Personville Mining Corporation, the First National Bank, two newspapers, and the "part owner of nearly every other enterprise of any importance," *and* the power behind a senator, a governor, a mayor, and most of the state legislature (*Complete Novels* 9–10). It is to Willsson's authority that the Op restores the cleansed city. Finally, there is Bill Quint, representing the ineffectual organization that opposes Willsson's regime, the International Workers of the World. Quint leaves town after orienting the Op in Chapter 1; the IWW has no place in the plans of any of the gangsters or of the Op (and certainly not in the plans of the grand capitalist, Willsson), and so, it seems, no place in the future of Personville.[16]

The organizations that compete for control of Personville differ radically from the Klan that has seized Clinton in "The Knights of the Open Palm." The Klan, as Carroll John Daly depicts it, is mere sound and fury, easily subdued by Race Williams's gun. The strong individual does not even need the assistance of others: Daly describes the Jabine family's defiance of Ku Klux Klan, but then has Williams prove that he does not need their clan to defeat the Klan. The gangs of Personville are well armed with guns, machine guns, dynamite, all of which they do not hesitate to deploy against their adversaries. They do not deflate when confronted by the Op. Nor are there any Jabines in Personville; the IWW is evidently as impotent against the criminal gangs as it was against the legal organizations of Elihu Willsson. Significantly, the major assistance that the Op receives comes from not from any organization in the city, but from one remarkable individual who has gone her independent way without affiliating with any of the gangs: the slovenly Dinah Brand. Dinah Brand has managed for a time to prosper by playing the gang leaders against one another; in the end she is killed by a flying piece of the shattering machinery, and only the fat Op survives.

The Op does call upon his Agency for two operatives, Mickey Linehan and Dick Foley, but they provide only a minimum of support; one of them—Dick Linehan—actually abandons the Op and returns to San Francisco when he comes to doubt the Op's innocence. The Op succeeds by identifying the appetites and the intentions of the gang leaders and manipulating appearances in order to have them direct their violence against one another. He cannot aim, as Sherlock Holmes did, to defeat a criminal organization by decapitating it: these crude American gangs are not run by brilliant minds capable of writing treatises on the binomial theorem. They are not fantasy organizations that depend upon the malignant intentions of a renegade professor; they are versions of the actual underworld organizations that emerged and took root in major American cities in the Prohibition Era (though, to be sure, improbably massed in a western mining town). Personville's gangs, all of them—including the police and the IWW—lack strategic minds at their head, and, however well-armed, are vulnerable to the operations of intelligent—and patient, industrious, unimaginative, and lucky—individual.

And the individual hands the cleansed city back to an individual; the Op fulfills his assignment by restoring Elihu Willsson's singular control over Personville. A lone Operative defies his Agency in order to eliminate competitive gangs and reinstitute the rule of a lone plutocrat over the Mining Corporation, the Bank, the newspapers, and nearly every other enterprise of any importance. That, at least, is the overt moral of the story. But, as the Op informs him, to secure his rule, Willsson must now request that the Governor call up the National Guard to patrol the city and this surely qualifies the lesson. However much Willsson "owns" the Governor, and however much the National Guard may be in service to the plutocracy (as it was in the labor unrest at the Anaconda mines that lies in the background of *Red Harvest*[17]), his authority does depend upon his command of large-scale organizations. The detective's extraordinary abilities guarantee he can uncover the truth, but that is the end—both the goal toward which he works and the terminus of his action. Once he exposes the sources of disorder, his work is done. It takes a militia—an organization—to maintain a rich man's control of a city.

Erle Stanley Gardner: Perry Mason

The third mainstay of *Black Mask* in the 1920s was the prolific Erle Stanley Gardner, who contributed dozens of stories to the magazine under several different pen names. They featured a variety of protagonists including Ed Jenkins, who first appeared in December 1923 (thus following by months Race Williams's debut in June and the Continental Op's in October), Bob Larkin, Speed Dash, and Black Barr. Gardner's signature creation, Perry Mason, never appeared in *Black Mask*, but his 82-novel career (1933–1973) does have some relevance to the hard-boiled detective's relation to organization.

On the one hand, Perry Mason never encounters gang violence of the sort that the Continental Op so often encountered; the villains in the Mason novels are always exposed as self-interested individuals or, occasionally, as conspiracies of two or three individuals.[18] But if Mason never has to fight a mob, his investigations *are* invariably carried out in opposition to a massive organization—the American criminal justice system, with its well-funded, well-manned police forces and District Attorney Offices. These complementary state agencies would come to be regularly embodied in the persons of LAPD Homicide detective Arthur Tragg and Los Angeles District Attorney Hamilton Burger, but the cop and the DA are clearly creatures of their respective bureaucracies. Mason is the determined David endlessly battling a misguided Goliath, with, in the final chapters of every novel, a California courtroom serving as the Valley of Elah.

But Perry Mason is never an utterly isolated David. He operates from an office, and, unlike Sam Spade's, Mason's office never disintegrates. He does, after the first few novels, lose his law clerk, Jackson, but his imaginative receptionist, Gertie, and his loyal secretary, Della Street, remain with him always and remain always, for four decades, the same. Paul Drake, technically an independent entrepreneur with his own office down the hall, full of secretaries and contracted operatives, is always available to supply the information that Mason demands from him. To be sure, neither Della nor Paul grasp the truth until Perry explains it, but they both are assigned active roles in virtually every case, and on rare occasions even take initiative. They contribute more in each case than Dick Foley or Mickey Linehan ever does. And while in the first novel Della Street gestures in the direction of Effie Perine by briefly doubting the rightness of Mason's actions, by the end of *The Case of the Velvet Claws*, her faith is restored, and it remains unshakeable for the next forty years and eighty-one cases. Paul Drake often warns Mason that this time he is skating on thin ice with a guilty client, but he too is steadfast in his loyalty.

Perry Mason's office is more than just a nod to verisimilitude. Readers may not know the logistics of a functioning detective agency; they do know that real lawyers normally maintain a suite of offices and employ a staff of assistants. But Mason's office signifies something more than a concession to common knowledge. Gardner—himself a lawyer who practiced criminal law with some success—is overlaying the fable of the individual who detects truth with the Anglo-American tradition that the truth emerges in a judicial contest between two legal units, the prosecution and the defense. The prosecution necessarily comprises a bureaucracy of legal and forensic experts that dedicates itself to making the case against the accused. There has to be a contrary bureaucracy making the case for the accused. There may be an imbalance in the resources available to each of the two bureaucracies—therein lies a key element of the defense-lawyer-as-hero—but the system's legitimacy depends upon the appearance of fairness. Insofar as he is a detective solving mysteries, Perry Mason is a man alone; insofar as he is a lawyer vindicating clients, he is the CEO of a firm.

Raymond Chandler: Philip Marlowe

Race Williams, Sam Spade, the Continental Op, and Perry Mason describe a spectrum of hard-boiled heroic individualisms that emerged between 1923 and 1933, with Williams the most radical outsider, Mason the closest thing to an insider, and the two Hammett models occupying a middle space. Race Williams gloried in his aloneness. Sam Spade always prided himself on his successful separation from others, but discovered the high the price of separation when he turned Brigid O'Shaughnessy in to the police. The Op was nominally bound in service to an Agency, but managed to act entirely on his own, with minimal assistance (or oversight) from the Agency. Perry Mason, as close to an organization man as the hard-boiled hero could come, incorporated himself, maintaining a hierarchical establishment that operated according to the code of the American legal system and the American Bar Association, but he acted as a strong individual who, whenever necessary—and he always found it necessary—was willing to ignore the letter of the code (and the caution of Della Street and Paul Drake) in order to discover truth and achieve justice.

Perry Mason—with his unprecedented number of best-selling appearances and his longevity—would remain an envied model, but an inimitable one. For the next several decades, American detective story writers would choose between Daly and Hammett (Hammett–Op or Hammett–Spade) as their model. Daly did have some influence: Robert Leslie Bellem's Dan Turner, Hollywood Detective (1933–1950) was surely sired by Race Williams. But it was Hammett who was recognized by editors, writers, and many readers as the fountainhead. And the chief of Hammett's heirs was Raymond Chandler, who began writing hard-boiled short stories for *Black Mask* in 1933, and in 1939 published the first Philip Marlowe novel, *The Big Sleep*. And Chandler, while acknowledging Hammett as his primary model, would actually position his detective closer to Race Williams than to Spade or the Op when it came to organization. Philip Marlowe would make the militantly unaffiliated private eye the baseline hard-boiled detective for the next generation.[19]

Chandler shared with Hammett the conviction that detective fiction need not necessarily abandon literary pretension; it could accommodate ambition: the detective story writer might explore serious social issues with the same artfulness that any writer might, and this clearly separates Hammett and Chandler from Daly or Gardner, whose ambitions were directed toward quite different goals. Gardner's self-deprecatory phrase, "fiction factory," has some accuracy, though neither his nor Daly's mass-produced prose is devoid of moral and even aesthetic interest. Significantly for the genre, Chandler's vision of the essential ethical character of the detective pushed him toward the Race Williams model of detached detective, though Marlowe's detachment has none of Williams's colorful braggadocio. Philip Marlowe is not the employee of a larger Agency, nor does he run even the minimal office to which Sam Spade returns at the end of *The Maltese Falcon*. "Samuel Spade" may replace "Spade & Archer" on the office's front door in Chapter 3, but he still employs Effie Perine in Chapter 20, and her disaffected voice carries weight. Marlowe is always alone. He was, as he tells his first client, General Sternwood, for a brief time part of the judicial bureaucracy—an investigator for the District Attorney—but he now operates defiantly alone: "I was fired. For insubordination. I test very high for insubordination, General" (*Stories & Early Novels* 594). He operates out of a minimalist office, with its file cabinets full of California climate. Lacking a chauffeur, he is technically even more isolated than was Race Williams. Marlowe is proud of his utter independence of any confining relationships; it is, as he told Lt. Breeze, the guarantee of an unfettered pursuit of the truth. But where Race Williams can simply boast of his unlimited freedom to act, Marlowe often expresses his awareness that there is a cost to his isolation from others.

Marlowe does have a few lasting relationships. Bernie Ohls, Marlowe's immediate superior when he was in the D.A.'s office, appears briefly in four of the seven novels, providing a referral or a recommendation and occasionally sharing an attitude or a drink. And in the final two novels (*The Long Goodbye* and *Playback*), Chandler was inspired to establish a sexual relationship between Marlowe and Linda Loring.[20] But otherwise, Philip Marlowe is not just alone, he is emphatically alone. In a much-discussed scene in the first novel, *The Big Sleep*, Marlowe returns to his apartment in the Hobart Arms, and finds that Carmen Sternwood has managed to enter it and is lying naked on his bed. He compels her to dress and depart, then "I put my empty glass down and tore the bed to pieces savagely" (709). His action—and especially the "savagely" that modifies it—has been examined as a clue to Marlowe's response to female sexuality. But, as Carmen's body is as well a radical violation of his privacy, it is also a statement about his need for inviolate aloneness: no one, male or female, should invade his private space.[21] He does not share his bed, nor does he share his office.

When, in *The Long Goodbye*, Chandler *does* have Marlowe share his bed with Linda Loring (and earlier in the same novel, permit Terry Lennox to stay overnight—*not* in his bed), the abrupt opening up of his living space is matched by a renewed emphasis upon the firmly closed character of his business space. His office has always been occupied by one alone; the contrast has usually been to police stations and prosecutor's offices (and jails) with their multitudes of officials of various grades and competencies coming and going and on call. In *The Long Goodbye*, Chandler sends Marlowe to a version of the Op's Continental Detective Agency in order to acquire the names and addresses of local doctors with shady reputations and last names beginning with V. The Carne Organization is "a flossy agency in Beverly Hills that specialized in protection for the carriage trade" (*Later Novels* 509). It fills its offices with much more than California climate: it keeps extensive (and useful) files, and its uniformly gray decor is, Marlowe observes, expensively designed to convey a message to prospective clients. The agents' offices are decorated with plaques bearing "a small inspirational legend in steely letters on a gray background": "A CARNE OPERATIVE DRESSES, SPEAKS AND BEHAVES LIKE A GENTLEMAN AT ALL TIMES AND IN ALL PLACES. THERE ARE NO EXCEPTIONS TO THIS RULE" (511). Marlowe, with his instinct for insubordination, is naturally averse to Carne's décor and his rule, but so is his friend, George Peters, who works for Carne because the money is good "and any time Carne starts acting like he thought I was doing time in that maximum-security prison he ran in England during the war, I'll pick up my check and blow." (512). Still, Peters carefully disconnects the microphone hidden behind one of the pictures hung in his office: even he pays the price of discretion when working for a bureaucratic, organization.[22]

The Carne organization occupies only a few pages in *The Long Goodbye*, enough to permit Marlowe to express disdain for the organization's character and to solicit access to its files. Somewhat more present, though still peripheral, is the criminal organization, here embodied in a pair of Las Vegas mobsters, Randy Starr and Mendy Menendez, and their henchmen. Like the Carne operation, the mobsters are efficient at what they do; unlike the Carne organization, they are quite colorful. Mendy Menendez especially plays the flamboyant tough gangster. But Marlowe expresses the same contempt for Menendez as he does for the colorless Carne. Marlowe reserves his respect for men who stand alone; in *The Long Goodbye*, these are enigmatic Terry Lennox and the novelist Roger Wade, both of whom engage in self-destructive behavior. Both men are flawed, and their flaws are evident immediately, but Marlowe can admire the fortitude—even the foolish fortitude—with which they face their problems. Wade is murdered and remains an object of admiration; Lennox appears to be murdered, and Marlowe makes a sentimental gesture in his memory, but when he discovers that Lennox has not been murdered and has chosen to adopt a new identity with the aid of the Las Vegas mob, Marlowe disowns him. The moral nihilism that leads to Lennox's failure belongs to Terry Lennox alone, but it is significant that it is facilitated by his friends in the mob.

The Carne Organization appears only in *The Long Goodbye*, but the other two organized authorities against which Marlowe posits his lonely self are ubiquitous in the Marlowe novels and in hard-boiled fiction generally. The Los Angeles justice system—sometimes its district attorneys, always its police (and, when nearby Bay City is included, often brutal and corrupt police)—is always present, and always mistrusted by Marlowe. The DAs are always vulnerable to pressure to act in the interest of the wealthiest citizens, and the police, coarsened by their regular contact with the worst of society are bound by standardized rules and—especially in Bay City—are capable of stark brutality and corruption. And, representing the organized underworld, mob bosses are frequently present in the background: Eddie Mars in *The Big Sleep*, Laird Brunette in *Farewell, My Lovely*, Steelgrave in *The Little Sister*. The central crime is always perpetrated by an individual for specific reasons, and it is always solved by an individual who is "a complete man and a common man and yet an unusual man" (*Later Novels* 992)—by Philip Marlowe. But the shadow of organized crime and organized crime fighting is always there.

The Truman Dicks: Hammer, Thursday, Archer, Wilde

The hard-boiled tradition had thus, by 1940, established a scale of private eye autonomy that would be familiar to readers.

- **The Regional/National Agency:** the detective subordinate to an immediate superior (an Old Man), enrolled with colleagues upon whom he calls for assistance, operating from a local bureaucracy (secretaries, errand boys, night men—with links to a wider bureaucracy) and governed by local and national regulations. Examples: the Continental Op, Doan[23]
- **The Established Office:** the detective as CEO, with an extended payroll (secretary, legal assistant, receptionist, with a contracted detective agency; and a suite of offices). Examples: Perry Mason, Nero Wolfe
- **The Established Partnership:** the detective plus a partner, a secretary, with a contracted lawyer; and a suite of offices. Example: Sam Spade, at the beginning of *The Maltese Falcon*
- **The Basic Office:** the detective plus a secretary. Examples: Sam Spade, at the end of *The Maltese Falcon*, Mike Shayne through most of his career
- **The Bare Office:** the detective alone. Examples: Race Williams, Philip Marlowe

With the exception of Perry Mason and Nero Wolfe, both of whom operate at the fringe of the hard-boiled, they are all shades of solitude. Even with national agencies behind them, the Continental Op and Doan function almost entirely as lone investigators. And none of them decorates whatever office (or, for that matter, home) that they occupy. Just as Dupin and Holmes distinguished themselves by their bohemian habits from the respectability that preoccupied the middle class of their time, the hard-boiled detectives separate themselves from the consumerism and conspicuous consumption of their time. They choose not to invest in the trappings of success.

The postwar writers working in the genre could select from these models of undistinguished solitude. The two most bureaucratic options—Regional/National Office and Established Office—were least favored. Bart Spicer's Carney Wilde would move in that direction; and when he achieved it—in the Eisenhower years—his career was over. The last two—the Basic Office or the Bare Office, the models in which the detective is least bound to any organization—were the most often adopted: Chandler's eulogy of the solitary complete, common, and yet an unusual man evidently resonated most deeply with writers and readers of the 1940s, perhaps because so many readers (and writers) were themselves transitioning from the regimentation of the military (or of the regimentation imposed by the stringencies of the war economy at home) into the pressure to conform imposed by the new corporate character of American business life. The detective of the 1940s embodies an independent alternative to the men in the gray flannel suits: he is a man who returns from war to work for himself—and in an adventurous line of work. It is his job to see for himself how the citizens of postwar America are leading and misleading their lives. He will work alone, or nearly alone. If he does work with someone else, that other person will be marked as different and as subordinate: as a secretary, not a fellow detective and certainly not as a supervisor; she will be female, not male, with a frisson of sexual attraction that makes her work for more just than her salary. With or without a secretary, the postwar hard-boiled detective remains a proletarian; a working man who ekes out a precarious living on a specified per diem (circa $25 in 1949). And he ekes it out on his own.

Three of the four principal writers adopted the Basic or the Bare Office. Mickey Spillane assigned Mike Hammer a Basic Office, with Velda as his competent and adoring secretary. It is clear from the beginning that Velda's primary function is to emphasize the manly prowess of the employer whom she explicitly desires to marry (though she will eventually, when the series resumes in 1962 after a decade-long hiatus, acquire some prowess of her own).[24] Ross Macdonald and Wade Miller placed their detectives in Bare Offices. Though he would be more socially conscious than most of his peers, Archer would also, until his final cases, be one of the loneliest. Max Thursday begins his career with no office at all; in his remaining appearances, he operates from a Bare Office (though he will keep a few undeveloped part-time agents on call). The fourth writer, Bart Spicer, made the unusual choice to have his detective grow his practice as business, beginning with a Bare Office and expanding steadily until he is himself an "Old Man," the CEO of a large Established Office.

Mickey Spillane: Mike Hammer

Mike Hammer would seem to be the natural heir to the Minimal Office favored by Race Williams, Spillane's avowed model for his detective. And Hammer's opening diatribe in *I, the Jury* against a sadistic murderer and a judicial system that offers such murderers an excess of benefits and delays would seem to set him firmly against all organized investigation. Hammer dismisses Captain Chambers's confidence that the police, with "every scientific facility at our disposal and of lot of men to do the legwork" (11), can beat Hammer to the solution of the crime, declaring that he is not, like Capt. Chambers, "tied down by rules and regulations" (8), and he is not, like the law, "cold and impartial" (7). His keys to successful detection are thus two: "I'm alone" and "I hate hard" (8). The hate proves to be crucial: throughout his career, Hammer's personal emotional commitments push him to endure and to administer the beatings that lead him to his killer. His self-absorption as he expresses his own feelings makes him the memorable figure at the murder scene in Chapter 1. Hammer's outrage at the murder of "about the best friend I ever had" (7) overshadows not only the anger of Lt. Chambers, but, as well, the quiet grief of his friend's fiancée. Pat Chambers also lost a friend; Myrna Devlin has lost the man that rescued her and was to marry her, but Hammer's emotion seems the only emotion in the chapter. Hammer's forceful voice makes him seem alone when he is not.

The qualification of Hammer's second assertion "I'm alone" is emphasized when he returns to his two-room office in the Hackard Building at the beginning of Chapter 2 and is greeted by a secretary. If the first chapter suggested that Mike Hammer was a more violent—a much more violent—version of the lonely Philip Marlowe, Hammer's employment of a secretary recalls instead Sam Spade's Effie Perine or even Perry Mason's Della Street. But Velda is no Effie, no Della. In addition to her million-dollar legs and her tight-fitting dresses, she has the competence to collect the information that she knows Hammer wants. She is herself a licensed private investigator, and thus—unlike Effie or Della—is presumably as tough as her employer. But Spillane makes immediately clear that Velda's strengths do not diminish her dependence. She is *more* dependent than Effie, who can oppose her sentiment to Spade's realism, or than Della, who declines Perry Mason's proposal of marriage because she would rather work for Mason in the office than stay at home as his wife. Velda is almost comically eager to marry Hammer throughout the series. There is a moment in *I, the Jury* when Hammer tricks Velda into saying "No" to a marriage proposal, to her great frustration. Hammer may covet Velda's legs and curves, but he does not touch them. His restraint, juxtaposed to her open desire to become Mrs. Hammer, marks him as the autonomous individual. And Velda's first word—"Poo!"—seems to infantilize her. She follows "Poo!" with a childishly reproachful, "You haven't been here in so long I can't tell you from another bill collector" (12). She is not an equal partner; she is an uncommonly strong, uncommonly attractive woman, but this serves only to make her submission to Hammer make him appear even stronger and even more attractive. Like Pat Chambers, she can actively support Mike Hammer's drive to solve a murder, but neither the cop nor the secretary can ever direct Hammer's behavior. He consults only his own impulses and intuitions, and in this crucial sense, he is indeed alone.

Hammer immediately contrasts the efficacy of his independence to the limitations that those "rules and regulations" impose upon the police. But Spillane makes clear Hammer's scorn for *all* organizations and their trappings. His dismissive attitude toward Charlotte Manning's pretentious secretary ("I was lower than the janitor in her estimation" 30) may echo a familiar hard-boiled disdain for the ornamental greeters that prosperous businessmen (and businesswoman) have to employ in their over-decorated waiting rooms. But his brief visit to the college in Parksdale again emphasizes the authority inherent in Hammer's confident individualism. Aroused by Hammer in the middle of the night, Russell Hilbar, Dean of Students, briefly attempts to assert his control ("I'm afraid that's impossible") but gets no further than, "Now if you'll please..." before Hammer's "Listen, buddy..." (122) backs Dean Hilbar up against a chair and compels his utter capitulation. Hammer then hurries over to a dorm room, and in an exchange of gunfire, kills George Kalecki. When the noise brings out a number of students, one of them armed with a rifle, Hammer gives them orders, and they too instinctively obey. He dismissively describes the student who helps to transmit his orders "Good ROTC material" (125). Elite academics and their wards prove instantly submissive to a stranger with confidence.

If benevolent organizations—police, psychiatric practices, colleges, the army's Reserved Officer Training Corps—produce at best well-intentioned but weak actors in *I, the Jury*, in later novels malevolent organizations—the Communist Party, the Mafia—prove to be much stronger forces—too strong and too clever for the nation's organized authorities. Those organizations are anomalous in the Mike Hammer novels of the Truman era: in four of the six novels, the villainy proves to have a single ill-willed person as its only begetter, and Mike Hammer's triumph is that of the stronger individual over the individual who *thought* that he or she was strong enough to violate moral laws with impunity.

In *The Big Kill*, Hammer's deflation of the Mafia's aura of invulnerability is one of two nearly independent actions. In the first if these, relating to the Mafia, he violently eliminates a number of major and minor gangsters in a red harvest that cleanses at least some of the social evil afflicting his city. If he doesn't completely eradicate it, as the Continental Op did (for the moment, anyway), he certainly achieves more than the police have been able to. But it is the second action, involving Lily Carver and Dr. Soberin that provides the climax of the novel. Killing malignant individuals who have physically harmed people Hammer cares for—in this case, torturing Velda: that is the real mission of Mike Hammer.

But it is in *One Lonely Knight* that Spillane emphasizes the malignity of organized criminality and the unique authority of the individual to combat that criminality. The Communist Party is the center of evil in *One Lonely Night*. Hammer's crusade against the Party is, as always, an action based upon personal motives, but it explicitly develops the detective's necessary role of defender of community that not only cannot defend itself; it does not even recognize the existential threat that is operating against it. Hammer, being Hammer, seeks vengeance—for the death of Paula Riis and the torture of Velda, but he also is driven by the need to justify himself against the condemnation of the Judge who had looked at Hammer "with a loathing louder than words," lashing him "with his eyes in front of a courtroom filled with people, every empty second another stroke of a steel-tipped whip" (6). Hammer walks from the crowded courtroom of humiliation through the empty snow-covered streets onto the George Washington Bridge. He is as alone as one can be in a city of eight million. And then, when the Communist assassin attempts to kill Paula Riis, he discovers the purpose of a man ostracized by the city: he alone can save the city. Neither the judge, nor the people in the courtroom, nor the police, nor the savviest of journalists can even see the threat posed against it by Russian thugs, American dupes, and, especially, the crazy fifth columnist, Oscar Deamer. Mike Hammer sees them, hates them, and shoots them down. And he does so on behalf of a populace that regards him and his methods as contemptible.

Spillane, like many Americans in what is sometimes called the McCarthy Era, may have mistaken the threat to America posed by the Soviet Union and by the Communist Party of the United States of America and its fellow travelers. He certainly exaggerated the impact that an isolated vigilante (one lonely knight) could have upon a well-armed Soviet-sponsored conspiracy. But Spillane was not writing history. Most of the Mike Hammer novels have him serving the community incidentally, by eliminating a series of bad actors who—sometimes in unrelated ways—represent threats to law and order. In *One Lonely Night*, the service to the community is not incidental; Mike Hammer deliberately sets himself not just against a set of brutish conspirators, but against the worldview—socialist, communitarian, certainly anti-individualist—that the conspirators embrace. It is Spillane's most profound sermon against the impulse to submit oneself to an organization. Three people die on the George Washington Bridge: the first is the Russian assassin whom the organization has assigned to kill a disenchanted person who wants to leave the organization; the second is that disenchanted person, who sees no escape from the organization and leaps to her death; the third is a fellow traveler and a mad man who is using the organization for self-aggrandizement. It may be hard for those who do not share Mike Hammer's sense of the peril embodied in the villainous Communists, but for those who did, *One Lonely Night* was a fable of the inevitable triumph of the most isolated individual over the most malign of organizations.

Mike Hammer's confidence in his judgment as to what needs to be done and in his ability to do what needs to be done is the unquestionable premise of his behavior. Most of the people he meets know this by his reputation or see it in his manner; the few who do not are invariably educated by his fist or his gun. His egoism would be monstrous were it not always justified by events. Because it *is* always justified, he emerges as a charismatic model of American manhood. The millions of men (and, presumably, some thousands of women) who purchased the Hammer novels saw the private eye as the ideal of the individual who submits to no external authority—not the American justice bureaucracy and certainly not to the unjust Mafia or Communist bureaucracies and works under no aegis. Hammer never wears a uniform, and behaves exactly the same, whether operating as a licensed P.I. or with his license suspended. His authority—with villains, women, civilians and uniformed cops—derives solely from the authority of his own mind and body.

Wade Miller: Max Thursday

Mike Hammer's charismatic self-confidence is on display in the first chapter of his first appearance. In the first chapter of his first appearance, Max Thursday is virtually anti-charismatic. He is an alcoholic, lying intoxicated in a bed in a shabby room in a run-down hotel, with his ex-wife trying to shake him awake. Even when he awakens from his torpor, determined to rescue his kidnapped son, he does not become, in *Guilty Bystander*, or in any of the succeeding novels, a charismatic character, with absolute confidence in the rightness of his actions. No one adores him; he never has a Velda: his wife has divorced him and his girlfriend for several novels eventually decides that her romantic future requires a different man. Lt. Clapp, his friend on the homicide squad, is never as deferential to him as Lt. Chambers is to Mike Hammer. The people he meets always eventually discover his virtues, but he never quickly stuns men or women into submission to his will. His self-doubt is sufficient to compel him to make the dramatic gesture of turning in his license to carry a firearm.

But Max Thursday is nonetheless presented as an individual who, because he operates according to his inner gyroscope, can outperform both the official authorities in a more or less friendly competition (more friendly with the police force; less friendly with the District Attorney's office). Because he has a marriage and a son in his past, Thursday begins his new career more emphatically alone than Mike Hammer ever is.[25] Thursday has lost a family; Hammer has never had one.[26] And, though he develops his relationship with Lt. Clapp and inaugurates a relationship with Merle Osborn, neither of these ever reaches the uncritical intimacy that Lt. Chambers and Velda maintain with Mike Hammer.

Both men find an ally on the Homicide Squad of the police force, but Lt. Clapp is far less compliant than is Lt. Chambers; Max Thursday is much less free to follow his own impulses. Like Hammer, at the end of his first case, Thursday shoots and kills a woman who might have diminished his loneliness, but the contrast is striking. Mike Hammer executes a woman whom he loves, and with whom he imagined living in marital bliss—Charlotte Manning would abandon her psychiatric practice and live as a housewife cooking fried chicken for her man when he returned from work. He kills a dream of deep togetherness. He is, in fact, haunted at times by the memory, but it does not inhibit him from making a succession of emotional and physical connections with women, and eventually proposing marriage to Velda. Max Thursday did not love the woman whom he kills; there was no dream of togetherness with her. She did rescue him when he was derelict and provide him with a room and the dignity of a job (as house detective), and she assisted him as he pursued the kidnappers of his son. She also betrayed him, but such as she was, she has been his only support, and killing her leaves him utterly on his own.

Villainy is more often organized in the Thursday novels than in the Hammer. Organized crime can graduated in three levels: nonce conspiracies of a few individuals, established conspiracies of several individuals on the model of Casper Gutman's Maltese Falcon cohort, and standing criminal mobs. Most detective fiction employs the lowest level, though an unexpected established conspiracy may be revealed in the end. Major corporate mobs are usually left to related genres such as gangster fiction (e.g., *Little Caesar*) for private crime organizations and espionage fiction for state-run criminal activities, though Prof. Moriarty provided a precedent and Hammett's *Red Harvest* showed that a private eye could also engage with gangsters. Mike Hammer faced the usual nonce conspiracies in most of his cases, though in two he did confront the *much* larger malignity of the Mafia and international Communism. Max Thursday does not ever face directly organized crime of these dimensions; he sends no messages to Uncle Joe. But criminal gangs are constantly operating on the periphery of his cases.

In *Guilty Bystander*, the kidnapping of Thursday's son is the result of a nonce conspiracy involving his employer, Smitty, and Smitty's conspiracy is built upon another nonce conspiracy in which Angel Spencer and Clifford O'Brien plot to steal a string of valuable pears from a genuine mob operation run by the Spagnoletti brothers. The Spagnoletti brothers, with their Italian surname and their elegance and their brutality represent stereotypical crime bosses, more fully realized than the Carl Evello who aspires to head the New York City mob in Spillane's *Kiss Me, Deadly*. Recovering his son from one nonce conspiracy and the pearls from another constitute the principal tasks that recall Thursday to his calling as detective, and his success in identifying the villains in both instances marks him as a successful private eye. But the Spagnolettis are responsible for a central scene in which Thursday is cruelly tied up and whipped. Throughout the series of novels, San Diego is presented as a city in which criminal gangs engaged in gambling, prostitution and drug-running are constantly part of the background.

In the penultimate novel of the series, *Murder Charge*, Wade Miller re-imagined Dashiell Hammett's *Red Harvest*, with San Diego's diverse gangs moving toward the center of the action. In Hammett's novel, the aging autocrat who once ran Personville had lost control to the competing gangs, who were now engaged in internecine conflict. In *Murder Charge*, it is the arrival of a potential new autocrat—an emissary from the well-established eastern mob—that precipitates the action. In *Red Harvest*, Elihu Willsson hires the Continental Detective Agency to recover his control, and the Op is sent as their agent. In *Murder Charge*, it is the San Diego Police Department and the F.B.I who recruit Max Thursday as a free-lance agent, assigning him the task of infiltrating the underworld to discover its full dimensions. Like the Op, Thursday succeeds by playing one faction against another. And the lesson of the novel is that the free-lance, improvisational private eye is, at least in certain crises, more competent than the local gangs, the national gang, the local police force, or the national police force. The man alone succeeds.

In *Shoot to Kill*, the final novel of the series, Wade Miller complicates the status of the lone private eye. On the one hand, Max Thursday has graduated from a one-man minimal operation; he has expanded his office. He still has no full-time secretary, but "Max Thursday—Private Investigations" is now supplemented by "Seaboard Investigation Service—Commercial & Industrial—Licensed & Bonded to the State of California" (*Shoot to Kill* 11). Thursday is Seaboard Investigation Service's sole full-time agent, but he has hired four part-time employees: two retired police matrons, a retired prison guard, and retired motorcycle patrolman who respond to his call: in the opening chapter, they assist him in discovering which salesperson is stealing money from his employer. None of them acquires a name, or displays initiative, but they are tools he can use.

On the other hand, Max Thursday is, in his personal life, again dramatically alone again. Merle Osborn has been a reliable companion in the middle four novels, but she has always continued to pursue her own career, and she has never expressed the submissive devotion to Thursday that Velda displays toward Mike Hammer. Thursday himself grows complacent about their relationship, and—despite being a professional detective—is shocked to learn not only that she has come to prefer another man, but that her relationship with other man has progressed so far as that she has accepted his proposal of marriage. And the distance between Mike Hammer's unerring egoism and Max Thursday's all-too-human imperfection is most evident in Thursday's response to this shock: he attempts to frame his rival for murder. To be sure, he has reason to think that the rival did commit the crime, he does fumble the effort to plant the evidence, and he is properly dressed down by Lt. Clapp, and spends the remainder of the novel in a quixotic effort to demonstrate—against the police certainty that the rival *is* guilty—the innocence of the man he tried to frame. Max Thursday has only himself to rely upon, but he never succumbs to the megalomania of Mike Hammer. Indeed, when a character denounces the rival as an "obscene little animal" that deserves punishment, Thursday can respond—as Mike Hammer never would—"Who am I to say what anybody deserves?" (*Shoot to Kill* 74). Embarrassed by his brief excursion into hasty judgment and falsifying evidence, he repudiates the authority to decide moral status. Max Thursday is always determined to pursue his investigation to its successful completion, fighting whatever forces stand in his way, but, unlike Mike Hammer, he will *not* be the jury.

Wade Miller inserts into *Shoot to Kill* a cautionary tale about the danger of socializing the ethos of the man alone. Kelly Dow, a prominent San Diego businessman, achieved some celebrity when he discovered the body of a missing girl that the police had been searching for. His success has led him to conceive of himself as one of the common, complete, and unusual men whom Chandler celebrated as the essential detective. But he does not, like the true detective, work alone. He sets himself up at the head of a group of mounted vigilantes, and when a murder suspect escapes from police custody and evades capture, Dow makes portentous claims that, given official failures, his amateur posse will bring the suspect in, dead or alive. Lt. Clapp and D.A. Benedict are naturally averse to Dow's untrained "Sunset Riders" attempting to usurp police functions; Dow's bluster and his Riders' undisciplined enthusiasm make them genuinely dangerous. Max Thursday, usually the object of official mistrust, joins them in contempt for Dow's vigilantism. And, if the shared judgment of cop, D.A., and private eye does not suffice, Wade Miller seals Kelly Dow's fate by making him the head not just of an anti-crime organization, but, as well, of a crime organization: Max Thursday proves him to be the backer of a crime organization that runs gambling in San Diego. The individual with a functioning inner-gyroscope is, is hard-boiled detective fiction, the ultimate detector of guilt and innocence; without that gyroscope, Kelly Dow not only falls into the error of creating a counter-productive public anti-crime organization, he is himself susceptible to the private excitement of criminal activity.

Ross Macdonald: Lew Archer

Lew Archer remains, until his final appearance in *The Blue Hammer*, the loneliest of detectives. He begins his career, like Max Thursday, as a divorced man, emphasizing the loss of an intimacy once possessed, and unlike Thursday, who never mentions his wife or son again, Archer will often refer to the Sue whom he has lost. Through eighteen novels, he never acquires a lasting friend or acquaintance. Uniquely among the major Truman private eyes (Hammer, Thursday, Mac, Wilde), he never develops a relationship with a cop. He never acquires a secretary, or employs either full or part-time assistants. He slowly reveals pieces of his own past, and he always proves deeply sympathetic to a number of people whom he encounters. But he never experiences the emotional or physical engagement with anyone that Mike Hammer has with Lt. Chambers, Velda, and a succession of full-bodied women and that Max Thursday has with Lt. Clapp and Merle Osborn. He seems utterly alone.

Macdonald had published four thrillers prior to inaugurating the Archer series in 1949: *The Dark Tunnel* (1944), *Trouble Follows Me* (1946), *Blue City* (1947), and *The Three Roads* (1948). The protagonists of each of these—Robert Branch, Sam Drake, John Weather, and Bret Taylor—are enmeshed in very complicated emotional relationships. Bret Taylor, for example, has been institutionalized for a mental disorder following a traumatic experience aboard a naval vessel in the war and, shortly after his return to the mainland, the traumatic discovery that his wife has been murdered. With the assistance of Paula West, who loves him, he struggles to deal with amnesia as he tries to discover who killed his promiscuous wife. Lew Archer will slowly reveal a few details about his childhood and adolescence, but he never enjoys real intimacy with anyone until he encounters Betty Siddon in *The Blue Hammer* (1976). His sympathy for others is his defining virtue, but he manages to avoid all deep or lasting relationships. Archer, with his slowly emerging and never more than lightly sketched past and his complete aversion to ongoing relationships with others, is thus, for Macdonald, a deliberate turn to the convention that the detective begins every novel essentially as a tabula rasa. Mike Hammer, with his recollection of Charlotte Manning in several later novels and the definite progress in his relationship with Velda, showed *some* signs of building upon his immediate past. Max Thursday, by losing his wife, then gaining, holding, and finally losing Merle Osborn and by developing over the course of the series an extended relationship with Lt. Clapp and, in the three later novels, with D.A. Benedict, goes a small step further in connecting one investigation with the next. Lew Archer is very much the heir of Philip Marlowe in his consistent habit of forgetting people and events from prior cases.[27] Self-reliance is the principle upon which he operates, and the complete absence of even potential support from a network of supportive allies and friends ensures that the reader sees him as essentially self-reliant.[28]

A telling contrast appears in the initial novel. Archer is brought in to investigate the disappearance of Ralph Sampson on the recommendation of Albert Graves. Archer had worked with Graves before the war, when Graves had been a young prosecutor with ambitions to run for Governor. At the end of the war, he ran a town in Bavaria for two years, and then returned to private practice, trying to make his fortune advising "old ladies." Though he has not prospered as much as he had hoped to and is operating his well-appointed ("This is just my front" 14) office with a single receptionist, he still the epitome of the organization man: his early ambitions, his service as a district attorney and in the army, and his present goals all mark him as man who succeeds by working within the system. And Archer has always— with a wartime interlude in military intelligence—been the lone operator.

Both Archer and Graves are taken with Miranda Sampson, the young, attractive daughter of Ralph Sampson. When the novel opens, Miranda is sunk in unrequited love for her father's chauffeur, the unsettled ex-fighter pilot, Alan Taggert. Graves nonetheless, and with her father's approval, hopes to marry her. When Taggert is killed and has proven to have been involved in the kidnapping of her father, Miranda offers to transfer her affections to Archer, who seems briefly tempted, but then declines what he recognizes as a false basis for a relationship. Albert Graves has no compunctions, and succeeds in persuading Miranda to marry him. Archer then demonstrates that, although Graves had no part in kidnapping Ralph Sampson, when the occasion arose, he did seize the opportunity to murder his bride-to-be's wealthy father. Albert Graves is not a deeply corrupt man; indeed, he seems fundamentally decent, and after Archer charges him with the murder, he delivers himself to the authorities and confesses to the crime. He may not have been a weak man *because* he has pursued advancement by pleasing superiors (and old ladies) within the judicial/military/ legal systems, but it appears that the weakness led him to pursue advancement in such venues is associated with the weakness that permitted him to strangle the captive Ralph Sampson. At novel's end, Graves will be spending the next portion of his life in the penal system. The self-reliant private eye returns alone from Santa Teresa to his home and office in Los Angeles.

In his Truman era novels, Macdonald consistently included gangsters as embodiments of corrupt organizations, and he regularly connects them with broader social issues. Dwight Troy, in *The Moving Target*, profits from the exploitation of illegal Mexican farm workers. Walter Kilbourne, in *The Drowning Pool*, made his money selling black-market cars in Detroit, then came to California and purchased respectability by investing his gains in an oil refining company that mars the landscape. Troy and Kilbourne are significant players in the novels in which they appear. In *The Way Some People Die*, the complex crime network that involves Dowser, Herman Speed, Mosquito, and the Tarantine brothers is more central to the novel's plot, but in the next novel, *The Ivory Grin*, the gangster element retreats again to an important, but secondary role. The once-powerful, now paretic Detroit mobster, Leo Durano, and his formidable sister Una are trying to retain control of his organization from their California exile, and they initiate the action by hiring Archer. When, in *Find a Victim* (1954), Archer returns after a brief hiatus (Macdonald had followed 1951's *The Ivory Grin* with a non–Archer novel in 1952), gangsters play no significant role, and nearly disappear from all of the succeeding novels.

Macdonald's early gangsters—Troy, Kilbourne, Dowser, Speed, Leo and Una Durano—are all colorful figures; indeed, Macdonald seems more interested in producing colorful figures with affectations and neuroses (Dowser is uneasy being alone) and psychoses (Leo Durano's paretic violence) than men who run organized crime. There is little representation of the actual operation of their criminal activities. Similarly, the police in the Archer novels almost always appear as individuals—as men whom Archer can express contempt for, or have fistfights with, or even cooperate with. They do not work as professional in teams (as Max Thursday's Lt. Clapp does) nor are they regularly said to have manpower at their disposal (as Mike Hammer's Lt. Chambers is said to have, though that manpower is almost never seen in action). Macdonald is just not interested in men in groups—either to disparage or admire them.

He is, throughout his career interested in exploring the dynamics of one form of social relations. The "organization" that lies at the basis of all crime in Ross Macdonald's fiction is the family, often three generations of family. He certainly express the orthodox hard-boiled view: organizations—legal and illegal—do consistently degrade the world in which his families find themselves. They exploit labor, drill for natural resources, and sell drugs; they are unsubtle and unhelpful in dealing with children living in (or fleeing from) unhealthy homes. Military men—usually ex-military men, whose characters have been molded by their service in uniform—consistently possess mentalities that deform the lives of spouses and children. In the late novels, corporate exploitation of natural resources even becomes a central emblem of malignity in America: the oil spill that fouls the ocean and the beach in *Sleeping Beauty* (1973). But it is the family itself network, and particularly the unhappy pressure of older generations upon the younger generations that most often lies at the roots of the problems with which Archer finds himself engaged. It is there from the beginning. Two of the daughters in the first three novels become murderers, with some sympathy for Cathy Slocum in *The Drowning Pool*, and little sympathy for Galley Lawrence in *The Way Some People Die*. Miranda Sampson, in *The Moving Target*, the first daughter in the series, lives in a troubled family, with a father unbalanced by the death of his son in the Second World War and a stepmother who now hopes only to survive that father; she is infatuated with a man who has no use for her; she marries a man who desires her, but whom she has never desired; and her advances to Lew Archer are repelled. As the series progresses, the trappings of gangsterdom fade and, especially after *The Galton Case* (1959), parents and children become the constant center of the troubles that Lew Archer is called to investigate.

Bart Spicer: Carney Wilde

Carney Wilde is the uncommon private eye who does seem to aspire to don a gray flannel suit in an Established Office. He wants, as he says in his initial case, "the vacations and new cars and long quiet afternoons in a sailboat" (*The Dark Light* 33). And these things, he realizes, will not come to him from investigations into a missing minister, which is the problem that occupies *The Dark Light*. They will come from his success is securing a regular contract for store protection from Eli Lazarus, the benevolent department store owner who has inherited a prominent six-story building in central Philadelphia. And Wilde understands that success securing Lazarus's store will be the basis for securing further contracts and expanding his business. The brief scene at the beginning of Chapter Six of *The Dark Light*, in which Wilde testifies in court to the care with which he pursued and caught a thief who stole a diamond ring from the Lazarus store (and caught, as well, the fence who accepted the ring) matters more for Wilde's future than the rest of the novel that is devoted to answering the question, "What happened to Rev. Kimball?" A piece of more or less routine good work for Eli Lazarus is much more profitable than the extended and successfully concluded inquiry into the minister's disappearance.

When Philip Marlowe meets his first client, General Sternwood, he reports that he was fired from the District Attorney's office because he "test[s] high on insubordination" (*Stories and Early Novels* 594). The General replies, "I always did myself": men—at least men with the soldier's eye, in Chandler's world and in the world of most fictional private eyes test high on insubordination. Even the humble Continental Op defied the Old Man in *Red Harvest*. Carney Wilde is tough and persistent in the cases he takes on, but he regularly and happily embraces his subordination to Eli Lazarus (later, Eli Jonas). He expresses his gratitude for the early and on-going support of Eli Lazarus in most novels, and when, in *The Long Green*, Eli Jonas calls from New Mexico for help in recovering his daughter, Wilde is on the next plane out of Philadelphia. Carney Wilde is never a sycophant, but he is also never willfully solitary. He wants to belong.

The two detectives of the late 1940s most often praised for their humane approach to their profession thus come to it representing opposite views of how a private eye operates. Lew Archer maintains the most minimalist of offices; there is little description of its furnishings, and the furnishings never include another person. Archer never needs a tangible base, and never desires support from anyone else. Carney Wilde aspires to—and in his final novel achieves—the most maximalist of offices: he becomes CEO of a mid-sized urban corporation, with a fancy office in the Equity Trust building, enclosed by a cordon of other offices and a host of employees. He wants support—from an employer, from an executive assistant, from employees, from a wife, and in the end, Spicer grants him all of these.

Nonetheless, in the early novels, Carney Wilde seems, like most private eyes, to center himself as an individual—at first with only a sublet office in the department store—who can outperform an organization—here the Philadelphia Police Department—in the investigation of homicides. He is as unattached as his peers; open, like Mike Hammer, to romantic interludes with attractive young women, but essentially a man on his own. Like Mike Hammer and Max Thursday, he has an ally in the police department, though his relationship with Lt. Grodnik (later Capt. Grodnik) evolves in ways that Hammer's and Thursday's relations with their police allies do not. Mike Hammer always takes Capt. Chambers for granted. Max Thursday has to recover Lt. Clapp's respect after losing his license and becoming an alcoholic, but once he does resume his profession, they can always rely on one another. Capt. Grodnik takes time to warm to Wilde. As late as the fourth of the seven novels, Grodnik can gruffly rebuff Wilde's offer of assistance (though Wilde, of course, presses on with his assistance anyway). Wilde briefly considers marriage with Grodnik's daughter, though she decides she prefers Wilde's assistant, Penn Maxwell.

And Maxwell is the real sign of Carney Wilde's difference. No major private eye had ever hired an assistant. He might hire a sensible female secretary (Effie Perine) or a stunning female secretary (Velda). But never an assistant. Maxwell never actively assists in an investigation; Wilde still acts entirely alone. But Maxwell does manage the office, and Carney Wilde's office has an ever-expanding roster of largely nameless employees needing management. Indeed, Carney Wilde has become, over twelve years, such a gray flannelled businessman that, in his final appearance, he has to be jolted back into detecting crime. The first chapters of *Exit, Running* have him returning from vacation with his wife to his corporate executive suite, where his overworked second-in-command, Penn Maxwell, has just negotiated the quarter-million-dollar acquisition of the inventory of a former competitor. Wilde signs the papers he is told to sign and shakes hands. The new business will be profitable, but not exciting: it will expand his firm's capacity to service the security needs of more department stores. Wilde now presides over an organization that employs hundreds of men (and some women as well), with the important but routine mission of deterring shoplifting and other forms of commercial theft.

Wilde's acuity as a business executive, however, quickly proves to be less than his acuity as a detective. He is unaware that, not having had his salary raised in years, Maxwell has quietly made plans to move to a competing agency that will better reward his merits. Only a spontaneous gesture of generosity to Maxwell—Wilde assigns him 45 percent ownership of the new "Wilde Protective System, Inc."—preempts Maxwell's resignation, but it is significant that exactly when Bart Spicer rewards his detective with all of the prerequisites of commercial success, he inserts this marker of the detective's incompetence in the field of commerce. The novel, *Exit, Running*, then depicts Wilde's usual competence in the field of detection. Tough persistence, the signature virtue of the private eye enables him to confront a peripheral threat from the Philadelphia mob and to solve the central problem of death of Quentin Christie. He does use bodyguards from his agency, but as a detective, he acts alone.

Conclusion

The Truman private eyes preserved the necessary individualism of the type: the essential fable of detective fiction that the man alone, whether he be an extraordinary man or an ordinary man, is the key to solving murder mysteries. As a hard-boiled dick, he was, of course, ordinary. But the aloneness of the uncommonly tough common guy was moving in different directions. He might express disdain for everyone who needed a police force or a courtroom to secure justice. He might oppose his unique self-confidence against the pretensions to authority of the New York City homicide squad, or of the national Mafia, or of Stalin's international Communist Party, and he always exposes their weakness. Or he might himself emerge from a state of weakness, having lost his essential connection to his wife, his son, and his policeman comrade, and tentatively build a new set of relationships— with a new woman, with his old comrade, and with the embryo of a business—and then lose the new woman. Or he might, having lost his wife, selflessly devote himself into intervening in the lives of others, with a special inclination to protecting the fragile egos of damaged young adults. Or he might, year by year, move toward more and more stable relationships with people who become admired patrons, trusted friends, valued employees, and spouses.

The options break in two directions: toward growth and integration into a community of intimates—fully achieved by Carney Wilde, partially achieved by Max Thursday—or toward constant isolation—fully achieved by the selfless Lew Archer, partially achieved by the self-centered Mike Hammer.

Lew Archer. Total isolation. Archer remains completely alone. Although in each of his cases, he reaches most deeply into the lives not just of the principal figures, but often into the lives of secondary characters, he never permits himself to respond deeply to anyone. He makes a point of being unable to judge others; but he also evidently is unable to bond to others. He needs no one to assist him in his practice, and, throughout all of the early novels, he engages in no developing relationships at all.

Mike Hammer. Partial isolation. Hammer is Lew Archer's antithesis; his egoism is titanic. He is always ready to touch other people's bodies—to compel them—men and women—to submit to his will, but no one else's subjective reality seems to really touch him. And yet Hammer is not quite alone. Mickey Spillane assigns him a pair of unbreakable personal bonds—with Pat Chambers and with Velda. Hammer may only need them as evidence of his ability to attract unquestioning loyalty, but they nonetheless make him always less alone than Lew Archer. And although Pat and Velda are indeed predictably loyal, there is some small indication of development in their relationship—Mike does eventually propose marriage; Pat eventually reveals that he too has desired Velda.

Max Thursday. Partial integration. Thursday begins and ends his career more dramatically alone than any of the four detectives. He first appears as a man broken by the loss of connection with his wife and his comrade; in the final novel he loses one of the two redeeming connections that he has made (that with Merle Osbern). Even if he proves unable, with both his wife and with Merle Osborn, to sustain a lasting intimate connection, he clearly wants and needs such a connection. Lew Archer doubtless wants such a connection, and Mike Hammer, with his proposal of marriage to Velda, technically achieves such a connection, but it is Max Thursday who actually engages himself—however inadequate his engagements prove to be—in ongoing relationships. The trust between him and Lt. Clapp actually grows; the mistrust between him and D.A. Bennett emerges through the final novels of the series. He loses a wife, briefly re-enters her life, then appears totally estranged from her; he meets a new romantic partner, relies upon her in a sequence of novels, and then loses her. And it is Max Thursday who faces the reality that a successful private eye needs to employ subordinates.

Carney Wilde. Full integration. Wilde is the thoroughly engaged private eye—engaged with his employer, with his employees, and, eventually, with his wife. He *wants* connections. Although solving the crime at hand is always his immediate goal, and he solves the crime, as all detectives do, alone, he is from the beginning aware that the successful life is not defined by solving individual crimes through individual persistence and thought. He needs a network of associates. Eli Lazarus, his patron, comes first; growing a trust with the homicide squad—Lt. Grodnik and Lt. Connolly—comes second; hiring trustworthy employees comes third; and finally he is ready to marry an attractive wife. He ends his career at the center of an acquired community.

* * *

The degree of the detective's physical and emotional isolation makes a significant point, but it can be misleading. The *quality* of his separation from others matters. Lew Archer builds no friendships or romantic attachments, but he involves himself sympathetically in the lives of the persons he encounters in each separate case. Mike Hammer tends to make extreme responses to the people that he meets: hatred, lust, and pity are the bright colors of his palette of emotion. And even his steady relationships with Pat and Velda have elements of adolescent intensity: his unshakeable buddy, his gorgeous crush. Nonetheless, both Max Thursday and—most clearly—Carney Wilde seem to be living more plausibly complete American adult lives not just compared to Mike Hammer, but also to does Lew Archer.

Complete lives were still not expected of private eyes in the Truman years. When Chandler extolled the detective as "a complete man and a common man and yet an unusual man," he still presumed a man set apart. His "completeness" meant that he did not need anyone else; he was self-sufficient: self-sufficient economically (able to pay rent for an apartment and an office; unable to hire employees), ethically (with inner gyroscope that kept him morally straight in despite of the corruptions of the city), and emotionally (needing no companion to fill a crucial empty space in his life). This completeness is what renders him immune to temptation and able to persist in his investigations. It makes him hard-boiled and being hard-boiled makes him successful. It is why, in the end, Mike Hammer is more hard-boiled than Lew Archer: Hammer has others (Pat, Velda) in his life, and Archer does not. But Hammer doesn't *need* the others he has; he would be himself without either Pat or Velda. Archer does seem to need others, but never seems to find the right person. Max Thursday needs others: without his wife he falls into a derelict existence as an alcoholic, and the moment he loses Merle Osborn, he plants false evidence. But he can succeed alone. He regains his license without regaining his wife, and he shuts Merle Osborn completely out of his work in *Murder Charge*. Carney Wilde is the least self-sufficient of the four detectives. He is, at his core and as a private eye, fully hard-boiled. But from the beginning, that core is qualified by a clear need for more than the rewards of investigation. Wilde wants the accouterments of material success—he wants to be a boss, drive nice cars, find an attractive wife. He is a complete private eye, but, without a business and a spouse, he is an incomplete man.

* * *

Carney Wilde came closest to heralding the next turning point in the genre. His need for business success, measured by an ever-expanding payroll and ever more elaborate offices, was, unfortunately, not embraced in the 1970s or 1980s. The detective as aspiring CEO was a dead end.[29] The qualities of a good manager seem antipathetic to those of a good detective, and Carney Wilde's ultimate achievement—buying the stock of an outclassed competitor—is not the dream of any private eye.

But the crucial validation Wilde's character received through his need for others—his wife Ellen, but also Eli Jonas, and Capt. Grodnik, and Lt. Connolly, and Penn Maxwell—points to the validation the major detectives of the 1970s and 1980s were obliged to receive from *their* significant others. Completeness defined as self-sufficiency, hitherto the standard definition from Dupin to Lew Archer, now appears to be a pathology. Effective private eyes are men and women who succeed in solving the problems of others because they themselves live their lives fully engaged with others. They are supported by a network of trusted relationships. They fashion families for themselves—almost always constructed families of chosen intimates. Robert B. Parker's Spenser acquires his true love, Susan Silverman, in the second novel of the series (*God Save the Child*), his trusted sidekick Hawk in the third novel (*Mortal Stakes*), and his adoptive son, Paul Giacomin, in the seventh novel (*Early Autumn*); all remain part of his life through nearly forty novels. Sue Grafton's Kinsey Millhone is twice-married, but the husbands play a small role in her life. More important are the chosen relationships with Henry Pitts, her octogenarian landlord, and his brother William; with Rosie, the tavern proprietor; and with men like the cop Jonah Robb and the private eye Robert Dietz. All of these characters appear frequently over the course of the twenty-five novels. (Millhone also, late in the series, acquires unchosen, blood relatives who also play a recurring role in her life.)

Much has gained from this expansion of the essential core of the detective's character. Not only is his or her core identity—sexual identity, racial and ethnic identity, class identity—been diversified, the community (or communities) with which he or she associates his or her self also broadens the moral basis from which he or she approaches the world. As a result, detective fiction—not just in the United States, but across the globe—has become a vehicle for the presentation to a broad readership of popular fiction of new perspectives on the pressing issues in any given society. The new detectives don't just find new answers; they see new problems.

Appendix I
Between *Black Mask* and the Truman Dicks: Stout, Davis, Halliday

Daly, Hammett, and Gardner were the stars of the *Black Mask* universe in its first decade and a half; a brief look at the role of organization in three other significant writers who built upon the *Black Mask*'s new model detective in the 1930s may amplify a bit the role of organization as the private eye moved beyond the pulp origins of hard-boiled detective fiction.

Nero Wolfe (33 novels, 41 novellas, 1934–75) was almost exactly contemporary with Perry Mason, also remaining popular through five different decades, though not as spectacularly popular as Mason. Cast more in the classical detective story mold (though with Archie Goodwin adding a soupçon of toughness through his narration), Wolfe provides a contrasting example of the American detective functioning happily as the CEO of an organization. Wolfe maintains a permanent staff inside his brownstone: Archie Goodwin, his assistant; Fritz Brenner, his cook; and Theodore Horstmann, his orchid-keeper; he also regularly employs supplemental detectives (Saul Panzer, Fred Durkin, Orrie Cather) who function like Dick Foley and Mickey Linehan, but with considerably more personality. But Wolfe's Brownstone New York City is midway between 221B Baker Street in London and Perry Mason's office in Los Angeles, but in the degree of its realization, it is much closer to London. Holmes's quarters are at once a place of commerce (where he can be consulted by clients) and an expression of his idiosyncratic, bohemian character. Watson, who cohabits there at times, makes little impress on the furnishings; the files, the chemistry table, the tobacco in the Persian slipper, the bullet holes in the wall are all Holmes. Mason's office is a place of commerce that expresses no personality at all; it is thinly sketched as a functional lawyer's office, with a desk and a bust of Blackstone upon which Mason can irreverently toss his hat. Wolfe imposes his formidable personality not just upon the furnishings of his brownstone, but also upon its inhabitants. Within it, he dominates his employees, his clients, his adversaries, the police; those he cannot dominate are not admitted into it (e.g., J. Edgar Hoover in *A Family Affair*). Wolfe makes his house a sanctuary in which a community of individuals live lives structured by order and ritual—*his* order and ritual. Because he does not ever willingly leave the house, it is always the place where other people's disorders are cured. Wolfe is the charismatic CEO who magically rectifies the lives of those who work for him as well as of those who consult him. Only in the most extreme circumstances does he go alone down the mean streets. He is the antithesis of the hard-boiled dick.

Norbert Davis began to write for *Black Mask* in 1932. To the surprise of those familiar with philosophy (and unfamiliar with the work of Norbert Davis), Davis was one of Ludwig Wittgenstein's favorite writers. His major work lay in his three Doan and Carstairs novels (1943–1946) that are remarkable for their humor: the detective team consists of a man (Doan) and a Great Dane of above-average size (Carstairs). A more eccentric duo is unlikely, and precisely for this reason Davis recalled Hammett's Continental Op model: the detective as employee. Doan is employed by the Severn International Detective Agency, with his immediate superior, J. S. Toggery, appearing briefly in one novel and A. Truegood, the head of the national organization appearing briefly in later novels. Doan's irreverence toward his superiors makes them parodies of the Old Man who runs the Continental Detective Agency, but however comical, they do reiterate the lesson that real detectives are most likely employees of larger firms.

Brett Halliday introduced Michael Shayne in 1939 the same year that Chandler introduced Philip Marlowe; unlike Marlowe who appeared in seven novels at intervals between 1939 and 1958, Shayne was featured in thirty novels by Halliday in those same decades (1939–1958), with ghost writers continuing the series until 1976. Shayne is never as eccentric as Davis's Doan was, but he was more individualized than the factory product that Perry Mason became. Shayne was a hero who performed with reliable toughness and retained a steady readership novel after novel. He was the epitome of the "normal" hard-boiled detective. Halliday did initially experiment with novelty: his tough self-employed detective meets Phyllis Brighton in the first novel (1939), engages himself to marry her at the end of the second novel (1940), and then abruptly loses her between the seventh and eighth book (both 1943). Shayne remains essentially solitary for the rest of his long career, though Halliday does sketch in a few Gardner-like connections—a secretary, a friendly cop and a friendly reporter, an unfriendly cop—as regular players in Shayne's Miami. The failure of the Phyllis Brighton experiment speaks to the necessary aloneness of the hard-boiled detective.

Appendix II
The Doheny Case/
The Cassidy Case

Officials Close Inquiry—*Los Angeles Times* headline, 19 February 1929

Edward L. Doheny was, in 1928, one of the wealthiest men in Los Angeles, and perhaps one of the wealthiest men in the world (La Botz xiii). He had been one of the city's first oil millionaires, sinking his first profitable well in the Los Angeles Oil Field in 1892 and then had built upon his success by expanding the operations of his Pan-American Petroleum and Transport Company into Mexico, creating "the largest fuel oil business in the world" (Ansell 1). He was also, in 1929, one of the most notorious wealthy men in America. Doheny was reputed to be richer than John D. Rockefeller in 1925; he was counted among "the new industrial elite of Los Angeles" (Ethington 194).

When Warren G. Harding became President in 1921, Doheny was one of two oil men who secured favorable leases from the government through the influence of Albert Fall, Warren Harding's Secretary of the Interior. Harry Sinclair, of Sinclair Oil, arranged to acquire the lease to the Navy's emergency petroleum reserve at Teapot Dome, Wyoming; Doheny arranged with his old friend Fall to acquire the lease to the Navy's emergency petroleum reserve at Elk Hills, California. It would be Sinclair's lease that gave the affair its name in the contemporary newspapers and in American history: the Teapot Dome Scandal, generally regarded as the greatest scandal in American politics until Watergate. And it would be Sinclair and Fall who would go to prison. In 1929 Fall would be convicted of accepting a $100,000 cash bribe from Doheny; with better lawyers, Doheny would be acquitted of offering the bribe in 1930. But from 1922, when the leases were first publicly questioned, Doheny's name was associated with the scandal, and for nearly a decade he faced the possibility of conviction and imprisonment.

Doheny had asked his son, Edward L. (Ned) Doheny, to carry the $100,000 from a New York City bank to Albert Fall in Washington, D.C., in 1922. Ned was accompanied on this assignment by his close friend (and "secretary"), Hugh Plunkett. The two men had been close companions for fifteen years.

At 10:30 on the evening of February 16, 1928, Ernest Clyde Fishbaugh, the Dohenys' family doctor, was called to Ned's mansion. Fishbaugh told the police that when he arrived at Greystone he was met by Ned's wife, Lucy, who told him that her thirty-five-year-old husband had been engaged in an argument with Hugh Plunkett in one of the guestrooms. Fishbaugh reported seeing Plunkett walk down the hall and shut a partition door; he then heard a shot. He found Plunkett dead in the hallway, and through the guestroom door, he saw the body of Ned Doheny dressed in a silk bathrobe. Both had died of bullet wounds to the head.

Fishbaugh (and others in the Doheny household) also testified that Plunkett had recently suffered a nervous breakdown brought on by a variety of troubles: a history of painfully abscessed teeth, a broken marriage, addiction to Veronal and other barbiturates, and the prospect of having to testify about his accompanying Ned to Washington to give Albert Fall that $100,000 in the upcoming bribery trial of Ned's father. Fishbaugh, Ned, and others had been trying to persuade Plunkett to commit himself to a sanitarium to recuperate, but Plunkett was strongly resisting, and quarreled with Ned over the issue. The obvious conclusion was that in a fit of remorse at having just killed his friend and patron, Plunkett had committed suicide. A lawyer for the Doheny family issued a statement: "Ned Doheny died the finest kind of death. He died trying to help a friend" (qtd. in La Botz 171). Ned was given a grand funeral and burial. His wife, Lucy, showing no ill-will, sent flowers to Hugh Plunkett's funeral, and her brothers served as Plunkett's pallbearers. Plunkett's sister and brother both fainted at his graveside. In honor of his son, E. L. Doheny paid for the construction of the grand Edward L. Doheny Jr. Memorial Library on the campus of the University of Southern California, Ned's alma mater.

But Leslie T. White, a young investigator for the D.A.'s office, had doubted the murder-suicide account from the time of his own arrival at Greystone at 2:00 a.m. on February 17. He found the testimony of all the witnesses—Dr. Fishbaugh, Lucy Doheny, and the large domestic staff—rather too neatly consistent: "The testimony dovetailed with remarkable accuracy" (White 4). There were powder burns—an indication of firing at close range—at the wound on the head of Ned Doheny, but not at the wound on the head of Hugh Plunkett. The gun, found under Plunkett's body, was inexplicably warm hours after the crime had been committed, and it was free of fingerprints. White noticed the direction that the blood from Ned's wound had flowed and forced Fishbaugh to confess that Ned was not dead when he arrived. Ned had lived for twenty minutes, and his body had been moved. White was advised by his superior, Lucien Wheeler, to report his reservations about which man was the suicide and which the murder victim directly to District Attorney Fitts. In his memoirs, White tells the result of his discoveries: "The new turn of events in the case caused a twenty-four hour sensation, then it was dead … dead" (7). On 18 February, the day White reported to Fitts, the *Los Angeles Times'* lead story was headlined "Doherty Murder Inquiry Discloses Controversy," with a secondary headline, "Fitts Pushes Inquiry into Doherty Murder." The next day, the *Times* headline read: "No Inquest on Doherty, Officials Close Inquiry" (La Botz 171–72). The officials explained that an inquest was not required "because the man who brought tragedy into one of America's wealthiest families also killed himself" (qtd. in La Botz 172).

White would eventually publish his doubts about the official story in Chapter 18 of *Me, Detective* (1936). The chapter ends with the lesson he took from the experience:

> when the case finally petered out, I took an awful beating from newspaper men and the other dicks in the bureau. I was accused of being everything from a faker to a plain damn fool. I was ready to agree to the latter definition.
>
> It was from one of the veteran "broken-arches" that I drew the most concise summary of the situation.
>
> "You were wrong, Les," he told me with a sigh. "You should have let sleeping dogs lie until you could definitely prove just what did happen."
>
> "But, damn it," I groaned. "How can you prove a thing like that unless you are allowed to investigate it?"
>
> The answer was a shrug. [7]

Seven years later White would use Chapter 18 of *Me, Detective* to publicize his unofficial version of what he thought had happened at Greystone on the night of 16 February 1929. The Los Angeles District Attorney, the *Los Angeles Times* (owned by Harry Chandler, another member of the Los Angeles's "industrial elite"), and the Edward L. Doheny Jr. Memorial Library might all argue for the official Doheny version that portrayed Hugh Plunkett as the mad killer and Ned as the victim, dying "the finest kind of death." If he was not allowed to complete his investigation of the crime, White could at least suggest that no one else had completed an investigation either, and that the unchallenged conclusion of the Los Angeles officials should be regarded at least as not proven.

White would quit the District Attorney's office in 1931 and go on to a career as a writer, publishing at least six novels between 1938 and 1948, several in the genre of crime fiction (e.g., *Harness Bull* 1936 and *Homicide* 1937), as well as screenplays (15 writing credits between 1932 and 1957), articles for magazines such as the *Saturday Evening Post*, and many pulp stories published in *Detective Story, Far Eastern Adventure, Detective Action Stories*, and *Black Mask* (Rayner 207). He attended the *Black Mask* dinner on 11 January 1936, where he seems to have taken the only photograph of Dashiell Hammett and Raymond Chandler together (Rayner 217). Chandler might thus have heard White's doubts about the Doheny case directly from White, or he might have read *Me, Detective*. Or, given Chandler's decade-long career (1922–32) in the Los Angeles oil industry—his company, the Dabney Oil Syndicate, was a significant player in the business, though not nearly on the scale of Doheny's Pan-American Petroleum and Transport Company—Chandler must surely have noticed the murder-suicide at Doheny's Greystone at the time it occurred.

Greystone's ostentatious grandeur—purchased with a fortune built on Los Angeles oil—may lie behind the Sternwood mansion in *The Big Sleep* (also purchased with a fortune built on Los Angeles oil), and perhaps as well behind the Grayle Mansion in *Farewell, My Lovely*. But the Doheny murder-suicide case enters Chandler's fiction most significantly in the middle of his third novel, *The High Window* (1942). Investigating the disappearance of Elizabeth Bright Murdock's gold coin (the Brasher Doubloon), Philip Marlowe has discovered the body of George Anson Phillips in Phillips' room in a boarding house. He reports it to the police, and Detective-Lieutenant Jesse Breeze is assigned to the case. In Chapter 15, Breeze and his young partner, Lieutenant Spangler visit Marlowe in Marlowe's own apartment, certain that he is withholding evidence in the case. Marlowe refuses to discuss the case which brought him into contact with Phillips. Breeze reminds him that this is a murder case. Marlowe responds that in fifteen years he has seen many murder cases. "Some have been solved, some couldn't be solved, and some could have been solved that were not solved. And one or two or three of them have been solved wrong" (1070–71). And as an example of the last sort, he tells the story of the Cassidy case.

Cassidy was a multimillionaire. The police are called to his house one night and discover Cassidy's adult son dead of a bullet wound to the head, and in a doorway they find the body of his secretary, with a bullet wound to his head. The secretary held a burned-out cigarette in his left hand. According to White, Hugh Plunkett "had a half-burned cigarette held in his left hand in such a way that it would have been impossible for him to have opened the door and threatened the witnesses as they so testified" (6). Chandler has Marlowe use the same detail to support a slightly different inference: the secretary was left-handed, and "even if you are right-handed, you don't change a cigarette over to your other hand and shoot a man while casually holding a cigarette" (1071). White found powder-burns around the wound in Ned Doheny's head, but "no such markings on Plunkett's head"

(4). Marlowe notes that the secretary's wound was "not a contact wound" (1071). Marlowe, like White, suspects that the family doctor and the family used their time to arrange the scene and to influence the investigators. The cops, Marlowe claims, "didn't want the truth. Cassidy was too big. But this was a murder case too, wasn't it?" (1072).

Breeze responds with the cynicism of a veteran Los Angeles policeman like the "veteran 'broken-arches'" who shrugged at Leslie White's dismay about the abrupt closing of the Doheny-Plunkett murder-suicide: "The guys were both dead.... What the hell difference did it make who shot who?" (1072). White, a subordinate official, had to end his chapter on the Doheny case with the veteran's shrug; Marlowe, an independent agent, can do more than shrug. He can protest. The secretary was also a man; he too might have been mourned—by a mother or a sister or a sweetheart with "their pride and their faith and their love for a kid who was made out to be a drunken paranoiac because his boss's father had a hundred million dollars" (1072). Hugh Plunkett was mourned by a mother, a sister, a wife, and a brother, and their pride-faith-love may well have been undermined by an official script designed to comfort E.L. Doheny. The official version of events might offer the false solace to the wealthy and the powerful, but it therefore also offered a false disillusionment to the powerless. And Marlowe, the P.I., can refuse the offer.

The Cassidy Case underlies Marlowe's mistrust of official versions. He tells Lt. Breeze, "until you guys own your own souls you don't own mine. Until you guys can be trusted every time and always, in all times and conditions, to seek the truth out and find it and let the chips fall where they may—until that time comes, I have a right to listen to my conscience, and protect my client the best way I can" (1072). The occasion allows Marlowe to assert a fundamental value that makes him the sort of hero that Chandler famously celebrates in the "down these mean streets a man must go" peroration to "The Simple Art of Murder." Marlowe is a man of, "to use a rather weathered phrase," honor, a man of integrity. Unlike "you guys," Marlowe owns his own soul, and he will search for hidden truth unrestrained by the influence of multimillionaires.

And yet the "client" Marlowe is protecting at this moment in *The High Window*, is a multimillionaire, not "a kid who was made out to be a drunken paranoiac." She is a wealthy widow with, from the moment she first appears, a disagreeable personality. She behaves rudely to Marlowe and to her secretary, Merle Davis; she treats her "damn fool of a son" with parsimonious disdain, and she wrongly accuses her son's wife of stealing a valuable coin. By the end of the novel, Marlowe discovers that she murdered her first husband, and then persuaded the vulnerable Merle that she—Merle—had committed the crime. And Marlowe does protect Mrs. Murdock: he tries to persuade Merle that she is innocent by showing her the proof of Mrs. Murdock's guilt, but he shows the proof to no one else. Marlowe makes the rich widow pays no other price for her crimes than the $500 that he extorts from her on behalf of Merle.

But Marlowe does not protect just one wealthy client. Mrs. Murdock's son, Leslie, has murdered the blackmailer, Louis Vannier. In another echo of the Doheny/Cassidy case, Marlowe has found Vannier's body dressed in a silk robe with a bullet wound to his head. He watches from a concealed position as the gangster Alex Morny tries to frame his wife, Lois, for the crime by forcing her fingerprints onto the gun. When Morny leaves, Marlowe wipes the gun clean, and then forces prints from Vannier's dead fingers onto the gun. The police are not happy about the result, but when Vannier is identified as the killer of George Anson Phillips, they are happy enough to accept the evidence of suicide and to close the case. Marlowe knows that Leslie Murdock is guilty of the murder—more precisely of the manslaughter, but Leslie was acting to protect his mother, and Marlowe decides to protect him.

Thus an inner-directed man who owns his own soul ends up permitting—or in the matter of Leslie Murdock's murder of Vannier—even abetting the rich escaping the consequences of their malign actions. Marlowe might express disgust for the wealthy in *The Big Sleep* ("To heal with the rich. They made me sick," *Stories & Early Novels* 636), but at the end of that novel, he lets Vivian Regan place her homicidal sister in an institution where she will be watched and leaves the murder of Rusty Regan officially unsolved. It would seem to be his own, personal Cassidy case. But Regan has apparently no mother, sister nor sweetheart, only a wife—Vivian—who knows and doesn't care: "I didn't love him. He was all right, I guess. He just didn't mean anything to me…" (763). The detective's hard-won and hard-to-maintain autonomy means only that he can do what is right, even when that benefits the already powerful.

Appendix III
Brief Lives of the Truman
Writers, 1915–1952

Detective story writers have surprisingly often been the subjects of excellent biographies. Ross Macdonald was certainly fortunate in having Tom Nolan undertake a sympathetic and in-depth examination of his life and career (*Ross Macdonald: A Biography*, 1999). And Macdonald himself has been uncommonly open in writing and talking about his life and his art (see especially his essays in *Self-Portrait* and the extensive record of his conversations in *It's All One Case*). Despite his notoriety, Spillane has yet to receive a full biographical treatment, although Max Allan Collins and James L. Traylor have produced two admiring studies, one of his fiction (*One Lonely Knight: Mickey Spillane's Mike Hammer*) and one of his (and Mike Hammer's) presence in Hollywood (*Mickey Spillane on Screen*). No major work has been done on Bart Spicer or Wade Miller, though fans have produced web pages dedicated to their work (Wade Miller has been especially fortunate: see, for example, *The Authors Who Were Wade Miller*, http://www.mysteryfile.com/Wade/Miller.html).

The Life of Ross Macdonald

Ross Macdonald (1915–1983) was an accidental Californian. Kenneth Millar was born in Los Gatos near San Francisco in 1915, during a brief period when his parents, both native Canadians, had migrated to California. The family soon returned to Canada, where, when Millar was four, his parents separated, and he lived with a succession of relatives—his grandmother and a succession of his aunts and uncles. It was, at times, an impoverished existence. When he was six, his mother's plan to leave him at an orphanage was abandoned only at the last minute by the intervention of an uncle. In his teenage years, he seems to have engaged in activities that might have marked him as a juvenile delinquent. He saw his father rarely, but an insurance benefit received upon his father's death in 1933 permitted Millar to enter Waterloo College in Ontario, and he began an academic career that lasted until 1944, when, as a doctoral candidate in the English Department of the University of Michigan, he chose to enlist in the U.S. Navy and spent several months at Harvard University studying to be a communications officer. (He would receive his doctorate after the war—and after publishing eight thrillers—in 1951.) In February 1945, Ensign Millar was assigned the aircraft carrier USS *Shipley Bay* as its coding officer. The *Shipley Bay* made regular runs between Pearl Harbor and the Philippines; its one engagement in conflict occurred when it participated in the attack on Okinawa in spring 1945.

While in Canada, Millar had married Margaret Sturm; as Margaret Millar, she began her own career as a writer of mystery novels with the publication of *The Invisible Worm* in 1941. Millar's own first novel, completed before joining the navy, would be published in 1944, and he would continue writing while serving on the *Shipley Bay* and then in the home his wife had purchased in Santa Barbara. By the time he began to write the first Lew Archer novel, *The Moving Target*, he had published four novels under the name of Kenneth Millar, one of them, *Blue City* (1947), an experiment in the very tough vein that Mickey Spillane would mine in *I, the Jury*, also published in 1947.[1] *Blue City* was Macdonald's first book with the firm of Knopf. When in 1949, Alfred Knopf agreed to publish the first Lew Archer novel, *The Moving Target* (now, for the first time, under the pen name John Macdonald[2]), the publisher was able to announce that in 1929 the firm had published Dashiell Hammett's first novel; in 1939 it had published Raymond Chandler's first novel; and in 1949, it was publishing John Macdonald's first Lew Archer novel. Macdonald was thus explicitly identified as his decade's heir to his two great predecessors.[3]

Macdonald would publish a total of 19 Lew Archer novels between *The Moving Target* in 1949 and *The Blue Hammer* in 1976. He would, as well, publish a volume of Archer short stories in 1955, plus two additional thrillers that did not feature Archer. The Archer novels of the 1960 and 1970s acquired a reputation for presenting complicated plots that involved the sins of the parents being visited upon their children and grandchildren. Macdonald had, from the beginning, been especially proud of the carefulness and the significance of his plotting—an aspect of detective fiction that hard-boiled writers such as Raymond Chandler seemed to dismiss as generic necessity. The seeming obsessiveness of Macdonald's later Freudian plots rendered his novels peculiarly interesting to many readers (and, to be sure, a bit tiresome to others). For a long time, Macdonald harbored the ambition to write a major novel outside the genre which he had mastered; when discussing fiction, he could express admiration for the work of Dashiell Hammett (and, at times, of Raymond Chandler), but he seemed to identify *The Great Gatsby* as his true Penelope.

The Life of Mickey Spillane

Mickey Spillane (1918–2006) was born in Brooklyn, New York. He graduated from Erasmus Hall High School in Brooklyn in 1936 and he spent a year at Kansas State Teachers College before deciding not to prepare himself for a career in law. He returned to New York City and began work as a scriptwriter for the comics (including Captain Marvel). He enlisted in the Army Air Forces in May 1942 and trained as an aviation cadet in Florida. The Army decided to employ him as a fighter pilot instructor in Greenwood, Mississippi, and he never saw combat. He was discharged as a First Lieutenant in October 1945.

In 1945, he married Mary Anne Pierce and, returning to New York, purchased four acres near Newburgh, on the Hudson River north of New York City. In order to pay for the house he planned to build, he wrote a novel in nine (or, by another account, nineteen) days. It was published by E.P. Dutton as *I, the Jury* in 1947. It sold moderately well, but the paperback edition published in 1948 sold immoderately well, and the career of Mike Hammer was launched. After issuing six super-selling Mike Hammer novels in five years (plus one hard-boiled non–Hammer novel), Spillane retired his detective for a decade. The hiatus is often connected with his 1952 religious conversion from the Roman Catholicism of his upbringing to the Jehovah's Witnesses. Mike Hammer returned in 1962 and would appear in seven more novels, the last in 1996. Attempting to exploit the James Bond phenomenon of the mid–1960s, Spillane also composed four Tiger Mann novels. And in a development that surprised many, Spillane later also published two popular young adult novels in 1979 and 1982.

Unlike Macdonald, who remained as much as possible a private man, Spillane enjoyed publicity. He worked briefly as a circus acrobat; he acted in films, playing Mike Hammer in the movie version of *The Girl Hunters* (1963); and in the 1980s he played a version of himself in a trench coat in a long series of television advertisements for Miller Lite beer. If Macdonald looked beyond Hammett to F. Scott Fitzgerald as the writer who produced the sort of fiction he aspired to produce, Spillane looked to Hammett's more popular *Black Mask* stablemate, Carroll John Daly, who made no pretensions to the production of art and was content, decade after decade, to compose the sort of story that sold best in the vehicles—pulp magazines such as *Black Mask*—that were available to him.

The Life of Bart Spicer

Albert Samuel "Bart" Spicer[4] (1918–1978) was born in Richmond, Virginia, and is said to have spent his early childhood in various parts of the British Commonwealth. Before the war, he worked as a journalist for the Scripps-Howard Syndicate and as a radio news writer. After Pearl Harbor, he enlisted in the army as a private, went on to earn three medals and five combat stars in the South Pacific, and was discharged as a Captain. For the first three years after returning to civilian life, he worked as a publicist to advance Universal Military Training (the 1947 proposal of George C. Marshall to require one year of basic military instruction for all males), and then worked one year for the World Affairs Council (an organization dating to 1918 that worked to oppose isolationism in America). When his first novel, *The Dark Light*, won the $1,000 Dodd Mead Red Badge Prize, he became a full-time writer.

In addition to the seven Carney Wilde novels, 1947–1959, Spicer also wrote two Col. Peregrine White novels (espionage; 1955, 1966), four Harry Butten novels (as Jay Barbette, in a collaboration with his wife; detective novels featuring newspaperman Butten; 1950–1960), and two Benson Kellogg novels (1962, 1969). The Kellogg novels were ambitious crime novels in the manner of Robert Traver's bestselling *Anatomy of a Murder* (1958), set in the American Southwest. Spicer's literary ambitions also led him to write thick historical novels such as *The Wild Ohio* (1953) and *The Tall Captains* (1957). Unlike either Macdonald or Spillane, who seemed to have been content to live their peacetime lives in the United States (although Macdonald, of course, spent crucial years in Canada, and before World War II he did briefly visit Hitler's Germany), the Spicers moved to Spain in the 1960s, and only returned to the States in the 1977 for health reasons (Spicer died in Tucson, Arizona, in 1978). He would claim to have lived in England, India, Africa, France, Spain, and Mexico. In Mexico, he was part of the artists' colony at Ajijic on Lake Chapala and was reported to be there writing full-time in the early 1950s ("Bart Spicer").

The Life of Wade Miller

The two men who collaborated to write the Max Thursday novels were Robert Wade (1920–2012) and Bill Miller (1920–1961). Wade was a native of San Diego; Miller was born in Garrett, Indiana. They met in junior high school in San Diego and attended San Diego State College together. When World War II began, they both enlisted in the Air Force, with Miller serving in the Pacific theater and Wade in the European; both were discharged as Sergeants. After the war, they were the first of the new generation to publish a private eye novel: *Deadly Weapon* (1946), featuring the detective Walter James (and including Lt Austin Clapp, who provides Max Thursday with conditional police support in every novel). Between 1947 and 1951 they issued the six Max Thursday novels, as well as a number of other crime novels under the Wade Miller nom de plume (and, beginning in 1955, under the name Whit Masterson). Before Miller died at the age of 41, they had written over thirty novels. By setting the Thursday novels concretely in the streets and buildings of San Diego, Wade Miller anticipated the movement away from the New York–Chicago–Los Angeles scenes that had become standard for hard-boiled fiction.

Robert Wade has left the most direct testimony of the impact of the war upon the veterans who returned to begin careers writing detective fiction: "WWII influenced my career profoundly, probably more than any other single event in my life. I spent two and a half years in combat situations, participated in two amphibious invasions, ... served on a counter-intelligence team in Tunisia and Sardinia, and covered the air war in the Mediterranean as an Air Force combat correspondent. From those varied vantage points, I was privileged to observe men under extreme stress and witness the many faces of courage, all experiences which served me well in my future writing" (Lynskey, "Interview"). In this respect, Wade resembles Raymond Chandler, who was profoundly affected by his experience serving in the Canadian army in World War I.

Wade Miller has had his admirers, and a web page titled "The Authors Who Were Wade Miller" presents a series of admiring articles along with an interview and a bibliography. Another well-illustrated web page covers "Locations in the Max Thursday Novels." But aside from entries in standard research volumes, the series has not received much academic attention.

The Life of Thomas B. Dewey

Thomas Blanchard Dewey (1915–1981) was the author of 17 Mac novels (1947–1969), as well as two less-hard-boiled series featuring Singer Batts (four novels, 1944–1951) and Pete and Jeanne Schofield (nine novels, 1957–1965). Born in the Midwest (Elkhart, Indiana), Dewey graduated from Kansas State Teachers College in 1936 (and thus departed campus a few months before Mickey Spillane arrived for his brief time in Emporia; the authors of the tough urban Mac and the notoriously tough urban Hammer thus nearly met in a small very Midwestern American college town). Dewey continued in academics at the University of Iowa and would eventually work as an assistant professor at Arizona State University (1971–77). During the war, he worked for the State Department in Washington, D.C., and then in advertising in Los Angeles before becoming a full-time novelist in 1952. He opened the Mac series by setting the detective in the mean streets of Chicago, but even in the second novel, he had Mac's case put him on a train heading to Los Angeles, and he would eventually transplant Mac's office to Los Angeles. Standard research volumes in detective fiction often cover Dewey's Mac novels, and the always useful *Thrilling Detective* website accords him an admiring page.

Chapter Notes

Introduction

1. This is certainly true in retrospect; histories of the detective story find the shift to common man model of detective—the Continental Op, Sam Spade—to be the crucial contribution of the American 1920s to the development of the genre. But to most readers in that decade (i.e., all of those who disdained to spend ten cents on a pulp publication), it doubtless seemed that the detective as uncommon individual—as an elitist aesthete (Philo Vance) or a Confucius-quoting "Chinaman" (Charlie Chan)—was still the rule.

2. "Return to Normalcy" was the slogan of Warren G. Harding's campaign. The nation's preference for Normalcy over Progress in 1920 led to the most decisive in U.S. history, with Harding's Republican ticket taking 60.3 percent of the vote and Cox's Democratic ticket only 34.1 percent (Socialist Eugene Debs took 3.4 percent).

3. Paretsky, like Grafton, acknowledged a debt to the advances that Ross Macdonald made in the hard-boiled style. She specifically cites his attention to the deformations imposed by those empowered by society upon those disempowered: "he, much more than Chandler, really has this sense of dislocation that people with a lot of power can perform on people without it" (quoted in Hamilton 6).

4. The 1949 debuts of Macdonald's Lew Archer, Spicer's Carney Wilde, and Dewey's Mac coincided with Chandler's reassertion, after six years of silence (the prior Marlowe novel, *The Lady in the Lake*, had appeared in 1943), of the eminence of Philip Marlowe. The continuity between the Coolidge tough guy and the Truman tough guy is signaled by the: the publication of the fifth Philip Marlowe novel, *The Little Sister* in 1949. Raymond Chandler was still setting the bar. And whereas the final two Marlowe novels (both published during the Eisenhower Presidency) would mark noticeable departures—*The Long Goodbye* being the longest and most ambitious (and for many readers the greatest) and *Playback* being the shortest (and for most readers the least appealing) of Chandler's novels—*The Little Sister* has all of the characteristic excellences of the prior four Marlowe novels. The innovations of the new generation could be directly juxtaposed to the practice of the master.

5. Phenomena such as Don Pendleton's long-running series of Mack Bolan novels (beginning in 1969) demonstrate that Spillane was not without some influence on later writers. Ernest Tidyman's John Shaft novels (beginning in 1968) can be seen as an African American turn on the line of very tough guys that Spillane exploited.

6. Throughout the Truman years, Kenneth Millar published his Archer novels under the name John Macdonald or John Ross Macdonald. Not until *The Barbarous Coast* in 1956 would Lew Archer appear in a novel by "Ross Macdonald."

7. In her "Introduction" to Tom Nolan's biography of Macdonald, Sue Grafton credits Macdonald with demonstrating that hard-boiled detective fiction was "no longer the exclusive domain of the whiskey-drinking gumshoe, fists flying, guns blazing, blonde bombshell perched on the edge of his desk. "Lew Archer was a man with a finely honed sensibility, whose passion for fairness permeated everything

he did," and, as a result, Ross Macdonald "gave the genre its current respectability" (Nolan 8). To be sure, three of the four writers discussed in *Truman's Gumshoes* were moving against the whiskey-drinking, the flying fists, the blazing guns, and the blonde bombshell, but Macdonald was certainly the one whose fine prose and right-minded politics made him the icon of the new gumshoe.

8. Despite its respectable magnitude, Philadelphia never ranked with New York, Los Angeles, Chicago, or even San Francisco on the map of hard-boiled America, but the San Diego of Wade Miller's Max Thursday novels is obviously the outlier here. Thursday's very concrete San Diego anticipates the trend in the 1970s and 1980s away from megalopolises and toward setting the detectives in secondary cities, or even non-urban regions of the country.

9. Work on the first Levittown on Long Island began in May 1947; five months later, in October, the first families were able to move in. No African American families were permitted to purchase houses in Levittown.

10. Of course, Mickey Spillane's enormous success lay precisely in creating a *Very* Wrong Place for Mike Hammer to operate in—a dark, rainy New York City corrupted by drugs and prostitution and subversion, and this scene does seem to recall that of Hammett's *Red Harvest* (and even more of Carroll John Daly's *The Snarl of the Beast*). But Spillane's melodramatic villains also do, in some degree, embody the 1940s tendency toward sociological analysis. They are not simply greedy and selfish; they often embody structural aspects of American culture that Spillane presents as unnatural or perverted.

11. Even the master was content to send his protagonist back into action largely unaltered. In *The Little Sister*, Chandler does have Marlowe explore the Hollywood precincts which he (Chandler) himself had recently been patrolling as a screenwriter (*Double Indemnity*, 1944; *Blue Dahlia* 1946), but a really significant alteration in the nature of Marlowe's character and investigations would not occur until 1953 with *The Long Goodbye*.

12. John Evans was the name under

which Howard Browne published his four hard-boiled Paul Pine novels.

13. Ross Macdonald was the name that Kenneth Millar finally settled upon as he attempted to distinguish his Lew Archer novels from the crime fiction of his wife, Margaret Millar, and his contemporary, John D. MacDonald.

14. Wade Miller was the name under which Robert Allison Wade and H. William (Bill) Miller published their six Max Thursday novels.

15. Evans was perhaps, in any event, better known for his science fiction novels, his screenplays, and his television scripts, which he produced under his birth name, Howard Browne.

16. Ross Macdonald probably would not describe "surpassing Chandler" as his ambition. He clearly drew upon Chandler, and he drew upon Chandler more than he did upon Hammett, but once he learned that Chandler had disparaged the first Archer novel in a private letter, his fraught relation to his obvious master was rendered even more fraught. Judging by the frequency of his references to F. Scott Fitzgerald and *The Great Gatsby* in his ruminations in *It's All One Case*, one suspects that Macdonald would prefer to identify the artistry of Fitzgerald as his true inspiration.

17. Ross Macdonald's first novel, *The Dark Tunnel*, a spy novel sent in a city resembling Ann Arbor, had also been published in the Dodd Mead Red Badge series, though it did not win a prize. In some precincts of the Internet, *The Dark Light* is reported to have been nominated for a 1949 Edgar Award in the category of Best First Novel. It was not. Nor was Macdonald's first Lew Archer novel, *The Moving Target*. The nominated novels in 1949 were by Mildred Davis, Richard Ellington, and Herbert Brean, with Davis's *The Room Upstairs* awarded the prize.

18. The novels of all four came out initially as hardcover books, but it was as paperbacks that they reached the widest audience. When the Mike Hammer novels were published in paperback, their sales were unprecedented—indeed, for a number of critics of literature and culture, disturbingly unprecedented. Only the last three novels of Ross Macdonald, published in the 1970s, made the hardback bestseller

lists, and their popularity was widely admired.

19. David Goodis (1917–1967), a native Philadelphian, did not write hard-boiled detective fiction, but he did make Philadelphia the scene of some of his noir novels.

20. By the time he was interviewed for *Life* magazine in June 1952, the five novels Spillane had already published had sold some 8 million copies.

21. One of the nine later novels, *The Twisted Thing* (1966) appeared as one of a burst of four Hammer novels issued between 1962 and 1967; it was, in fact, the second Hammer novel that Spillane wrote in the 1940s. His publishers declined to publish it. On the one hand, it represents a significant early stage in Spillane's pre–Eisenhower conception of Mike Hammer, but, on the other hand, it would play no part in the development of the reading public's conception of the detective during the Truman Presidency.

22. Bart Spicer too would experiment with other detectives, producing—with his wife as co-author—the Harry Butten series (four novels, 1950–1960) and the Col. Peregrine White series (two novels, 1955, 1966). With the relatively early end of the Carney Wilde series, Spicer would also move toward writing large novels on social issues and historical events.

Chapter 1

1. In 1966, Boucher retracted at least a measure of his dismissal of Spillane's fiction: "For almost twenty years I have been one of the leaders in the attacks on Spillane; but of late I begin to wonder whether we reviewers, understandably offended by Spillane's excesses of brutality and his outrageously antidemocratic doctrines, may not have underestimated his virtues" (*The New York Times* 27 February 1966).

2. To be sure, Race Williams's "method" lacks the subtlety of Dupin's "analysis" or Holmes's "Science of Deduction." Williams declares on the first page of *The Snarl of the Beast*: "I have brains, I suppose. But a sharp eye, a quick draw, and a steady trigger finger drove me into the game.... The police don't like me. The crooks don't like me. I'm just a halfway house between the law and crime; sort of working both ends against

the middle" (1). Race Williams is hardly a ruminative investigator, but Daly still felt the need to have his character explain himself before narrating his experience. Hammer will, from page one, define himself essentially by feelings and actions.

3. A memorable instance: through a combination of well-planned, quick action and brute strength, Spade disarms Caspar Gutman's young gunsel in a hotel corridor. Then, as he returns the guns in Gutman's hotel room, he emphasizes his mastery— to Gutman as well as to the humiliated Wilmer, with a wisecrack—"A crippled newsie took them away from him, but I made him give them back" (497). Mike Hammer occasionally essays a wisecrack, but his shows of mastery are almost always entirely matters of quickness and brute strength.

4. Significant surnames were a common device in hard-boiled fiction, and the Truman authors often followed the tradition. Carney Wilde is not a wild man; indeed, he is quite civil. (There is, however, a carnival element to the pointedly titled *The Taming of Carney Wilde*.) Thomas B. Dewey's Mac answers to no name other than this most nondescript identity.

5. Pressing the pace of his narrative, Spillane can slip into nonsense and solecism. The coroner tentatively places Jack Williams's death at 3:15; Pat Chambers claims that the autopsy "may be able to narrow it down even further" (10), as though 3:15 were not already absurdly precise. Later, discussing Hal Kines's practice of seducing college girls in order to press them into prostitution, Charlotte Manning says he was enrolled in her class "ostensibly to procure women for this vice syndicate" (105). Kines's "ostensible" motive was to attend class; his *actual* motive was to procure women for this vice syndicate. (It is easy enough to score Spillane's solecisms; it is also necessary to observe that they do not matter: Spillane's readers were not pedants, and they were not competitively parsing his prose to identify the clues that the Great Detective would assemble into a conclusive solution. Whatever its crudity at times, Spillane's narratives always move.)

6. Throughout the large middle of *The Maltese Falcon*, the investigation into the death of Miles Archer is almost forgotten in a narrative focused on the fantastic

conspiracy. It compels Spade to deal with Iva Archer and with Lieutenant Dundy and Detective-Sergeant Tom Polhaus, but until the final chapter, when it becomes a decisive factor, Archer's death seems quite secondary.

7. Although Spillane is often identified as a misogynistic reactionary and Hammett is celebrated as a hero of the Left, it is worth noting that Spillane's detective finds himself attracted to a working professional woman, while the object of Sam Spade's attentions is what, in his time, would be called an adventuress. Brigid O'Shaughnessy seeks to prosper by attaching herself to a sequence of susceptible men; Charlotte Manning has acquired advanced university degrees and maintains a successful psychiatric practice (and runs a profitable drug ring on the side). And, in fact, all of the significant women in Hammett's fiction—Dinah Brand, Gabrielle Dain, Janet Henry, Nora Charles—are unemployed women who live off their wits or their inheritances. Few of the women Mike Hammer meets are so fortunate. Some have been compelled to resort to prostitution; most are nurses, models, advertising executives, waitresses, even licensed private eyes. This does not, of course, make Spillane enlightened. Mike Hammer does insist that Charlotte abandon her psychiatric practice and take up huswifery, and Charlotte does happily acquiesce. Man as sole breadwinner and woman as homemaker is, in Spillane's world, the natural order. But Mike Hammer clearly likes strong women and meets many of them; he just knows that, at their core, they want not to achieve, but to submit.

8. And unlike the damage that he sometimes boasts he has inflicted upon the faces (and especially the teeth) of some of his adversaries, those who sap Hammer do not permanently alter his appearance, which, he admits, is ugly anyway—ugly but magnetically ugly.

9. Robert Gale has tabulated the high mortality rate that characterizes Hammer's world: 48 people die in the first four Hammer novels, 34 of them completely innocent of involvement in the instigating crime (22). Gale does not count the survivors who have been badly beaten.

10. Spillane takes the MVD (the Soviet Union's Ministry of Internal Affairs) to be the agency in charge of security and espionage. This seems to be in error. When the MVD was created in 1946 as the successor to the NKVD (the People's Commissariat for Internal Affairs), the security and espionage responsibilities of the NKVD were assigned to the new MGB (Ministry of State Security) and then, in 1954, to the KGB (Committee for State Security). But, of course, the niceties of the bureaucratic arrangement of the divisions of Soviet state security have little significance in the New York City of *One Lonely Night*. The novel makes the point that the Communist threat has multiple sources: one is direct Soviet agents, whether operating under the aegis of the NKVD, the MVD, the MGB, or the KGB; a second source is the class of weak-minded American sympathizers; and the third source would be a small class of power-hungry (and in one important instance, clinically insane) American revolutionaries.

11. Hammer's virulent and simple-minded anti-Communism offended liberal sensibilities at the time, and ever since. But as a reminder that it was not simply mindless, it should be noted that Francis Cardinal Spellman—no liberal, certainly, but no low-browed simpleton either—specifically praised *One Lonely Night*: "In private Spellman, as usual, was even blunter about Communism than he was in public. His notion of what to do about the Reds was summarized in *One Lonely Night*, a Mickey Spillane novel. Spellman urged priests to read the book, so taken was he with Spillane's solution: 'Don't arrest them, don't treat them with the dignity of the democratic process of the courts of law … do the same thing they'd do to you! Treat 'em to the inglorious taste of sudden death....'" (Cooney 148).

12. The line about "truth, justice, and the American way" is always associated with Superman. It first appeared in the Superman radio serial in 1942 (Duncan 225) and was a fixture on the television series (1952–1958). It neatly encapsulates Hammer's pursuits in *One Lonely Night*. Truth is, of course, the object of all detective inquiries. Justice—that the detective must be judge, jury, and executioner—is the special object of every Mike Hammer investigation, and it is embodied in the title of the first novel, *I, the Jury*. Like all detectives, Mike Hammer always discovers the truth. Like few detectives, he always delivers the justice. In *One*

Lonely Night, he also vigorously defends the American way of life—a way of life that, he finds, too few Americans are willing or capable of defending.

13. As Max Allan Collins and James L. Traylor point out, abandoning Mike Hammer did not mean a retreat into silence. Between 1952 and 1962 Spillane published more than a dozen non-Hammer novelettes, produced a year's worth of scripts for a Mike Hammer comic strip, and wrote a number of non-fiction pieces (*On Screen* 13).

14. Senator Estes Kefauver from Tennessee was the Chair of the Senate Special Committee to Investigate Crime in Interstate Commerce. The Committee was established in May 1950 and over the next year held televised hearings in 14 cities on the depredations of organized crime. It brought "Mafia" into the national vocabulary.

Spillane's shift from the external threat of Russian Communism (with its Fifth Column American dupes and madmen) in *One Lonely Night* to the internal threat (with a Sicilian accent) in *Kiss Me, Deadly* is underscored in Thomas Heise's analysis of the latter novel: "Through a narrative of detection and revenge, *Kiss Me, Deadly* records postwar social anxieties over an expanding liberal government's infiltration into the daily lives of American citizens, rising urban crime, and the efficacy of bourgeois law, and redirects them onto an immigrant criminal underworld that is inside the body of the nation and yet alien to it" (59). What was embodied as an essentially foreign ideology that was corrupting and weakening the nation has become an essentially native practice that is corrupting and weakening the nation. The key figure in Spillane's Mafia does have an "immigrant" surname—Evello, but the Mafia cohort also includes Billy Mist, Sugar Smallhouse, and Charlie Max. Spillane does not overemphasize the ethnicity of the mobsters: they are avaricious like all of the villains who populate his novels and are distinguished by their ability to organize their avarice into a corporation that functions with the efficiency of all great American corporations. They are certainly "inside the body of the nation"; but not so alien to it. It is their corrupted Americanness, not their foreignness that disturbs Spillane.

15. To be precise, Hammer strangles Evello nearly to death, and then arranges for one of Evello's bodyguards to enter the darkened room and, thinking the unconscious body is Hammer's, push a knife into his heart. Hammer then clubs the bodyguard to death.

16. When *I, the Jury* replays the plot of *The Maltese Falcon*, the one thing it omits is the Maltese Falcon: there is no MacGuffin pursued by all the players. In *Kiss Me, Deadly*, the cache of narcotics *is* a MacGuffin, and an action that seems to focus upon a crusade against the Mafia ends up as a search for the Mafia's hidden stash. If Hammer defeats the Mafia, it is not by cutting off its head, but by seriously undermining its finances: he does locate the two containers holding the narcotics; they are the real things, not leaden facsimiles; and he does have Velda convey the containers to the police. (That this task is delegated to Velda, and never depicted, indicates that the real drive of the narrative is toward executing embodied evil-doers—Dr. Soberin and Lily Carver—not defeating the Mafia.)

Chapter 2

1. That Robert Wade and Bill Miller wrote as a team was not an innovation in the genre; Frederic Dannay and Manfred Lee began writing as Ellery Queen in 1929 and made that nom de plume one of the best-known authors in all of detective fiction. In the 1960s Maj Sjöwall and Per Wahlöö (under both names) and Mary J. Latsis and Martha Henissart (as Emma Lathen) would also produce important detective novel series. But in the subgenre of hard-boiled detective fiction, Wade and Miller were clearly the most remarkable team.

2. The private eye's reliable ally on the homicide squad becomes a standard feature in the Truman era: Capt. Chambers bends with what is at times embarrassing deference to the assertiveness of Mike Hammer; Lt. Clapp's steady but not unduly submissive attitude toward Max Thursday is echoed in Capt. Grodnik's evolving relationship with Carney Wilde, and Lt. Donovan's backing of Mac. Hammett's Continental Op had always cooperated with local policemen, but he never acquired a constant official sponsor. Philip Marlowe had Lt. Bernie

Ohls to recommend him on occasion, but Ohls was not a regular backer of the detective. Ross Macdonald stands apart among the Truman private eyes in lacking even a Bernie Ohls behind him.

3. Both 1947 detectives are, in this respect, significantly different from 1929's Sam Spade. Hammett makes it clear that Spade has not trusted Miss Wonderly/Miss LeBlanc/Brigid O'Shaughnessy from the moment he meets her. Her devious performances are, in fact, a source of his attraction to her. Hammer and Thursday have trusted implicitly their woman throughout the entire action of the novel; the discovery of the women's deceptions, slowly explicated by the detective, comes as the necessary shock that proceeds (and presumably justifies) the shocking violence of the detective killing the false female. Spade expects the women in *The Maltese Falcon* to be as self-serving as the men; Hammer and Thursday are genuinely surprised to discover women are more self-serving than men.

4. Wade Miller has done the research (as had Dashiell Hammett). Velázquez's *El Bufón Calabacilla* (1637–1639) does hang in the Prado. Abrahán Niza and Count von Raschke claim that the museum painting is actually a copy by Velázquez's nephew, Juan Bautista del Mazo Martínez. Juan Bautista Martínez del Mazo (1612–1667) seems to have been Velázquez's son-in-law, not his nephew; but he was probably Velázquez's apprentice before marrying the painter's daughter, and he did certainly make copies of some of his father-in-law's work.

5. It is surely a coincidence, but the Mike Hammer novel that Mickey Spillane published in 1950 also features an exclusive woman-run agency that covers for an extensive blackmail operation. But Juno Reeves is much less an ambiguous figure than Quincy Day: she is Hammer's seductive ally until the moment she is exposed as a blackmailer, a murderer, and a man. Quincy Day is cast more in the ambivalent Brigid O'Shaughnessy/April Ames mold; she is never thoroughly with the detective nor is she ever thoroughly against him.

6. In addition to the two Max Thursday novels, Wade Miller also published two non-series novels, *Devil May Care* and *Stolen Woman*, in 1950.

7. Tana French uses the same improbable premise in her 2008 very interesting novel, *The Likeness*, which also features a cop (in Dublin, Ireland), whose resemblance to a woman whose death can be kept secret allows the police to arrange for her to rejoin the peculiar group of friends with whom the dead woman was associated in order to uncover the mystery of the woman's death. French's interest in the situation is, of course, very different from that of Wade Miller. The psychological implications of the improbable impersonation are much more complex, and the world of a mid-twentieth century American hard-boiled detective novel is far from that of an early twentieth century Dublin police mystery. The contrast between the two is revealing. (Tana French was, in fact, born an American, but has lived for decades in Dublin).

Chapter 3

1. Macdonald was the husband of Margaret Millar, who had not only published eight novels in the mystery genre under her married name before 1949, she had also enjoyed success as a screenwriter in Hollywood. Macdonald was, thus, when he submitted the first Lew Archer novel to Alfred Knopf, much less of a novice as a writer and much more familiar with the practical aspects of publishing popular fiction than Mickey Spillane or Wade Miller had been. Margaret Millar would continue to publish novels into the 1980s. None of Mickey Spillane's wives were writers, though his second wife, Sherri Malinou Spillane did pose nude for the cover of his 1972 novel, *The Erection Set*. There is no evidence of spousal involvement in the literary careers of either half of Wade Miller (Bob Wade or Bill Miller). Bart Spicer's wife, Betty Coe Spicer, joined her husband as co-author of four mystery novels featuring newspaperman Harry Butten (1950–1960), published under the name Jay Barbette.

2. Chandler was, in any event, an unlikely model for artful plotters. He at times openly disdained plot and was clearly much more interested in character and dialogue; Macdonald always valued plot highly, and always carefully constructed his

plots to carry meaning as well as to culminate in the obligatory surprise.

3. Sue Grafton, who also lived in Santa Barbara, placed Kinsey Millhone in "Santa Teresa" as a deliberate homage to Ross Macdonald and Lew Archer.

4. There would be three transitional novels—*Find a Victim* (1954), *The Barbarous Coast* (1956), and *The Doomsters* (1958)—before he produced what he regarded as the watershed novel in which the detective traces a problem of violence and identity to its true sources in family trauma, *The Galton Case* (1959).

5. Himes began his Harlem Detective novels in Paris for the French publisher Gallimard's Serie Noire; the French translation of *For the Love of Imabelle* (*La Reine des pommes*) would appear in 1958. 1957 would also see publication of Ed Lacy's first Toussaint Marcus Moore novel by Ed Lacy was the pen name of Leonard S. Zinberg (1911–1968). Though himself white, Lacy was married to an African American woman and attempted a serious portrait of a thoughtful Black detective. The Eisenhower presidency (1953–1960), during which these Black detectives debuted, would see the landmark Supreme Court desegregation case, *Brown v. Topeka Board of Education* (1954), and the dramatic integration of Central High School in Little Rock, Arkansas.

6. Michael Kreyling observes: "One obvious reason Macdonald claimed 'social range' for *The Ivory Grin* is that, by registering the presence of 'the Negro Problem' in America more strongly than in any of his previous novels (and, arguably, in the genre), he had turned a popular form toward a social problem rather than away from it" (69). *The Ivory Grin* is indeed a more sympathetic (and less political) treatment of "the Problem" than Macdonald's earlier novel, *Trouble Follows Me*. It is not, however, a "stronger" treatment than Bart Spicer's two earlier novels—*The Dark Light* (1949) and *Blues for the Prince* (1950).

7. The 1943 Detroit race riot was a major episode in African American history. The movement of African Americans north in the Great Migration of the early 20th century had been supplemented by the arrival of nearly 400,000 Black and white migrants from the South during the industrial boom caused by the Second World War. The initial provocation came when the Packard Motor Car Company promoted some Black workers on its assembly line in June 1943, leading to a strike by white workers. The rioting continued for several days, and federal troops were required to quell it. Thirty-four people were killed, most of them Black. Ross Macdonald was working at his graduate studies at the University of Michigan, Ann Arbor—40 miles west of Detroit—at the time.

8. To compensate for the formidable and treasonous Hector Land, Macdonald also includes a polite African American Pullman Car porter, who responds to Ensign Drake's respectful inquiries (Drake carefully inserts a "Mr." in front of the man's name) with information about Black Israel, of which both he and his Brotherhood of Sleeping Car Porters disapprove.

9. *The Ivory Grin* provides a rare instance of a private eye ending his investigation by shooting to death the very client who initially hired him. When he fires at Una Durano, Archer is explicit: "I shot to kill" (240). Una Durano has, to be sure, just shot and killed Bess Wionowski and probably will aim for Archer next. But executing one's homicidal client is, perhaps, not so far from executing one's homicidal fiancée.

10. It is also proper to see Macdonald's focus on the troubles of youth as a response to his own troubled youth, and, in the 1960s and 1970s, with that of his daughter's troubled youth. Biography is, of course, relevant, but Macdonald's repeated references to F. Scott Fitzgerald's *The Great Gatsby* (in his responses to questions in *It's All One Case* and elsewhere) makes clear his sense that the fable of a young man (or a young woman) attempting to rise by any means necessary—and to measure one's altitude by one's material goods—is *the* fable of his century. The key difference is that for Jimmy Gatz, the status is a means to recovering his beloved; for Macdonald's young men and women, it is often to escape—or to find—their parents.

Chapter 4

1. The year after introducing Carney Wilde as a very typical private eye with an office and a client, Bart Spicer collaborated with his wife, Betty Coe Spicer, to begin a

second series of hard-boiled novels featuring Harry Butten, who is *not* typical. Harry is a newspaperman, not a private eye, but he is most distinguished by being bound to a wheelchair. Because he is, in *Final Copy* (1950), looking for the person who left him paralyzed from the waist down, he is his own client. And, although this personal motive never reaches the intensity felt by Hammer or Thursday, it does align him with those avengers. Harry Butten would return in three more novels (1953, 1958, 1960).

2. Boucher at least once added Thomas B. Dewey's Mac novels to the admirable alternatives to Mike Hammer: "Thomas B. Dewey continues to exemplify better than any other writer save Ross Macdonald and Bart Spicer humanity of hardness" ("Criminals at Large," 15 July 1956: 166).

3. Eli Lazarus will inexplicably morph into "Eli Jonas" in *Black Sheep, Run* and all of the later Carney Wilde novels. Under either name, he is evidently a version of John Wanamaker, founder of the landmark John Wanamaker Department Store near City Hall in Philadelphia (or perhaps version of John Wanamaker's son and heir, Rodman Wanamaker, though Rodman [1863–1928] also died well before Carney Wilde set up his detective agency).

4. Ross Macdonald is the notable exception here: he never provides Lew Archer with a reliable supporting cop, and, indeed, several times implicates the apparent official authority—policeman, sheriff, district attorney—in the tangled skein of the crime.

5. To be sure, the usual cop, by the 1940s, is more complex than the Prefect G—or the Lestrade or the Inspector Japp—that the earliest detectives had to tolerate. Even Pat Chambers will reveal an unexpected dimension when, in the return of Mike Hammer in 1962, it is revealed that he too has been in love with Velda. Both Max Thursday's Lt. Clapp and Mac's Lt. Donovan are, from the beginning, more than simply the abettors of the protagonists. They do not provide unqualified support to the private eyes. But Lt. Grodnik, with his emerging family and hobbies, is certainly a more rounded character.

6. Spade's renouncing of Brigid O'Shaughnessy is a complicated gesture. Marlowe renounces a whole series of women until, after renouncing Linda

Loring in *The Long Good-bye* he seems to retract the renunciation in *Playback*.

7. The memorial evening when Manny Brenner leads the players with his clarinet and Martha Prince plays the piano can be compared to the ending of James Baldwin's "Sonny's Blues." Baldwin writes from within the Black experience, and the course of the lives of the narrator and Sonny are crucial to what Sonny says through his playing and what his brother hears through Sonny's playing. Bart Spicer cannot achieve all that James Baldwin can. But he does achieve something quite remarkable for a hard-boiled novel.

8. The Minute Men are echoed by Kelly Dow's vigilante Sunset Riders in the final Max Thursday novel, *Shoot to Kill* (also 1951). Although Dow appears as a bombastic opportunist, his armed Sunset Riders are regarded as a serious nuisance by the authorities. Olmsted's Minute Men are a nuisance in *Black Sheep, Run*, but a minor nuisance.

9. Spicer may be exploiting the national concern about the Mafia evoked by the 1950 Kefauver hearings (as does Spillane in *Kiss Me, Deadly*, 1952), but Bernie Sokol operates on a small scale, independent of major organized crime syndicates; driven from the Philadelphia, he operates carefully from a roadhouse in New Jersey, and seems more a throwback to the enterprising gangsters of early hard-boiled fiction rather than to the menacing prospect of national syndicates.

10. Wade Miller had used the device effectively in *Calamity Fair* (1950).

11. An additional motive for setting a Carney Wilde novel in the southwest was Spicer's own longstanding interest in the region. He lived for a time in Ajijac, Mexico (near Guadalajara) and when he returned to the States from Europe for health reasons in the late 1970s, he relocated to Tucson, Arizona. His two long Benson Kellogg crime novels (*Act of Anger*, 1962, and *Kellogg Junction*, 1969) would be set in Arizona, and would reflect a strong effort to represent the natural, social, and political aspects of the Southwest.

12. Thomas B. Dewey's detective will grow emotionally attached to the small boy, Roger Mitchell, in the second novel in the Mac series, *Every Bet's a Sure Thing* (1953), and children will reappear as principal figures in his later, post–Truman novels. Lew

Archer's usual attachment throughout his career is with slightly older children, adolescents and youth adults who have reached the age of questioning their own identities and their places in their families and their world; he is more a sympathetic observer than a crusader.

13. Velda does somewhat complicates Mike Hammer's economic solitude. As his secretary, she does not diminish his status as the singular productive member of his office: success depends entirely upon what he chooses to do (and upon the outcome of his choices). But when she is revealed herself to possess a P.I.'s license (and, when Hammer's license is suspended, to operate the agency on the basis of her license) and, after the 1952–62 hiatus, is revealed to have as an espionage agent in Europe during the Second World War, then Velda becomes what would, in any other world, clearly a partner. In Mike Hammer's world, however, Hammer's forcefulness and Velda's submissiveness to Hammer's forcefulness leave him effectively the singular productive member of the Hammer agency.

14. The obvious contrast is with Mike Hammer, who assumes that after their marriage Charlotte Manning will simply close her upscale psychiatric practice and keep house for her masculine provider.

15. Carney Wilde's ultimate choice—with his wife's blessing—to re-arm himself contrasts with Max Thursday's unrevoked decision to disarm himself. To be sure, Thursday's repudiation of his gun was a moral decision after he has shot and killed four people; Carney Wilde's self-disarmament was a gesture intended to reassure Ellen Pomeroy. But the two contrary responses do emphasize that Wilde, despite his unusual growth in both the public and private spheres remains rooted in the hard-boiled tradition, while Thursday represents a qualified movement away from the extreme of violence that that tradition often celebrated.

Chapter 5

1. In 1955, Sloan Wilson's bestselling novel, *The Man in the Gray Flannel Suit*, had made the figure of the upwardly mobile, mid-level executive commuting from his family's comfortable but insufficiently modish home in Connecticut to work in public relations for the massive United Broadcasting Corporation, which represents the new industrial model of media in America. Tom Rath is not, like Steinbeck's Mr. Pritchard, a conformist company head; he aims only for the middle—and always the higher middle. He returns from the War to pursue advancement within existing economic structures, first as "assistant to the director of the Schanenhauser Foundation" (20) and then, to secure a significant improvement in salary, as assistant to the media mogul who heads the UBC. Rath is entirely a creature of that broad and remunerative class of middle management. He wears the eponymous gray flannel suit as the uniform adopted not only by his colleagues at UBC, but by all of his upwardly mobile, mid-level fellow commuters on the train. In the end, despite some remarkable success, Rath decides that the stress on his life and upon his relations with his wife and children requires him to abandon the flannel-suited life, decline an upward promotion, and accept a position in the company that pays well but will end his chances for further advancement. The film version of the novel featuring Gregory Peck and Jennifer Jones that appeared the following year was, like the novel, very popular: Americans—at least those who read popular novels and viewed popular movies—were clearly interested in the price that corporate conformity exacted from the ranks of its white-collar workers.

2. Or, in the rare instances she has been a woman, a gyroscopic woman: Miss Marple and Bertha Cool, to take two quite different examples, are insistently their own women. Bertha Cool is belligerently assertive of her values. Miss Marple does seem to derive her strength from belonging to the village of St. Mary Mead, and in some respects might be placed in Riesman's category of tradition-directed. But her defiant (though not intolerant) embrace of Victorian values in a twentieth century that largely deprecates those values would seem to mark her too as a person who has chosen her ethics, not simply inherited it. She is certainly a centered person, and not one to adopt the values of the others who surround her.

3. The anecdote is based upon the actual 1928 murder-suicide of Ned Doheny, heir

to the Doheny fortune, and his friend/secretary, Hugh Plunkett. See Appendix II: The Doheny Case/The Cassidy Case.

4. The police procedural is a useful exception with which to prove the rule. Successful procedural series—Jack Webb's *Dragnet*, the Martin Beck novels of Maj Sjöwall and Per Wahlöö, Ed McBain's 87th Precinct novels—*do* emphasize the necessity of teamwork, the importance of departmental specialists, and the value of following of established procedures. This separates them radically from the main lines of detective fiction. The procedural detectives distinguish themselves through their initiative, their persistence, and, at times, even through their brilliant analysis of clues. But the premise of their subgenre is that ultimately it is the system of the evolved (and evolving) methodologies adopted by the police department, not the peculiar intelligence of a singular policeman, that reliably solves crimes that identifies the criminal.

And even so, the procedural often betrays its sympathy to the genre's bias toward individualism. Police procedurals tend to feature one member of the team—Sgt. Friday, Martin Beck, Steve Carella—who becomes the individual with whom readers can regularly identify. They remain cops; they do not emanate the aura of superior (and arbitrary) insight that Great Detectives invariably possess, but they are distinctively perceptive members of the teams that with whom they serve.

5. A prominent exception would be R. Austin Freeman's Dr. Thorndyke, who, in addition to a professional colleague (and narrator) like Jervis, for most of his career, employs an assistant who contributes materially to his investigations: Nathaniel Polton, the factotum who not only manufactures useful devices and develops useful photographs, but also contributes suggestions. Dr. Thorndyke is the genius, but in a gesture toward realism—and Freeman prided himself upon the scientific basis of all of his stories—the genius requires the practical input of at least one or two reliable team members.

6. Father Brown is, in this regard, another important exception. He too operates as an individual. In his name and his manner, he is so insistently commonplace as to be distinctive. But his authority is attached essentially, not accidentally, to his identity as an ordained member of the Catholic Church. G.K. Chesterton was not a Roman Catholic when he created Father Brown, but he was explicit, beginning with the first story, "The Blue Cross," that the priest's humility—his character—and his wisdom—his method—are both derived from his attachment to the universal church.

7. Early in the second Inspector French novel, *The Cheyne Mystery* (1926), Crofts explicitly juxtaposes the English private investigator with the English official investigator. The novel's protagonist, Maxwell Cheyne, having first been drugged in a hotel's cocktail lounge and then discovered that his home has been burgled, decides to consult Mr. Speedwell, a somewhat shady private detective whom the hotel had employed to investigate the drugging. In offering his services, Speedwell explains, "Now individually the private detective is every bit as good as the police; better, in fact, because he's not so tied up with red tape. But he hasn't their organization" (33). This fundamental contrast—the police have the benefit of the enormous resources of their organization but must also pay the price of "red tape," the rubric for a host of limitations that extend well beyond paperwork—becomes the always assumed (and sometimes expressed) credo of private detectives, especially of those American hard-boiled detectives. In *The Cheyne Mystery*, Speedwell does prove himself to be an effective, if not an entirely scrupulous, detective. But it will be Inspector French who ultimately solves all of the mysteries that surround Maxwell Cheyne's experiences. And Inspector French does so essentially on his own. When, for example, he notices the final letters of an ink-stamp on a torn paper receipt, he infers that it comes from a hotel whose name ends in "-lon" located in a continental city within a certain distance from London whose name ends in "-s." He then, on his own and "for a considerable time," consults a library of tour books, identifies a likely hotel in Belgium, travels overnight to the hotel, and when he discovers it is not in fact the required location, continues to mull the problem until inspiration strikes and find the right hotel in the right city. French does consult his superior for permission to follow his lead,

and reports his success to the same superior, but all of the thinking and all of the following up on the thinking are performed by the Inspector alone. Inspector French may have an organization behind him, but he doesn't actually use it; he may have to deal with red tape, but it doesn't visibly hinder him. He does not, to be sure, detect with an air of whimsy; he must remain earnest. But as an investigator, he is essentially as liberated from direction from above, coordination with peers, and supervision of subordinates as that flippant and insistently übermenschliche Philo Vance, who dismisses the guidance—even the authority—of the New York City Police Department (and, as well, of the New York City District Attorney's Office).

8. They were almost invariably men. The most notable exception was Bertha Cool, the hard-boiled manager of her own firm of private investigators. But Erle Stanley Gardner did not inaugurate the Bertha Cool series until 1939, and the more active and invariably successful investigator in the 29 or 30 Cool/Lam novels is always the pint-sized but definitely masculine narrator, Donald Lam.

9. The first Continental Op novel, *Red Harvest* (1929), which is the first important hard-boiled detective novel and which is centrally concerned with not one, but several gangs that compete to dominate Personville, stands as the remarkable exception to this rule.

10. Race Williams had been preceded by Daly's two earlier gestures toward hard-boiled detective fiction. In December 1922, *Black Mask* published his "False Burton Combs" and in May 1922 it had published his "Three Gun Terry." Both stories feature essential elements that would feature in Race Williams and his world, but it was Race Williams who would come to embody Daly's version of "hard-boiled," appearing 54 times in *Black Mask* from his debut in October 1923 to his final appearance in November 1934 (he would appear 17 more times between 1935 and 1955 in *Dime Detective*, *Thrilling Detective*, and, eventually, in *Smashing Detective Stories*).

11. Sean McCann's *Gumshoe America* has an excellent chapter, "Constructing Race Williams: The Ku Klux Klan and the Making of Hard-Boiled Crime Fiction" (39–86). As he observes, some of the Klan stories in *Black Mask* took a favorable view of the Klan's potential as a community-based alternative to the "class parasites and social decadence" that seemed to be prevailing in an urbanized America (40).

12. In this respect, Ralph Dezzeia functions more as Minister D—in "The Purloined Letter"—than the Ourang-Outang that rampaged through the apartments on the Rue Morgue).

13. To be sure, Daly has Race make the point that while simultaneity of thought and action are his typical mode of behavior, he can, when the occasion demands it, stop and think through a situation. When he returns home and notices the flickering of a light in his brownstone and then hears a blast from a car horn, he grabs his gun and prepares to burst into the room. But then he pauses and follows that first thought and first action with a paragraph of further thought. Though hardly comparable to the full nights that Sherlock Holmes may devote to thinking through his three-pipe problems, Race does have moments of cogitation. The moment passes quickly; he takes off his shoes and undertakes a stealthy roundabout way to the confrontation and gunfire that inevitably follows. "I'm a man of action but I can think occasionally," he remarks (63).

14. Neither *The Glass Key* nor *The Thin Man* was serialized in *Black Mask* as Hammett's first three novels had been. The more complicated relationship between the detective and his community in those novels fit less easily in the pulp magazine. (Of course, Hammett's literary ambition and Knopf's enticements, not *Black Mask*'s discomfort, surely motivated the exit.)

15. Active fictional detectives never marry, until they do. There are always anomalies. Most directly relevant to Hammett's valedictory novel would be the Pam and Jerry North novels of Frances and Richard Lockridge, a series of 26 novels which began in 1936, two years after the publication of *The Thin Man*. Like the police procedural, married sleuths comprise a special subgenre of detective fiction. Agatha Christie's Tommy and Tuppence, who featured in four novels and a volume of short stories 1922–1973, would be an early pair in the Golden Age tradition (and their status, as Christie's third-string,

trailing Hercule Poirot and Miss Marple by a good distance, is an indication of the relative importance of the subgenre—until the 1970s). Gideon Fell was married, though his wife rarely appeared in the series. Lord Peter Wimsey became a married detective in the final novel of his series, though he had been deeply engaged with Harriet Vane in four of Sayers's eleven Wimsey novels. And that final novel, *Busman's Honeymoon*, takes as a subtitle, "a love story with detective interruptions in which Lord Peter plays the leading part." Dorothy Sayers knew that detectives *in detective stories* did not marry.

16. The central role of multiple gangs in Hammett's first novel makes *Red Harvest* a useful text here, but criminal gangs figure frequently in the Op stories that precede it: "The House in Turk Street," "Dead Yellow Women," "The Gutting of Couffinagel," and "The Big Knockover" all involve violent gangs of some sort.

17. Hammett was among the Pinkerton agents sent to Butte, Montana to defend the Anaconda Copper Mining Company from the IWW in 1920. He told Lillian Hellman that he had been offered $5,000 to eliminate Frank Little, the chief IWW organizer.

18. The moral vision of the unprecedentedly popular Perry Mason series insists upon individual responsibility. Gardner's virtuous characters are always entrepreneurs; even his wealthy clients have almost always earned, not inherited their wealth, and he clearly prefers his young men and women to be self-reliant. Similarly, Gardner's villains are always greedy, parasitic individuals who seek to acquire illegitimately wealth that others have earned.

19. Chandler's debt to Hammett is unmistakable; neither he himself nor any critic then or now has overlooked it. He was, however, personally on friendly terms with Erle Stanley Gardner and he expressed admiration for some aspects of Gardner's fiction. In a 1939 letter to Gardner, Chandler declared that early on in his apprenticeship as a writer, he tried to master the form of the detective story by taking a synopsis of a Gardner story and then trying to write his own version, comparing his version to Gardner's, and then trying another rewrite, "and so on" (Chandler, *Letters* 8). In a 1946, he expressed specifically his admiration of the character of Perry Mason: "I

think he is just about perfect" (*Letters* 70). But when he imagined his hero—that complete, common, and yet unusual man—Chandler rejected the shell of organization that Gardner found expedient to construct for Perry Mason and made his detective more alone than either Sam Spade or the Continental Op.

20. Marlowe's affair with Linda Loring is fraught, but much less fraught than Spade's relationship with Brigid O'Shaughnessy. And Chandler has Philip Marlowe engage with Linda Loring at least in part to refute an emerging critical view that Marlowe's fierce celibacy in the first five novels was to be decoded as repressed homosexuality, not as proof of admirable moral autonomy.

21. This provides another contrast with Spade, who welcomes Brigid O'Shaughnessy to his apartment (and his bed). He also eventually welcomes Joel Cairo, Caspar Gutman, Wilmer Cook, Tom Polhaus, and Lt. Dundy into the apartment: just as he accepts Effie Perine and Miles Archer as natural inhabitants of the offices of Spade & Archer, he accepts that people—lovers, adversaries, cops—will occupy his apartment. Indeed, he may prefer to meet them on his ground. Until *The Long Goodbye*, Marlowe never willingly meets anyone in his apartment, and aside from relatively rare scenes when clients actually do visit it, his office too seems a fortress of solitude.

22. The advantage of Carne's militarized bureaucracy, aside from such incidental rewards as the expensive cigar that a client gives to George Peters, is that it works. Carne's organization maintains a file system that provides Marlowe with the names of three doctors who practice in gray areas of medicine and whose names begin with V. One of the three turns out indeed to be the Dr. V whose rural sanatorium is holding the novelist that Marlowe has been hired to locate.

(The "Dr. V" clue is not Chandler's strongest plotting device, but it is unimaginable without a large organization. The original of Carne's fruitful file system was that of the actual Pinkerton National Detective Agency: "The ultimate heart of the Pinkertons' continued success was this criminal file. Through contacts as varied as frontier sheriffs, city policemen, and underworld snitches, the Pinkertons collected all known data concerning criminals, including their origins, associates, methods of operation, meeting places, and known and suspected crimes. One constant source of information was the newspaper: As crimes and criminals were reported, field agents clipped and sent in the stories, along with extra notations, all stored diligently in the criminal's file.... The mug shot, a Pinkerton innovation, soon spread to the police and other detective agencies" (Jackson 105).

23. For brief discussions of Doan, Wolfe, and Shayne, see Appendix 1.

24. Interestingly, in the second Hammer novel, *The Twisted Thing*, written immediately after *I, the Jury* but not published until 1966, Velda has vanished. She returns in the second published novel, *My Gun Is Quick*, and remains a fixture thereafter. There is no lack of women smitten by Mike Hammer's virility in *The Twisted Thing*, but when Spillane produced his second published Hammer novel, he evidently decided to retain Velda's reliable adoration as a necessary marker of Hammer's manly appeal.

25. In a series of stories published in *Manhunt* in 1953–1954 (and then collected in a 1958 Gold Medal paperback titled *I Like 'em Tough*, Curt Cannon adopted the broken-marriage premise Wade Miller used in *Guilty Bystander* and used it to make the protagonist even more alone. Curt Cannon (the name of the hero as well as of the author), like Max Thursday, lives a drunken and derelict life after separating from his wife. His scene is the Bowery, not San Diego, and his separation was a violent one: catching his wife in flagrante, he severely beats up the lover, and as a result, loses his license. Unlike Max Thursday, he does not redeem himself by exercising his talents to rescue a son; he never recovers his license. And he pursues, in a very hard-boiled manner, the problems that are forced upon his attention. Curt Cannon provides a look at how Mike Hammer might have responded, had he been Max Thursday's situation. (Curt Cannon was an early pseudonym taken by Salvatore Lombino/Evan Hunter, who, as Ed McBain, wrote the widely admired police procedurals featuring the 87th Precinct.)

26. With very rare exceptions, no detective before the developments of the 1970s appears to have parents or siblings. Lord Peter Wimsey is the conspicuous exception, entertaining a dowager mother, a brother and a sister-in-law, a sister and a brother-in-law, and eventually, of course, a wife. Sherlock Holmes did eventually acknowledge his superior brother, Mycroft.

27. Both Philip Marlowe and Lew Archer do experience a minimal degree of continuity over the course of their careers. A few minor characters do reappear. The very brief recollection of *The Moving Target*'s Miranda Sampson two years later in *The Way Some People Die* is a rare example in the Archer series.

28. Archer's autonomy is, in part, a consequence of Macdonald's view that the detective is not, in fact, the protagonist of the Archer novels. "But, you know, there is a sense in which Archer is not the main character at all. He is, essentially the observer and narrator.... He observes what happens to my central figures who are always changing" (Macdonald, *Self-Portrait* 89). Macdonald deliberately avoids adding substance—details about his life and his relationships—that would diminish the neutrality that permits Archer to be the insightful observer. It is interesting that the writers of the 1980s and after who properly admire Macdonald's writing style and his insights into character and society move conspicuously in the opposite direction, making the detective a very substantial character, with a life history and crucial intimate relationships. The insights of their detectives are validated precisely by these emotional and intellectual engagements.

29. Emma Lathen's John Putnam Thatcher (24 novels, 1961–1997) would prove the rule. Though an established, not an aspiring, businessman—he is a senior vice president of the Sloan Guaranty Trust—Thatcher is the epitome of corporate success. The novels were well-written and the series was well-received. But it began no vogue for executive detectives. Outside of police procedurals, detectives belong to networks of intimates, not to structured organizations.

Appendix III

1. *The Long Wait*, Spillane's version of the basic plot of *Blue City*—a hard-boiled son returns to the tough city in which his murdered father had been a leading figure

and restores order—would not appear until 1951.

2. Due to a contretemps with John D. MacDonald, who in the Truman years was also establishing himself as writer of fiction in the same hard-boiled field (though it would not be until 1964 that he would begin his own series of Travis McGee novels), "John Macdonald" was expanded to "John Ross Macdonald" for the second Archer novel, *The Drowning Pool* (1950), and finally reduced to "Ross Macdonald" with *The Barbarous Coast* in 1956. "Ross Macdonald" would then be retroactively be designated the author of all of Kenneth Millar's books.

3. Hammett had ceased publishing novels when Chandler succeeded to the throne in 1939. Chandler had *not* ceased to publish novels in 1949; in that very year he published *The Little Sister* (shifting publishers to Houghton Mifflin), and he would publish two more Marlowe novels in the 1950s. When Chandler wrote to James Sandoe in 1949, he expressed strong, specific reservations concerning the artfulness of his new rival's prose. When the letter was published in *Raymond Chandler Speaking* in 1962, Ross Macdonald read it, and was evidently deeply hurt; this led him to depreciate Chandler's influence on his own fiction.

4. Spicer seems to have legally changed his given name to "Bart" in 1964.

Bibliography

Ansel, Martin R. *Oil Baron of the Southwest.* Columbus: Ohio State University Press, 1998.

Auden, W. H. "The Guilty Vicarage: Notes on the detective story, by an addict." *Harper's Magazine.* May 1948. https://harpers.org/archive/1948/05/the-guilty-vicarage/ .

Baker, Robert Allen, and Michael T. Nietzel. *Private Eyes: 101 Knights: A Survey of American Detective Fiction 1922–1984.* Bowling Green: Bowling Green University Popular Press, 1985.

Barbette, Jay. *Final Copy.* New York: Bantam, 1953.

"Bart Spicer, writer of detective and spy mysteries." *Lake Capala Authors.* Web. 8 July 2020. http://lakechapalaartists.com/?p=1561.

Chandler, Raymond. *Later Novels and Other Writings.* New York: Library of America, 1995.

_____. *Selected Letters of Raymond Chandler.* Ed. Frank MacShane. New York: Columbia University Press, 1981.

_____. *Stories and Early Novels.* New York: Library of America, 1995.

Collins, Max Allan. "Lady, Go Die! A Behind the Scenes Look at Completing Mickey Spillane's Lost 'Mike Hammer' Novels." 7 May 2012. https://litreactor.com/columns/lady-go-die-a-behind-the-scenes-look-at-completing-mickey-spillanes-unpublished-mike-hammer.

Collins, Max Allan, and James L. Traylor. *Mickey Spillane On Screen.* Jefferson, NC: McFarland, 2012.

_____. *One Lonely Knight: Mickey Spillane's Mike Hammer.* Bowling Green: Bowling Green State University Popular Press, 1984.

Cooney, John. *The American Pope: The Life and Times of Francis Cardinal Spellman.* New York: Times Books, 1984.

"Criminals at Large." *The New York Times.* 25 September 1949.

_____. *The New York Times Book Review.* 18 November 1951: BR 28

_____. *The New York Times Book Review.* 3 August 1947: BR14.

_____. *The New York Times.* 12 February 1950: 183.

_____. *The New York Times.* 15 July 1956: 166.

_____. *The New York Times.* 5 August 1951: 185.

Crofts, Freeman Wills. *The Cheyne Mystery.* Baltimore: Penguin, 1965.

Daly, Carroll John. "Knights of the Open Palm." In *The Great American Detective.* Ed. William Kittredge and Steven M. Krauzer. New York: New American Library, 1978: 18–38.

_____. *The Snarl of the Beast.* New York: HarperPerennial, 1992.

Davis, J. Madison. "His 'customers' were the jury." *World Literature Today* 81.2 (May/April 2007: 6–8)

Dewey, Thomas B. *Draw the Curtain Close.* New York: Pocket Books, 1968.

_____. *Every Bet's a Sure Thing.* New York: Simon & Schuster, 1953.

Duncan, Randy. "Travelling Hopefully in Search of American National Identity: The 'Grounded' Superman as a 21st Century Picaro." In *The Ages of Superman.* Ed. Joseph J. Darowski. Jefferson, NC: McFarland, 2012. 219–30.

Dunnar, Andrew J. *America in the Fifties.* Syracuse: Syracuse University Press, 2006.

Etheridge, Chuck. "Carroll John Daly." In *American Hard-boiled Crime Writers*. Ed. George Parker Anderson and Julie B. Anderson. Gale 2000. *Dictionary of Literary Biography* Vol. 226. *Gale Literature Resource Center.* https://link.gale.com. Accessed 2 March 2020.

Ethington, Philip J. "Ab Urbe Condita: Regional Regimes Since 13,000 Before Present." In *A Companion to Los Angeles*. Malden, MA: Wiley, 2014. 177–215.

Gale, Robert L. *A Mickey Spillane Companion*. Westport, CT: Greenwood, 2003.

Geherin, David. *The American Private Eye: The Image in Fiction*. New York: Frederick Ungar, 1985.

Goldman, Eric F. *The Crucial Decade and After: American, 1945–1960*. New York: Vintage, 1960.

Graebner, William. *The Age of Doubt: American Thought and Culture in the 1940s*. Boston: Twayne, 1991.

Hamilton, Cynthia S. *Sara Paretsky: Detective Fiction as Trauma Literature*. Manchester: Manchester UP, 2015.

Hammett, Dashiell. *Complete Novels*. New York: Library of America, 1999.

_____. *Crime Stories and Other Writings*. New York: Library of America, 1999.

Heise, Thomas. "The Crimes of Punishment: The Tortured Logic of Mickey Spillane's *Kiss Me, Deadly*." *Journal of Popular Culture* 45.1 (February 2012): 56–78.

Holland, Steve. "Mickey Spillane: Hard-boiled's most extreme stylist or cynical exploiter of Machismo?" *Crime Time* 2.6 (December 1999). http://www.mysteryfile.com/Spillane/Verdict.html

Jackson, Joe. *Leavenworth Train*. New York: Carroll & Graf, 2001.

Kreyling, Michael. *The Novels of Ross Macdonald*. Columbia: University of South Carolina Press, 2005.

La Botz, Dan. *Edward L. Doheny*. New York: Praeger, 1991.

Lachman, Marvin. "The Man Who Was Thursday." *The Authors Who Were Wade Miller*. http://www.mysteryfile.com/Wade/Miller.html. 13 July 2020. Web.

_____. "Thomas B(lanchard) Dewey." In *American Hard-Boiled Crime Fiction*. Ed. George Parker Anderson and Julie B. Anderson. DLB Volume 226. Gale, 2000.

Lingeman, Richard. *The Noir Forties: The American People from Victory to Cold War*. New York: Nation Books, 2012.

"Locations in the Max Thursday Novels." http://mistymansion.com/locs.html. 13 July 2020. Web.

Lynskey, Ed. "One-Two Punch: The Author Duo of Wade Miller." *The Authors Who Were Wade Miller*. http://www.mysteryfile.com/Wade/Miller.html. 13 July 2020. Web.

Lynskey, Ed, Steve Lewis, and Bill Pronzini. "Interview with Mr. Robert Wade." *The Authors Who Were Wade Miller*. http://www.mysteryfile.com/Wade/Miller.html. 13 July 2020. Web.

Macdonald, Ross. *The Drowning Pool*. New York: Pocket Books, 1959.

_____. *Find a Victim*. New York: Bantam, 1972.

_____. *The Ivory Grin*. New York: Bantam, 1971.

_____. *The Moving Target*. New York: Pocket Books, 1959.

_____. *Self-Portrait, Ceaselessly into the Past*. Ed. Ralph B. Sipper. San Bernardino: Brownstone Books, 1995.

_____. *Trouble Follows Me*. New York: Bantam, 1972.

_____. *The Way Some People Die*. New York: Bantam, 1971.

Macdonald, Ross, Paul Nelson, Kevin Avery, Jeff Wong, and Jerome Charyn. *It's All One Case: The Illustrated Ross Macdonald Archives,* Seattle: Fantagraphics, 2016.

Masterman, Whit. *A Hammer in His Hand*. New York: Bantam, 1963.

McCann, Sean. *Gumshoe America: Hard-Boiled Crime Fiction and the Rise and Fall of the New Deal*. Durham: Duke University Press, 2000.

McCullough, David. *Truman*. New York: Simon & Schuster, 1993.

Miller, Wade. *Calamity Fair*. New York: HarperPerennial, 1993.

_____. *Deadly Weapon*. https://www.sandiegoreader.com/news/1999/sep/23/cover-deadly-weapon-murder-at-the-burlesque/. 13 July 2020. Web.

_____. *Fatal Step*. Cincinnati: Prologue Books, 1975. Kindle ed.

_____. *Guilty Bystander*. New York: Signet, 1958.

_____. *Murder Charge.* New York: Signet, 1961.

_____. *Shoot to Kill.* New York: Signet, 1957.

_____. *Uneasy Street.* Cincinnati: Prologue Books, 1975. Kindle ed.

Mills, C. Wright. *The Power Elite.* New York: Oxford University Press, 1956.

Moore, Richard. "The Early Wade Miller." *The Authors Who Were Wade Miller.* http://www.mysteryfile.com/Wade/Miller.html. 13 July 2020. Web.

"Nick Carter." *Thrilling Detective.* http://www.thrillingdetective.com/carter.html. 13 July 2020. Web.

Niebuhr, Gary Warren. "The Max Thursday File." *The Authors Who Were Wade Miller.* http://www.mysteryfile.com/Wade/Miller.html. 13 July 2020. Web.

Nolan, Tom. *Ross Macdonald: A Biography.* Scottsdale: Poisoned Pen Press, 1999.

"Old King Brady." *Thrilling Detective.* http://www.thrillingdetective.com/more_eyes/old_king_brady.html. Web.

O'Neill, William L. *American High: The Years of Confidence 1945–1960.* New York: Free Press, 1986.

Panek, LeRoy. *Reading Early Hammett: A Critical Study of the Fiction Prior to The Maltese Falcon.* Jefferson, NC: McFarland, 2004.

Pierce, J. Kingston. "The Case of the Split Man: Biographer Tom Nolan Examines Both the Brilliant and Darker Sides of Ross Macdonald's Contradictory Life." *January Magazine.* April 1999. http://www.januarymagazine.com/profiles/nolan.html. 23 August 2020. Web.

Rayner, Richard. *A Bright and Guilty Place.* New York: Anchor Books, 2010.

Riesman, David, Nathan Glazer, Reuel Denney. *The Lonely Crowd.* Garden City: Doubleday Anchor, 1950.

Ritt, Brian. "Thomas B. Dewey." *Thrilling Detective Web Site.* http://www.thrillingdetective.com/trivia/thomas_b_dewey.html. 14 July 2020. Web.

_____. "Wade Miller." *Thrilling Detective Web Site.* http://www.thrillingdetective.com/trivia/wade_miller.html. 13 July 2020. Web.

Severo, Richard. "Obituary: Mickey Spillane, 88, wrote Mike Hammer detective novels—Americas—International Herald Tribune." July 18, 2006 Web. https://www.nytimes.com/2006/07/18/arts/18spillane.html.

Smith, Kevin Burton. "Paul Pine." *Thrilling Detective Web Site.* https://thrillingdetective.wordpress.com/2020/01/21/paul-pine/. 14 July 2020. Web.

Spicer, Bart. *Black Sheep, Run.* New York: Bantam, 1952.

_____. *Blues for the Prince.* Harpenden: No Exit Press, 1989.

_____. *The Dark Light.* New York: American Mercury Mysteries, 1949.

_____. *Exit, Running.* New York: Dodd, Mead, 1959.

_____. *The Golden Door.* New York: Dodd, Mead, 1951.

_____. *The Long Green.* New York: Dodd, Mead, 1952.

_____. *The Taming of Carney Wilde.* New York: Bantam, 1954.

Spillane, Mickey. *I, the Jury.* (1947) New York: Signet, 1947

_____. *Kiss Me, Deadly.* (1952) New York: Signet, 1952

_____. *My Gun Is Quick.* (1950) New York: Signet, 1957

_____. *One Lonely Night.* (1951) New York: Signet, 1962

_____. *The Twisted Thing.* (1966) New York: Signet, 1966

_____. *Vengeance Is Mine.* (1950). New York: Signet, 1959.

Steinbeck, John. *The Wayward Bus.* New York: Bantam, 1973.

Wade, Robert. "Interview with Mr. Robert Wade; Conducted by Ed Lynskey, Steve Lewis & Bill Pronzini." The Authors Who Were Wade Miller. 15 September 2020. Web. http://www.mysteryfile.com/Wade/Miller.html.

Weber, Max. "Politics as a Vocation." In *From Max Weber.* Edited by H. H. Gerth and C. Wright Mills. New York: Oxford University Press, 1946.

_____. *The Theory of Social and Economic Organization.* Ed. Talcott Parsons. New York: Free Press, 1947.

Whyte, William H. Jr. *The Organization Man.* Garden City: Doubleday Anchor, 1956.

White, Leslie T. *Me, Detective.* New York: Harcourt, 1936.

Wilson, Sloan. *The Man in the Gray Flannel Suit.* New York: Dell, 1966.

Index

Adams, Cleve 15
African Americans 3, 9, 11, 12, 13, 19, 30, 31–32, 82–84, 90–92, 95, 97, 99, 167, 168, 173
Auden, W.H. 14, 31

Baldwin, James 174
Barbette, Jay *see* Spicer, Bart
Bellem, Robert Leslie 15, 16, 132
Black Mask 3, 6, 10, 18, 24, 26, 117, 118, 119, 121, 125, 126, 130, 153, 154, 158, 163–4, 177
Block, Lawrence 8
Boucher, Anthony 24, 48, 91, 169, 174
Brown, Howard *see* Evans, John
Buchan, John 66

Cannon, Curt 179; *see also* McBain, Ed
Capone, Al 59
Chandler, Raymond 2, 8, 10, 14, 15, 16, 17, 23, 24, 27, 34, 35, 58, 62, 65, 66, 67–71, 74, 75, 88, 90, 108, 111, 131–34, 135, 143, 147, 151, 154, 157–160, 162–63, 165, 167, 168, 172, 178, 180; *The Big Sleep* 8, 34, 57, 67, 68, 69, 74, 78, 133, 134, 158, 160; *Farewell, My Lovely* 70, 90, 134, 158; *The High Window* 111–12, 115, 158–60; *The Lady in the Lake* 167; *The Little Sister* 167, 168; *The Long Goodbye* 133–34, 167, 168, 174, 178; *Playback* 167; "The Simple Art of Murder" 108, 159
Chesterton, G.K. 92, 176
Christie, Agatha 177–78
Cold War 12, 42
Collins, Max Allan 24, 161, 170
Communism 12, 13, 39–42, 44, 45, 46, 48, 138, 139, 140, 141, 149, 170,171
Conan Doyle, Arthur 1, 6, 116; "The Adventure of the Blue Carbuncle" 127; "The Adventure of the Crooked Man" 115; "The Adventure of the Devil's Foot" 79, 127; *Sign of Four* 115; *A Study in Scarlet* 115–16
Coolidge, Calvin 5–7, 8, 9, 10, 11, 13, 167
Cox, James M. 7, 167
"Criminals at Large" 23, 34, 91, 174
Crofts, Freeman Wills 117, 176–77

Daly, Carroll John 1, 6, 15, 24, 26, 27, 75, 118, 119–23, 128, 132, 153, 163, 168, 169,

177;"Knights of the Open Palm" 118–21; *Snarl of the Beast* 25, 27, 121–22, 125, 168, 169; "Three Thousand to the Good" 121
Davis, Norbert 16, 108, 154
Debs, Eugene 167
detectives, fictional: Archer, Lew 1, 10, 14, 15, 17, 19–21, 23, 27–28, 65–89, 90, 94, 99, 100, 105, 108, 136, 143–47, 148, 150, 151, 152, 162, 167, 168, 169–170,172, 173, 174, 175,178, 179, 180; Beck, Martin 104, 176; Bolan, Mack 167; Bond, James (spy) 20, 163, 174; Brady, Old King 118; Brandstetter, Dave 9; Brown, Father 92, 176; Butten, Harry 164, 169, 172, 174; Cannon, Curt 179; Carter, Nick 118; Chambers, Pete 15, 17; Chan, Charlie 167; Charles, Nick 105, 124; Continental Op 6–7, 10, 13–14, 26, 27, 66, 71, 80, 89, 93, 100, 108, 118, 124–130, 131, 133, 135, 138, 142, 147, 154, 167, 171, 177, 178; Cool, Bertha 175, 177; Doan 16, 108, 135, 154; Dupin, Auguste 5–6, 25, 82, 108, 111, 114–15, 116, 118, 119, 122, 127, 128, 135, 152, 169; 87th Precinct 176, 179; Fell, Gideon 178; French, Inspector Joseph 116, 117, 176–77; Hammer, Mike 1, 10, 14, 15, 16, 17, 18, 19, 20, 21, 23–48, 49, 51–53, 55, 60, 61, 62, 63, 66, 70, 71, 72, 73–74, 77, 78, 79, 80, 83, 85, 91, 93, 94, 99, 102, 105, 107, 108, 113, 136–44, 146, 148, 150–51, 163, 166, 168, 169, 170, 171, 172, 174, 175, 179; Holmes, Sherlock 25, 79, 82, 90, 108, 111, 114–19, 122, 126–27, 129, 135, 153, 169, 177, 179; James, Walter 18; Johnson, Coffin Ed 9, 83; Jones, Gravedigger 9, 83; Leaphorn, Joe 9, 102; Liddell, Johnny 15, 17, 18; Mac 15, 17, 67, 94, 165–66, 167, 169, 174; Mann, Tiger 20, 163; Marlowe, Philip 10, 14, 15, 27, 34–35, 57–58, 67–69, 71, 74–76, 78, 88–89, 93, 94, 99, 100, 111–13, 131–34, 135, 137, 144, 147, 154, 158–160, 167, 168, 171, 174, 178, 179, 180; Marple, Miss 175, 178; Mason, Perry 43, 130–31, 135, 137, 153, 154, 178; McBride, Rex 15; McCone, Sharon 9; Millhone, Kinsey 9, 152, 173; Moore, Toussaint Marcus 173; North, Jerry 105, 177; North, Pam 105, 177; Pine, Paul 15, 16, 168; Poirot, Hercule 118, 126, 127, 178;

185